THE SON THAT WASN'T

Book One of the Beyond the Crossroads Series
A Novel
Erica Fimbrez

Erica's Story House

Published by Erica's Story House

First edition 2025

Print ISBN: 979-8-9929578-1-5
eBook ISBN: 979-8-9929578-0-8

Cover update for series branding

Book Cover by Sienna Rose

Printed in the United States of America

Contents

Prologue

1937—Superior, Arizona

Five-year-old Nora Hernandez stood in the small, dimly lit kitchen, her cheeks burning from the sharp words of her mother's cousins, Elena and Isadora.

It was a beautiful Saturday afternoon. All Nora wanted was to play outside with her older brother, Ramon, and the neighborhood children.

But instead, she was stuck inside, burdened with chores she didn't even have time to finish before more were piled on her.

Elena said to her, "Eres una niña estúpida, no sirves para nada."

You're a stupid girl, you're good for nothing.

Nora flinched, staring down at her tiny hands, wrinkled from scrubbing dishes in the chipped ceramic sink.

Isadora chimed in with a sharper command. "Cuando termines de lavar los platos, recoge nuestra ropa y tráenosla. Después de que tu tía Elena y yo la lavemos, la colgarás para que se sequen." *When you finish washing the dishes, pick up our clothes and bring them to us. After your Aunt Elena and I wash them, you will hang them to dry.*

Nora swallowed hard, holding back tears.

She hated it when her mother worked Saturdays, leaving her at home with her strict and demanding cousins.

It meant no playing outside, no freedom, only chores.

Her mother always let her play outside when she was home.

In her mother's sleeping space, Nora pulled out her worn, faded yellow dress from the bottom drawer of her mother's nightstand and slid her little tattered shoes out from under the bed.

She quickly dressed herself, her hands fumbling with the buttons.

She could hear Elena and Isadora growing distant as they moved to the back of the house to wash clothes.

Nora's heart raced with both fear and excitement.

She had a plan.

She waited until Elena and Isadora were fully engrossed in their laundry and until Ramon and the other children outside were too immersed in their play to notice her.

Then, like a small, determined shadow, Nora darted out of the house.

Neither Elena, Isadora, nor the children noticed as Nora slipped away. She moved like a shadow, quick and silent, her small figure weaving through the yard.

She darted behind bushes and peeked around trees, her breaths coming fast and shallow as she ensured she was out of sight.

Her faded yellow dress clung to her slender frame, its hem frayed from countless washes and adventures.

Her shoes, little more than thin, tattered scraps, kicked up small puffs of Arizona dust as she ran.

Tears streaked her dirt-smudged face, carving clean lines down her cheeks.

Her brown hair, tied haphazardly into a short ponytail, bounced with every hurried step.

Nora's destination was clear.

She ran toward the mountains, *her* mountains. *The Superstition Mountains*, or Las Montañas de la Superstición, as her mother called them.

This was her escape, her refuge from the relentless weight of her world.

The mountains loomed in the distance, their rugged silhouettes framed against the endless blue sky.

To others, they might seem foreboding, but to Nora, they were comforting.

The wind whispered secrets through the rocky terrain, and the towering peaks felt like protective sentinels.

Here, she found solace.

Here, she talked to Anio.

Nora's parents, Jorge and Rosa, had once dreamed of a brighter future. They met in Ray, Arizona, a bustling mining town in Pinal County. Jorge worked tirelessly in the mines, his hands calloused and his spirit worn by the labor. When Ramon was born, followed three years later by Nora, Jorge decided to return to Sonora, Mexico, his home state, where life might offer a softer rhythm.

For a while, they found a semblance of peace in Sonora, but tragedy struck two years ago when Jorge succumbed to tuberculosis. His death left Rosa with no choice but to return to the United States, where opportunities, though scarce, were still more abundant than in Mexico. She brought her children to Superior, where she found a cramped, two-room house on the edge of town. The peeling paint and sagging walls showed their age like tired old bones. Rosa worked tirelessly as a house cleaner and waitress at a local bar, scraping by to keep her family afloat.

Elena and Isadora followed to "help," but to Nora, it felt more like control.

They assigned her endless chores, criticized her every move, and robbed her of a chance to simply enjoy her childhood.

But here, at the foot of the Superstition Mountains, none of that mattered. The dry desert air wrapped around Nora like an embrace, and the towering cliffs seemed to tell her that everything would be okay.

She wiped her tear-streaked face with her hand and stood still, letting the mountains' quiet strength fill her small body.

This was her place, *her* escape. Here, she could dream of a world far beyond the confines of her two-room house. Here, she could simply be Nora.

Nora did not find it unusual, nor was she alarmed by the fact that she was sitting at the top of a mountain she didn't remember climbing. At just five years old, such details didn't matter. She only knew that whenever she walked toward the mountain, she always reached her destination. And there, at the summit, she found her safe haven—a place where sadness faded and comfort waited. It was where she sat with Anio.

The spot was as familiar to her as her own reflection.

The trees stood tall and protective, encircling two large rocks.

The rocks served as benches for her and Anio, their surfaces smoothed by time and weather.

It was a place of peace, a space she instinctively turned to when her family's words or actions left her feeling small or hurt.

Strangely, she never remembered the journey up the mountain. Before she knew it, she sat upon the rock, still and quiet, as the whispering trees swayed through the wind. Anio stood beside her, his presence steady, ancient, and knowing.

She was so young when she first met him that she couldn't say his name, Antonio. Instead, she called him Anio.

Anio was a middle-aged man with a medium-dark skin tone and shoulder-length hair, tied back and streaked with salt and pepper. His warm, kind eyes held an ageless wisdom, and his very presence seemed to radiate calm.

Around his neck, Anio wore a chain with a peculiar charm: a small, round crystal globe ball. Encased within the ball was a portion of the Earth's continents, their shapes perfectly detailed.

Strangely, no matter which side of the sphere Nora looked at, it always displayed the same view, except one side had a faint blue hue, while the other had a faint red hue. The difference was subtle but unmistakable, and it fascinated her. A brass ring encircled the ball vertically, seamlessly dividing its surface, and was attached to a long, six-inch chain.

"Don't be sad, mi pequeña," Anio would say, his voice low and soothing. "Your life will have many changes, some good, some not so good. But no matter what happens, always remember this: I am with you. I will help you through the sadness, and I will rejoice with you in your triumphs."

Anio's expression softened as he spoke, his voice low and steady.

"This will be our last visit here on this mountain. There will be changes in your life soon. You will move to another place, far away from this mountain."

Nora's heart sank. Tears began to form in her wide, innocent eyes, her chest tightening as the thought of leaving her sanctuary, and Anio, filled her with sadness. Before she could let out a cry, her attention shifted to Anio, who was removing the chain from around his neck.

Her breath caught as she watched him hold the crystal globe in the palm of his hand. The chain dangled loosely between his thumb and index finger, glinting faintly in the sunlight. Slowly, Anio closed his hand around the globe, and to Nora's amazement, a bright blue glow seeped through the spaces between his fingers. The light was vibrant and alive, pulsing faintly as if it held a heartbeat of its own.

Nora didn't speak. She simply stared, her tears momentarily forgotten, her eyes wide with astonishment.

Anio smiled gently, his voice warm and soothing. "Take this," he said, extending the glowing ball toward her. "It belongs to you. Let it remind you that you are loved and protected. It will guide you when you need it."

With trembling little hands, Nora accepted the globe and cradled it in her dirty palms. The glow faded almost instantly, and the ball returned to its ordinary, glass-like state. For a moment, her face fell, a flicker of disappointment crossing her features.

Anio, noticing her expression, crouched down to her eye level. He took her hand, gently helping her to her feet. "It is time to leave," he said softly. He placed the chain in her hands, folding her small fingers around it.

"What I say to you now, your young mind may not remember," he continued, his voice taking on a deeper, almost otherworldly tone.

"Your soul will retain this information. One day, when your hair has turned white, when time has shaped your body with age, your mind will drift into another world. There you will remain, except for brief moments of clarity. Moments when the universe allows you to return. Moments when you are needed."

Nora's eyes stayed locked on his, her small chest rising and falling as if she could sense the weight of his words, even if their meaning escaped her young mind.

"You will have children," Anio went on, his gaze unwavering, "and they will have experiences that are not of this world. Your daughter, whose mind and body will travel to a world parallel to this one, will need your help. Your children will need your guidance."

Anio bent down further, cupping her face gently in his hands. His touch was warm. Nora felt an unexplainable comfort wash over her.

"I will be with you. Not even time can take me away from you," he said, his voice no louder than a whisper, but filled with profound certainty.

For a moment, the world seemed to stand still. The sunlight filtering through the trees danced around them, and the gentle breeze carried a faint hum, the wind rippling through her skin as if the mountain itself were whispering secrets only she could hear.

Nora clutched the necklace to her chest, her small fingers gripping it tightly, as if she already understood its importance.

Chapter 1

They say the past never truly leaves us. Maybe that's true.

My name is Andri Perez, though my birth certificate says Andrea. No one calls me that, not even my mother. I'm just Andri.

I grew up knowing the world wasn't as ordinary as most people believed. My family had their share of strange moments, things we couldn't explain, things we didn't talk about outside our own walls. It was as if we lived on the edge of something unseen, something old, something that had always been there.

My mother, my grandmother, and those before them. They all had their stories. Whispers of things that didn't fit within the world's rules. Warnings wrapped in bedtime tales. I never paid much mind to them, never thought they would matter to me.

But even with that, I thought I had a grasp on reality. I thought I understood the limits of the unexplainable.

Turns out I had no idea. Because the Earth I knew (the one beneath a blue sky) was only half the truth.

There's another Earth, one I never imagined. An Earth where the sky burns red.

Strange things happen to people every day. But what happened to me wasn't just strange. It shattered everything I thought I knew about myself, about the past, about the very world I lived in. And maybe, just maybe, it had all started long before I was born.

Now I know anything is possible.

This is my story.

1984—San Jose, California

Victor Costa and I hadn't dated long before we decided to elope. Why? Good question. If you'd asked me then, I probably would've mumbled something about love and fate. But honestly? I'm not sure I knew the answer. I doubt Victor did either.

Maybe at twenty we thought time was slipping away faster than it really was. We were young, impulsive, and full of half-baked ideas about love and forever. So we did what any reckless love-struck fools would do. We ran off and got hitched.

Afterward, we broke the news to our families.

My family took it in stride.

Neither my mother, Nora Hernandez Perez, nor my older sister, Leanne, were surprised. They had a way of sensing life's twists and turns before they happened. If I had told them I was moving to Mars, they probably would've just asked if I'd packed enough warm clothes.

Mom liked Victor well enough and wished us happiness. My father, Frank Perez, lived out of town, so he didn't meet Victor until months later.

My parents had been divorced for years, so Dad's absence didn't raise many eyebrows.

Victor's family, on the other hand, reacted as if we had burned down the church instead of just skipping it altogether.

His father, Felipe Costa, was furious. We endured an hour-long lecture about tradition, respect, and responsibility, during which I nodded solemnly while Victor sat stiff-backed, enduring it like a soldier.

Felipe finally cooled off after exhausting every possible way to remind us how foolish we were.

His mother, Julia, was more reserved, but I could tell she wasn't thrilled. She offered a small, polite smile that never quite reached her eyes.

Unlike Felipe, she wasn't prone to dramatics. His younger sister, Bridgette, seemed surprised and suspicious about our sudden marriage, but she was too wrapped up in her own life to dwell on ours.

I knew his family had hoped for something different: a wedding that united the families, something more traditional, more meaningful.

Maybe if we'd done things the way they wanted, it would've turned out differently.

But at twenty, you don't think about consequences. You think about adventure. And marriage, for all its seriousness, had felt like an adventure we were meant to take.

In December, I sat in the sterile, overly bright office of my gynecologist, staring down at a positive pregnancy test.

The reality of it settled over me in slow waves: excitement, nervousness, a twinge of fear. I wasn't just Andri Perez anymore. I was Andri Costa, and I was going to be a mother.

The doctor handed me a card with my next appointment date, scheduled for January, when I would officially begin prenatal care.

The moment felt surreal, like I was standing at the threshold of something enormous, something life-changing. And I was.

1985–January, San Jose, California

Dr. Wong conducted his examination and asked me a series of questions. Since it was still too early to detect the baby's heartbeat, he didn't attempt to listen for it. Instead, he reassured me that we could check at my next appointment.

I was given a due date of July 25, 1985.

"Andrea Costa!" the office assistant called out.

"Yes, but I go by Andri," I said.

She handed me a card with my next appointment date, February, for prenatal care.

At my next visit, Dr. Wong was able to detect a faint heartbeat. He listened carefully, then measured my abdomen.

"All clear," he said with a reassuring smile. But despite his words, I couldn't shake the unease lingering in the back of my mind.

Nine days later, I returned to the clinic, worried about some light spotting. Dr. Wong performed another check, partly to ensure everything was fine, but mostly to ease my nerves. This time, the heartbeat was stronger, and I heard it clearly through the Doppler. We both smiled.

"It's not uncommon," he explained gently. "I'm not concerned unless it gets heavier. If that happens, come back right away."

I spoke with other women who had gone through healthy pregnancies. They assured me it was normal, that spotting happened to plenty of expectant mothers.

"As long as your doctor isn't worried, you shouldn't be," they said. So, I tried to believe them.

As March arrived and I returned for my third prenatal visit, everything appeared to be going well. The spotting had stopped, and my small baby bump had begun to show: a visible reminder that this was real, that life was truly growing inside me.

Dr. Wong moved the Doppler device across my abdomen, his usual calm expression focused. But after a few passes, something shifted in his face.

His brows knitted slightly. His lips pressed together. He was struggling to detect the heartbeat.

A cold wave of anxiety crept up my spine. I searched his face for reassurance, willing him to say something, anything, that would steady the panic building inside me.

He must have sensed it (the tension in my posture, the silent plea in my eyes) because he quickly met my gaze and offered a calm, practiced reassurance. "I'm going to send you for an ultrasound to double-check everything," he said gently. "It could just be that the fetus is positioned too far back in the uterus, or the dates might be slightly off. Your uterus is enlarged, so we want to be certain of what's happening."

I nodded, trying to swallow the lump forming in my throat.

Everything was probably fine.

It had to be fine.

⸺◆⸺

The ultrasound was scheduled for the following Monday.

Victor, who was working the day shift, rearranged his schedule so he could come with me.

I wasn't overly worried; at least, that's what I told myself.

Mostly, I was curious. The thought of seeing my baby on the screen brought a small thrill of anticipation, a flicker of wonder at the life growing inside me.

Would the baby have Victor's strong jaw? My dark eyes? Tiny fingers, already curled into a fist?

I clung to that thought, letting it drown out the faint unease still lingering at the edges of my mind.

The day of the ultrasound arrived, and Victor waited in the reception area, flipping through an old magazine, though I doubted he was reading a single word.

Inside the dimly lit room, the sonogram technologist prepped me for the procedure. She spread a cool layer of gel across my abdomen, the sudden chill making me shiver.

"Sorry about that," she said with a small smile. "It'll warm up quickly."

I nodded, offering a tight smile in return.

With practiced ease, she began guiding the wand over my skin.

I turned my attention to the screen, my heart picking up speed.

Any moment now, I'd see something: a tiny shape, a flicker of movement, a heartbeat.

But the screen remained a blur, shifting shadows, grainy movements, nothing I could make sense of.

My chest tightened as I searched the technologist's face, hoping for reassurance. A smile. A nod. Some indication that everything was fine.

But her expression remained neutral, her focus locked on the screen.

The room felt too quiet.

A faint unease curled around me, pressing down like a slow-moving fog.

Something wasn't right.

This was just routine. Everything was fine. It had to be.

The wand moved in slow, deliberate passes across my abdomen, the room heavy with silence.

Then, at last, the technologist spoke.

Her tone was measured but careful. "Your uterus is a little enlarged and full of clotted blood."

Her words hit me like a punch to the gut.

Clotted blood?

My stomach tightened. My fingers curled into the paper sheet beneath me.

"What does that mean?" I asked, my voice unsteady.

She hesitated. "The ultrasound is only detecting clotted blood."

Only blood. No baby.

She continued, keeping her voice professional and neutral. "I'll send the findings to your doctor right away. You should call his office later. He may want to see you."

The ground felt like it had shifted beneath me.

This wasn't what I expected.

I had come here eager to see my baby, to experience the joy of watching a tiny heartbeat flicker on the screen.

Instead, I was leaving with more fear than answers.

Later that day, I met with Dr. Wong. His explanation left me with even more uncertainty.

"Sometimes the Doppler picks up your own heartbeat," he said. "It happens occasionally."

I stared at him, waiting for more, something definitive, something reassuring.

But he kept glancing at the chart, his brows knitted in confusion. His usual calm, reassuring demeanor was absent, replaced with something else.

He looked just as perplexed as I felt.

"For both appointments?" I pressed, folding my arms across my chest. "How often does this happen? Because I feel like I'm breaking some kind of medical record here."

Dr. Wong gave me a half-smile (the kind meant to reassure, but that did nothing of the sort).

He avoided my gaze, flipping through my file as if the answers were hiding between the pages.

"Okay, I'll let you get dressed," he said, sidestepping my question with the grace of a seasoned politician.

I narrowed my eyes. "So, Doctor, does this mean there's no baby? That I am not pregnant?"

My voice lifted slightly, making sure he heard me loud and clear.

Dr. Wong, already halfway out the door, hesitated.

For a split second, he stood there, his back half-turned, his hand gripping the doorknob.

Then, he slowly turned back, though his gaze barely met mine.

"Yes, that's what it means."

And just like that, he stepped out and shut the door behind him. The conversation was over.

I sat there, staring at the sterile white walls, the weight of his words pressing down on me.

One minute, I was planning a future with my baby, thinking about names, imagining tiny hands gripping my fingers.

And the next... I wasn't.

The silence in the room felt too loud. The crinkled paper beneath me. The faint hum of fluorescent lights. It all felt distant. Unreal. As if the last few months had been nothing more than a cruel mistake.

Four weeks later, I had a menstrual period, heavier than normal.

I passed what had once been inside my uterus.

A slow, hollow realization settled over me.

If I wasn't pregnant, why had my uterus grown?

And if I was... what had happened to my baby?

I'll probably never get an answer.

In time, I pushed those questions aside. Life moved on, and so did I.

Or at least, that's what I told myself.

It wasn't until January 1994, when our daughter Molly was born, that those memories resurfaced.

I was thrilled when I found out I was pregnant again.

But the moment I saw the first signs of spotting, a cold dread settled deep in my chest.

My heart pounded.

Not again.

My mind raced, flipping through every possible explanation, grasping for logic.

But logic was drowned out by fear.

What if this pregnancy ended the same way?

What if this baby disappears too?

I left work immediately, my hands gripping the steering wheel tightly, as I drove straight to my new doctor's office.

My breath was shallow. My pulse erratic.

Every stoplight felt like an eternity.

The past had a way of creeping in, turning rational thought into panic.

Thankfully, the spotting stopped after a week, and the pregnancy progressed without complications.

When Molly was born, healthy and perfect, I finally felt like I could breathe again.

I held her tiny body against my chest, inhaling that soft, newborn scent, my entire being overwhelmed with relief, love, and something else: something deeper.

That earlier loss still lingered, like a shadow that never fully faded.

It wasn't something I thought about every day.

But it was always there.

A part of me I never quite escaped.

Chapter 2

2016—Ridgefield, Nebraska

"Mom, I'm not coming home this weekend. I have to study for a project that's due next week," Molly said over the phone.

"Okay, Molly, I want you to do well on your project," I replied. "I'll take Grandma into town next week, and maybe we can have lunch."

"Sounds good, Mom. I'll see you then," she said before we hung up.

I set the phone down, staring at it for a moment longer than necessary.

Molly was twenty-two now, away at college just an hour from home. It was hard to believe how much life had changed since she was little.

She had always been a striking girl, with long, dark, wavy hair that tumbled past her shoulders, a porcelain complexion reminiscent of her Aunt Bridgette. She had a petite frame that barely reached 5'1."

But beyond her appearance, Molly had an independent streak, a quiet determination that had always been there, even as a child.

She had never been the type to seek permission. Even as a toddler, she'd figure things out on her own, whether it was learning to ride a bike, picking out her own clothes before she could even tie her shoes.

That fierce independence had only grown over the years.

And though I was proud of the woman she was becoming, I couldn't ignore the hollow ache that came with her growing distance.

After a long separation, Victor and I finalized our divorce in 2000. The truth was, we had hardly seen each other even before that. His passion for bass fishing tournaments kept him away more often than not, traveling, competing, always chasing the next big catch.

At first, I used to come along, enjoying the trips, the early mornings by the water, the energy of the tournaments.

But with work and a small child, it became impossible.

He couldn't give it up.

And I couldn't keep up.

I had grown used to his absence long before our marriage officially ended.

Eventually, I remarried Greg Ross, and we had a son, Lanix.

That marriage didn't last long either, but Greg and I remained on friendly terms.

The same went for Victor and me.

Life moved on, as it always did.

A few months ago, I met Drew, a local man who had a way of making the world feel a little lighter. He was retired but still full of life, always finding ways to stay busy. We spent time together, first as friends, then as something more. There was a connection, unexpected but undeniable. It had been so long since I'd felt that kind of pull toward someone, and with Drew, it just felt... right.

Through it all, Lanix was growing up fast. He was twelve now, but you wouldn't know it just by looking at him.

With his sandy blond hair, wide blue eyes, he looked small for his age; he could easily pass for eight.

Strangers often assumed he was younger, something that frustrated him to no end, especially when they used that sing-song voice adults reserve on little kids.

But Lanix was sharp. Quick-witted. Observant.

Sometimes, the things he noticed, the way he could read people, the way he questioned things most kids wouldn't think twice about, made me forget just how young he really was.

After retiring from my government job in Northern California, I decided to relocate to Ridgefield, Nebraska, a small, rural town in the Midwest.

I wanted quiet.

A life where you wake up to the sound of birds, not the hum of traffic.

Where the biggest worry is choosing between a trip to town or waiting for the weekend to come around.

Where life moves slow enough to finally breathe.

The neighbors are kind, but not nosy. They wave as they pass and offer to lend a hand when needed.

I found myself settling into a rhythm I hadn't known I'd been missing.

Even the creaks of the old floorboards and the wind whistling through the eaves felt like part of the charm.

For the first time in years, I didn't feel rushed. I felt... home.

One night in late October, as a chill settled into the house, I walked into Mom's room to help her get ready for bed.

The soft glow of her bedside lamp cast long shadows against the walls, and the faint scent of lavender lingered in the air from the sachet she kept in her top drawer.

As I opened it to put away her glasses, my eyes fell on something familiar.

The necklace. I hesitated, reaching for it.

The delicate crystal globe dangled from its chain, catching the light, its surface shimmering as if it held something more than just crystal and air.

It was beautiful in an old, almost otherworldly way.

I had seen it a few times throughout my life, always tucked away, never worn.

And yet, every time I asked about it, Mom would simply smile, the kind of smile that held more secrets than answers.

I turned toward her, the necklace resting in my palm. "Mom, where did you get this?"

She glanced at it, and there it was again, that same faint, mysterious smile.

"Oh, I got that when I used to see Anio at the Superstition Mountains," she said casually, as if it were the most ordinary thing in the world.

I smiled, amused.

That was always her answer whenever someone asked.

She never changed her story, never hesitated, never wavered in her reply, as if the truth of it was as solid as the bed she sat on.

Of course, my siblings and I had always struggled to believe her tale.

A man in a billowing white robe with long hair, gifting her a necklace?

It sounded too fantastical to be real, like something out of an old legend whispered around campfires, meant to dazzle children rather than stand the test of time.

And yet, Mom never wavered.

Then again, she wasn't the only one who believed it.

Years ago, when I was just a teenager, I met an old Apache elder, a man named Thomas Graywolf, who had once lived near the base of those mountains.

He was quiet but sharp-eyed, the kind of man who could see straight through a person with just one look.

One summer afternoon, I mentioned Mom's story to him in passing, half-expecting him to chuckle at the absurdity of it.

Instead, he went still, his dark eyes studying me carefully before saying in a voice low and steady:

"Some stories aren't meant to be believed. They're meant to be understood."

Back then, I didn't give his words much thought.

But now, as I gently placed the necklace back into the drawer and slid it shut, his voice echoed in my mind, a whisper on the wind.

I stood there for a long moment, hand resting on the nightstand, thinking about all the things I used to dismiss.

Maybe Thomas had known more than he let on.

Maybe Mom had too.

And maybe, just maybe, there was still more I was meant to understand.

◆

Helping Mom into bed, I tucked the blankets around her frail shoulders, unable to shake the lingering curiosity about her story or the mysterious necklace that had always been just out of reach.

"Good night, Mom," I said softly, switching off the light in her room.

The soft click of the lamp echoed in the stillness, casting the room into gentle shadows.

As I stepped into the hallway, I hesitated for a moment.

Listening to the quiet. Then, shaking off the thoughts that threatened to keep me awake, I crossed the hallway to my bedroom.

I settled into my usual spot by the window, where I liked to sit with the lights off.

My phone buzzed. A message from Drew.

Drew: *I missed seeing you today, but I enjoyed our conversation earlier.*

A small smile tugged at my lips as I typed back.

Me: *I always enjoy our conversations. I hope we can have one in person soon.*

A few moments later, my phone lit up again.

Drew: *Well, let's be sure to make that happen.*

Me: *For sure. Call me tomorrow; we'll make a plan.*

Drew: *I will. Good night.*

Me: *Good night.*

I shut off the phone and placed it on the nightstand.

The night stretched before me, vast and quiet.

On clear nights, the stars shimmered like tiny lanterns in the darkness, each one a distant mystery, a story untold.

I had always found comfort in them, their presence unwavering, even when everything else in life shifted like sand beneath my feet.

This was my time to think.

To reflect.

As I stared into the endless sky, my thoughts wandered, tracing paths not taken.

What would life have been like if I'd made different choices?

If I had stayed in California?

If I had pursued the dreams I once held close, instead of setting them aside.

Was that truly the more practical choice?

A chill prickled along my skin, though the room wasn't cold.

Then, out of nowhere, a vivid vision, or was it a dream, took hold of me.

The Dream, The Vision

The world around me shifted.

The next thing I knew, I was driving.

Molly sat beside me as we cruised down a desolate, two-lane road in rural Texas.

The horizon stretched endlessly, painted in muted shades of gold and brown.

The land flat, unforgiving, and vast.

But the sky...

The sky was wrong.

A deep, dusky red bled across it, casting an eerie glow over the empty landscape. It wasn't the warm amber of a Texas sunset, nor the soft pastels of dawn. It was unnatural.

Almost oppressive, as though something unseen loomed just beyond the clouds.

A faint unease coiled in my chest, but I pushed it away.

Dust swirled in the dry air, kicked up by the tires as we rolled on, the car's rhythmic hum the only sound beneath Molly's excited chatter.

She talked, unaware, unbothered. As if she didn't see the sky bleeding above us.

She was beaming, animated, her hands in motion as she talked about spending time with her big brother, David.

She could barely sit still, her words tumbling over each other in a rush of excitement.

Molly would be staying at his home for the long weekend, eager to bond with his three young daughters.

Our meeting place was an unremarkable crossroads, where two empty rural roads met at a lonely intersection.

Just a dusty road and silence.

And a late-model white SUV, parked off to the side, its tires half-buried in the dry earth.

David was already waiting.

He stood outside the vehicle, arms loose at his sides, watching as we approached.

There was something oddly familiar about him, though I couldn't immediately place it.

He looked to be in his late twenties or early thirties, standing around six feet tall.

His build was solid but not bulky, the kind of strength that came from years of hard work, not a gym.

His dark brown hair was short, the sides faded, the strange red light catching faint auburn undertones.

His medium-to-light complexion mirrored my own.

Then I saw his eyes. They were light brown, his father's eyes.

But the rest...

My breath caught.

He carried my features. *My son?*

The thought struck me like a whisper and a thunderclap all at once.

Molly jumped out the moment we stopped, brimming with excitement.

She darted to the trunk to grab her bags.

But David was faster.

With an easy motion, he took them from her hands before she could lift them.

She didn't protest.

She beamed up at him, falling into step beside him as they walked toward his SUV, as if they'd known each other forever.

I watched him place the bags inside, then turn and pull Molly into a warm hug.

His voice dropped to a near whisper.

"Is she okay? Is she sober?"

A chill prickled along my spine.

"Yes," Molly answered softly. "She just had coffee and water this morning."

Confusion washed over me.

What did he mean by that?

Did they think I had a drinking problem?

And why were we meeting here, of all places?

Why not at my house, or his?

Something was wrong.

The more I tried to think, the less sense it made.

It was as if a fog had settled over my mind.

A disorienting haze dulling my ability to grasp logic.

Molly turned to me and wrapped her arms around me.

"Drive carefully, Mom. See you in a few days."

Her voice was casual, light.

But her words tugged at something buried deep inside me.

I was supposed to return here to pick her up.

Yet, I couldn't recall ever being in this place before.

And still...

There was something unsettlingly familiar about it.

Like a fragmented memory teasing the edges of my consciousness, there, but just out of reach.

Refusing to surface.

"Molly, get in the car and wait for me. I want to talk to Andrea for a minute," David said.

"Okay," she responded without hesitation, slipping into the SUV.

I stood there, confused.

Why did he refer to me as Andrea?

How did he know I was bringing Molly to meet him?

David.

My son.

The words felt alien in my mind.

My son.

I repeated the thought, testing its reality.

But it didn't stick.

It felt both true and impossible.

Like holding two opposing truths at once.

I didn't know him.

A tightness coiled in my chest, bewilderment, unease.

Who was this man?

He spoke to me with familiarity.

With a hint of judgment.

Like he knew me.

But I didn't know him.

David leaned against his car, one leg crossed casually over the other, arms folded across his chest.

"It looks like you've been taking good care of Molly. I'm glad to see it," he said.

His words caught me off guard. *Why would he say that?*

Why wouldn't I take good care of her?

She's not a child. She's an adult now.

But there was something in his tone.

An undertone I couldn't ignore.

Like he doubted me.

I felt it.

An air of suspicion, aimed squarely at me.

Then I looked up and realized he was watching me closely, his gaze locked on mine.

Waiting.

So I met his stare, unwavering.

For a moment, the rest of the world fell away.

His gaze was piercing.

Searching...

As if he were trying to unearth a truth I didn't yet know myself.

My voice faltered slightly as I asked him a question.

A strange question.

Strange for him.

But not for me.

"When is your birthday?"

David looked at me, raising an eyebrow.

"July 23, 1985," he said.

The date hit me like a physical blow.

I just stared at him.

For a moment, silence stretched between us, heavy and unspoken.

"I guess you forgot," he said.

His voice was even. Unreadable.

I couldn't tell if it was rhetorical, or just laced with sarcasm.

Either way, I didn't respond.

I couldn't.

My mind was reeling.

Spinning with questions that had no immediate answers.

How could this be?

Who was he, really?

Why did the name, the date, the familiarity feel like puzzle pieces I didn't even realize I'd been trying to fit together?

I knew about his life.

I knew he lived in Texas and had three daughters.

I could picture their little faces.

But had I met them?

I didn't remember meeting any of them.

My mind was a terrible fog.

What is happening here?

The thought echoed through me.

I knew this man as my son.

I knew I was in Texas.

And yet...

Had I ever even been to Texas?

Lanix is my only son.

So how could this be?

And then he asked, "Why didn't you raise me?"

The question hit me harder than I expected.

I stared at him blankly, unable to speak.

I knew I hadn't raised him.

But I couldn't understand why.

But I raise my children, I thought.

Then...

A vision flashed through my mind.

It was vivid, haunting.

My ex-mother-in-law stood before me, holding a baby.

My baby.

Her face twisted into a wicked grin as she laughed.

A sharp, mocking sound that echoed through my head.

She stole my baby.

The realization struck like a hammer.

But how?

And why?

The questions swirled, threatening to drown me.

I snapped back to the present and met David's eyes.

He was watching me closely.

His gaze sharp, unyielding.

As if he could see the storm raging inside me.

He must've noticed the depth of reflection in my face.

I looked at him again, desperate to bridge the chasm between us.

But no words came.

He didn't get an answer.

And truthfully...

Neither did I.

Chapter 3

The soft click-click-click of tiny nails on hardwood floors stirred me from sleep.

I rolled out of bed, following the familiar sound into the living room.

Mom sat in her usual spot, her robe wrapped snugly around her shoulders, watching her small dog Chulo make his morning rounds. "Good morning, Babe," she said. To Mom, I was either babe or Mija.

"Good morning, Mom. Sounds like somebody is due for a nail trim," I murmured, my voice still thick with sleep.

Mom just smiled knowingly, shaking her head. "He's ready for his breakfast."

Of course, he was. He was always ready to eat.

As if on cue, Chulo trotted toward the kitchen, and Catfish, my cat, sat regally by her bowl, radiating the self-important patience of a queen waiting for her meal.

I set to work making breakfast for Mom and Lanix.

The scent of frying bacon filled the kitchen, curling into the air and blending with the aroma of fresh coffee. Eggs sizzled in the pan, their edges crisping into golden perfection, while diced potatoes browned in the skillet, popping softly in the oil. I warmed the homemade tortillas I made the night before.

Soon, plates were set, coffee poured, and, as always, Mom and I settled in for our morning chat over steaming cups of coffee.

I reminded her about the pregnancy long ago, the one that had ended without explanation, leaving only questions time never quite erased.

Then I told her about the dream.

No, the experience.

I hesitated, fingers tightening around my cup. "Mom, it was bizarre," I said, still unsettled by its vividness. "I don't know if it was a vision or a dream, but... he told me his birthday was July 23, 1985."

I swallowed, my pulse quickening. "My due date was July 25, 1985."

"And his name is David."

I paused, shaking my head. "Mom, I wasn't even thinking about it. I haven't thought about it in years."

Mom set her coffee down with quiet care, her fingers lightly tracing the rim of the mug.

Then, in that gentle, knowing voice of hers, she said, "Sometimes dreams are more than just dreams. Maybe they are glimpses of something real, something we're meant to remember. Maybe it's God's way of letting you meet your son who wasn't born in this life."

Her words settled over me, soft but undeniable. Her openness didn't surprise me.

Mom had always been attuned to the mystical, no stranger to things that couldn't be explained.

In her younger years, she read cards for friends and family, offering insights that often left people shaken by their accuracy.

My siblings and I grew up surrounded by the unexplainable.

As if the strange and otherworldly things were simply a part of everyday life.

Some might dismiss such things as coincidences. Tricks of the mind. Overactive imaginations.

But we knew better. We had lived it.

For me, the veil between worlds had always been thin.

Remote viewing, the ability to see people or places without physically being there.

Out-of-body journeys.

Glimpses into parallel lives.

These weren't just abstract concepts. They were experiences etched into my reality.

I had once stepped into a life that wasn't quite my own.

Waking to find my home subtly rearranged.

My husband present when he should have been miles away.

My backyard beautifully landscaped, no trace of the muddy chaos our dog had made it.

It was as if I had shifted into a version of my life that had taken a different path.

Quiet proof that realities could diverge and overlap in ways we don't yet understand.

And then there were the faces.

When I closed my eyes, they would appear.

People living their lives.

Sometimes in our time. Sometimes long past.

Strangers whose stories flickered before me, echoes from another existence.

My older sister Leanne carried her own burden.

As a child, cemeteries were never places of quiet reflection.

For her, they were loud. Restless. Filled with voices only she could hear.

And most of them were not kind.

Later, she tried to control it. Tried to turn the curse into something useful.

She joined paranormal investigations, using her abilities to assist where others relied on technology: recorders, meters, ghost boxes.

She didn't need them. She could hear the voices directly—speak with them.

She could sense what was waiting in the shadows before a case was even accepted.

But the darkness she encountered was not without consequence.

Some things don't want to be seen. Don't want to be known.

And she paid the price for it.

In the end, she chose to walk away.

To silence the voices as best she could.

Though they never truly left.

And then there was my younger brother, Joe.

He had kept quiet for years, unwilling to be dismissed as just another guy seeing things in the sky.

But he wasn't just seeing things.

As a young man, he would sit by campfires with friends, staring up at the night while the others swapped stories and laughed.

Unaware of the craft hovering above them.

They never saw what he did.

Never noticed the shapes cutting through the stars, moving in ways no man-made object ever could.

He learned to keep it to himself.

Until one day, Leanne convinced him to go fishing.

That time, he wasn't alone. The craft was unmistakable, hanging above them in the sky.

He saw it. Clear as day.

Leanne saw it too.

An unseen presence pressing against the air itself.

Over the years, the sightings continued.

Growing bolder. More frequent.

Once, while working a night shift in a busy town, he watched as a massive craft hovered just above him, undeniable in its size and presence.

He turned, expecting the city to react.

Expecting people to point. To stop. To acknowledge what was there.

But no one else saw it.

Not his coworkers.

Not the drivers on the road.

No one.

It was as if the moment existed only for him.

A silent revelation in a world that wasn't ready to see.

These weren't just stories.

They were fragments of something bigger.

Pieces of a puzzle we were still trying to understand.

And maybe.

Just maybe.

There was a reason we had lived them.

Yet not everyone believed.

Michael, my older brother from California, was the outlier in our family.

A man of science. Driven by logic and reason.

A scientist who sought answers through data and theory rather than intuition.

He didn't dismiss us outright, but viewed our experiences with the detached curiosity of a scientist studying an anomaly under a microscope.

I often wondered if he truly believed us.

Or if he simply humored our stories out of familial obligation.

But regardless of belief, there was one undeniable truth.

We were all woven into the same strange tapestry.

At the center of it all was Mom.

Mom had always been the grounding force in these conversations, offering wisdom and reassurance when the unknown crept too close.

Whether it was Leanne's encounters with spirits, Joe's experiences with unidentified aerial phenomena, or my own brushes with remote viewing and parallel travel, she never dismissed what we shared. Instead, she listened.

She nodded with that quiet, knowing look, as if she understood more than she ever let on.

But now, looking at her, I couldn't help wondering how much she still understood when we talked.

The dementia had come like a slow-moving tide, gradual but unstoppable.

Diagnosed just a few months ago, she still spoke with conviction, still offered advice, but the gaps were undeniable.

Conversations drifted. Moments slipped.

Sometimes, she would pause mid-thought, her eyes searching, as if the words had abandoned her.

The sadness pressed down on me, heavy and unrelenting.

Mom and I had always been close.

Our conversations had been my anchor, my safe harbor in a world that often felt too chaotic.

She had a way of making the impossible seem possible, of easing my fears with a simple touch of her hand.

But now...

Each moment felt both precious and fragile.

Like holding onto a wisp of smoke, knowing it would eventually slip through my fingers.

After finishing my coffee, I retreated to my bedroom, drawn by the need to be alone with my thoughts.

The dream, no, the vision, still clung to me, its weight lingering in the quiet of the house.

I sat by the window, staring out at the bare trees swaying in the morning breeze, my mind circling back to the images that had been seared into me.

David.

The name felt both foreign and familiar.

A life that never was, a path never walked.

But in that dream, I had walked it.

I had existed in it.

It had felt more than real; it had felt lived.

And in that moment, I was his mother.

But the question lingered, gnawing at the edges of my thoughts.

Was his mother also Molly's mother?

It didn't make sense, but then again, none of it did.

Dreams could be strange, tangled things, slipping between reality and something else entirely.

But this, this wasn't a typical dream.

It wasn't hazy or fragmented like the fleeting remnants of sleep.

It had been vivid. Structured.

Grounded in something deeper.

Maybe Mom was right.

Maybe God had given me a chance to meet the son that wasn't.

I wiped at the corner of my eye, catching a tear before it could fall. There was no room for unraveling now.

Tonight, I was supposed to meet Drew.

I sat in front of the mirror, blending eyeshadow across my lids with careful strokes.

The plan was simple: Patsy Cline tribute show at the theater, then beer and chicken wings at the local pub. Nothing extravagant.

But somehow, it felt different. I was looking forward to seeing him.

Excited, even.

And nervous.

I shouldn't be.

◆

When I arrived, I found a parking spot down the street and stepped out into the cool evening air. The theater ahead was alive with energy; people gathered outside, chatting, some already making their way in. The warm glow of the marquee lights flickered against the pavement.

And then I saw him.

Drew stood near the entrance, tall and relaxed, his hands casually tucked into his pockets. The moment his eyes found mine, a wide grin spread across his face, one that sent an unexpected warmth through me.

I hadn't realized I was smiling just as big.

As I walked toward him, I took in the familiar details of him. His lean frame, the dark hair streaked with gray at the temples, the way his kind brown eyes watched me with quiet appreciation.

He held out his hand. Without hesitation, I took it.

Chapter 4

Red Earth 1984—Gilson, Texas

Andrea Perez, twenty years old and desperate, clutched the phone so tightly her knuckles turned white.

She could feel Victor slipping away, and she wasn't about to let that happen.

The thought of losing him sent a jagged bolt of panic through her chest.

Her mind raced, grasping for something, anything, that could make him stay.

She'd spent the past week watching his affection dwindle, his patience wear thin.

The way he looked at her had changed: no more warmth, no more longing. Just distance.

After five unanswered calls, he finally picked up.

Her breath hitched. For a moment, she couldn't speak.

When she finally did, her voice trembled, thick with desperation.

"Please, Victor, let's work it out," she begged, tears threatening to spill over. "Don't leave me."

Silence.

She squeezed her eyes shut, gripping the phone like a lifeline.

"Just... just love me again," she whispered. "Stay."

The silence stretched, unbearable.

For a fleeting second, she thought he might soften.

That he might say the words she needed to hear.

But deep down, she knew better.

She knew how to get what she wanted: charm, manipulation, even the occasional victim act when it served her.

But this was different.

This wasn't just about keeping Victor.

This was about control. About survival.

If he left, what would she have left?

She had come too far to let it all slip through her fingers.

———◦———

Andrea grew up in San Jose, California. She was raised by her mother, Nora Hernandez Perez, alongside her older sister, Leanne, and her younger brother, Joseph "Joe" Perez.

Her father, Frank Perez, walked out when she was just seven, vanishing from their lives without so much as a backward glance.

He left behind an aching void, one her mother, Nora, never truly filled.

Instead, Nora worked full time, scraping together just enough to keep food on the table and a roof over their heads.

But when she wasn't working, she was out.

The nights were long when Nora wasn't home, and Andrea learned early that loneliness had a way of creeping into the corners of a quiet house.

The walls of their small apartment felt too big.

The television always felt too loud in the silence.

It was Leanne who made it bearable, stepping into the role of caretaker without hesitation.

She made sure Andrea and Joe had dinner, brushed Andrea's hair before school, kept the laundry done, and told them everything was fine, when it wasn't.

Leanne was the only person in Andrea's life who made her feel truly cared for.

Then, at thirteen, Andrea's world shattered.

The memory was burned into her like a scar.

Walking down the hall. Calling for Leanne.

Expecting an answer.

Instead...

She found her sister crumpled on the bedroom floor.

A metal ladder tipped onto its side.

Shards from a shattered light bulb glittered around her like broken glass teeth.

For a moment, Andrea stood frozen, her mind refusing to understand what she was seeing.

Then came the screaming.

The cause of death was ruled an accident.

A fatal blow to the head from a fall while changing a light bulb.

The explanation was ordinary. Simple. But Andrea could never shake the feeling that something about it was wrong.

Nora didn't take it well.

Grief has a way of hollowing people out.

For Nora, grief came with a bottle in hand.

The drinking started slow, just enough to dull the edges, but soon it consumed her.

She drowned herself in it, losing hours. Days. Whole stretches of time in a fog.

Andrea was devastated, not just by Leanne's death, but by everything that came after.

She needed her mother.

But instead of stepping up, Nora checked out.

Andrea resented her for it.

Hated her for it.

How could she just disappear like that?

How could she leave Andrea and Joe to fend for themselves when the only person holding them together was gone?

It was during those years Andrea learned a hard truth: If you didn't fight for what was yours, it would be taken from you.

And Andrea wasn't about to let that happen again.

She drifted through those next few years like a ghost, her rage and grief simmering just beneath the surface.

In the years following Leanne's death, Andrea's life unraveled.

School became an afterthought, a place she attended less and less until she stopped going altogether.

The streets of San Jose became her classroom.

And the people she ran with, fast-talking, hard-living, untamed, became her teachers.

She fell in with neighborhood delinquents, the ones who knew how to work the system and take what they wanted without getting caught.

Days bled into nights filled with the curl of smoke from stolen joints, the bitter burn of cheap liquor, and the adrenaline of fights that left her knuckles bruised and her heart racing.

Stealing became second nature.

Money.

Food.

Anything not nailed down was fair game.

There was no remorse, no guilt.

If someone was foolish enough to leave something unguarded, they didn't deserve to keep it.

That was how the world worked.

And Andrea learned quickly:

Use or be used.

Trust was for fools.

Love was a weakness.

People existed to be manipulated, to serve a purpose.

And anyone who didn't?

They were obstacles. Meant to be stepped over, pushed aside, or removed entirely.

Andrea didn't flinch at that reality.

She embraced it.

For a while, it even gave her power.

———◆———

Months after her mother's death in 1980, Andrea moved to Texas.

Liver failure, the doctors had said. Years of drinking had finally caught up with Nora, stealing what was left of her before Andrea had the chance to make peace.

Not that she'd been looking for it.

Their relationship had been fractured for years.

And when Andrea got the call, she wasn't even sure how to feel.

Sad? Angry? Indifferent?

All she knew was that California suddenly felt smaller, suffocating.

The memories.

The ghosts.

The people who knew too much.

It was too much.

So when her childhood friend Marisa and her family relocated to San Antonio, Andrea saw Texas as a way out.

A fresh start.

A chance to reinvent herself.

But Texas didn't change her.

If anything, it sped up the inevitable.

The arrests.

The fights.

The endless nights spent chasing a high, through alcohol or reckless choices.

Everything blurred together in a haze of mistakes and regret-soaked mornings.

Then came the night she went too far.

The details were hazy: too many drinks, too much rage.

When it ended, she was in handcuffs.

And Marisa's family was done with her.

That was when reality hit.

She was alone.

With nowhere to turn, the court ordered her to a four-month rehabilitation home.

Andrea went.

Not because she wanted to change.

But because she had to.

It was either that, or something worse.

She completed the program, going through the motions like a performer hitting her marks.

Saying the right things.

Acting remorseful.

Showing just enough effort to keep the counselors from looking too closely.

She got through it.

And for three years, she kept her drinking to a minimum.

It wasn't a clean slate, but it was enough to stay out of trouble.

Then she met Victor.

Andrea had been drawn to him immediately.

His thick, dark hair was always neatly combed back; his jawline sharp; his confidence steady but never arrogant.

His light brown eyes were different, honest, steady, without cruelty.

And his strong, muscular build only added to the sense of safety he seemed to radiate.

Victor was a good man.

A decent man.

And that was the problem. Andrea had known from the start, life with Victor would be stable, predictable, safe.

But deep down, she feared that safety would suffocate her.

The very thing she craved, stability, could become a cage.

She had spent her life fighting, manipulating, surviving.

Could she really live in a world where love wasn't earned through pain or power?

She didn't know how to function in that kind of life.

And now, with Victor pulling away, the old panic was creeping in.

Because if she lost him... what did that say about her?

To Andrea, Victor had always been convenient.

He was steady. Reliable.

And most importantly, he adored her.

He fed her ego, made her feel untouchable.

But now, he had dumped her.

The blow to her pride stung more than she wanted to admit.

She had seen it coming.

Of course she had.

The way his patience had worn thin.

The sighs after their arguments.

The colder look in his eyes, something final.

She had been screwing up.

The drinking. The bad attitude. The recklessness.

And he had told her as much.

Still, she justified it. *I don't drink that much. I'm just having fun.*

If Victor stayed, she could quit, just for a while.

Enough to keep him.

But taking responsibility? Actually *owning* her mistakes?

That was something Andrea wasn't willing to do.

Admitting her flaws felt impossible.

It felt like cutting herself open.

So instead, she did what she always did: blamed everyone else.

It wasn't her fault. It was his.

He was being dramatic, overreacting.

He wanted her to be someone she wasn't.

If he couldn't handle her, fine. Let him leave.

He wasn't the first. He wouldn't be the last.

To Andrea, most people were of little consequence.

Just pieces in a game she believed she could control.

Andrea Perez met Victor Costa at an Elvis Presley concert in April 1983.

She had won the tickets from a local radio station, caller number nine. She'd screamed into the phone, already picturing the night.

Not that she was a huge Elvis fan, but she never turned down a chance to be somewhere exciting.

Victor hadn't even planned to go. He'd been dragged there by his friend Adam, who was the real Elvis fan.

Victor knew only a few songs and spent most of the night with his arms crossed, waiting for it to end.

Until he saw Andrea.

She was all energy, leaning over the railing, singing too loud, laughing with wild, uninhibited confidence.

There was something magnetic about her. She noticed him, too.

By the end of the night, she made sure they crossed paths.

Andrea was good at that: positioning herself, flashing that slow, knowing smile, making a man feel like the only one in the room.

Victor didn't stand a chance.

They hit it off, and their relationship began, though from the start, it was an on-again, off-again mess.

Victor genuinely cared for her.

There was something about Andrea that hooked him.

He was drawn to her straight, dark hair, her full lips curling into that teasing smirk, her laugh, loud and contagious.

Her humor made her easy to be around, effortless in a way that made life feel lighter.

But over time, that lightness faded. The cracks grew.

Andrea's drinking went from casual to habitual, then toxic.

Laughter turned to shouting.

Teasing became sharp-edged insults.

Nights turned into long, drawn-out fights.

Especially when drunk, her moods turned cruel and unpredictable.

One moment she was the woman he loved. The next, she was cold, venomous, cutting him down with words that bled.

Victor's parents saw it before he did. They saw the toll, his exhaustion, his heavy silence. They begged him to leave her before she dragged him down.

And though he tried many times. His feelings always pulled him back.

Every time she swore she'd change.

Every time she sobbed in his arms, he believed her.
He wanted to believe her. And so the cycle turned. Over and over.
Until neither of them knew how to stop it.

Chapter 5

One evening, after downing a few drinks at Freddy's Bar, Andrea found herself wandering the town alone. The liquor burned in her veins, but not enough to drown the nagging thoughts in her head.

Victor had been distant again. The last time she saw him, he barely looked at her.

Something was off.

She stumbled along the sidewalk, the neon glow of passing signs flickering in her peripheral vision. Then, across the street, she spotted him.

Victor.

Walking out of Sam's Burgers.

With a woman.

Her blood ran cold, then hot. Her pulse pounded against her skull.

Without hesitation, she darted across the street, boots slamming against pavement as she weaved between moving cars. Horns blared. Brakes screeched. Angry shouts rang out.

But none of it registered.

All she saw was them.

She called him earlier and asked him to meet her at Freddy's. He'd only offered a vague maybe.

But now, there he was.

Standing with another woman, while she sat drinking alone, waiting for him.

Her vision tunneled, rage and alcohol mixing into something volatile.

And in that moment, only one thought pulsed in her mind: *He belongs to me.*

She stormed up to them, heart pounding in her chest, her vision narrowed to a pinpoint of fury.

Without thinking, without caring, she shoved the woman hard.

"Who is this bitch?" Andrea screamed, her voice raw with fury.

The woman stumbled backward, her heels scraping against the pavement before she collapsed with a sharp gasp.

Victor's face twisted in shock and rage. He lunged toward the woman, crouching down to help her up. His hands hovered protectively over her shoulders, steadying her as she winced.

"Get the hell away from us, Andrea. You're drunk again!" he roared, his voice slicing through the night like a slap.

Andrea's breath hitched. The alcohol in her veins fueled the fire in her chest.

She barely noticed the cars passing or the murmur of voices from the restaurant.

All she saw was Victor touching this woman. Shielding her.

Protecting her.

Her stomach twisted violently.

Who was she?

The woman was petite, too small to fight back. Her dark hair framed a delicate face; her porcelain complexion glowing beneath the streetlight.

She was pretty. Soft. The kind of woman men chose over girls like Andrea, the wild, unpredictable ones.

This is why. He's leaving me.

It felt like betrayal.

Her Victor, the one who once promised never to hurt her, was defending someone else.

Andrea's jealousy seethed, twisting into something dark and dangerous.

"You're cheating on me!" she spat, her voice like a blade.

Victor's head snapped toward her, his jaw clenched. "What the hell are you talking about?"

The woman flinched but said nothing, her eyes darting nervously between them.

Andrea didn't care. She had seen enough.

Victor was hers.

And no woman, especially not this one, was going to take him away.

What Andrea failed to realize, what her rage-blinded mind refused to see, was the truth standing right in front of her.

The woman wasn't a lover.

She wasn't a threat.

She was Victor's sister.

Bridgette.

And Andrea had just attacked her.

They had a massive argument that night, one that echoed through the empty streets long after Andrea's drunken fury burned into exhausted desperation.

She begged. She screamed. She threw accusations like daggers, clawing for any shred of control she had left.

But Victor was done.

The endless cycle of breakups and reconciliations, the drinking, the fights.

It all came to a head in that moment.

There was no reasoning with her. No reaching the Andrea he'd once cared about.

So, for the first time...

He walked away.

For good.

Andrea didn't believe it at first.

Victor had left before, only to come back. He always came back.

She told herself this was just another fight, another bad night.

In a few days, maybe a week, he'd cool off.

Things would go back to the way they were.

But this time was different.

Victor didn't call.

He didn't come looking for her.

He didn't want her back.

His parents were relieved, especially his mother, Julia.

Julia had never hidden her disdain for Andrea. She watched her with wary, disapproving eyes, always warning Victor: She's nothing but trouble. She'll ruin you if you let her.

For years, Victor had defended Andrea, insisting she just needed love.

That she wasn't as bad as people made her out to be.

But now?

Now he saw it.

And he wasn't going to be the one to save her.

Andrea, however, wasn't capable or willing to reflect on her own behavior.

In her mind, Victor had abandoned her.

He had betrayed her. He was the problem. Not her.

So, she did what she always did. She numbed herself.

She drank. Heavily. Recklessly.

What once felt like fun turned into a full-blown escape.

She wasn't just partying anymore.

She was drowning.

Consequences didn't matter.

The more she drank, the less she cared.

The arrests came soon after.

Drunk and disorderly. Public intoxication.

A bar fight here. A stolen wallet there.

Each time she landed in a holding cell, the rage flared.

But never at herself.

It was the cops. The bartender. The nosy stranger who called the police instead of minding their own damn business.

And when jail time wasn't enough to sober her up, there were the court-mandated rehab centers.

Live-in programs. Inpatient treatments.

Places that promised to fix her. But Andrea didn't want to be fixed.

She wanted to get by.

She wanted what she needed.

And she had a talent for manipulating people into giving it.

Her next drink.

A place to stay.

Someone to feel sorry enough to bail her out.

And for a while, it worked.

Until it didn't.

The Perfect Target

For the past few months, Andrea had been working as a cashier at a small, run-down convenience store, minimum wage, long hours, but enough to keep her afloat. It wasn't the life she imagined, but it was better than rock bottom.

After Victor dumped her, she was left with nothing.

Just herself and the endless days behind the counter.

Until the store hired someone new.

That's when she met Rachel Vega.

Rachel was different.

She was kind in a way most people weren't. She smiled easily, spoke gently, and carried a warmth that felt genuine, a rare trait in a world of cranky, self-serving people who only looked out for themselves.

At first, Andrea didn't think much of her. People like Rachel were weak, too nice for their own good.

But the more they worked together, the more Rachel's kindness stood out.

She went out of her way to help, covering shifts when Andrea needed time off, bringing her coffee without being asked, listening without judgment when Andrea vented about her life.

And that's when Andrea realized something:

She had no one else.

No family. No real friends.

And if she wanted to stay afloat, she needed someone.

So, she did what she always did. She took advantage.

She knew she had to tread carefully, didn't want to come on too strong and scare off the opportunity.

Instead, she crafted a narrative.

Played the victim.

The "poor me" routine she'd perfected over the years.

She let Rachel believe what she wanted.

That she was just a woman trying to get her life back together.

That she was trying.

And Rachel?

Rachel believed her.

Just like Andrea knew she would.

Maybe she'll offer me some money, Andrea thought, eyeing her with quiet calculation. *Or a place to stay.*

Her time was running out.

With only a few days left at her temporary housing, she needed a solution fast.

No backup plan. No savings. No one else to turn to.

And Rachel?

Rachel was the only person in her life who seemed to actually care.

That made Rachel the perfect mark.

Andrea wasn't stupid. She knew Rachel was kindhearted, generous to a fault.

The type of person who couldn't turn away someone in need.

So, she played the role.

Just enough vulnerability.

Just enough "poor me" to steer Rachel exactly where she wanted.

And predictably, Rachel didn't hesitate.

She invited Andrea to move into her parents' home, offering her a place to stay when no one else would.

It was almost too easy.

At first, things were fine.

Rachel did what she could, believing Andrea just needed a little support, just enough encouragement to get back on track.

She tried to guide her, especially when it came to the drinking.

But Andrea didn't want help.

She wanted freedom.

And now that she had a place to stay, her reckless habits only worsened.

Ron and Stephanie Vega, Rachel's parents, quickly grew uneasy.

They had agreed to let Andrea stay out of kindness because Rachel had asked and they trusted their daughter's judgment.

But Andrea?

Andrea was a different story.

She was polite enough at first.

But the cracks showed quickly.

She came home late, always late.

Unsteady footsteps on the porch signaled another night of drinking.

She stumbled in, breath thick with the sharp tang of alcohol, her eyes glassy, unfocused.

The smell clung to her, seeping into the air, impossible to ignore.

At first, Rachel made excuses.

"She's just adjusting."

"She had a bad day."

"She's trying, Mom, really, she is."

But Stephanie wasn't so sure.

She watched as Andrea's supposed effort unraveled into nothing more than excuses.

Her presence in the house shifted from guest to burden. Andrea never cleaned up after herself.

Dishes piled. Crumbs scattered. Counters always a mess.

Empty bottles tucked into corners, as if hiding them made the evidence disappear.

And every single time, it was Stephanie or Rachel cleaning up after her.

The final straw came with Ron.

Ron had been patient.

But patience has limits. And Andrea was testing his.

He'd welcomed her under his roof, on one condition: that she respected it.

But Andrea had no respect for anything.

And he was beginning to wonder if she ever would.

⸻ ◆ ⸻

One night, long past midnight, Andrea stumbled in, reeking of alcohol.

Ron sat in his recliner, hand on the TV dial, flipping through channels with slow, deliberate clicks, his expression unreadable.

Andrea barely acknowledged him.

She just muttered something incoherent and disappeared down the hall, slamming the bedroom door behind her.

Ron exhaled slowly, jaw tight, his hand heavy on the armrest.

From the kitchen doorway, Stephanie caught his eye.

"She can't stay here much longer," Ron said, his voice low but firm.

Stephanie nodded.

Rachel might not see it yet, but her parents did.

Andrea wasn't looking for a fresh start.

She was looking for a free ride.

And Ron wasn't going to let her take advantage of their kindness much longer.

Ron Vega had always been a patient man.

But his patience was gone.

And tonight, he'd had enough.

"Rachel, how many chances have we already given her?" he demanded, pacing the living room.

His voice was edged with frustration, his jaw tight, his hands clenched at his sides.

"She doesn't help around the house.

She disrespects our home.

And I won't allow it anymore."

Rachel sat on the couch, arms crossed, her face tight with worry.

She had known this conversation was coming.

She just hadn't expected it tonight.

"Dad, she has nowhere to go," she said, her voice soft, almost pleading.

"I'm trying to convince her to go back to rehab. I really think she'll agree soon. Just give me more time to work on it. I promise I'll take better care of the situation."

Ron exhaled sharply, running a hand through his graying hair.

"More time? Rachel," he said, shaking his head.

"I know she's your friend, though I can't understand why, but you're taking on a responsibility that isn't yours to bear."

Rachel bit her lip, his disappointment pressing down like a weight.

She knew Andrea wasn't making things easy.

She knew her parents had every right to be frustrated.

But deep down, she still believed Andrea could turn things around.

That if she just tried hard enough, she could convince her to get help.

But how much longer could she keep making excuses?

And more importantly...

How much longer would her parents put up with it?

"I know, Dad. I wish you could know the Andrea that I know.

She really is fun, a great person to be around when she's not drinking," Rachel replied softly, twisting the hem of her sweater between her fingers.

"But once she starts the rehab program, I think it'll help her.

And things will be better for all of us."

She wanted to believe that.

Needed to believe that.

Rachel still clung to the hope that she could make a difference.

It was that version of Andrea, the one she glimpsed in rare, sober moments, funny, charming, even vulnerable that Rachel still held onto.

The real Andrea, buried under the weight of addiction.

Ron sighed, his frustration giving way to reluctant understanding.

He pulled Rachel into a hug, kissing her forehead the way he had when she was a little girl.

"You've always had a big heart for the people you care about," he murmured.

"I just hope you can convince her soon."

Rachel leaned into the embrace, drawing comfort from it.

"I will convince her, Dad, but I'll have to give her an ultimatum."

"An ultimatum?" Ron asked.

Rachel looked up at him, "Yes, if you and Mom can just give me a little more time, I'll figure something out."

Ron nodded, "Your Mom and I trust your judgment.

We know you'll come up with the best outcome for her."

"Thanks, Dad," she said, her voice hopeful, though doubt lingered at the edges of her mind.

She watched him walk away, then stood alone for a moment, turning everything over in her head.

Convincing Andrea wouldn't be easy.

But Rachel had never relied on charm or showy speeches.

She had always approached the world differently.

Rachel had never been considered conventionally pretty or popular. She didn't turn heads when she walked into a room, and she was fine with that.

Her strength wasn't in her looks, but in the quiet kindness she carried, reflected in the warm depths of her large, bright brown eyes.

She had a way of making people feel seen, heard, understood without judgment, without expectation. Something rare on this Red Earth.

And Andrea?

Andrea had noticed that. And she was more than willing to exploit it.

Where Rachel's warmth was understated, Andrea's presence was impossible to ignore.

Standing at about 5'3", with dark, straight hair that framed her face just right, and brown eyes that sparkled with mischief, she had a magnetism men found intoxicating.

She knew how to laugh at the right moments.

How to make someone feel like they were the most interesting person in the room, even when she couldn't care less.

It was easy to be drawn to her.

To get swept up in her lively, flirtatious energy.

But beneath the charm, beneath the effortless laughter, lurked something else.

Andrea wasn't just charming. She was manipulative. Calculating.

She had learned long ago that the world was a game.

And people were just pieces to be moved, used, and discarded when they no longer served her.

And Rachel?

Rachel was just another piece. A convenient one.

One Andrea had no intention of letting go of.

Not until she had drained her of everything she could offer.

Andrea's struggle to maintain stable employment was nothing new.

It was a cycle, one she had neither the interest nor the discipline to break.

Most of her jobs had been at gas stations, grocery stores, and other dead-end places that barely paid enough to keep her afloat.

She never lasted long.

She got bored.

Showed up late too many times.

Or helped herself to a little extra cash when she thought no one was watching.

But there was one job she actually enjoyed.

For three brief months, she worked at a car dealership.

It was different from the usual places.

Clean. Professional. A step above the mind-numbing routine of scanning barcodes and stocking shelves.

She liked the way people looked at her when she walked into the showroom, dressed sharp, exuding confidence, pretending she knew more about the vehicles than she actually did.

She liked the thrill of talking fast.

The satisfaction of convincing someone they needed the upgraded model.

The rush of success with each sale.

For a moment, just a moment, she thought maybe this was a job she could keep.

Then... she screwed it up.

It started small, just a couple of vodka shots during her lunch break, hidden in the bottom of a soda cup.

Just enough to take the edge off.

But by the time she returned to the lot, her balance was off, her judgment hazy.

When she got behind the wheel to move one of the brand-new cars, she miscalculated.

The sickening crunch of metal on metal rang out as she scraped the side of another vehicle, leaving a deep, unmistakable dent.

She froze, heart hammering.

For a split second, she considered lying.

Making up an excuse, maybe saying someone else had done it. That she'd found the car like that.

But she didn't get the chance.

Her manager stormed out before she could even process what had happened, his face red with fury.

The dealership wasn't about to tolerate an employee who wrecked their inventory, especially not one who reeked of alcohol.

She was fired on the spot.

And though she told herself she didn't care...

Though she laughed it off and blamed her boss for overreacting...

Deep down, it disappointed her. Briefly.

Andrea didn't dwell on things.

Regret was useless. A weakness.

Something other people clung to.

If she let herself feel guilty every time she screwed up, she'd never get through the day.

So, like always, she shoved the disappointment aside, poured herself another drink...

And moved on.

Chapter 6

Andrea woke up with a slight hangover around 1:30 p.m. on a cool winter Sunday. As soon as she opened her eyes, she saw Rachel standing in the doorway, staring at her.

Andrea sat up, her voice hoarse and laced with snark.

"Rachel? What do you want?"

Rachel stepped into the room and sat on the edge of the bed. The stale scent of alcohol and morning breath made her wrinkle her nose.

"We need to talk," she said firmly.

Andrea rolled her eyes and flopped back onto the pillow.

"Ugh. Not that again," she groaned.

"Yes, Andrea. That again," Rachel replied.

"It's time, Andrea. My parents don't think they can let you stay here anymore, and honestly... I'm sorry to say this, but I believe you're taking advantage of me, and of them."

Andrea sat up slowly, narrowing her eyes.

"Rachel, you're being dramatic. I'm a good friend to you, and you know how much I love your parents. I would never do anything to hurt them."

Love her parents?

Did I really just say that?

"Andrea, I think rehab would be the best thing for you," Rachel said, rising from her seat and moving toward the door. Her hand rested on the knob for a moment before she turned back, her face set with quiet determination.

"You'll have to decide. Rehab or not. If you choose to go, I'll help you in any way I can. If you don't, you'll need to move out by Thursday morning."

Without another word, Rachel stepped out and gently closed the door behind her. Andrea grabbed a pillow and hurled it at the door. It bounced off and crumbled to the floor, silent, like the empty room she was left in.

The two women sat in the living room the next day, the dull murmur of the television filling the silence.

Andrea wasn't really watching. It was just background noise.

A distraction from the unease still clinging to her after Rachel's ultimatum.

Outside, the wind howled against the house, cold air sneaking in through the old windowpanes. A shiver ran down Andrea's spine, but she ignored it, pulling the blanket tighter around her shoulders.

Ron walked in carrying a couple of logs for the fireplace. The scent of fresh-cut wood clung to him, mingling with the faint smokiness from earlier burns.

Without a word, he knelt by the hearth and began arranging the logs with practiced care.

Andrea barely looked up. Her fingers drummed idly on the couch cushion.

Ron wasn't a man of many words when it came to her. He tolerated her, sure, but she'd always sensed his disapproval, subtle but ever-present. Like he'd been waiting for her to screw up again.

Which is why his next words caught her completely off guard.

Without looking up, he spoke.

"Andrea, I heard about a good rehab program here in Gilson, the Applegate Rehabilitation Center."

His voice was steady. Casual. As if he were discussing the weather.

Andrea stiffened.

"We can all check it out together if you'd like," he continued, adjusting the logs one final time before turning to face her.

"Rachel, Stephanie and I will support you however we can while you're there."

Andrea's eyes widened, a flicker of surprise breaking through her usual mask of indifference.

Mr. Vega?

Talking to me about rehab?

That wasn't how this usually went.

Her gaze flicked toward Rachel, half-expecting her to jump in.

To soften the moment.

To take the weight off Ron's words.

But to her surprise, Rachel looked just as caught off guard.

Because this... this wasn't Rachel gently urging her to get help.

This was Ron Vega.

The man who had barely spoken to her beyond polite tolerance.

Laying it out plainly.

And somehow…

That made it feel more real, more final.

Andrea turned to Ron and forced a half-hearted smile.

It felt more like a grimace.

"Thank you, Mr. Vega," she muttered, her voice unusually subdued. It was all she could manage without letting her real feelings slip through.

Inside, she was fuming.

How dare he?

How dare he sit there, acting like some benevolent father figure, offering her rehab like she was some pathetic idiot?

She wanted to snap back.

To roll her eyes.

To say, *Oh wow, rehab? What an original idea. Why didn't I think of that?*

But she bit her tongue.

Because Andrea might have been reckless.

But she wasn't stupid.

She couldn't risk losing her warm bed tonight.

So instead… she just sat there.

Her face hot.

Her pulse pounding beneath her skin.

The reality of her situation settled like a weight in her chest.

Rachel wasn't bluffing.

Rehab or move out.

There was no in-between.

She stared at the television, the colors flashing across the screen in a blur, but the images meant nothing.

Her mind was racing, flipping through options, grasping for an escape.

But for the first time in a long time, she had none.

Out of the corner of her eye, she caught Rachel watching her.

Not saying anything.

Just… watching.

Rachel could see it, the storm brewing beneath Andrea's carefully guarded expression.

But she didn't push.

Didn't speak.

And somehow, that silence was worse.

It stretched, thick and heavy, filling the room like a challenge neither of them wanted to address.

Andrea clenched her jaw, her chest tightening.

The walls were closing in.

And for the first time since moving in.

She was scared.

Suddenly, Andrea stood, her chair scraping loudly across the floor.

Without a word, she strode to her room, yanked her jacket from the hook, and shoved her boots on. Her hands trembled as she grabbed her bag.

"Where are you going?" Rachel's voice was cautious, with an edge Andrea didn't like.

"You said I had to make a decision, right?" she snapped, her voice tight.

"Well, I'm going for a walk. To think."

She didn't wait for a response.

She yanked the door open and stepped outside.

The icy winter air hit her like a slap, biting at her cheeks, cutting through her coat.

She walked fast, aimless but fueled by panic. Her boots crunched over the frozen sidewalk, each step harder than the last.

Tears burned hot trails down her face, only to vanish in the wind.

Above, the sky, usually an unsettling red, was choked with thick clouds, casting a pinkish-gray glow over everything.

Muted. Lifeless.

Like she was trapped in a limbo between choices.

The cold clawed at her bones, but she welcomed it.

At least it was something to feel.

Shit just got real, she thought bitterly. *I'm one decision away from being home-less.*

Her throat tightened.

And I don't want to go back to rehab.

It didn't work the first time, or the second. Or the third. It won't work now either.

She let out a shaky breath, watching it curl in the air, evaporating like every bit of control she'd once had.

I'm so screwed.

Her mind wandered to Victor.

It had been a while since they'd spoken, but the last time still burned in her memory.

She'd gone to his house, knocked on the door.

He never answered her calls anymore.

She remembered his face, cold, unreadable.

"Andrea, don't come here. I don't want to see you anymore."

She'd pleaded.

"I didn't know she was your sister! Let me apologize. Please, Victor, give me another chance."

There'd been a flicker in his eyes, something hurt, something unfinished.

But it didn't matter. His anger was louder.

Final.

"No. We're done."

Those words had shattered something inside her.

Even now, they echoed in the hollow space where hope used to be.

Victor wouldn't help her.

He wouldn't even look at her.

⸺◦⸺

Andrea pushed through the door of Burt's convenience store, the warmth inside slamming into her like a wave.

She headed straight for the refrigerated section.

"I just need a drink to calm down. To think," she muttered to herself.

Her fingers curled around a bottle...

But then she paused.

An idea struck.

It bloomed so fast, so fully, she couldn't help but grin.

"Yes, good idea, Andrea," she murmured, giving herself a pat on the back as if to celebrate her own cleverness.

She spotted the payphone outside and made a beeline for it. The booth was cracked, dirty—but it would do. She dropped in some coins, heart pounding.

Stephanie answered.

"Mrs. Vega, can I talk to Rachel?" Andrea asked, forcing her voice to sound steady.

"Sure!" came the chipper reply.

A brief pause. Then...

"Andrea? Where the hell are you?"

Rachel's voice sliced through the static.

Andrea gripped the receiver tighter, trying to draw courage from Rachel's voice.

"I'll go to rehab," she said, barely above a whisper. "I don't want to... but I will."

Silence.

Then Rachel's voice softened. "Okay. We'll help you, and—"

"There's something else."

Andrea hadn't meant to blurt it out. She'd planned to ease into it, to find the right words to make it sound believable. But it just spilled out before she could stop it.

Another pause. Rachel's voice turned sharp. "What?"

Andrea swallowed hard. "I'm pregnant."

Saying it aloud made it feel heavier.

Real.

"I didn't want to tell you or your parents because I was afraid you'd kick me out."

Silence.

Long enough to make Andrea wonder if Rachel had hung up.

Then, "Is it Victor's?"

"Yes," Andrea whispered.

"But he won't talk to me. He won't answer my calls."

Rachel exhaled. Her voice, when it returned, was steady.

"Then forget about Victor for now. What matters most is you getting treatment."

Andrea closed her eyes.

It wasn't the reaction she'd hoped for.

She'd expected concern, maybe a delay.

Instead, Rachel stayed firm.

Rehab.

No detour. No loophole.

Andrea mumbled a goodbye and hung up.

Her hand lingered on the metal receiver.

The cold of it sank into her bones.

Then she turned, walked back inside the store.

The buzzing fluorescent lights cast a sterile light over everything. The shelves, the floor, the tired cashier.

Andrea's feet moved on their own, past the snacks, the dusty cleaning supplies, straight to the back.

She grabbed a bottle of orange juice, cold, grounding.

Then she spotted the vodka.

Lined up like soldiers behind the counter.

She hesitated.

Then grabbed two minis.

And one big one.

She snatched a plastic cup on the way to the register.

The cashier, a middle-aged woman with a sour expression, didn't even glance at Andrea before snapping, "Hey! You gotta pay for that cup. No free shit around here."

Andrea rolled her eyes, exhaled through her nose.

Of course, they're charging for a stupid plastic cup.

"How much is the damn thing?" she muttered, fishing in her pockets.

The woman scoffed. "I don't have time for your crap. Can't you see I've got a line?"

She thrust her hand out. Fingers twitching.

Eyes flicking to the growing line behind Andrea.

Andrea froze.

Then smiled.

Slow. Icy.

She dropped a few coins onto the counter with a loud clatter.

"There's your money," she said sweetly.

"Now you can shove them up your ass, bitch."

A gasp sounded from behind her.

Andrea didn't wait to see whose.

She grabbed her stuff, shoved the door open, and stepped back into the cold.

The wind knifed across her face.

She gritted her teeth, jacket pulled tight.

Screw that lady. Screw this town.

She had bigger problems.

⸺◆⸺

Outside, the streets were quiet.

Just the occasional rumble of a car or shuffle of footsteps.

Near the store's entrance, a couple of beggars huddled together.

Layered in tattered coats, their breath fogging the air.

One of them.

A plump, disheveled old woman.

Caught Andrea's eye.

Her white hair hung in greasy strands around a bloated, weathered face.

Her eyes darted rapidly, wild and oddly alert. She grinned.

Her teeth were a disaster: yellow, cracked, some missing entirely.

Andrea looked away, heart kicking.

Something about the woman set her on edge.

She quickened her pace, crossing the street toward the park.

Wind rattled through the trees like dry bones.

The playground creaked.

Empty benches sat frosted and lifeless.

Andrea shoved her hands into her pockets.

Just get to the bench. One drink. That's all.

Her whole body shook.

She just needed to be alone.

To drink.

To think.

She was sure the park would be empty.

But she was wrong.

Chapter 7

As she settled onto the icy wooden bench, fumbling to unscrew the cap of her orange juice, movement caught in the corner of her eye made her freeze.

The old woman from the store.

Andrea's breath hitched as she watched her shuffle across the street, heavy boots scraping the concrete with each slow, deliberate step.

The way she moved made Andrea's stomach coil with unease. There was purpose behind each step, too much purpose.

The woman grinned. Too wide.

Her toothless smile stretched unnaturally across her weathered face.

"Hello," she rasped, oddly cheerful, plopping herself down on the bench beside Andrea.

Andrea stiffened.

A sharp, instinctive warning flared in her gut.

Something was wrong.

Up close, the woman smelled of something sour and damp, like rotting leaves soaked in wool. Her watery eyes gleamed with something unreadable, something that crawled under Andrea's skin like static.

She couldn't explain it, but she felt it, an unseen force, an energy that clung to the woman like an invisible fog.

It wasn't just the cold making her shiver now.

She tightened her grip on the plastic cup, forcing herself to stay composed.

She didn't want conversation.

She didn't want to be asked for money, or worse, to share her drink.

Without looking at the woman, she muttered, "Hello," hoping that would be enough to end it.

But the woman wasn't deterred.

"My name's Sonya. Sonya Mercer. And you are?"

Andrea exhaled sharply, irritation rising.

"Wanting to be alone. Thank you," she said, her tone clipped.

Sonya chuckled softly, unfazed.

"Well, I can see something's troubling you. Maybe I can help."

Andrea turned toward her, eyes narrowing.

"Look, lady, I don't care what your name is. I have no money, and I'm not sharing my drink, so get the hell away from me."

Still smiling, Sonya leaned back on the bench like she hadn't been insulted at all.

"I'm not here for your money or your drink," she said calmly. "At least, not right now."

Andrea stared, confused.

"You summoned me here, and I accepted," Sonya added, her voice light, unnervingly sure.

Andrea wrinkled her nose.

"I summoned *you?"* She dragged the word out in disbelief.

"I don't think so. Why would I do that? Get lost, lady, and take a bath. Yuck."

Sonya chuckled again.

"Not intentionally, of course. But energy doesn't lie.

Like attracts like.

I can feel it. You want something. Badly. And I can help."

Andrea's sarcasm faded to suspicion.

How does she know that?

She turned toward Sonya, her voice low and skeptical.

"Okay, so tell me, what do you think I want?"

She crossed her arms, smirking.

Daring her to answer.

Sonya's smile widened.

Her eyes glittered.

"It's Sonya," she corrected with a wink. "Call me Sonya."

Then her tone shifted, sharp, focused.

"That man of yours... what's his name?"

Andrea flinched.

"Victor, right?"

Her stomach dropped.

Before she could react, Sonya burst into a hearty laugh, deep, toothless, and far too loud for the quiet park.

The sound sent a chill racing down Andrea's spine.

How does this old lady know his name?

Then Sonya leaned in, her voice low and velvet-smooth.

"I can help you keep him. Make it hard for him to ever want to leave you again."

Andrea froze.

Her heart pounded.

She was both intrigued and terrified.

A flush crept over her skin, burning hot despite the frigid air.

And suddenly, she realized just how cold it was. Too cold to linger.

This woman knew about Victor. Andrea's breath quickened. Panic tightened in her chest.

Without a word, she gathered her things in jerky movements.

She downed the last of her drink, the citrus biting her throat, and tossed the empty cup into the trash.

She walked fast, her boots crunching hard against the icy path.

But she couldn't help it. She glanced back. Sonya was still there. Still smiling.

"Miss Andrea," Sonya called, her voice light and lilting. "You can find me here in the park... whenever you need me."

Andrea didn't respond. She just walked faster.

Behind her, Sonya whispered to herself,

"You'll be back."

As soon as Andrea disappeared down the path, Sonya stood and shuffled over to the trash can. She peered inside, checking the cup for leftover drops, but found none.

Andrea, now halfway down the path, stopped suddenly. A nagging thought tugged at the edge of her mind.

She turned back. Her breath curled in the air.

"How did you know my name?" she called, voice louder than she meant.

"I never told you my name!"

Sonya tilted her head, still grinning. Her eyes glinted.

Then, in a voice soft and sly, she said.

"Hmm... didn't you?"

The words slithered through the air like smoke, wrapping around Andrea, clinging to her even as she turned away.

She didn't answer. She couldn't.

Andrea's steps quickened.

But Sonya's voice, and the chill it carried, lingered long after she left the park.

Could this strange woman really help her get what she wanted?

Andrea didn't know. But she was curious.

Curious enough to return to the park in the morning.

———◆———

The next day, it was slightly warmer. Andrea sipped her coffee, grabbed her jacket, and headed for the door.

As she turned to close it, Rachel appeared behind her, resting a hand on the doorknob.

"Andrea, where are you going so early?" Rachel asked.

Andrea shrugged. "Just going for a walk. Oh, and I made coffee. Enjoy."

Rachel slowly shut the door, only to find Ron standing beside her.

"When does she start rehab?" he asked.

Rachel smiled faintly.

"She checks in on Thursday."

Ron looked out the window, watching Andrea disappear down the street.

"Thursday can't come soon enough," he muttered.

"What?" Rachel asked.

Ron shook his head and wrapped an arm around her shoulders.

"Oh, nothing. Come on. Let's get some of that coffee she made."

———◆———

Andrea walked straight to Sunrise Park, the same bench, the same worn path. The memory of Sonya Mercer had lingered all night, needling at her thoughts. Part of her wondered if it had even happened. Maybe she'd imagined the whole thing.

"Old lady, I hope you're at the park. I need to talk to you," she muttered.

When she arrived, her eyes scanned the area. A few dog walkers passed by, bundled against the cold, but the benches were mostly empty. Andrea sat on the same one as yesterday and waited.

Birds chirped. Distant traffic hummed. But there was no sign of Sonya.

Frustrated, she stood and crossed the street toward Burt's convenience store.

"I think a drink's in order while I wait," she murmured.

She still had some cash left from her last paycheck. Rachel, knowing Andrea would be checking into rehab soon, had told her to keep it rather than pay rent.

At the store entrance, Andrea cast one last glance toward the park.

No sign of her. Nothing. A slight pang of disappointment hit her.

She entered the store and grabbed two large bottles of vodka, a bottle of tequila for later, orange juice, and two plastic cups, just in case.

As she stepped back onto the sidewalk, waiting for the streetlight to change, her gaze drifted again toward the park.

Her breath caught.

There, sitting exactly where she'd been yesterday, was Sonya Mercer.

Andrea crossed the street, brown paper bag in hand. The bottles inside clinked softly. She sat on the opposite end of the bench without a word. Sonya glanced at the bag but said nothing.

"Let's get to the point," Andrea snapped. "What exactly do you want?"

Sonya tilted her head, her tone calm. "The question is, what do *you* want?"

Andrea crossed her arms. "Since you seem to know everything about my life, I'll make it easy: I want Victor back. I want him to take care of me. I'm tired of struggling. I know he could provide for me. His family owns property. They've got influence. But right now? He won't even speak to me."

The wind picked up, rustling the bare branches like dry bones. The park was nearly deserted, save for a few hunched figures moving quickly along winding paths. Damp earth and decaying leaves perfumed the air, autumn's remnants stubbornly clinging to frozen ground.

Andrea stared straight ahead, arms crossed, fists clenched in her lap. Sonya sat beside her, eerily still, her thin coat hardly moving in the wind. Her sharp eyes studied Andrea as if she'd been waiting for this confession.

"I'm supposed to check into Applegate Rehab on Thursday," Andrea blurted, her voice muffled by the wind. "I told my friend Rachel and her parents I'm pregnant. With Victor's baby."

She gave a bitter laugh. "I'm not, of course. I just... I thought it'd buy me time. But it didn't."

Her voice wavered.

"They still expect me to leave on Thursday. So, you see, old lady... I need to be pregnant."

She turned to Sonya. "Can you pull that off? With your witchcraft, magic, whatever it is? Because if you can..." She hesitated. "I know Victor will come back. He wouldn't abandon his child."

A gust of wind howled through the trees. Andrea flinched but didn't break eye contact.

Sonya just watched her. Her expression didn't change. Only the faintest smile curled at the corners of her lips. Calm. Expectant.

"Is that all you ask?" she finally said, voice almost amused. "To be pregnant when you are not, at this time?"

Andrea blinked.

"Yes," she said quickly.

Sonya's eyes gleamed. "With Victor's child?"

Andrea hesitated, then nodded. "Yes."

Sonya hummed as if weighing something ancient and strange. "That will take time."

Andrea leaned forward, desperate. "How much time? I need it to happen now. I calculated. It has to be now, or he won't believe it's his!"

Sonya didn't flinch.

The wind picked up again, swirling like it too was listening.

"Miss Andrea," Sonya said at last. "You must give me twenty-four hours. Meet me here tomorrow morning. Bring a pregnancy test."

Andrea frowned. "That's it?"

Sonya's gaze sharpened. "And I will require partial payment. Up front."

Andrea bristled. "What? Partial payment? Seriously?"

"You said you are not pregnant now," Sonya replied evenly. "If you do not pay, there will be no chance of it."

Andrea groaned and rummaged through her bag. Her fingers brushed the cool neck of the full vodka bottle. She yanked it out, along with a plastic cup, and shoved them at Sonya.

"Here," she growled. "If you burn me, you'll regret it. I'll see to that. And get your own damn orange juice."

Sonya took them without hesitation, her fingers curling around the bottle like it belonged to her.

Then, she looked up.

"Full name?" she asked. "I need Victor's full name."

Andrea stiffened. Her hand tightened on the bag.

"Why do you need his full name? Who are you, really?" she asked, her voice low. "Who is Sonya Mercer?"

Sonya's expression didn't change. Her voice dropped into something older than the wind itself.

"I am a seer. A mystic across time and of this world, and others."

Andrea's blood chilled. Her breath fogged before her in sharp little bursts.

Still, she pressed on. "His full name is Victor Costa," she said, voice taut.

Sonya nodded slowly, letting the name settle like dust over old stone. Then she turned and began walking away, but not before flashing a chilling, toothless grin.

Raising the vodka bottle in a mock toast, she rasped, "I'll consider this a down payment."

Andrea narrowed her eyes, but said nothing.

Something in Sonya's tone. Playful. Menacing. Final. Stuck with her.

She turned away and walked fast, arms crossed tight over her chest. The wind stung her face, but it wasn't the cold that made her shiver.

Behind her, barely audible, Sonya chuckled.

"You think you're the first desperate soul to come to me?" she murmured to no one.

Her words scattered on the wind.

She tilted her head back, took a swig from the bottle, and sighed, eyes distant, heavy with memories.

Once, a long time ago, she had begged for a wish too.

But wishes always had a cost.

They always did.

Chapter 8

Sonya

Sonya knew exactly who the Costa family was: an influential name in these parts, synonymous with wealth and power, their fortune built on real estate.

As she left the park, she moved with purpose, her heels clicking softly against the pavement. Two blocks down, she reached her home. A modest yet comfortable two-bedroom house. Unassuming to outsiders, but laced with unseen power.

The moment she stepped inside, she placed the bag with the vodka on the table and headed to her bedroom. In the bedroom, she shed the layers of deception. Her coat slid from her shoulders, followed by her dress, her wig, and finally, the false teeth that masked her true visage.

She turned to the ornate hand mirror resting on a velvet-draped table and gazed into it, watching as her reflection slowly shifted. Wrinkles smoothed, skin tightened, and her true face emerged: a woman of thirty-four, with straight, light brown hair threaded with hints of auburn, cascading past her shoulders.

After a steaming shower, she entered the dimly lit guest room. The air was thick with incense and whispered promises. At the center of the room, a single black candle flickered, casting jagged shadows along the walls.

She knelt before it, inhaled deeply, and began the summoning:

"Shadow-born, beyond the veil,
I call thee forth through night's black trail.
Anio, whisper of fate long spun,
By blood and dark, your power unfolds.
Come now, rise, heed my plea...
From depths unseen, unbind to me."

The candle's flame twisted unnaturally, darkening at its core. The mirror's surface rippled, as though the glass had turned to liquid. From its depths, a shadowed form began to take shape.

Anio's presence filled the space, unseen, yet oppressive. His voice slithered into her mind like a silky rasp.

"Speak."

Sonya steadied herself. The presence of Anio always unsettled her. His voice was a whisper woven through shadow, ancient and knowing.

"I met with her, as you instructed. She'll return tomorrow. But what she asks…" She hesitated, the weight of doubt pressing against her ribs. "I don't think—"

Anio's voice sliced through the space between them, cold and absolute.

"I know what she asks. And it shall be."

A pause followed, heavy with unseen force.

"Do you doubt me, Sonya?"

A ripple of unease passed through her, but she forced herself to speak.

"No… I just…" The words faltered. She could never lie to him. He already knew.

"She will return tomorrow," Anio continued, his tone laced with eerie certainty. "A child will be in her womb, but not until March."

Sonya exhaled slowly. "She wishes for it now."

"The soil is not yet ready," Anio murmured. "Not until March."

Sonya lowered her head in submission. "I will handle it."

"See that you do."

His voice rumbled low, like a storm gathering just beyond the horizon.

The figure in the mirror pulsed, only a suggestion of movement within the swirling darkness.

"The time will come when she will serve her purpose," he said, his voice slow, deliberate, like the turning of ancient gears. "For now, she must remain in place, unaware. When the moment arrives, she will be the key to a door that cannot yet be opened."

Sonya spoke hesitantly. "She asked to carry the child of Victor Costa. I'm not sure how that could be accomplished. Could that be?"

Anio's voice roared, shaking the air:

"It could be… and it will be. But not until March. There is a counterpart of Andrea. She lives in the earth you came from. She is pregnant with the counterpart of Victor. That fetus will be ready to transport into Andrea's womb in March."

Sonya swallowed. "And until then?"

A low, guttural chuckle echoed from the mirror, reverberating through the room like distant thunder, unsettling and inescapable.

"Until then... we let her believe she has a choice."

Anio's image faded from the mirror. Then he was gone.

Sonya wrapped the mirror in its usual dark green velvet cloth and returned it to the velvet-draped table. She blew out the candle, then walked to the kitchen and pulled a beer from the refrigerator.

Taking a long drink, she made her way to the living room and sank into a chair.

She replayed her conversation with Anio over and over.

She was disgusted by his words: "The fetus will be ready to be transported into Andrea's womb."

Stealing a woman's baby straight out of her body? Sonya's stomach turned.

How would Andrea feel if she knew the truth, that the child growing inside her wasn't hers, but stolen from another woman?

Something tells her that Andrea won't give it a second thought.

Each word echoed like a whisper from the past, tightening invisible chains around her. She took another sip, the bitterness grounding her for a moment.

But as the liquid burned down her throat, her thoughts slipped further into the past.

Back to how she ended up in this mess.

Back to the moment everything changed.

The moment that led her here,

To this life,

To this nightmare,

To the inescapable shadow that loomed over her.

Blue Earth 1957–Superior, Arizona

Identical twins Sonya and Tanya Mercer were born in 1950 in Superior, Arizona.

At age seven, Tanya invited Sonya to a place she called "the mountain top," claiming she had a friend there.

Skeptical but curious, Sonya agreed to go.

One Saturday afternoon, while their mother prepared lunch and their father helped a neighbor, Tanya declared it was time. As they walked, Sonya suddenly found herself standing on a mountain.

There, she watched Tanya approach an older man with long black-and-white hair tied in a ponytail, dressed entirely in white.

Tanya called him Anio.

Sonya watched silently as Anio handed Tanya a necklace, a brown chain with an indistinct ball at the end, and placed it gently around her neck.

Sonya tried hard to hear what they were saying, straining through the wind, but their voices remained just out of reach.

Then, after watching Anio pull Tanya into a warm hug, the girls were suddenly back in their yard, as if nothing had happened at all.

Sonya never got a good look at the necklace.

But she couldn't stop wondering, bitterly, why she didn't have a kind friend to give her special gifts. Why Tanya and not her? They looked exactly alike.

From that moment on, a quiet, simmering jealousy began to take root in her heart, a jealousy that never quite let go.

Blue Earth 1968–Superior, Arizona

Sonya

Sonya sat on her neatly made bed, tapping her foot impatiently. The thought of Tanya outshining her gnawed at her pride.

She reached for the AM radio on the nightstand and twisted the dial until the static gave way to a gritty guitar riff. Cream's *"Sunshine of Your Love"* pulsed through the small speaker, filling the room with heat and swagger. It was her kind of sound: bold, unapologetic.

She stared at the dress Tanya had shown her earlier, a simple navy A-line with lace trim. It was nice but not dazzling. It was safe. And Tanya was anything but safe. She was quieter, more reserved, but when she made a statement, people noticed.

"I bet she's hiding it in her closet," Sonya muttered, eyes narrowing toward Tanya's side of the room.

Her closet door was slightly ajar, teasing her curiosity.

Sonya knew she shouldn't snoop. But the fear of being overshadowed at their high school graduation party outweighed any guilt.

She rose from the bed and tiptoed across the room, her heartbeat quickening with each step. Glancing back at the door to make sure Tanya wasn't coming, she eased the closet open.

Inside, Tanya's belongings were arranged with meticulous care, far more organized than Sonya's side. Dresses hung in a tidy row, but none stood out. Still, Sonya couldn't shake the feeling that something was hidden.

She rifled carefully through the hangers until her hand brushed against something tucked behind the others, a garment bag.

Her stomach twisted with a mix of excitement and dread as she unzipped it.

Inside lay a stunning scarlet cocktail dress, its intricate beading shimmering even in the dim light. It was bold, glamorous, and everything Tanya claimed not to be.

Sonya's jaw clenched. She was right.

"That sneaky little bitch," she hissed.

She didn't know whether to confront Tanya or find a way to outshine her.

But one thing was certain: she wasn't going to let her twin steal the spotlight at the biggest party of their high school lives.

Her eyes drifted toward Tanya's dresser, the unspoken boundary between them.

They had an agreement: no snooping through each other's drawers. But the top drawer, the so-called *stuff drawer,* had always tugged at her curiosity.

Today, that tug became irresistible.

Taking a breath, Sonya crossed the room and placed her hand on the handle.

Her fingers trembled slightly before she pulled it open. The faint creak of wood broke the silence.

The first thing she saw made her heart stop.

Lying atop a small yellow box was the old brass necklace, the one with the strange little globe.

The sight of it jolted her back to the mountaintop, to Anio, and to Tanya's necklace.

A memory she had nearly buried.

Sonya could still feel the crisp mountain air, still see Anio placing the necklace around Tanya's neck, the way she had tucked it away and never mentioned it again.

She shook her head.

Had that really happened?

For years, she'd questioned the reality of that day. But now, seeing the necklace, tangible and real, sent a chill down her spine.

It was real. Every bit of it.

She strained to hear any movement outside the room.

All she could hear was the sound of the radio.

Sonya reached into the drawer, her fingers brushing the cool brass chain. She picked it up and held it to the light.

The globe hung suspended from the chain, small but intricate.

Two identical maps of the world were etched on either side of the crystal, separated by a thin brass ring. It wasn't a traditional globe that wrapped around, but rather a mirrored flattening, like two Earths facing each other.

Her brow furrowed as she turned it over in her hand. Something about the design felt... wrong.

Could it mean something? Could it be tied to her and Tanya being identical twins?

Or was it just some bizarre trinket gifted by a strange old man?

The absurdity of it made her laugh under her breath, the sound cracking through the tension.

But the laugh didn't last long.

The necklace felt heavier now, like it carried more than metal and crystal.

This wasn't just some ugly piece of junk.

Without fully understanding why, Sonya slipped the necklace over her head.

Just as Tanya burst into the room.

"NO! It's not for you!"

Sonya spun around. Tanya and their mother stood frozen in the doorway, their faces pale with terror.

They screamed.

A red light flooded the room, vibrating the walls as if the house itself had come alive.

Sonya tried to speak. *What's happening?* But no sound left her lips.

The room shook violently.

The crimson light blinded her. Dizzy and nauseated, she reached for something to hold on to.

Then everything went black.

Red Earth 1968—Superior, Arizona

Sonya

Sonya awoke in her room, disoriented. Her father stood beside her bed, while Aunt Helen sat rocking in a chair nearby.

Groggily, Sonya asked, "Where's Mom and Tanya?"

Her father and Aunt Helen exchanged a quick glance.

"What kind of stupid question is that? Have you lost your mind, girl?" Aunt Helen snapped, her voice dripping with disdain.

The words hit Sonya like a slap, pulling her back. Aunt Helen was her father's sister. And definitely not Sonya's favorite aunt. To Sonya, she was a sarcastic thorn in her side, much like her father and her sharp-tongued grandmother.

Sonya glanced up at her father, who frowned and said, "You know your mom's been dead for years. And who the hell is Tanya? Get up. You're fine. There's work to do, and you need to help your aunt with the laundry."

Still groggy, Sonya looked around the room. Her bed was familiar, but the other bed, on the opposite side of the room, was Aunt Helen's.

We share a room? she thought, confused.

Shaking off her discomfort, she got up and wandered into the living room, where something peculiar caught her attention: a faint red glow filtering through the windows.

Curious, Sonya moved closer and peered outside. The sky was red, not dark or fiery, just vividly crimson where blue skies should have been.

"Why is the sky red? Is there a fire?" she asked, her voice tinged with unease.

The question hung in the air, unanswered, as the crimson light cast its unsettling glow across the room.

She looked over at her father, who, along with Aunt Helen, stared at her as if she'd grown three heads.

"What are you talking about? Why wouldn't the sky be red? What color do you think it should be?" Aunt Helen asked, her tone sharp.

Her father frowned. "If you keep talking crazy like this, Sonya, we'll have to take you to see Dr. Martin. You'll have to work your ass off to pay that bill, so I suggest you get it together."

Sonya forced a smile, trying to steady her voice. "No, I'm fine. I just need some water."

Her father's gaze lingered on her, sharp and suspicious, as he pulled a cigarette from his shirt pocket, struck a match, and lit it with practiced ease. Without a word, he headed out the front door.

Sonya watched him go, biting back the question that burned on the tip of her tongue: Since when does Dad smoke?

She turned back to the window, where the red sky seemed to glare back at her, oppressive and unnerving. It wasn't just strange; it felt wrong, deeply unsettling.

Her thoughts were interrupted by Aunt Helen's sharp voice. "It's such a beautiful day. Perfect for drying clothes. Get out there and hang them on the line!"

Sonya grabbed the basket of laundry, balancing a packet of clothespins on top, and stepped out the back door. The red sky loomed overhead, casting an eerie hue over everything.

As she stared at it, a cold certainty settled in her chest: this wasn't her world. It was a different world entirely.

She was in a *red world.*

—◇—

The night air in the house was thick with tension. It had been a few days since Sonya appeared in this hellhole, and every moment since had been a battle. She and Aunt Helen clashed daily, their arguments driving her father to the brink.

During one of their latest spats, Sonya clenched her fists as Aunt Helen's sharp voice lashed into her like a whip.

"You're nothing but a worthless, selfish girl, a burden, just like your mother was!" Aunt Helen spat, her face contorted in disgust. "Maybe that's why she's in an early grave. Maybe she knew you'd turn out like this!"

Sonya's blood boiled. "You're a bitter, hateful bitch! That's all you are!" she snapped, her voice shaking.

Aunt Helen's hand twitched, as if she wanted to strike her, but before she could, Sonya's father stormed into the room. His expression was cold, unmoving. He had already chosen a side, and it wasn't hers.

"Sonya, get to your damn room."

"No!" she fired back. "She started it... she's always—"

Her father grabbed her by the arm and shoved her backward, sending her stumbling into the hallway. "Enough! I don't want to hear your damn mouth! You're gonna shut up, and you're gonna stay in that room until I say otherwise."

From behind her father, Aunt Helen stood smirking, a curl of satisfaction on her lips. The sight made Sonya's stomach twist. He had never pushed her before.

"I said go!"

When she hesitated, he grabbed the door, shoved her inside, and locked it from the outside.

Sonya pounded on the door, hot tears burning her eyes. "Let me out! You can't just lock me in here, you bastard!"

Silence.

Then, footsteps walking away.

Her hands curled into fists. Her breath came fast and ragged. She wouldn't stay here. She couldn't.

A few minutes later, Sonya pried open the bedroom window, heart racing as she slipped out into the cool night air. She landed softly in the grass and took off without looking back.

She had no idea where she was going, only that she had to get as far away as possible.

⚬

The bus stop was empty, bathed in the unnatural red glow of the sky. Sonya dropped onto the bench, her hands shaking from anger and exhaustion.

She barely noticed the man in the dark suit sitting beside her until he spoke.

"Going somewhere, Sonya?"

She stiffened, her head snapping toward him.

He was too clean, too composed for this world. His black suit was crisp. His hair neatly combed back. He looked out of place, but something about him felt even more wrong than the sky above.

She hadn't told him her name.

"How do you know my name? And who the hell are you?" she asked warily.

The man smiled. Too calm. Too knowing.

"I know many things," he said smoothly. "I know you feel trapped. I know you don't belong here. And I know," he paused, tilting his head ever so slightly. "That you had a sister."

Sonya's stomach dropped.

Her breath caught in her throat. *He knew.*

Her legs tensed, ready to bolt. *No one here knew about Tanya. No one.*

She forced herself to play it cool. "What are you talking about?"

The man's smile didn't waver. He just studied her, eyes gleaming like a predator toying with its prey.

"You don't have to pretend with me, Sonya. I know about Tanya. I know what was taken from you."

Her throat went dry. "How do you know about her?"

"I know many things," he said again, his voice softer this time, almost comforting. "More importantly, I know how you can stop being the forgotten one. You don't have to be second-best anymore, Sonya."

The words sank their hooks deep into her chest. Second-best. That's all she had ever been. Even here. Even now.

The man leaned forward, his voice a whisper in the heavy air.

"What if I told you I could give you power?"

Sonya swallowed hard. She should leave. Every instinct screamed at her to run.

But she didn't. She stayed.

She let him speak.

And that's when everything changed.

He didn't demand. He listened. He let her spill her frustrations, her anger toward Tanya, toward a life where she always came second.

"You were meant for more, Sonya," he murmured. "What if I told you I could change things... shape the world around you?"

She scoffed. "That's impossible."

"Is it?" He gestured toward her neck, toward the globe necklace hanging there.

"That trinket isn't just jewelry," he whispered. "It's a key. And with it, you could have something your sister never did—real power."

Sonya hesitated.

"Go ahead," he urged. "Make a wish. Something small."

She thought for a moment, then muttered, "I wish Aunt Helen would shut up for once."

The air crackled. A gust of unseen force swept through the town.

He smiled, just slightly. "Go home and see for yourself."

Sonya frowned, uneasy. But she couldn't resist.

She ran back to the house, heart pounding. He followed.

When she reached the porch, she heard it; silence.

Aunt Helen sat in the living room, her mouth open, eyes wide with panic. She was trying to speak, but no sound escaped her lips.

Sonya gasped. "What... what did I just do?"

The man smiled. "You're learning."

A shiver ran through her as she met his gaze. "Who are you?" she asked, her voice barely above a whisper.

He smirked. "You can call me Anio."

***

As the years passed, the power she once craved became a noose tightening around her neck.

Yes, he provided her with a home, met her every basic need, but at a cost. As long as she carried out his will, his evil deeds.

He thrived on chaos and fear, drinking in the energy they unleashed. So he sent her into town, stirring unrest, spreading fear and anger. Feeding his hunger.

She wanted out.

But Anio knew. He always knew.

"You can't stop, Sonya. You can't just walk away." His voice was darker now, less patient. Hungrier.

"I don't care," she whispered. "I'm done."

Anio laughed, not loud, not forced. Just a deep, knowing amusement.

"You think you have a choice?"

For years he had waited. Patiently. Because he already knew exactly what he would take from her.

And then, one night, she woke, gasping for breath, the necklace searing hot against her skin.

The walls shifted. The shadows oozed along the corners, stretching.

And he was there. Watching from the corner of her room.

Not entering. Not appearing. Just there.

"Anio?" Her voice wavered, laced with fear.

"It's time, Sonya," he said, his tone unyielding.

She sat up abruptly, eyes wide. "Time for what?"

His gaze flicked to the necklace. "Give it to me." His voice was smooth, inevitable.

"No."

He stepped closer. The shadows followed.

"Give. It. To. Me."

Her fingers refused to obey. But the moment the necklace left her hands, the ground trembled.

The red sky flared.

Anio exhaled a long, shuddering breath, like a man who had been starving for centuries.

"You were never the important one, Sonya," he whispered as he turned away. "You were just the first step."

And just like that, she was powerless again.

Sonya watched, her breath caught in her throat.

Anio was changing before her eyes, his form shifting like a mirage solidifying into something more ominous. More real.

The slick, sharp-dressed man was gone.

Before her stood his true form.

Tall and imposing, his long salt-and-pepper hair was slicked back and tied, but shadows clung to it unnaturally. His eyes, too dark, did not reflect light but swallowed it whole, as if they were endless voids. His skin, worn with an ancient quality, carried the weight of something beyond time itself.

He wore a simple, robe-like garment, but it was not the light, welcoming fabric she remembered. This one was earth-toned, like the crimson soil of Red Earth, with ragged strips along the arms. The fabric, rough and woven, should have been ordinary, yet something about it felt wrong, unnatural in its drape, as though it did not fully belong to this world.

And his feet—there were no feet.

He hovered just above the ground, his presence stretching beyond the physical, an entity bound not by Earth, but by something else entirely.

Sonya's heart pounded in her chest as realization dawned upon her.

It was him.

The man Tanya had encountered on the mountain all those years ago.

But that Anio, Tanya's Anio, was different. He had been just as tall, just as commanding, but his eyes were brown, bright and warm, full of wisdom and kindness. His robe had been light in color, a reflection of the comfort and peace he once exuded.

This Anio was wrong.

This Anio was something else entirely.

Chapter 9

Red Earth 1984—Gilson, Texas

Andrea returned to the same bench the next morning, nerves wound tight as she clutched the pregnancy test she'd brought with her.

Twenty-four hours had passed since her deal with Sonya, and her anxiety was at an all-time high. She scanned the path, fingers tightening around the test.

"Where are you, old lady?" she muttered under her breath.

Sinking onto the bench, she let out a long, shaky exhale. Doubts crept in like shadows at the edges of her thoughts.

This is ridiculous. How could some old woman conjure a baby inside me? Victor's child, no less?

She glanced down at the test in her hands, suddenly feeling foolish.

What am I even doing? Sitting here with a pregnancy test, actually thinking this could happen?

Moments later, she spotted Sonya walking down the path, her steps deliberate, her expression unreadable. Andrea shifted over, making room on the bench.

"Well? Can I take the test now?" she blurted before Sonya even sat down.

Sonya lowered herself onto the bench and replied calmly, "You can, but it will be negative."

Andrea's anger flared. "What do you mean it'll be negative? Are you playing games with me?"

"No," Sonya said evenly. "You'll have to fake a pregnancy until March. But come March, you *will* be carrying Victor's child."

Andrea's eyes narrowed. Her fists clenched at her sides. "Why the hell do I have to fake it until then? What does that even mean? Wait until the baby is Victor's? And how do I know you're not full of it? Prove it!"

Sonya stood slowly, brushing invisible dust from her skirt. Her expression was unreadable. "What if I told you the baby will have to be taken from someone else... so you can finally get what you want?" Andrea's brows pulled together. "Taken from someone else?" She shrugged. "As long as it's Victor's, what do I care?"

Sonya shook her head slowly, almost in disbelief. "Yes... that's what I thought." She paused, then added, "If I prove I'm telling the truth, will you agree to the terms? Will you agree to fake your pregnancy until March?"

Andrea hesitated.

Distrust churned inside her, but so did desperation.

Every instinct screamed *don't trust her,* but the longing in her gut, her need for this to be real, was stronger.

Sonya scanned the area. Seeing no one nearby, she reached into her bag and pulled out a small container filled with a crimson liquid.

"Drink this," she said, holding it out. "It will give you all the symptoms of pregnancy. Any test you take until March will show positive."

Andrea eyed the container skeptically. "So I'm supposed to drink this and poof, everything magically works out?" Her voice dripped with sarcasm.

Sonya didn't answer. She simply met Andrea's gaze, unblinking.

Andrea rolled her eyes. "Oh, what the hell," she muttered, grabbing the container and raising it to her lips.

"Wait!" Sonya's voice cut through the air, sharp and commanding. "I must say the words to seal the magic."

Lowering the container, Andrea watched as Sonya glanced around, then began to chant:

"By moon's soft glow and earth's embrace,
Seed of change, now find your place.
Through blood and breath, this path be spun,
A mother's gift at last begun.
Body rise to mimic life,
Veil the truth, conceal the strife.
Let signs align, the truth be blurred,
Until the promise is assured.
As I will it, so shall it be,
A binding spell of certainty."

Sonya nodded. "Now. Drink."

Andrea hesitated for a beat, then tipped the container back.

The liquid burned faintly as it slid down her throat.

"You can take the test now," Sonya said evenly.

Andrea narrowed her eyes.

"I'll go to the park restroom and take it. And you're coming with me."

Sonya shrugged a shoulder and followed without a word.

Inside the stall, Andrea hovered near the tiny test tube, heart racing as the minutes crawled by. The longer she waited, the more doubt crept in. She glanced again, squinting hard. There it was. A faint blue ring forming at the bottom of the tube.

Her breath caught.

"Positive," she whispered, then louder: "It worked!"

Bursting from the stall, test tube clutched tight, she turned, expecting Sonya's knowing smile.

But the restroom was empty.

Sonya was gone.

Confused, Andrea's gaze fell on an envelope lying on the floor.

The old parchment paper looked oddly out of place, almost glowing in the dim light.

She picked it up, opened it, and read the message inside:

Our business is far from over. What is now in motion cannot be undone. Be ready, Andrea, the time will come.

Andrea laughed bitterly and crumpled the paper, tossing it into the trash.

But as she turned to leave, a chill crept down her spine.

She couldn't shake the feeling that Sonya's message wasn't just a warning.

It was a promise.

⸻ ◆ ⸻

After leaving the park, Andrea began the slow walk back to Rachel's parents' house. Fatigue hit her like a wave. Her body felt heavy, and a faint nausea churned in her stomach.

She smiled faintly to herself.

The magic was at work.

Her thoughts drifted to Victor.

Now she could tell him she was pregnant with his child.

The image played out in her mind: Victor returning to her, offering her a home, caring for her and the baby.

The thought filled her with cautious hope.

But then her mind turned to March, the time when a real baby would be growing inside her.

A flicker of doubt crept in. *Do I really need a baby?* she wondered.

All I need is for Victor to believe I'm pregnant.

The timing is perfect; he'll think it's his.

Her steps slowed as the weight of her plan settled on her.

She brushed off the unease.

Oh well.

Whatever it takes to bind him to me.

As Andrea crossed the street, she spotted Victor leaving Burt's market with a woman.

Her heart raced. It's him.

But the woman wasn't his sister, Bridgette.

No, it was someone else.

Victor's new girlfriend.

Serena.

She walked beside him with confident grace.

Her glossy chestnut hair fell in soft waves around delicate features, and her hazel eyes shimmered with quiet allure.

As they moved together, Victor casually draped his arm around her waist, an intimate, effortless gesture that spoke of tenderness.

Strangers turned to admire them.

Andrea hesitated, the sight of their affection sending a fresh wave of emotions crashing into her.

Victor's eyes widened when he saw her.

Serena looked at him, then at Andrea with confusion.

"Can I help you?" Serena asked, her tone sharp with suspicion.

"I just want to talk with Victor for a minute," Andrea replied, locking eyes with him.

Victor turned to Serena, visibly uneasy. "Give me a minute."

Serena stiffened. "No! If some woman wants to talk to my man, she can say it in front of me."

My man? Andrea's stomach turned.

She wanted lash out at her.

But thought better of it.

Victor faced her, his voice cold. "Say what you have to say and then leave me alone."

Andrea didn't flinch. "Fine. I just wanted you to know… you're going to be a dad in July. We'll need to talk about this, so contact me through Rachel."

Victor's face reddened. "I don't believe you!" he snapped. "You probably heard I have a girlfriend and now you're trying to start trouble. And even if you are pregnant, it's not mine. Leave me alone."

Andrea stood frozen, his words slicing through her.

A girlfriend? This can't be happening.

Red Earth 1985–Gilson, Texas

Andrea gave birth to a healthy baby boy on July 23, 1985.

That morning, Rachel called Victor to inform him. He hadn't seen or heard from Andrea since the day he denied her pregnancy. He had moved on with Serena, their life unfolding without interruption.

"She had the baby this morning, Victor. You're a dad," Rachel said over the phone. There was a pause.

"Victor? Are you still there?" she asked.

"Uh… yeah. She just had the baby? Where? Um…" he stammered, clearly caught off guard.

"Andrea and the baby are at Gilson Medical Center," Rachel said. "She told you she was pregnant. You didn't believe her, but she was telling the truth."

Victor snapped, "How do I even know it's mine?" Rachel hesitated, choosing her words. "You don't. Not completely. Especially if you're already suspicious. But Andrea's been living at my parents' house since before she got pregnant. She hasn't dated anyone. I'm her best friend. I'd know if she had. But it's your decision whether to believe me."

Victor said nothing.

Rachel continued, "She asked me to call because the rehab center won't allow the baby to stay. She still has five months left in the program. She's asking if you'll care for the baby until then."

Victor paused. "I'll… I'll call you back and let you know."

"Okay, but there's not much time. Please call tonight or tomorrow at the latest."

"Rachel?" Victor asked suddenly.

"Yeah?"

"Is it a boy or a girl?"

"You have a healthy son," Rachel replied. "His name is David."

Victor slowly set the phone down, his thoughts spiraling.

A strange mix of emotions washed over him: relief, pride, maybe even something softer he didn't want to name.

It had to be his, because the idea of Andrea having another man's baby made his blood boil.

The strength of that feeling startled him.

He shouldn't be reacting like this. He was with Serena. He loved Serena. So why did the idea of Andrea, of Andrea's child, cut so deep?

Victor dropped into a nearby chair, staring at his hands. He didn't understand it, and he didn't want to.

But deep inside, something still hadn't let go.

He picked up the phone again and dialed his parents.

He didn't mention his doubts.

He kept it simple.

"You're grandparents now," he said quietly. "I have a son."

⸻◦⸻

Andrea and her newborn returned to Applegate Rehabilitation Center, where they were greeted by Jillian Grayson, the assistant director.

"The baby can stay with you for the next two weeks," Jillian said, her tone firm. "But after that, you'll need to find a suitable home for him. Otherwise, you'll have to leave Applegate."

Before Andrea could respond, a soft knock interrupted them.

The receptionist stepped in.

"Ms. Grayson, there's a Mrs. Costa and her attorney, Mr. Jackson, here. Mr. Jackson has requested to speak with Andrea Perez."

Andrea's heart skipped.

Jillian frowned, then nodded. "Show him in."

A tall, lean man in his late forties entered, briefcase in hand.

His salt-and-pepper hair was neatly combed, and his calculating eyes peered from behind thin glasses. His navy-blue suit was crisp. His posture upright and precise. Everything about him was deliberate.

"I'm looking for Andrea Perez," he said. "I represent Mr. Victor Costa, who is here with his mother, Mrs. Costa. They're prepared to care for the baby, as requested."

Andrea stood abruptly. "I'm Andrea Perez!"

Jillian looked to her. "Are you okay with this?"

Andrea nodded, still processing. "Yes."

Jillian gave her a supportive nod before stepping out and closing the door.

Mr. Jackson turned toward Andrea. "My clients claim you've asked for assistance with the baby, so you can focus on your goals and starting fresh." His tone was neutral, but each word seemed carefully placed.

Andrea, unaware of the subtle undertone, took the statement at face value.

She believed this arrangement was temporary. Just until she finished her program.

Maybe even until Victor came back to her.

For a moment, hope flickered.

Is he here... for me?

She frowned. "Why do they need a lawyer? And why is Julia here instead of Victor? Where is Victor?"

Mr. Jackson replied smoothly, "Mr. Costa stepped outside and Mrs. Costa is assisting with paperwork. When the time comes, the baby will be released into their care. It's just legal formalities."

He studied her carefully, noting her tentative nod.

Satisfied, he placed a stack of papers in front of her.

"I'll need your signature," he said.

Before Andrea could respond, the door opened again.

A petite, well-dressed woman entered with a wide, practiced smile.

Her lipstick was red, her makeup expertly done, her gray pantsuit crisp and professional.

"This is Anita," Mr. Jackson said. "My assistant. She's also a notary."

Andrea glanced warily at the paperwork as Anita approached, her warm, disarming smile.

"I'll need your ID," Anita said cheerfully.

Andrea retrieved it from the nightstand and handed it over.

"It'll take me some time to read through all this," Andrea said, her voice cautious.

Anita exchanged a quick glance with Mr. Jackson, but her smile held steady.

"Oh, don't worry about the wording," she said kindly.

"It's just as Mr. Jackson explained: Victor Costa will care for the baby while you focus on getting your life back in order. That's all."

Her cheerful demeanor never faltered as she handed back Andrea's ID.

Andrea felt comforted by Anita's warm presence.

The intimidation she had felt from Mr. Jackson faded; Anita's trusting energy reassured her.

Convinced there was nothing to worry about, Andrea signed the papers without reading them, ignoring what she was agreeing to.

Anita quickly notarized the document, her smile never wavering.

Mr. Jackson gathered the papers, placed them in his briefcase, and handed Andrea an envelope.

"Everything's in order now," he said before he and Anita headed for the door.

Andrea smiled, relieved.

She felt at ease, believing little David would be safe with his father until she completed her recovery program.

As Mr. Jackson walked toward the door, he paused and turned back to Andrea.

"The Costas will be here tonight to pick up the baby," he said, his tone matter-of-fact.

Andrea's face paled, her distress immediate. "Wait! I was told I had two more weeks with him—they can't take him tonight!" she shouted, her voice trembling.

Mr. Jackson's lips curled into a devious smirk.

"Yes, they can, and they will," he replied coldly.

"The envelope I gave you contains copies of the documents you signed. My assistant will send you copies of the signed and notarized documents once we're back at the office. Have a good afternoon."

Without waiting for a response, he turned and walked out the door, leaving Andrea stunned and reeling.

———— ❖ ————

That night, Victor and his mother arrived at the rehab center.

While Victor waited in the reception lobby, Julia entered Andrea's room, accompanied by Ms. Grayson.

Julia's eyes landed immediately on the baby in Andrea's arms.

Her sharp gaze softened, just slightly, as she took in how much the infant resembled Victor as a newborn.

Then she looked up, and her expression hardened.

"We're here to pick up the baby," Julia said flatly.

Andrea glared at her. "I had permission to keep him for two weeks! Why are you taking him now?"

Julia straightened, her chin lifting. "I will not have a degenerate like you raising my grandchild," she replied coldly.

Andrea shot to her feet, ready to lash out, but Ms. Grayson stepped between them.

"Andrea, please," she said gently but firmly. "You've had a long day. Get some rest. I'm sure they'll bring the baby by to visit you soon."

Andrea looked down at her son, kissed his forehead, and whispered, "Be good for Daddy."

Julia snorted. "No. It's Nana. It's Daddy and Nana," she corrected, a smirk twisting her lips.

In truth, Andrea wasn't as devastated by them taking the baby as she was furious that Julia had outmaneuvered her.

She had won.

The baby had been Andrea's leverage: her plan to bring Victor back.

And now that leverage was gone.

The thought burned in her chest, igniting a fire of rage and determination.

The only thing she could focus on now was finishing the program.

So she could make them all pay.

In truth, Andrea wasn't as devastated by them taking the baby as she was

---

The years slipped away like water through Andrea's fingers, each one marking another failed attempt to see her son, another battle lost against Julia's fortress of influence.

It wasn't just Julia's wealth that intimidated Andrea; it was her unshakable grip on power. She had an army at her disposal: silver-tongued lawyers, judges in her pocket, and a network of elite connections that could bury someone in legal quicksand.

Andrea never stood a chance.

She tried everything: letters, phone calls, even showing up outside Julia's estate in a desperate bid to catch a glimpse of David. Every attempt was crushed.

Restraining orders were filed. Police were called.

Andrea quickly learned that if she stepped too far out of line, Julia would make sure she disappeared.

By 1987, Andrea's life had unraveled. The weight of her failures pressed against her like suffocation.

She bounced from job to job, her heart never in any of it.

Nothing ever felt like a fresh start, just temporary places to hide from the truth.

No direction. No passion. Only a past that refused to let go.

Then came the mistake that sealed her fate.

She had been working at a rundown movie theater, selling popcorn to bored teenagers and tearing ticket stubs without thought, when temptation whispered.

The cash drawer was always right there. Twenties nestled between crumpled ones, the till full and easy to reach.

At first, it was just skimming, small bills, barely noticeable. But desperation is a hungry thing.

Soon, small amounts turned into hundreds. Then thousands.

The night she took four thousand dollars was the night everything fell apart.

She thought she'd been discreet. She thought no one had noticed. But the manager did. The books didn't lie. Within days, the police were at her door.

The trial was swift. Too swift. Julia's name was never spoken aloud, but Andrea felt her influence in every moment.

She had no money for a decent lawyer. No one to speak on her behalf. No character witnesses.

The prosecution painted her as a thief without conscience. A woman who had stolen from her employer, betrayed trust, and spiraled out of control.

The verdict was inevitable.

Andrea Perez was sentenced to five years at Adams Correctional Institution for Women.

Chapter 10

Prison was worse than Andrea had imagined.

Cold cement floors. The hum of fluorescent lights that never truly turned off. The stale scent of sweat and bleach lingering in the air.

The days bled into one another, weeks slipping by in an agonizing cycle of monotony.

But the worst part wasn't the bars or the confinement.

It was knowing she had nobody waiting for her.

She had once believed Sonya's words. The old woman had sworn that Victor would return when he learned she was pregnant. That he would come back for her. To build the family she had always dreamed of.

Victor had come back.

But not for her.

Only for the baby.

During her incarceration, Andrea endured a painful silence. Days blurred into weeks, then months, stretching the void between her and the life she once knew. No letters came from Victor. No word of David.

It was as if they had vanished.

Or worse...

As if she had.

In the beginning, she clung to hope. She told herself Victor might soften. That despite everything, he wouldn't erase her entirely from David's life.

But hope is a fragile thing.

And it chipped away, piece by piece.

Her only lifeline was Rachel.

Through the sterile walls of the prison, Rachel's letters arrived like small rays of light in an otherwise endless night. She never missed a week. And in those neatly penned pages, Andrea found her only tether to the outside world.

Rachel wrote about everything: her job, the people they used to know, and the small, forgettable details that made life feel real.

"It's getting colder out here, but the damn neighbor still insists on mowing his lawn at the crack of dawn. If you were here, you'd be throwing something at him. I just know it. "I ran into Bridgette last week. She pretended not to see me, but I know she did. Same old high-and-mighty act."

Rachel never made empty promises. She never said she could fix things or get Andrea out. She never told Andrea what she wanted to hear, only what she could tell her.

That honesty made her letters all the more precious.

They were proof that someone still remembered her.

That she hadn't been completely erased.

Without them, Andrea wasn't sure she would've survived the years that followed.

Red Earth 1992–Gilson, Texas

A few months after her release, Andrea took a calculated risk.

Through Rachel, she sent a message to Victor. Ostensibly requesting to see her son.

But deep down, she had ulterior motives.

She framed it as a simple request.

A supervised visit.

A mother wanting to reconnect with the child she'd been torn away from.

But in truth, Andrea saw it as the first move in a larger game.

Victor's initial response was swift and merciless: No.

For two agonizing weeks, Andrea lived in limbo.

She told herself he might reconsider.

That he would see reason.

Each day that passed without a reply gnawed at her.

Still, she refused to give up.

Then, the call came.

Rachel's steady voice wavered with something unreadable. "Victor agreed."

Andrea nearly dropped the phone. "What?"

"But only under strict conditions," Rachel warned. "He'll meet you at Sunrise Park this Saturday at two p.m., for thirty minutes. No longer."

Andrea gripped the receiver tighter, the plastic pressing into her palm. "Thank you, girl. I owe you."

As she hung up, a storm of emotions surged through her: relief, anxiety, hope, and something more dangerous: expectation.

This could be it.

Not just a chance to see David, but a turning point.

A path back to the life that had been stolen from her.

But doubt twisted in her gut.

Had Victor moved on?

Was there another woman in his life?

Did David even know who she was?

The thought of someone else raising her son, calling her mom, made bile rise in her throat.

It was bad enough knowing Julia was raising him.

She forced herself to stay focused.

One step at a time.

Since her release, she had remained sober.

She was determined to prove, if not to Victor, then at least to herself, that she could change.

That she had changed.

She would walk into that park as the woman she wanted him to see.

Someone worthy of forgiveness.

Someone worthy of redemption.

And maybe...

Someone Victor could love again.

Arriving at Sunrise Park, Andrea eased her rented car into a space near the entrance.

The late afternoon sun hung low in the sky, casting a deep crimson glow across the landscape.

The trees, their leaves darkened by the eerie light, swayed gently in the breeze.

Shadows stretched long across the manicured grass. The sky, tinged in rust and scarlet, gave everything a dreamlike quality.

Andrea had grown used to it. But never comfortable.

The scent of freshly cut grass and barbecue smoke mingled with the faint metallic sharpness that always seemed to ride the wind in Red Earth.

She barely noticed.

Her pulse thrummed in her ears.

As she stepped onto the path, she scanned the park.

Families gathered beneath the trees, faces bathed in amber haze.

Children laughed on the playground, but even their joy felt dim under the blood-tinged sky.

Andrea wasn't looking at them.

Her eyes locked onto two figures beneath a sprawling oak tree.

Victor sat with his arms resting on his thighs, his light brown eyes shaded beneath the brim of his cap.

Beside him, little David fidgeted with something in his hands, a toy or a rock he'd found near the bench.

Andrea drew a breath and straightened her shoulders.

This was it.

She summoned the charm that had once captivated Victor—the easy confidence she had rehearsed in the mirror over and over.

That first meeting set the tone.

One meeting became another.

Then another.

Eventually, it became a routine: Saturdays in Gilson, sometimes in San Antonio.

It felt like progress.

Like the slow unraveling of the years between them.

But over time, things shifted.

David stopped coming to the meetings.

The visits that began as a chance to reconnect with her son... had become something else entirely.

They had become a chance to reconnect with each other.

They had become exactly what Andrea had hoped for.

Victor began confiding in her, sharing fragments of his life she'd never been privy to before.

He had never married, though he'd spent years in a stagnant relationship with Serena.

There was no passion left, no shared future.

They stayed together out of habit, roommates, not lovers.

Meanwhile, David was being raised by Victor's parents, Felipe and Julia.

Andrea listened.

She nodded.

She offered sympathetic murmurs at all the right moments.

But inwardly, she was calculating. Wondering.

What does this mean?
What do we mean?
She saw how he looked at her now, how his guarded expression had softened.
How he lingered just a little longer after their meetings.
He noticed her changes, too.
She knew it was working.

Andrea had fought to rebuild her life since her release, and Victor saw it.

Just months out of prison, she had secured a job at a car dealership, working long hours but grateful for the stability.

She'd moved into a small but decent studio apartment in San Antonio. Nothing fancy, but it was hers.

Most importantly, she was sober.

She was different.

Better.

And Victor couldn't ignore it.

Her humor, the quick wit that had once drawn him in, was back.

That effortless charm, the spark in her eyes when she spoke, it was all there again, wrapping around him like a familiar embrace.

Each week, their conversations stretched longer.

Their moments together lingered past what was necessary.

Victor found himself drawn to her again.

Not out of obligation.

Not out of guilt.

But because he wanted to be.

Eventually, their talks turned to the future. Their future.

One evening, as they sat together beneath the hazy red sky, Victor placed a hand on her shoulder.

His touch was warm, steady, grounding in a way Andrea had almost forgotten.

The distant hum of crickets filled the air, blending with the occasional rustle of wind through brittle leaves.

The air smelled of warm dust and that faint metallic sharpness that always hung in Red Earth's twilight.

Victor's voice was thick with emotion as he turned to face her, his light brown eyes, searching, vulnerable, holding the weight of something unspoken.

"You know you're the one," he said. "In my heart, it's always been you."

Andrea's breath hitched, not from love, but from the intoxicating power of his devotion.

The way he needed her.

The way he'd convinced himself she was the missing piece, the one thing that could make his life whole again.

She let him pull her closer, her lashes lowering just enough to play into the moment, the perfect balance of coy and receptive.

Victor exhaled, his thumb tracing absent-minded circles along her arm, his heart wide open.

"I'm glad to see that the woman I fell for is back."

And then he kissed her.

Softly at first, as if testing the waters.

A gentle press of lips.

A quiet hesitation.

Then deeper, needier, filled with longing.

The kind that came from years of convincing himself she was the only woman he had ever truly loved.

Andrea let herself melt into it, surrendering.

Not to love.

But to the way he made her feel.

The warmth.

The admiration.

The way his touch fed her ego and wrapped her in a glow of importance.

She kissed him back.

Not out of affection.

But because she liked the way he loved her.

And so she let him believe in a love that had never truly belonged to him.

◆

For Andrea, staying sober wasn't easy.

Temptation clawed at her daily, whispering in quiet moments, in the stillness of her small apartment, in the restless nights when sleep refused to come.

The craving was always there, curling at the edges of her resolve like smoke, waiting for the right moment to consume her.

But she held firm.

Not because she believed in redemption.

Not because she wanted to be better.

Because she had no choice.

Prison had been a brutal wake-up call. A stark reminder of how easily she could be discarded, locked away, forgotten.

She would never go back.

She wouldn't give anyone, especially Julia, that satisfaction.

Andrea craved stability.

Security.

And she saw Victor as her ticket to both.

Her motivations weren't pure. They never had been.

She wasn't in love with Victor.

She didn't love anyone.

The only person she had ever truly cared for was her sister, Leanne.

But Victor?

Victor was a means to an end.

It was never about rekindling some lost romance.

There was no warmth when he kissed her. No ache of longing when he held her.

If anything, she had to remind herself to react the way he expected.

To soften under his touch.

To meet his gaze with just enough vulnerability to keep him tethered.

This wasn't about love. It was about revenge.

Taking Victor, and possibly even David, away from Julia would be the ultimate retribution.

For the years Julia had stolen from her.

For the life she could have had.

For the son she barely knew.

Andrea smiled to herself, the taste of victory already sweet on her tongue.

She just had to play the game a little longer.

Chapter 11

As Andrea's charm wove its way back into Victor's life, the fragile threads holding his relationship with Serena finally snapped.

Their bond had been unraveling long before Andrea's return, strained since the day David was born.

Serena had never fully accepted the idea of her man fathering another woman's child, especially Andrea's child.

She had stayed with Victor out of convenience, out of the stubborn hope that, given enough time, things would settle. That he would grow to love her the way she wanted. That she would be enough.

But she wasn't.

She had always known it, no matter how many times she told herself otherwise.

So when Victor finally ended things, the words didn't shock her. They were simply confirmation of what she had been dreading for years.

Still, it hurt.

She wanted to be angry, to scream, to break something, to hate him.

But the worst part?

She couldn't even blame him.

Because deep down, she knew.

She had always known.

Victor had never truly belonged to her.

He had always belonged to *her*. To Andrea.

Serena felt sick just thinking about it: the way his eyes softened at the sound of Andrea's name, the way his thoughts would drift, as if pulled by some invisible thread back to a past he never let go of.

And now, he was running straight back into the arms of the woman who had already destroyed him once.

The pathetic, broken drunk.

Serena clenched her fists, her nails biting into her palms.

Andrea didn't deserve him.
But it didn't matter.
Victor had made his choice.
And it sure as hell wasn't her.

⸻ ◆ ⸻

Victor soon left his job in Gilson, walking away from the family's real estate and investment business, a decision that sent shockwaves through his already fragile relationship with his parents.

Felipe and Julia were furious.

They had spent years grooming Victor to take over the business, entrusting him with the family's financial legacy, only for him to throw it all away.

For her.

They felt betrayed. Humiliated. And they made no effort to hide who they blamed.

"This is Andrea's doing," Julia hissed in private, her voice dripping venom.

"She's sinking her claws into him again," Felipe fumed. "Just like before."

Victor dismissed their anger, brushing off their accusations as nothing more than baseless paranoia.

But the damage was done.

The rift between him and his parents widened, a wound that festered with each passing day.

Andrea?

She didn't mind the blame.

Let them believe it was all her doing.

Let them seethe.

It only made her victory taste sweeter.

The move to San Antonio marked a new beginning, a beginning she had carefully orchestrated.

With Victor now living under her roof, their lives entwined once again, everything was falling perfectly into place.

Soon after, they rented a modest house, setting the stage for their picture-perfect reunion.

David began staying with them every other weekend.

To the outside world, it was a story of redemption.

Andrea played the part effortlessly: a mother rebuilding her bond with her son, a woman mending the shattered pieces of her past.

She asked about David's schooling. Cooked his favorite meals. Offered just enough maternal warmth to make it convincing.

But behind her carefully crafted smile, Andrea relished the storm she had stirred.

She saw the resentment simmering in Julia's eyes whenever she caught wind of the arrangement. She heard the disapproval in Felipe's voice; the way Victor's family bristled at the mere mention of her name.

Good.

She wanted them to squirm.

Victor's family, however, was not so easily fooled.

Julia, fiercely protective of David, refused flatly and without negotiation to allow him to live with them full time.

No amount of pleading, arguing, or sugarcoated promises could sway her.

The standoff between Victor and his mother only deepened the cracks already forming in their relationship.

Tension crackled through every conversation, every strained phone call.

And Andrea, ever the silent puppeteer, pulled the strings with expert precision.

She fed Victor's frustrations in careful, measured doses, always subtle, never overt.

"She's always controlling you," she whispered in the dark, her fingers tracing soft circles along his arm.

"She doesn't trust you to make decisions for your own son."

"David should be here, with us, not being raised by someone who sees me as the enemy."

Victor stewed, jaw tight, fists clenched.

And then, one night, he said the words she'd been waiting to hear:

"Maybe I should take legal action."

Andrea smiled in the dark.

Yes.

David should live with his father and mother.

Victor was certain of it now.

It wasn't just about principle. It was about what was right.

He had spent too long letting Julia dictate the terms of his relationship with his own son.

That had to end.

He was David's father.

He should be the one making decisions.

Not his overbearing mother.

Victor became determined to fight for full custody.

Andrea, however, was indifferent.

Whether David lived with them full time or not didn't matter to her.

She played along, nodding in agreement, offering quiet affirmations. Of course, he was right.

Of course, David belonged with them.

Every step that unraveled Julia's carefully controlled world sent a thrill through Andrea's veins.

She savored the cracks forming in Julia's once-impenetrable façade, the way her grip on Victor, and by extension, David, was slipping.

And the best part?

Victor was on her side.

Completely.

She had molded him into an ally without him even realizing it.

Every fight with Julia, every act of defiance, only tightened Andrea's grip on him.

It was intoxicating.

The power.

The chaos.

The knowledge that she was the one pulling the strings.

Andrea leaned back, watching Victor stew in his frustration, the tension in his jaw growing tighter by the minute.

She let him believe he was leading the charge.

But in truth, he was following the path she had so carefully laid.

Victor wasn't the only one being manipulated.

Unbeknownst to him, Julia had already begun poisoning David's young mind against Andrea.

Nana, as he called her, filled his head with quiet warnings.

"There are good mothers and bad mothers," she would say. "Andrea might pretend to be good, but she isn't.

It wouldn't be safe for you to live with her."

David remained polite during visits, but his wariness was obvious.

There was a distance in his eyes, a hesitation in his voice.

He watched Andrea carefully, mirroring the caution instilled in him.

Confusion clouded his young mind.

He knew Andrea was his mother, but he didn't understand why she hadn't been there like the other moms he saw.

Why she felt like a stranger.

The doubts Julia had planted took root.

Andrea noticed the tension but didn't care.

David's discomfort was just another inconvenience, one more wrinkle in the larger game she was winning.

This was never about love.

It was about power.

And Andrea was done playing the victim.

Now it was her turn to pull the strings.

Red Earth 1993–June, San Antonio, Texas

The late afternoon sun bathed San Antonio in a deep red glow, its light stretching across the sky in hues of rust and ember. Warm air clung to the city, thick with the scent of pavement baked under the relentless heat.

Andrea and Victor stepped out of the doctor's office, their hearts pounding with excitement. The news they'd just received was nothing short of life-changing.

They were expecting their second child.

A baby.

Another chance.

Andrea cradled her stomach, though it was far too soon to feel anything, let alone show. But the knowledge alone was powerful.

A fresh start.

A new chapter.

By the end of December or early January, their child would be here.

Victor had taken off early from work for the appointment, eager to be there for her. And now, they had another appointment to schedule: a meeting with their attorney.

The goal was clear: secure full custody of David.

Everything was lining up perfectly.

Andrea could already picture it, Victor at her side, their lawyer outlining the case, the inevitable battle with Julia that they were bound to win.

David belonged with them.

When the day of the appointment arrived, Andrea felt a surge of anticipation. Victor was leaving work early, 1:30 p.m. sharp, to swing by the house and pick her up for their 2:30 meeting.

But when 2:30 came and went, unease prickled in her chest.

She checked the clock.

Then again.

Where is he?

Her thoughts spiraled.

Maybe he changed his mind. Maybe he doesn't want to fight his mother after all.

No, that was ridiculous. He had been so sure, so determined.

And legally, they should win.

So where the hell was Victor?

Victor already had custody as David's father, and she was his biological mother. The courts had to see it their way.

Didn't they?

Andrea paced the small living room, her fingers tightening around the phone as she dialed Victor's workplace.

The line clicked, and a woman's voice answered.

"Yes, he left at 1:30. Right on time."

Her pulse quickened. *Then where the hell was he?*

The meeting was scheduled for 2:30.

And now it was already past that.

A sick feeling churned in her stomach.

Had Julia gotten to him? Had she convinced him to back out at the last second?

She grabbed the phone again and called the attorney's office.

"No, he never showed up," the receptionist informed her.

Andrea froze.

The silence that followed was deafening.

An hour passed.

Then...

A knock at the door.

Sharp. Sudden.

The sound shattered the tension in the air, sending a jolt through her spine.

She moved toward the door, dread pooling in her gut.

As she swung it open, two uniformed officers stood on the other side.

San Antonio Police Department.

Andrea's breath caught in her throat.

"Ma'am, we need to speak with you."

Their voices were calm. Too calm.

A hollow ringing filled her ears as they spoke the words that brought her world to a standstill.

Victor had stopped by the bank to get cash.

As he was leaving, he was confronted by two masked men attempting to rob him.

He was shot.

He hadn't survived.

The room swayed.

The floor seemed to drop out beneath her.

She barely registered the officers still speaking, their voices distant, distorted, like echoes at the end of a long tunnel.

Victor was gone. Just like that.

And with him, the future she had so carefully crafted.

Andrea's breath caught.

Not from grief, but from sheer frustration.

How could he be so careless? This wasn't part of the plan.

They had been on the verge of winning.

Of securing custody of David. Of tearing Julia's world apart.

And now, just like that, Victor was gone.

Everything was in jeopardy.

She clenched her jaw, refusing to give the officers anything.

No tears.

No reaction.

Not a single crack in the mask.

They didn't need to know how close she'd come to reclaiming what was rightfully hers.

This wasn't grief. It was rage.

Cold, sharp, and rising.

⸺◆⸺

The fallout was swift and merciless.

Since she and Victor had never married, Andrea had no legal claim to anything.

No rights.

No say.

And Julia made damn sure she knew it.

Smug as ever, Julia took complete control of the funeral arrangements, shutting Andrea out entirely.

No invitation.

No acknowledgment.

As if she had never been a part of Victor's life at all.

Andrea didn't bother fighting it.

She could already picture Julia playing the grieving mother, basking in the sympathy of friends and family, using Victor's death as yet another excuse to cast Andrea as the villain.

Andrea knew Julia didn't love Victor the way a mother should.

And when Victor left with her, Julia had been furious.

Furious about the custody battle over David. She was manipulative and losing control.

How does Andrea know that?

Because it takes one to know one.

As for David?

Predictably, he stayed with his grandparents.

That's where he belongs anyway, Andrea thought bitterly.

She didn't love the boy. She never had.

Sure, he had been a pawn, a crucial part of her plan, but beyond that?

There was nothing. No bond. No attachment.

It's not like David and I ever really bonded, she reassured herself coldly.

She had no time to dwell on the boy or the life she had been so close to manipulating.

She had to focus on herself.

Because if there was one thing Andrea knew, it was how to survive.

And one thing was certain: Julia could not find out about her pregnancy. If she did, it would give the woman far too much power.

And Andrea had already lost enough ground.

So, with methodical precision, she took control of what little she had left.

She emptied her joint bank account with Victor, taking every last dollar before his family could freeze the funds.

She packed her belongings, discarding anything that tied her to San Antonio.

And left without looking back.

She headed north.

To Fort Worth.

Rachel and her husband, Jim, welcomed her into their home in Fort Worth, though Andrea knew that generosity came with unspoken conditions.

She played the part of the grateful houseguest: cooking, cleaning, keeping her head down.

Never taking up too much space.

Never giving them a reason to regret their decision.

She understood the rules of survival: blend in, give them what they wanted, and never, ever overstay her welcome.

Her pregnancy did little to change that.

Andrea stayed sober, not out of concern for the baby, but out of necessity. Losing Rachel and Jim's goodwill would leave her stranded, and she refused to let that happen.

So, she played along.

Smiled when required.

Accepted their concern with quiet humility.

And when, after months of calculated effort, she finally gave birth.

She felt something unexpected.

Not love.

But something close to satisfaction.

A daughter.

She named her Molly.

For the first time, a flicker of something unfamiliar stirred in Andrea's chest.

Not affection. Never that.

But a sense of pride.

This child was hers.

Hers to shape.

Hers to control.

Chapter 12

After maternity leave, Andrea left her part-time job at Goodwill and secured a better position at a car dealership.

The work suited her.

She thrived in the world of sales, where manipulation and persuasion weren't just useful.

They were necessary.

Reading people.

Bending conversations to her advantage.

Making others believe exactly what she wanted them to.

It was second nature.

Rachel and Jim doted on Molly, easing the pressures of motherhood in a way that worked to Andrea's advantage.

They were the perfect buffer.

They took care of Molly, allowing Andrea to focus on her career while maintaining the façade of a devoted mother.

But in truth?

Andrea saw Molly for exactly what she was.

Not a child to be cherished.

Not a daughter to be loved.

But a guarantee.

A safeguard for survival.

And Andrea had no intention of losing.

Red Earth 2007—Fort Worth, Texas

Molly was now thirteen, and with every passing day, she looked more and more like her paternal grandmother, Julia.

The resemblance was uncanny, from her sharp, striking features to those piercing, watchful eyes.

As much as Andrea despised Julia, she had to admit, begrudgingly, that it was fortunate the woman had been a handsome one.

Molly's beauty would be an *asset*, Andrea thought.

Still, the constant reminder of Julia's bloodline ignited a simmering resentment she could never quite extinguish.

Andrea still lived on Rachel and Jim Durazo's property, sharing the two-bedroom guest house with Molly.

The arrangement was a lifeline Andrea couldn't afford to lose.

Jim had inherited the home, a sprawling property set on two acres, after his parents passed. The main house now bustled with their growing family, including their five-year-old son, Little Jimmy.

Rachel and Jim charged Andrea a modest rent, but there was one non-negotiable rule: *no alcohol.*

Rachel had made it clear from the start.

And for years, Andrea had managed to follow it.

Not out of discipline.

Not out of love for Molly.

But because Rachel had warned her, plain and simple:

If you fall back into your old habits, Julia will find out about Molly.

And she will take her away.

Andrea hadn't had a drink in years, though the late '90s had tested her.

When Molly was a toddler, there had been slip-ups, long, blurry nights that ended in shameful mornings.

Rachel, ever the rescuer, had stepped in and helped her get back on track.

For that, Andrea felt a quiet, begrudging debt.

But she kept that sentiment buried deep.

Now, she worked tirelessly to maintain her image of stability, at least on the surface.

She paid rent on time.

Followed Rachel's rules.

Kept her cravings on a tight leash.

But inside, the old bitterness still churned.

The guest house felt like a cage.

Rachel's charity, a leash.

Andrea hated feeling beholden to anyone, even if it meant security for Molly.

Lately, that sense of being trapped had only grown worse, especially with Molly's relentless pleading to visit her father's grave. After weeks of dodging the subject, Andrea finally gave in. It wasn't a decision she made lightly.

She had avoided Gilson for years, mainly to steer clear of Julia, but now Rachel had planted the seed in Molly's mind, nurturing her curiosity, Andrea had worked hard to keep buried.

Molly wanted to honor Victor.

To feel a connection.

And Andrea couldn't put her off forever.

------●------

As they approached Victor's grave, Andrea spotted a small black sedan parked off to the side.

She dismissed it as nothing.

Her focus was on Molly, on her daughter's quiet, determined steps.

When they reached the headstone, Molly knelt and gently placed a bouquet of flowers at its base. She said nothing.

Andrea wrapped an arm around her, masking the discomfort that always came with pretending.

She began telling Molly stories about Victor, carefully curated tales that painted him in a favorable light.

Molly smiled faintly, her eyes never leaving the grave.

Then...

Footsteps.

Andrea tensed.

She turned.

And her breath caught.

Her face paled.

She forced a nervous, strained smile.

Standing just feet away, holding the hand of a small girl, was a grown man she instantly recognized.

It was David.

"Andrea?"

David's voice was cautious.

"Yes," she answered, her voice barely above a whisper.

David looked at her, then at Molly, his eyes narrowing as he pieced it together.

"This is Molly," Andrea said quickly, her voice faltering. "Your sister."

David froze, his expression a mix of shock and disbelief.

"My sister?" he echoed, glancing down at Molly, who stared back at him with wide, curious eyes.

Molly turned to Andrea, confusion flickering across her face.

Having been told about her older brother, she asked, "Mom, is this him? My brother?"

Andrea nodded.

Before she could respond, the little girl by David's side tugged at his hand. He scooped her up effortlessly, holding her close.

"This is Paula," he said, voice soft but guarded. "My daughter."

Andrea felt the air leave her lungs.

A strange numbness crept in as she stared at the child in his arms.

My granddaughter.

The realization hit her like a wave.

She wasn't one for sentiment, but something about the little girl's innocent gaze stirred an unexpected emotion.

Her eyes welled.

For the first time in years, Andrea couldn't suppress the tears.

David noticed.

He felt a flicker of something he couldn't quite name.

Maybe it was satisfaction.

Maybe it was pity.

But he didn't let it show.

He remembered all too well the woman in front of him.

The mother who had abandoned him.

The drinker who had chosen her addiction over him.

Nana had told him everything, including how Andrea was the reason his dad was lying in that grave.

Still, his eyes softened when he looked at Molly.

"Hey, big brother," Molly said with a bright smile, breaking the tension.

David didn't respond right away.

He just looked at her, then back at Andrea.

Finally, he reached out and pulled Molly into an embrace.

She hugged him tightly, and after a moment's hesitation, he hugged her back just as firmly.

Holding Paula in one arm and Molly in the other, David felt a strange warmth he hadn't expected.

"Andrea," he said, his voice quieter now, "Molly is yours and Victor's?"

Andrea nodded. "I was pregnant when... when he died."

David's expression darkened momentarily.

Then he exhaled and looked at Molly again.

His features softened.

To Andrea's surprise, he handed Paula to her, then pulled Molly into another hug.

Little Paula, now cradled awkwardly in Andrea's arms, watched the scene unfold.

She saw Andrea's watery eyes.

She saw the tight embrace between her father and her aunt.

And confusion crept across her tiny face.

Her lip quivered.

A moment later, she was crying too.

Andrea shifted her in her arms, still overwhelmed by the moment.

She stared at David and Molly, both teary-eyed, both clinging to each other, and for the first time in a long while, she felt something stir deep within her.

A flicker of regret. Longing. And something else she couldn't name.

"This is our first time here," Andrea said, glancing at David. "It's a coincidence that we both showed up at practically the same time."

David gave a small, humorless smile. "Not really," he replied. "I saw you walk over here."

Andrea's eyes narrowed.

"That your black car over there?"

"Yeah," David said, shifting Paula in his arms.

"So how did you know..." Andrea started, but David cut her off.

"Your friend Rachel. Her cousin Ruben is a good friend of mine. She asked him to have me call her. I called last night. She told me you'd be here. But she didn't mention..."

He glanced at Molly.

"She didn't mention I had a sister."

Andrea's expression shifted.

She forced a smile.

"Rachel's been my best friend for years. She's a good person," she said, her voice overly cheerful to mask her unease.

Her mind raced.

Maybe this was a chance, a way to rebuild something with David. She decided to test the waters.

"David, if you're not busy, maybe we could stop for something to eat before Molly and I head home. We could talk about—"

"No."

His tone was firm. Polite, but cold.

"I don't think so. But maybe I can pick up Molly for some weekend visits?"

Andrea froze. His words hit like a slap.

"Pick up Molly? But..."

Her voice trailed off when she saw Molly's hopeful expression.

Andrea took a breath, then turned to her daughter.

"Molly, why don't you take Paula down the row of tombstones? Let me talk to your brother for a minute."

Molly hesitated but nodded. She took Paula's hand and gently led her away.

Once they were out of earshot, Andrea turned back to David.

"David," she began cautiously, "the real reason I stayed away so long... I was pregnant. I didn't want Julia, your grandmother, to find out. I was terrified she'd get her lawyers involved and take Molly away from me. I couldn't let that happen."

David folded his arms, eyeing her carefully.

"The only way she could do that is if she could prove you're an unfit mother."

His gaze sharpened.

"Are you?"

Andrea's face darkened.

"Am I what?" she snapped.

"An unfit mother," he said evenly.

"No," Andrea barked, eyes narrowing.

David raised a brow but didn't argue.

"Then I don't think you should worry so much. Molly has a right to know her family. And Nana has a right to know her."

Andrea's jaw tightened. Her stomach churned. She was losing control.

"I've done everything to protect Molly," she said through clenched teeth.

"Maybe it's time to stop protecting her from something that isn't a threat," David replied. "Maybe it's time to think about what Molly wants, not just what you're afraid of."

Before Andrea could respond, Molly and Paula returned, hand in hand.

Molly looked between them, sensing the tension.

David crouched, softening his voice.

"Molly, I'd really like to spend some time with you soon. Would that be okay?"

Molly's face lit up. "I'd like that."

Andrea forced a smile. But inside, a storm churned.

She should have anticipated this.

Of course David would side with Julia. He'd spent his life hearing her version of the story.

Still, his subtle dismissal stung.

"Well, David, I'll have to think about this," Andrea said coolly. "I need time. But you're welcome to come to Fort Worth to see her."

David tilted his head slightly, brows raised.

"Fort Worth? Rachel didn't mention that. I thought you were still in San Antonio."

"No," Andrea replied, brushing a strand of hair behind her ear. "I moved right after... Victor was killed. I was terrified of Julia and her lawyers."

David's lips twitched into a faint smirk.

Then...

A subtle eye-roll.

The gesture wasn't lost on Andrea. Her annoyance flared.

She folded her arms, narrowing her eyes.

"David, if you're willing, we really need to sit down and talk. Just the two of us. There's a lot we need to discuss."

David shrugged.

"Why? I don't think it's necessary. What's done is done. We just have to move on."

The dismissive remark made her blood boil. She clenched her jaw, holding back the urge to explode.

Why do I even bother with him? she thought bitterly.

He's such an arrogant asshole! I don't give a fuck about him. I'm doing this for Molly. If I lose my temper, she'll blame me.

She forced herself to stop the thought from growing. Letting this escalate wasn't worth it.

Andrea reached into her purse, pulling out a pen and a scrap of paper. She scribbled down her number and handed it to David.

"Here," she said stiffly. "Keep in touch. If not with me, then at least with Molly."

David hesitated, then took the paper. Tucked it into his pocket without a word.

Andrea watched him. Her irritation still simmered, but she kept it buried.

"Let me know when you want to see her," she said flatly.

David gave a small nod, his gaze drifting to Molly and Paula.

"I'll think about it," he replied, voice distant.

Andrea turned away, her fists tight as she walked toward Molly.

Forcing a smile, she called out, "Come on, Molly, let's go."

But even as the words left her lips, an unease settled over her.

She couldn't shake the feeling that she'd lost something.

That the power she once held was slipping.

That she had just met her match. It left a bitter taste in her mouth. And she hated it.

As Molly hurried to her side, Andrea stole one last glance over her shoulder.

David was still standing at the grave, his focus on the headstone.

Andrea turned back toward the car, her thoughts swirling with frustration, resentment.

And the faintest trace of fear.

Chapter 13

David

David carefully buckled Paula into her car seat, making sure she was secure. As he slid into the driver's seat, he started the engine and pulled out of the cemetery. His mind was spinning.

Rounding a corner, he spotted a gas station and decided to pull into a parking spot near one of the phone booths. He didn't want to be too close to the taco truck, where people were gathered, laughing and chatting over their meals.

He parked the car, cut the engine, and let the silence settle around him. It felt heavy, pressing down on his chest, but he welcomed it. Anything to quiet the chaos in his mind. Leaning back against the headrest, he stared through the windshield without really seeing, trying to untangle his thoughts.

Glancing into the rearview mirror, he saw Paula fast asleep, her tiny chest rising and falling steadily. For a moment, he felt a pang of envy at her peacefulness, so untouched by the tangled web of emotions he was grappling with.

David exhaled slowly, replaying his interaction with Andrea. It hadn't gone the way he'd expected. Then again, he wasn't even sure what he'd expected. What he did know was that the encounter had stirred something intense within him. A mix of emotions he couldn't quite unravel: anticipation, excitement, and anger.

The anger was the most familiar, a bitterness he'd carried for years. He thought he'd buried it long ago, but seeing Andrea again had unearthed it with startling force.

There was a question he had wanted to ask her, one that had lingered in his mind for years. But he'd decided not to.

Why was I raised by my grandparents? Why is she raising Molly, but she couldn't raise me?

He knew what Nana had told him: the reasons, the explanations, the justifications. But he was an adult now. He understood the truth often had more than one side. And part of him wondered if there was more to the story than he'd been led to believe.

Andrea had tried to talk to him, even extend an olive branch of sorts. And he'd pushed it away. Why? Because she didn't deserve his forgiveness? Because he wanted her to feel the weight of her failures? Or because he wasn't ready to face the possibility of healing?

His thoughts drifted to his wife, Kathy. *All she wants to do is argue. She's so uptight, just like Nana. Just like the rest of my family, for that matter.*

His headache returned, a relentless pounding at his temples. A familiar torment, one he'd endured his entire life.

Frustration gnawed at him as he started the engine.

Glancing in the rearview mirror, he admired Paula, sleeping so soundly, so peacefully, without a care in the world. But just as he was about to shift into gear, his breath hitched. His gaze locked onto the parking lot behind him.

Something was wrong.

For a split second, he wasn't sure if his mind was playing tricks on him. He blinked, gripping the wheel tighter. *I can't believe what I'm seeing.*

It was Nana and Grandpa, standing in the parking lot, trying to yank Andrea out of her car.

What the hell?

Heart pounding, David pushed open the car door but hesitated, glancing back at Paula, still fast asleep.

Just then, movement caught his eye. Molly. She had spotted him and was already darting toward him; her face twisted in panic.

"Help! They're trying to hurt Mom!" she cried.

David crouched, gripping her shoulders. "Molly, listen to me. Get in my car, roll up the windows, lock the doors, and watch over Paula. Do you understand?"

Molly nodded frantically. "Okay!" She scrambled inside and did as he instructed.

Straightening, David rushed toward his grandfather. "What the hell is going on? Why are you doing this?"

Julia, startled by David's presence, loosened her grip on Andrea's blouse. Andrea seized the moment, pulling back into the safety of her car and quickly locking the door.

David turned to his grandparents, his pulse hammering in his ears. *What were they thinking?*

Felipe exhaled, his face hard but unreadable. "Your Nana wanted to talk to Andrea, but they started arguing. Then I saw Andrea push your Nana, so I stepped in to make sure she didn't get hurt."

David's eyes widened. "But... what are you both doing here?"

Felipe and Julia exchanged a glance, each silently hoping the other would speak first.

"We saw the taco truck, stopped for some tacos, and then we saw her there," Felipe said.

David, now irritated, asked, "But what are you doing here on this side of town?"

"We heard you were at the cemetery... that you were meeting with Andrea," Nana finally said, her voice firm and laced with disapproval. She hesitated before continuing. "I told you about her, David. She isn't someone you want in your life. We were just trying to stop it."

David's jaw tightened. "How did you even know she'd be at the cemetery?"

Julia shifted uncomfortably, her eyes flickering past David's shoulder as if searching for an escape from the question. Instead of answering, she deflected.

"Where is Paula?"

David didn't budge. His tone sharpened.

"She's fine. Now answer my question."

Felipe's expression darkened. "Hey, hey," he warned, stepping forward. "Don't talk to your Nana like that. Show some respect."

David shot Felipe a glance before turning his focus back to Julia, waiting.

Finally, Julia relented with a sigh.

"Kathy told us. She said you would be here, meeting with Andrea. At the grave of our son, your father, no less!"

Her voice trembled with indignation, as if Andrea's presence alone was an insult to his father's memory.

But David knew the real reason Andrea was there. And he wasn't about to tell them about Molly.

At least not now.

After tonight? Maybe never.

David stiffened. *Kathy told them?*

But why?

"Why would Kathy tell you that?" he pressed, watching as Felipe turned and headed back to his car.

Julia's lips tightened.

"Because she's concerned. Just like we are."

David scoffed.

"Nana, you don't even like Kathy."

Julia didn't answer.

David exhaled sharply, his frustration mounting.

"Then tell me. Why were you trying to pull Andrea out of her car?"

Julia's face hardened.

"I told her to stay away from you. We're not going to stand by and watch you end up like your father."

David tilted his head, eyes narrowing. "Why did you say that? Are you saying you think she killed him?"

Julia straightened, lifted her chin. "I think she must have had something to do with it. She's evil."

David stared at her, absorbing the weight of her words. His chest tightened, but he pushed the emotion down.

Without another word, he gently took Julia's hand and led her toward Felipe's car, where his grandfather sat behind the wheel, engine already running. He guided Julia into the passenger seat, buckled her in, then crouched beside her.

"Don't worry about me," he said softly. "She won't harm me. I'll send her home now, so you can go home too. We'll talk later."

He shut the door and stepped back as Felipe pulled away.

David watched their car disappear down the road, making sure they were truly gone before turning toward Andrea's car. He approached and motioned for her to roll down the window. She hesitated, then reluctantly complied.

Before he could speak, Andrea's voice broke the silence, rapid and unsteady.

"Look, before you take her side, because I know you will, just hear me out. She started it. She came up to me like a damn lunatic! I don't want Molly anywhere near her."

Her hands gripped the steering wheel so tightly her knuckles turned white.

"The only reason I didn't kick her ass was because I was afraid Molly would see. And with Felipe there, I knew he'd help her drag me out of the car."

She glanced away, catching her breath, her heart still pounding as she tried to make him understand before he could jump to conclusions.

David exhaled.

"Molly's in my car. I'll go get her."

Molly hurried over to Andrea's window.

"Mom, David said to drive straight home. Don't stop for anyone. He'll call me later."

Andrea nodded, her expression still tense.

David stood by his car, watching as she pulled away, only relaxing once she was out of sight. He slid into the driver's seat, letting out a breath he hadn't realized he was holding.

He glanced at Paula, still fast asleep, completely unaware of the chaos that had unfolded. His nerves were shot. His temples pounding.

I can't believe them.

His grandparents. Their behavior tonight was beyond anything he could have imagined.

And then Kathy?

What the hell was she thinking?

His headache intensified as his thoughts drifted to his newborn twin daughters, Daphne and Delilah, waiting for him at home with Kathy.

Why would Kathy call my grandparents?

He rubbed his temples, shaking his head.

My family's a damn mess.

Red Earth 2012–Rural Texas

As David made his way down the long, rural route from Gilson to the meeting spot with Andrea and Molly, he turned off the radio, letting the hum of tires on the cracked highway fill the silence. The empty fields stretched for miles on either side, broken by weathered fences and the occasional leaning mailbox. With nothing but open road ahead, his thoughts began to wander, drifting back over the past few years, to the slow unraveling of everything he once thought was solid.

His marriage to Kathy had been dying long before either of them admitted it. Now, it clung to life by the thinnest of threads: their daughters. Without them, it would have ended long ago.

Kathy was hardly ever home, spending most weekends with his ex-friend Ruben. At first, David had believed her when she claimed she needed "time for herself." Raising three young daughters, Paula, and the twins, Daphne and Delilah, was exhausting, she'd say. She just needed a break. A chance to breathe. And David, wanting to be a good husband and father, had done everything he could to support her.

He worked long hours managing the family business, making sure they never went without. On weekends, when Kathy insisted she needed space, he took all three girls with him to the office, setting up a small play area in the corner so Paula could color while he kept an eye on her little sisters. He thought he was being considerate. Thought he was holding things together.

But all the while, Kathy wasn't using that time to recharge. She wasn't taking a break from the stress of motherhood.

She was with Ruben.

His best friend.

The man who had once stood beside him at his wedding, toasting to his happiness. The man he had trusted and confided in. The man his daughters called Uncle Ruben.

David found out the truth in the cruelest way imaginable.

One evening, after a particularly long day at work, he decided to surprise Kathy with dinner from her favorite restaurant. She had told him earlier she wasn't feeling well and planned to take some ibuprofen and lie down.

He wanted to do something nice, to remind her that despite their struggles, despite the distance, he still cared. He still loved her.

But when he pulled into their driveway, her car wasn't there.

A sinking feeling took hold of him.

From the backseat, Daphne asked,

"Where's Mommy?" Her voice was innocent, unknowing.

David worried. She told him she was not feeling well.

He forced a smile. "She's probably just out running errands. Let's go find her."

He turned the car around, heading toward Ruben's house, just a few streets away.

"Maybe Ruben can watch the girls while I looked for Kathy," he thought.

What he found instead shattered him.

Her car was parked in Ruben's driveway. The porch light was off, but through the partially drawn curtains, he saw them, Kathy and Ruben, wrapped up in each other. Laughing. Drinking. Touching. The kind of intimacy that used to belong to him.

David's heart slammed against his ribs. His throat tightened.

For a long moment, he just sat there, gripping the steering wheel so tightly his knuckles turned white. His daughters were in the back, oblivious to the moment their father's world was crumbling.

"Daddy?" Paula's small voice pulled him from the haze.

"Can we go home now?"

David swallowed hard, blinking away the burning in his eyes.

He wanted to storm inside and take Ruben down with his fist. He wanted to demand answers, to make sense of the betrayal.

But he couldn't.

Not with his daughters in the car. Not when he felt like he was coming apart at the seams.

So he drove away.

That night, Kathy came home as if nothing had happened. She kissed the girls goodnight, barely sparing David a glance.

He didn't confront her. Not yet. He couldn't bear to see the lie in her eyes, the denial, the indifference.

But something inside him had changed.

After that night, he saw her for who she really was. The woman who once held his heart in her hands had crushed it without a second thought.

David filed for divorce the next morning.

Still caught between hurt, betrayal, and anger, he drove straight to Ruben's house.

When Ruben opened the door, his eyes widened in surprise at the sight of David, his expression dark, fury burning in his eyes. Before Ruben could react, a sharp blow to the jaw sent him crashing to the floor.

Kathy rushed over, kneeling beside Ruben. She glared up at David.

He hadn't realized she was there, hadn't seen her car in the driveway. But what did it matter now?

"If you're here, where are the girls?" he asked, working to keep his voice steady, to mask the pain beneath.

"They're with Mrs. Fernandez," Kathy answered, guilt flickering across her face.

David turned to leave, but at the last moment, he paused and glanced back at her.

"By the way, expect to be served with divorce papers. I filed this morning," he said, his voice calm and measured.

"And I'm requesting custody of the girls."

Then, without another word, he walked away.
Kathy shut the door.

———◆———

A few months back, the divorce had finally been finalized. Kathy took what she could, alimony included, and had no real interest in their daughters. As long as she got her share of the money, she was content leaving them with David. And David, he had spent the last year picking up the pieces for himself, for Paula, Daphne, and Delilah, for a love that died long before he realized it.

Chapter 14

As David continued his drive through the rural backroads, the memory of what happened just months after Kathy's betrayal pressed its way into his thoughts. He had thought the worst was behind him until life proved otherwise.

One morning in 2009, his grandfather, Felipe, called and asked David to come by the house to help with some repairs to the horse stables. David agreed, and when he and the girls arrived, they greeted Julia, then raced upstairs to find Aunt Bridgette, as they usually did.

As David stepped inside, he noticed a man sitting at the kitchen table, a man he'd never seen before. He looked to be around Aunt Bridgette's age, and his guarded expression immediately set David on edge. Figuring he must be a new boyfriend, David walked up and offered his hand for a shake.

"I'm David," he said, polite but firm.

The man hesitated, glancing at Julia before reluctantly taking David's hand. He didn't say his name, just gave a quick shake and looked away.

Julia forced a tight smile.

"He's the son of a good friend of mine," she said, a hint of strain in her voice.

David narrowed his eyes, shifting his gaze between the man and Julia.

"Which friend?" he asked, his voice low and unyielding.

Julia stiffened, caught off guard by the bluntness. Embarrassment flickered across her face, but she straightened her back and lifted her chin, determined not to let him intimidate her.

"She's an old friend I haven't seen in a while," she replied coolly, holding his gaze as if daring him to challenge her.

David smirked, clearly unconvinced.

"Where's Grandpa?"

Julia let out a breath, trying to mask her relief.

"He's out back at the horse stables," she said, her voice calmer now.

Without another word, David turned and headed outside, his mind already racing with questions about the stranger and Julia's unusually tense demeanor.

David spotted Felipe over by the horse stables. After getting instructions on what needed repairs, he got to work securing a loose board while Felipe moved to the other side of the stable to measure a piece of wood.

After a few minutes, David glanced over.

"Who's the man Nana's talking to in the kitchen?"

Felipe stopped and looked up, his expression neutral.

"He's a cousin of hers. Comes around maybe a couple times a month to visit."

David chuckled, wiping his hands on his jeans.

"How come you didn't get *him* to come out here and help you?"

Felipe shook his head.

"Nah, he's a strange one."

David smirked and went back to work, but something about it didn't sit right. His mind replayed the conversation with Julia. He narrowed his eyes, then straightened up as a thought hit him.

"Grandpa," he called out, "did you say he's her cousin? Because she just told me he was the son of an old friend of hers."

Felipe paused, brow furrowing.

"She said that?"

David nodded, jaw tightening.

"She did. What's his name?"

Felipe hesitated, rubbing the back of his neck.

"Come to think of it, I don't think I was ever told his name."

David's face grew serious, the uneasy feeling digging deeper into his gut.

"I don't like this. My daughters are in the house with that weirdo. Let's go find out who he is. Once and for all."

Felipe set down his measuring tape, giving David a cautious look.

"Alright. Let's get to the bottom of it."

They started toward the house, determination and suspicion driving every step. But then Felipe paused, glancing back toward the stable.

David paused and glanced over his shoulder.

"What is it?"

"I forgot somethin'," Felipe muttered. He walked to the shelf, grabbed something small, and slipped it into his pants pocket.

David caught a glint of metal.

The old revolver.

It was the emergency piece Felipe always kept around. David didn't ask. He just nodded, and they continued toward the house.

As they approached the kitchen, low, heated whispers filtered through the air. They halted, exchanged wary glances, then crept closer, hiding behind the wall to listen.

Julia's voice came first, trembling but defiant.

"You've been coming here for years to blackmail me. I pay you every time. What more do you want from me?"

The man let out a low, mocking chuckle, a wicked grin in his voice.

"I could take that grandson of yours out, just like I did your son. Instead of paying me to have your son killed all those years ago, now you can pay me to keep your grandson alive."

David's blood ran cold. His fists clenched at his sides. He looked at Felipe, whose face had turned a dangerous shade of red.

Julia's voice cracked.

"Stop it! Leave my grandson out of this." She paused, then steadied her tone. "Besides, I paid you to take out both of them... not just Victor. And you failed at that."

The man snickered.

"I told you, she wasn't with him. I can do it now... for a price."

Julia's voice turned steely.

"No. Andrea's no threat to me now. I got what I wanted. And I don't want you coming around anymore."

He smirked, unfazed.

"Or maybe your daughter?"

Julia's expression darkened, disgust flashing in her eyes.

"I paid you. Leave. Now."

He shrugged, feigning nonchalance.

"Okay... but I'll be back, cousin."

His voice dripped with mockery as he let out a cruel laugh and turned toward the door.

The man froze when he saw David and Felipe standing there, both glaring daggers at him.

Julia's eyes widened, fear and panic creeping over her face, unsure how much they had overheard.

Felipe stepped forward, his voice cold and steady.

"You got about three seconds to explain yourself before I put you down right here."

The man's smirk faltered, his gaze darting between Felipe and David, calculating his next move. David stayed silent, every muscle tense, ready to strike at the first sign of danger.

"Oh, Felipe! Please, it's not what you think!" Julia shrieked, her voice panicked and shrill.

Felipe hesitated, turning slightly toward her. That split-second distraction was all the man needed. He bolted, but David moved fast, sticking out his leg and tripping him to the floor. The man scrambled to get up, but David was on him, kicking him hard in the ribs.

"You killed my father, motherfucker!" David growled, each kick fueled by years of buried rage.

He wasn't thinking, just reacting. Letting the fury pour out in waves.

Suddenly, a loud thump echoed behind him.

David froze, breathing hard, and turned just in time to see Felipe crumple to the floor.

Stunned and confused, he looked at Julia, who stood there, staring at Felipe with wide, horrified eyes, unable to move.

The man staggered to his feet, taking advantage of David's diverted attention, and swung, landing a brutal punch to David's jaw.

David hit the ground, the pain exploding through his skull. The man turned to make his escape, but the sharp sound of two gunshots stopped him cold.

Still dazed, David pushed himself to his feet and looked toward the source.

The man collapsed to the floor, lifeless, a dark stain spreading across his shirt.

David turned to see Bridgette, standing in the doorway, holding Felipe's revolver with both hands. She trembled violently, her face pale, eyes wide, locked on the man she'd just shot.

⸺⸻◆⸻⸺

Bridgette had been on her way to the kitchen to bring cookies upstairs to the girls.

As she neared the entrance, she heard muffled voices. Curious, she slowed, listening.

The closer she got, the clearer the conversation became, and what she heard stopped her dead in her tracks.

"...you had him killed. You killed my son," Felipe rasped, his voice weak, trembling with disbelief and pain.

Bridgette froze, her heart pounding so loudly it drowned out everything else.

She leaned against the doorway, gripping the frame to steady herself.

"He was going to take David from us," Julia sobbed. "She, Andrea, was going to raise him, and I couldn't allow that."

Bridgette's face went pale, her mouth falling open as the weight of her mother's words crashed over her like a tidal wave.

The realization hit so hard her legs trembled.

She forced herself to take a breath, but it came out a choked whisper.

"He killed... my brother?" she managed to say, the words slipping out in shock.

Her eyes darted from Julia to Felipe, trying to make sense of what she'd just heard. "She had him killed."

Then she saw her father on the ground... the man fighting with David... trying to escape.

She spotted Felipe's revolver on the floor, grabbed it with both hands, and fired two shots.

The man fell.

Then she turned the gun on Julia.

David rushed over and gently took the gun from her trembling grip, guiding her to sit down.

"It's okay, Aunt Bridgette. It's over," he whispered, trying to calm her as her whole body shook with shock.

Julia stared at Bridgette, her face awash with guilt and regret.

For a fleeting moment, her lips parted, as if to deny it. To take it all back. But there was nothing left to say.

The truth was out. And the look in her daughter's eyes shattered what little remained of Julia's resolve.

Bridgette stared at her mother in disbelief and horror.

She didn't recognize the woman in front of her, the woman who could have her son murdered.

Everything she thought she knew was unraveling, and she didn't know how to put the pieces back together.

Julia dropped to her knees beside Felipe, her hands frantically touching his face. "Felipe! Felipe!" David knelt beside him, his heart pounding.

"Grandpa, what happened?" he asked, trying to get him to focus.

Felipe's dulled eyes drifted to Julia's face.

His voice was faint, barely a whisper, repeating the same words:

"You, you had him killed. You killed my son."

Julia sobbed, pressing her hands to her mouth.

"And I told you... he was going to take David from us," she cried, her voice trembling. "She, Andrea, was going to raise him, and I couldn't allow that."

Felipe kept repeating the same words, and Julia, the same defense, clinging to her twisted justification.

Then she turned to David. "I did it for you! You understand, *don't you?*"

David stared at her, struggling to process the horror of what he was hearing.

He couldn't believe it, couldn't wrap his mind around the reality that his grandmother was responsible for his father's death.

Suddenly, Felipe's hand went to his chest.

His breathing turned ragged and shallow.

David recognized the signs instantly. His grandfather was having a heart attack.

David jumped up and snatched the phone, dialing emergency services with shaking hands.

"We need an ambulance and the police," he said, forcing calm into his voice as he gave the address.

As he hung up, he noticed small figures slowly descending the stairs.

The girls.

He quickly nodded toward them, raising a hand and gesturing upstairs.

"Paula, take your sisters back up. I'll call Mrs. Fernandez to come get you."

Once they disappeared from view, he made the call, his voice tight and strained as he asked Mrs. Fernandez to come pick them up.

When he hung up, he looked back at Felipe, whose breaths came in short, painful gasps.

Julia knelt beside him, still sobbing and pleading for forgiveness.

David could do nothing but watch, his mind a chaotic blur of anger, grief, and disbelief.

———◦———

Felipe passed away not long after the confrontation, and Julia was arrested.

The charges stacked up quickly: first-Degree murder, conspiracy to commit murder, murder for hire, and obstruction of justice. Even her lawyers couldn't dig her out of this one. She was sentenced to life in prison, eligible for the death penalty.

David blamed her for Felipe's death too.

Now he understood just how dangerous Julia really was.

As much as he hated to admit it, Andrea had been right. She had every reason to fear Julia.

As for Bridgette, no one knew.

She went missing a few weeks after Julia's conviction. Once she was cleared of all charges, she vanished.

Before she disappeared, Bridgette sold the family business, the one David had poured years into managing.

He didn't fight her on it. He was too emotionally drained to care.

The business was gone.

And so was his sense of stability, slipping through his fingers like sand.

Despite everything, Bridgette made sure David and the girls would be taken care of. She arranged for him to receive monthly payments from the Costa family trust, ensuring he could stay home with his daughters and live comfortably.

But even with that safety net, it still felt like his world had turned upside down.

Bridgette remained the trustee of the trust, maintaining control over the finances, even in her absence.

David thought about searching for her. But about a month after her disappearance, he found an envelope slipped under his front door. No return address. No markings. Just his name, scrawled in neat, familiar handwriting.

With a sinking feeling, he opened it and unfolded the single sheet of paper.

The message was short and blunt: *Don't bother to look for me. I'm not the person I once was.*

David stared at the words, his chest tightening. He didn't need a signature to know it was from his Aunt Bridgette.

The meaning was clear. She couldn't face what had happened.

She couldn't live with the truth of what their family had become. And David understood that feeling all too well.

If it weren't for the girls. And for Molly, he might have disappeared, too.

There were days when the weight of everything threatened to crush him.

When he wondered how much more he could take.

But he couldn't walk away. Not from his daughters. Not from the only family he had left.

He folded the note carefully and slipped it into his pocket, letting out a long, shaky breath.

Somewhere out there, Bridgette was trying to outrun her demons. Maybe she'd find peace. Or maybe she'd stay lost forever.

Either way, David knew he couldn't follow.

He had to hold on. If not for himself, then for the girls.

Three years had passed since the betrayal of Kathy, Ruben, and Julia.

Grief had a strange way of layering itself, pressing down in ways David never saw coming.

Just when he thought he had a grip on reality, another wave would hit. Unexpected and relentless.

Chapter 15

David

Now, the only family David had left, outside of his daughters, was Molly.

Andrea didn't count.

She never really had.

As for Molly, they spoke once or twice a week, and she often spent weekends at his house, helping with the girls. She was good with them, patient, kind. But lately, he'd noticed something.

She was different.

Crankier than usual.

Stressed over things that never used to bother her.

Then again, who wasn't? Life had a way of wearing people down.

But for some reason, David felt it more than most.

The relentless headaches. The weight of exhaustion pressing down on him. No matter how much he tried to push through, there was always that gnawing feeling in the back of his mind. Something wasn't right.

As for Andrea, they barely spoke. Their only connection was Molly.

They had an unspoken agreement: Andrea would drive Molly to their meeting spot, a quiet stretch between Gilson and Fort Worth.

She never wanted to run into Julia. Never wanted her to know about Molly.

David understood that then.

But now his grandparents were gone. Molly was eighteen. What difference did it make anymore?

Still, Andrea insisted.

So, as always, they agreed to meet at their usual spot, the old crossroads off Texas State Highway 16, just past Cherokee.

David pulled off SH 16, dust kicking up beneath his tires as he slowed to a stop at the desolate intersection. The sun hung heavy in the Red Earth's sky, casting an unnatural reddish hue over the barren landscape, a constant reminder that nothing here was quite right.

He climbed out of his SUV, scanning the horizon as he adjusted his stance. No signs of life. No movement. Just silence.

A second car approached, tires crunching against the gravel shoulder. He exhaled, steeling himself.

The moment the car rolled to a stop, Molly jumped out, full of excitement. She barely waited for the engine to park before yanking the trunk open.

David reached for her bags, taking them from her hands before she could lift them.

"I got it," he murmured, nodding toward the SUV.

She didn't argue.

As they walked together toward his vehicle, he leaned in, lowering his voice.

"Is she okay? Is she sober?"

Molly hesitated, then whispered back, "Yes. She just had coffee and water this morning."

David let out a slow breath. Good.

He turned toward the car. Andrea sat behind the wheel, watching them.

David wasn't sure what to expect, not after everything. Every time they met here, it was something. Either she was rude, or she faked kindness for money or favors. Other times, she ignored him completely.

But this time... something was different.

Not in a way he'd ever seen before.

He met her eyes through the windshield, and a flicker of something stirred in his chest—unease, recognition... doubt.

Does she even know where she is?

There was confusion shadowing her face, her brows knitting together as if she were trying to grasp something just beyond her reach. Like she was slipping through reality without even knowing why.

Molly crossed the space between them and leaned into the window, giving Andrea a hug.

"Drive carefully, Mom. See you in a few days."

Something was wrong.

This wasn't just a meeting place. This was something else.

Something more.

David narrowed his eyes, suspicion growing.

Is she drunk?

"Molly, get in the car and wait for me. I want to talk to Andrea for a minute," he said.

"Okay." Molly climbed into the SUV without hesitation.

David stayed put, arms folded, leaning against his car as he watched Andrea closely.

She was acting strange, stranger than he'd expected.

But there was no scent of alcohol.

At first, she just sat there, staring at him, her expression shifting, flickering between confusion and something deeper.

Then she spoke.

"When is your birthday?"

David blinked.

What kind of question is that?

Still, he answered, "July 23, 1985."

As soon as the words left his mouth, something in her shifted.

The color drained from her face.

She just stared at him, unmoving, unblinking.

The silence stretched, too long, too heavy.

David's stomach tightened.

What the hell is wrong with her?

"I guess you forgot," he said, keeping his tone neutral. But inside, his mind was racing.

She didn't respond. She didn't even blink.

She just stood there, stuck in some kind of loop, lost in her own head.

David shifted his stance, uneasy.

Does she even know where she is?

Something about the way she looked at him unnerved him. It wasn't just confusion. This was deeper, like she was questioning reality itself.

And then she whispered something under her breath.

David barely caught it.

"I know you... but I don't remember you."

A chill ran up his spine.

It was as if she existed in two realities at once.

And David didn't know which one she belonged to.

He took a slow breath, steadying himself before asking the question that had weighed on him for years.

"Why didn't you raise me?"

The moment the words left his mouth, he saw something flicker in Andrea.

She froze.

Her expression went blank. Her eyes locked onto his, but she wasn't really seeing him. It was as if she had left the moment entirely.

David's fingers tightened around his crossed arms, watching her closely.

She didn't answer.

Did she not know?

Did she not remember?

Andrea's lips parted slightly, but no words came out. Her breathing shifted, shallow, uneven, like she'd just been struck by something invisible.

What was it?

What had just flashed through her mind?

His patience thinned.

He needed answers. He'd waited long enough.

But Andrea just stood there, silent, as if she were warring with something only she could see.

The seconds dragged.

Still, nothing came.

David exhaled, jaw tight.

She wasn't going to answer him.

Maybe because she didn't have an answer.

Or maybe, just maybe, because she didn't know the truth any more than he did.

Red Earth 2017–December, Gilson, Texas

Molly sat on the porch of David's house, her arms wrapped around her knees, staring out at the vast red-hued Texas sky. The sun hung bright and steady, its deep amber glow stretching across the horizon, casting long, rust-colored shadows over the yard. A light breeze stirred the December air, crisp but still comfortable, carrying the faint scent of dry earth and grass, still tinged with the coolness of the day.

She exhaled, checking the time again. Still nothing.

Behind her, David leaned against the doorframe, arms crossed.

"Did she say she'd call?"

Molly nodded, jaw tight.

"Yeah. She promised."

David let out a slow breath, rubbing the back of his neck.

"You really think she's gonna show?"

Molly shrugged her shoulders.

Andrea had been screwing up a lot lately, drinking too much, lying, picking fights, acting like the world owed her something.

Rachel and her husband had finally put their foot down and told her she had to leave.

Molly was allowed to stay on their property because she was an adult now.

But Andrea? Andrea had burned too many bridges.

The plan was simple: Andrea was supposed to pack her things, drive to Gilson, pick up Molly, and head straight back to Fort Worth.

But knowing her mother, plans never stayed plans for long.

David nudged her foot gently with his own.

"You want me to call her?"

Molly scoffed.

"She's not at the house anymore. Remember I told you Jim and Rachel kicked her out?"

David frowned.

"Touchy, touchy, there, little sister."

Molly sighed, rubbing her temples.

"I guess I'm just a little cranky. Mom will do that to you if you're around her long enough. Sorry I took it out on you."

They sat in silence for a moment, the weight of unspoken thoughts thick between them. Then Molly exhaled sharply and pushed herself up from the porch, heading inside.

David watched her go, curiosity gnawing at him.

He heard the soft clatter of the phone being lifted from the cradle, and a moment later, the unmistakable sound of dialing.

Before he could ask, Molly spoke over her shoulder.

"I'm calling Rachel."

His eyebrows lifted slightly, but he said nothing.

Rachel answered on the second ring.

"Hello?"

Molly didn't bother with small talk.

"Rachel? This is Molly. Have you heard from my mom?"

A pause. Then a sigh.

"No. I take it she hasn't called you?"

"Nope."

Another pause.

"Alright," Rachel said finally. "I'll come get you."

"You don't have to—"

"Hush," Rachel said, her tone firm but warm. "It's still early. I can be there in a few hours."

Molly hung up and glanced at David.

"She's coming."

David nodded.

"Probably for the best."

"I knew I should've driven here myself," Molly muttered, shaking her head. "But Mom didn't want me making the trip alone. She insisted on picking me up."

David glanced at her.

"Molly, I know you just started your new job, and you don't want to mess that up by missing tomorrow. I can drive you home. I'll have to make arrangements—"

"No, Rachel's already on her way," Molly replied. "Besides, you need to make sure Mrs. Fernandez comes by to pick up the girls."

Later that afternoon, Rachel's car pulled into the driveway, kicking up a cloud of dust. She climbed out, sunglasses perched on her head, looking tired but unsurprised.

"Well," she said, shutting the car door, "another promise Andrea couldn't keep."

Molly grabbed her bag and tossed it into the backseat, but David stopped her.

"Before you two head out, how about we grab something to eat?"

Rachel checked the time. "It's getting late."

"Come on," David said. "I know a good diner in town. You've been on the road, and Paula and the twins are staying with Mrs. Fernandez for a few days. Besides, Molly hasn't eaten since breakfast."

Rachel raised a brow. "Mrs. Fernandez?"

David nodded. "Yeah. She was my grandmother's friend. Now that Kathy's gone and hasn't bothered to see or contact the girls in years, Mrs. Fernandez looks after them when I need her to. But now that they're older, she mostly just enjoys having them over."

Molly glanced at Rachel. "I could eat."

Rachel exhaled through her nose, shaking her head. "Fine. But y'all are buying."

David smirked. "Deal."

⸺◆⸺

The diner was a small, old-school spot with cracked leather booths and a jukebox that hadn't worked in years. The three of them sat in a booth near the window, picking at their meals.

"Any idea where she actually is?" Rachel asked between sips of iced tea.

David shrugged. "Hell if I know."

Molly stabbed a fry with her fork. "She was supposed to pack her stuff and drive here, but she hasn't called, so..."

"She probably got sidetracked," Rachel muttered.

Molly looked up. "You really think she's coming? She knows I just started a job I love, and missing work tomorrow won't do me any favors."

Rachel sighed. "Sweetheart, I've known your mama a long time. And I know she's got her own way of thinking. If she planned to drive here, she probably did."

Molly frowned. "Then why hasn't she shown up?"

Rachel hesitated. "Because she got distracted by something she wanted more."

Silence settled between them. They all knew what that something was.

David rubbed at his temples and let out a slow exhale. "Damn headache," he muttered.

Rachel raised an eyebrow. "Again?"

"Yeah. Feels like something's squeezing my skull." He kneaded his fingers against the sides of his head, wincing. "I've had these my whole life, but lately... they've been worse."

Molly reached into her bag and pulled out a small bottle of ibuprofen, shaking two pills into her palm. "Here." David took them and dry swallowed with a grimace.

"Maybe you should get checked out," Rachel suggested. "Could be migraines."

"Yeah, maybe," David murmured, but deep down, he knew something felt off. The air always felt heavy. The sky, pressing down like a weight he couldn't shake.

It was like his body was wired for somewhere else. Somewhere less suffocating. He just didn't know why.

David checked his watch. "We should probably head back before it gets too late." They paid the bill and left the diner, climbing into Rachel's car.

They were halfway back to David's house when they saw it.

A faded maroon sedan, parked crookedly in front of a run-down bar, one tire up on the curb.

Molly saw it first. She sat up straighter, her pulse kicking up. "Wait."

Rachel slowed the car, squinting at the vehicle.

David leaned forward. "Is that Andrea's car?"

No one had to answer.

They knew.

Rachel pulled over, and the three of them got out.

Chapter 16

The air was crisp. It was December, after all, but this was Texas, so the chill was mild, even pleasant.

The distant sound of voices mixed with the muffled buzz of music spilling from inside the bar.

David exhaled sharply, raking a hand through his hair.

"Goddammit Andrea," David muttered.

They walked toward the entrance, their footsteps crunching across the gravel lot.

The door swung open just as they reached it.

Andrea staggered out, her hair wild, her balance unsteady. She blinked at them through glassy eyes, lips curling into a drunken sneer.

"Well, look who it is," she slurred, throwing her arms out dramatically. "The whole damn search party."

Molly's stomach dropped.

"Andrea," Rachel said firmly, stepping forward. "Give me your keys." Andrea snorted. "I don't think so."

Molly lunged before she could reach the car.

"Mom, stop. You can't drive like this."

Andrea rolled her eyes. "Oh, please." She fumbled with the door handle, missing it twice before finally yanking it open.

Rachel stepped in.

"Andrea, give me the damn keys. You're not driving like this."

Andrea's grip tightened on them.

"I can do whatever the hell I want. You ain't my mother."

David cursed under his breath.

"I gotta move the car before we get blocked in," he told Rachel, backing away. "Don't let her go anywhere."

Rachel nodded and tossed him the keys.

David jogged back to the car. He moved the car, scanning for a parking spot.

He found one just down the street, pulled in, and shut off the engine.

By the time he looked back, everything had gone to hell.

***

Andrea was already in the driver's seat. Molly sat in the passenger seat, fighting for the keys. And Rachel, Jesus, Rachel was hanging halfway into the car, gripping Molly's arm.

David slammed his door and sprinted back.

"Molly! Rachel!"

Andrea floored the gas.

Rachel had no choice. She hurled herself fully into the backseat just as the car peeled off, tires screaming against the asphalt.

David watched, breathless, as the taillights disappeared down the road.

"Shit."

He bolted for the car, yanked the door open, heart hammering. He threw it into drive and took off after them.

Andrea was speeding.

But David wouldn't chase her, not aggressively.

Not with Molly and Rachel in the car.

He was just going to follow. That was all he could safely do now.

Andrea drove aimlessly, her grip unsteady on the wheel, her foot heavy on the gas. There was no destination, just the road stretching endlessly ahead.

"Mom, please, pull over," Molly begged, her voice tight with panic.

Rachel leaned forward from the back seat, gripping the headrest.

"You've really done it this time!" she snapped. "Pull this damn car over now!"

But Andrea wasn't listening.

The alcohol blurred everything, logic, fear, consequences. Their voices clawed at the edges of her mind. Too much. Too loud. She needed to get away.

From the nagging. From the judgment. From herself.

She made a sudden, reckless turn onto a rural road outside of Gilson. She wasn't sure if it was the right way back to Fort Worth, but north was north, and that was good enough.

Molly's heart pounded.

"Mom, slow down!"

She reached for the wheel, lightly, carefully, trying not to overcorrect.

Andrea reacted instantly. Her backhand struck Molly's face with a brutal slap.

Molly gasped, her head whipping to the side, her cheek stinging.

Rachel's eyes blazed with fury.

"That's it!" she roared. "Andrea! STOP THE DAMN CAR!"

But Andrea only pressed the gas harder.

Molly turned to Rachel, her breath shaky.

They were trapped in a speeding death trap.

But then...

Headlights in the rearview mirror.

Molly's breath caught. David.

Relief washed over her, and she exhaled, hands trembling.

"It's David," she whispered. "He's behind us."

Rachel turned to look. So did Andrea.

And in her drunken, paranoid haze, she didn't see rescue; she saw pursuit.

Her jaw clenched.

"Oh, you wanna play hero, do you?" she muttered under her breath.

Then, without warning, she floored it.

The car lurched forward, the engine roaring.

Molly's relief twisted into terror.

"No! Mom, Stop!"

Rachel gripped the seat.

"Jesus, Andrea, slow the hell down!"

The car tore down the narrow road, dust billowing behind them.

The speedometer climbed.

60.

70.

80.

David was gaining ground, trying to catch up.

Andrea clenched the wheel tighter, her vision tunneling. The road ahead was winding, narrowing...

but she refused to let off the gas.

Then...

A sharp corner.

Molly saw it first. Her breath caught in her throat.

"MOM!"

Rachel grabbed the seat, eyes wide with horror.

But Andrea didn't slow down. Didn't even try.

The car hit the curve at full speed.

Tires screeched.

The world flipped.

The right side slammed down first, where Molly and Rachel sat.

Metal crunched.

Glass shattered.

A sickening force crushed into them.

Then...

Another violent roll.

The car tumbled again before coming to a brutal stop, upside down.

Silence.

Smoke curled from the wreckage.

One of the wheels spun idly, the sound eerily out of place.

David's car screeched to a halt.

His breath came fast, body frozen for a fraction of a second as he stared at the overturned vehicle.

His stomach dropped.

This can't be real.

But his legs were already moving before his mind caught up. He ran.

His heart pounded against his ribs as he reached the wreckage, dropping to his knees beside the shattered window.

Dear God...

What was he about to see?

His throat went dry.

His hands shook as he reached inside.

And then he saw them.

⚬

David reached into the wreckage, hands trembling as he grasped for someone, *anyone.*

His fingers brushed against an arm.

Small. Too small.

His breath hitched.

Molly.

A tremor ran through him as his eyes followed the shape of her body, twisted, still.

Her neck bent at an unnatural angle.

Wrong.

All wrong.

A sharp, suffocating pressure clamped down on his chest.

No.

His hands hovered over her, pleading, shaking.

A breath. A flutter. Anything. Please.

But the silence pressed in, deafening.

His vision blurred as the truth sank in, ruthless and unrelenting.

Molly was gone.

A raw, broken sound escaped his throat. He hadn't even realized he'd made it.

The weight of it, her absence, crushed him.

Drowned out the world.

Not her.

Not like this.

He reached for her, fingertips brushing against cold skin.

Too late.

And for the first time in his life, David had no idea how to move forward.

Through the crushing fog of shock and grief, he forced himself to shift—*Rachel.*

His hands found another arm, warm, trembling.

Still alive.

With careful, desperate urgency, he worked to free her, mindful of the shattered glass and tangled wreckage.

She let out a weak groan, so fragile it barely reached him.

Alive. But just barely.

Then, voices.

Across the road, porch lights flickered on from a nearby farmhouse. A woman let out a gasp, her hand flying to her mouth before she turned and bolted inside, calling for emergency services.

A man rushed toward the wreckage, boots crunching on gravel.

"Let's get her out," he said, crouching beside David to help with Rachel.

Together, they lifted her from the wreck and carried her to the roadside. The man checked her vitals, his brow furrowed.

"She's alive," he said. "Barely, but she's alive."

David barely heard him.

His eyes were locked on Molly.

The man moved next to her, placing two fingers against her throat. He already knew. But he checked anyway.

Nothing.

No life.

The man swallowed hard and looked at David, who was already consumed by silent shock.

"Did you see what happened?" the man asked, assuming David was just a passer-by who'd stopped to help.

Before David could answer...

A groan.

Movement.

They both turned sharply, eyes snapping toward the wreck.

David's stomach twisted.

He rushed to the other side of the car just as a figure stirred in the shadows.

Andrea.

David clenched his fists.

Of course she survived.

His whole body burned with rage as she blinked groggily, disoriented. Her breath reeked of alcohol.

She tried to push herself up, her head lolling slightly.

Her eyes found David's, confusion flickering across her bruised face.

"What... what happened?"

David snapped.

"What happened?" His voice cracked with fury. "You killed your daughter, that's what happened!"

His voice ripped through the thick evening air, shaking with rage, disbelief, something so raw it barely felt real.

"She was my little sister!" he shouted, voice cracking. "My sister! It should have been you! It should have been—"

His voice fractured into a whisper as his strength gave out, and he collapsed to his knees, broken.

The fading sunlight cast long shadows, stretching across the wreckage like silent witnesses to his fury.

Andrea blinked again, slow, unfocused, like she wasn't fully processing his words.

The man beside David stepped in, gently moving him aside before reaching down to pull Andrea from the wreck.

She stumbled as he steadied her, swaying on unsteady legs.

She was alive.

Alive when Molly wasn't.

Alive when Rachel barely was.

David's hands clenched at his sides. His chest heaved. His head pounded.

Andrea looked around, dazed.

"Molly?"

David turned away, unable to look at her.

The evening around them swelled with approaching sirens. Help was coming.

But nothing could undo what had already been done.

Even in her drunken haze, Andrea began to understand.

The wreck.

The voices.

The flashing porch lights from the farmhouse across the road.

The overwhelming stench of burnt rubber and blood.

She sat on the cold pavement, arms wrapped around herself, her body aching but intact. The alcohol still dulled her senses, but something was starting to pierce the fog.

A woman knelt beside her, speaking gently.

"Don't you worry now. Emergency services are on their way."

Andrea froze.

Emergency services.

Police.

Her stomach lurched, nausea climbing her throat.

Her breath quickened, shallow and uneven. She turned her head slightly, her gaze locking on David.

He was crouched beside Rachel, carefully draping a blanket over her. His voice was low, steady, trying to comfort her. Trying to keep her conscious.

His hands, miraculously steady, checked her breathing. Her pulse.

Andrea's eyes shifted again.

The man who had helped was now standing near the wreckage.

Placing a sheet over Molly.

A sheet.

Andrea couldn't breathe.

Her mind recoiled, rejecting the truth of it.

No. No. This wasn't happening.

Her body acted before her mind could catch up.

She bolted.

Her legs, sore, scraped, but still strong, carried her on instinct.

Andrea ran toward Rachel's car.

David had left it parked on the side of the road, keys still in the ignition.

At first, she thought about hiding behind it.

Or maybe slipping inside, curling up in the backseat, disappearing from sight.

But then...

Her eyes landed on the keys.

The engine still running.

Her pulse pounded in her ears.

She had to get out of here.

Without a second thought, she yanked the door open and slid into the driver's seat.

Tires crunched over gravel as she threw the car into reverse, a cloud of dust kicking up behind her.

She didn't look back.

Not once.

She just drove.

⋯⋯◆⋯⋯

David tucked the blanket around Rachel, his hands steady despite the chaos unraveling inside his mind.

His voice was low, gentle.

"Just hang in there, Rachel. Help's almost here."

Beside him, the man from the farmhouse stood solemnly near Molly's still form, his shoulders sagging under the weight of what had just happened.

Then, movement.

The hum of an engine.

David looked up, brows furrowing.

Rachel's car, the one he had driven here, was backing up.

The headlights swung in a wide arc as it made a sharp U-turn, then tore off down the road.

At first, he was confused.

Then the realization slammed into him like a freight train.

His head whipped toward the spot where Andrea had been sitting just moments ago.

She was gone.

His stomach clenched.

"No—"

A voice rang out behind him.

"The woman just drove off in that car!"

He turned.

The woman from the farmhouse stood there, face twisted in disbelief, her hands clenched at her sides.

His blood went cold.

Andrea.

She had survived. She had seen the destruction she caused. She had looked at her dead daughter... under a sheet, at Rachel, still barely clinging to life.

And she ran.

David rose to his feet, breath ragged, body tight with fury.

His eyes locked on the fading red taillights, disappearing into the blood-red dusk stretching across the horizon.

His jaw clenched so hard it ached.

His fists curled at his sides.

His heart pounded, not with fear. Not even with grief.

But with a cold, burning rage.

Through gritted teeth, he murmured, low and steady, a promise, not a threat:

"You selfish bitch! I'll find you. You're not escaping me."

Just then, the wail of sirens shattered the silence.

Red and blue lights flashed across the wreckage, color bouncing off the twisted metal and shattered glass. Dust kicked up around the emergency vehicles as they pulled onto the road, tires crunching gravel beneath them.

But David didn't flinch.

Didn't look away.

Didn't even blink.

He kept his eyes locked on the road.

On the direction she'd vanished.

Because this wasn't over.

Not by a long shot.

Chapter 17

Andrea sped into Gilson, her pulse hammering, her thoughts buzzing in a chaotic loop.

She pulled into an empty lot, her hands trembling as she left the keys in the ignition.

Without a second thought, she bolted from the car, putting as much distance between herself and the vehicle as possible.

Her breath came in short, ragged gasps as she ran, her mind spinning.

Where could she go?

What could she do?

Her legs carried her instinctively to Sunrise Park.

The familiar sight of the deserted benches and towering trees offered a fleeting sense of relief.

She collapsed onto a bench, pressing her hands to her temples, trying, failing, to still her thoughts.

Her fingers dug into her scalp.

This wasn't her fault.

They had come after her.

They had tried to control her, gang up on her.

Andrea swallowed hard, her dry throat burning.

"It was all Rachel," she muttered, clinging to the thought, rewriting reality in her favor.

She hunched forward, elbows on her knees, her mind spiraling.

She had to think. Had to figure out what to do next.

But just as she sank deeper into her panic, a flicker of movement snapped her back to the present.

She tensed.

Slowly, she turned her head, dread curling in her stomach.

Law enforcement?

Or worse, *David?*

Her muscles coiled, ready to bolt. But then she froze.

A figure had appeared on the bench beside her.

Not walked up.

Not approached.

Appeared.

A woman. Calmly sipping from a cup.

Andrea's breath caught. Her whole body went cold.

No. It couldn't be.

Sonya.

She had been old back then.

She should have been long gone.

And yet, here she was.

Alive. Unaged. Watching her.

Andrea couldn't move. Couldn't breathe.

The old woman simply smiled, as if she'd been waiting for this moment all along.

Andrea's pulse pounded with disbelief. Her breath stuck in her throat.

That face, the same one from decades ago, was unchanged. She sat across from her, raising her cup in a casual, mocking salute.

Andrea swallowed, her voice hoarse. "You... it's you. After all these years."

Sonya's sharp eyes crinkled at the corners. "Hello, Andrea. Been a long time, hasn't it?"

Andrea shifted on the bench, glancing around the park.

Her instincts screamed for her to run...

but fear, and something else, held her in place.

"Why are you here?" she demanded. "And how... how are you still alive?"

Sonya's smile stayed put, serene and deeply unsettling.

"Time isn't the same for people like me, dear."

Andrea's skin prickled.

"That doesn't explain why you look exactly the same."

Sonya exhaled, mildly amused.

"Oh, Andrea. You always did ask the wrong questions."

Andrea clenched her fists.

"What do you want from me? Why now?"

Sonya studied her, eyes unreadable.

Then, softly:

"Come with me. I can offer you a way out of all this... chaos."

Andrea's jaw tightened.

"A way out?"

Sonya nodded.

"I have a safe place. No police. No judgment."

Her voice lowered, calm but purposeful.

"No, David."

Andrea stiffened.

She couldn't deny the wave of relief those two words brought.

But her pulse quickened again.

How did she know?

Andrea's voice dropped to a whisper, laced with suspicion.

"Why would you help me?"

Sonya smiled again, cool, patient.

"Because I did you a favor once. And I always take care of the people I help."

Andrea frowned.

"That doesn't sound like a favor. So... why?"

Sonya let out a soft chuckle.

"Now you're asking the right questions."

She stood, gesturing toward the path winding out of the park.

"Come. All answers will come in time."

A breeze stirred the trees, but the air around Sonya remained completely still.

Andrea hesitated, only for a moment, before rising to follow.

She didn't know it yet, but the moment her foot touched that path, she was walking straight into something far bigger than herself.

Toward the truth.

Toward the force behind Sonya's power.

Toward Anio.

When Andrea stepped into Sonya's house, she paused just inside the doorway, eyebrows raised.

"Whose house is this?"

Sonya turned with a grin.

"It's mine."

Andrea blinked.

"No way."

Sonya said nothing, her expression unreadable as she removed her tattered coat. In one slow, deliberate motion, she pulled off her wig, then slipped out her false teeth.

Andrea's breath caught in her throat.

Her eyes widened, realization crashing down like a suffocating weight.

This woman had deceived her.

She opened her mouth to demand answers, but Sonya held up a hand, a silent, commanding gesture.

"Before you ask anything, I'll explain everything."

Andrea clenched her jaw but said nothing, following Sonya into the living room. They sank into the chairs, the air thick with tension.

And then Sonya began.

She spoke of their first meeting in 1984.

Of how she had disguised herself as an old woman, when in truth, she'd only been in her mid-thirties.

She revealed that she had been sent on a mission.

That Andrea had been her target.

Andrea stiffened.

"A mission? What kind of mission?"

Sonya's expression didn't change.

"I was never told why *you* were chosen. Only that you were. And now, after all these years…" She leaned forward, voice dropping to a whisper. "It's time to pay what's owed."

Andrea's eyes flashed.

"What's owed? If you're talking about the pregnancy thing, well, it didn't work! Victor didn't stay with me. His mother took my son from me. So, you see? I don't owe you anything. Your promise was worthless."

Sonya's smile didn't fade. It sharpened.

"Oh, wasn't it? You *did* get together, didn't you?"

Andrea scoffed.

"That's not fair! It was years later.

And he was killed not long after we finally settled in."

Sonya leaned forward. Her smile softened, her posture less rigid now.

Without the disguise, she looked older; her real self. A woman in her late sixties, with silver threads woven through shoulder-length light brown hair.

"Well, my dear," she said gently, "I never told you when he'd be with you, or for how long. Only that he would never want to leave you. And he didn't, did he? It just took him longer to realize it."

Andrea swallowed hard.

A chill crept down her spine.

"What does this all mean?" she asked, voice cautious. Wary.

Sonya met her gaze.

"It means you have a mission now. A very important one."

Andrea frowned.

"What mission?"

Sonya's smile deepened.

"Not from me. I'm not the one asking."

She stood and gestured for Andrea to follow.

"Anio is."

Andrea hesitated.

"Who's Anio?"

But Sonya didn't answer.

Instead, she led Andrea down a hallway into a darkened room.

⸻◆⸻

Shadows stretched across the walls as Sonya moved with careful precision, lighting two black candles.

Their flickering glow cast eerie, shifting shapes over the space.

From a table draped in velvet, Sonya retrieved a small handheld mirror, hidden beneath a dark green cloth. She lifted it, glanced at Andrea, then turned her focus to the glass.

Her voice dropped to a whisper, a chant slipping from her lips:

"By the pact we share, I summon you.

By the shadows and blood that bind us, appear before me.

Come forth, Keeper of Darkness, speak your will, and it shall be done.

Reveal yourself to me now."

As Sonya pressed her fingers to the mirror's surface, an image rippled into view.

Andrea inhaled sharply.

The figure in the mirror... and Sonya... both turned to look at her.

Her heart pounded.

No.

This isn't real. It can't be.

She opened her mouth to protest, to demand answers, to scream...

But Sonya raised a single finger to her lips.

Not now.

Andrea swallowed her words, the weight of the unknown pressing hard against her chest as the image in the mirror stared back, waiting.

The figure's lips curled into a satisfied smile.

A slow nod of approval followed, and then Anio's voice filled the room, smooth and commanding:

"Mission well done."

Sonya remained silent. But a flicker of uncertainty crossed her face.

She had followed orders without question. Yet even now, she didn't know why.

Why Andrea?

Why now?

But she didn't ask.

She simply inclined her head in silent acknowledgment.

Andrea, however, felt a cold unease creeping up her spine.

Anio's gaze turned fully to her, intense and unwavering.

"We do not have much time."

Andrea parted her lips to speak, but before a word could form, his voice cut through the air like a blade:

"Do not speak."

A jolt of fear locked her in place. She swallowed hard, her body instinctively tensing.

The air thickened, charged with something unseen.

Then...

Anio's gaze darkened.

And his next words sent a chill down her spine:

"Now, for your mission."

Both Sonya and Andrea held their breath.

"The necklace."

Sonya's eyes widened.

Could he mean *that* necklace?

The one he demanded all those years ago?

Anio continued, his expression unreadable.

"This necklace."

He held it up through the mirror's surface, the chain gleaming, the pendant pulsing with an eerie, unnatural glow.

"This was meant to be mine. Without it, I, we..." his eyes flicked to Sonya, "would not hold the power we have now. But there is another. We need that necklace."

His words dripped with persuasion, wrapping around them like silk, weaving illusion and purpose into something larger than themselves.

Then his gaze snapped back to Andrea.

"Your mission is to obtain that necklace. And when you succeed, you will be granted power beyond anything you can imagine."

Andrea's breath hitched.

Power?

The word echoed through her, seductive and dangerous.

Before she could respond, Anio raised the necklace again.

A soft red haze rippled outward, distorting the air like heat rising from pavement.

And then...

He stepped through.

The mirror shimmered. The surface rippled.

And in the next heartbeat...

Anio stood before them.

Real.

Tangible.

No longer just a reflection.

Andrea's pulse thundered.

The room darkened around them, something unnatural pressing in.

She had no idea what she had just been pulled into.

Trembling slightly, she asked, "What do I have to do to get the other necklace?"

Anio's lips curved upward in something resembling a smile, but his eyes remained cold, unreadable.

"You will be sent to another place," he said smoothly. "Another world. The necklace is there."

Andrea's breath caught.

Another world?

Anio's voice slithered through the room like smoke.

"You will travel to a world parallel to this one," he said. "You will be switched with the version of you that exists there. You must become her because the necklace is in her home. Once there, search the house, find the necklace, and return to the exact spot where you arrived. From there, take it to the Mystic Crossroads and show it to the owner. Only the owner. No one else."

Andrea swallowed hard.

"Another version of me?"

Sonya nodded.

"She lives in that world. Her name is Andrea too, but there they call her Andri. So remember to answer to that name when you're there."

"And then?" Andrea asked, voice tight with apprehension.

Anio's gaze darkened.

"Once the shopkeeper's eyes fall upon the necklace, it will emit a blue and red haze. That is the final step. Your mission will be complete."

His words twisted around her like a vice, thick with promise, heavy with power.

"And then, Andrea... you will have the privilege of using my power. Power beyond what you can fathom."

Andrea hesitated, uncertainty flickering in her eyes.

"That's all I have to do?" She let out a shaky laugh the simplicity of it almost absurd.

"Just pretend to be myself, I mean, Andri, find the necklace, bring it to the store owner, and I'll have power like Sonya's?"

Her lips parted in sudden realization.

"I can do that."

Anio's smirk deepened.

"Of course you can. And you will."

His voice dripped with satisfaction, sensing her naivety, the buried spark of selfish ambition.

"But understand this..."

His tone shifted, cool, razor-sharp.

"...once the necklace is in our possession, our power will not just grow... it will become unstoppable."

Andrea didn't even hear the shift in his tone.

She was too far gone.

Too consumed by the promise of power.

And that... was exactly what Anio wanted.

Chapter 18

A surge of nervous excitement shot through Andrea, a thrill she hadn't felt in years. Her sense of adventure sparked to life, pushing aside any lingering doubt. Even in her fifties, she was confident she could pull this off.

And once she had the power...

She'd reshape everything.

She pictured it now: youthful, radiant, with a stunning figure and, of course, larger boobs.

She'd travel the world, turn heads, live in luxury.

No worries. No struggles.

Just power, beauty, and the life of a queen.

Nothing and no one would hold her back.

"So, when do I leave?" Andrea asked, her voice brimming with anticipation.

"In a few minutes. You must prepare," Anio replied, his tone sharp, commanding.

He turned to Sonya.

"Hold out the mirror."

Sonya obeyed, lifting the handheld glass. Anio's fingers hovered over its surface.

Within seconds, an image flickered to life.

Andri...

Shopping at a store.

Anio's voice was smooth and deliberate.

"Make sure she is dressed as closely as possible: same clothing, same hairstyle."

Sonya studied the reflection, her breath catching as she noted the background.

A store exit.

And beyond it.

A blue sky.

Home.

The thought slammed into her like a punch to the chest.

If he could send Andrea there...

Why hadn't he sent her back?

All this time...

He could have sent her home.

A swell of betrayal rose in her throat, but she swallowed it down.

Not now.

Not in front of him.

She forced her focus back to the task: Andrea's outfit, her hair.

The more Sonya looked, the more the details locked into place.

Jeans. Shoulder-length dark hair. Neutral colors.

But then...

Her eyes caught someone standing near Andri.

A woman with long gray hair.

Sonya blinked.

No...

She looked again. A closer stare. And...

Tanya.

Recognition slammed through her.

Her breath hitched. Her pulse roared in her ears.

Tanya.

It was her sister.

She kept her expression neutral, fighting the flood of emotion surging inside her.

She couldn't let Anio see.

Couldn't let him ask questions.

Forcing her voice steady, detached, she turned to Andrea.

"You're wearing jeans. That's good, so is she."

She glanced back at the mirror, assessing again.

"Your top's a different color, but keep your sweater. It'll hide it. Andri's wearing a jacket, but your sweater's close enough. It'll do."

She pushed the rising ache in her chest down deep.

Was that really Tanya? Or just another trick?

Her throat tightened, but she kept moving.

"Your shoes are off.

She's wearing tennis shoes.

You're in ankle boots."

She turned toward Anio.

"She needs shoes like the ones Andri is wearing for the mission."

Anio didn't hesitate.

He waved a hand toward the front room.

"They are there."

Sonya nodded.

Then turned to Andrea.

"Go to the front room. There'll be shoes for you to use."

Andrea frowned.

"But how do you know what size—"

"They'll fit," Sonya snapped, sharper than she intended.

Andrea paused, meeting her gaze.

But after a beat, she turned and walked toward the front room.

As soon as she was out of sight, Sonya exhaled slowly, her chest rising and falling with tension.

Tanya...was it really her?

Or was this another of Anio's twisted illusions?

She didn't know.

But something deep inside her said, yes.

It was her.

And now...

Everything had changed.

As soon as Andrea left the room, Sonya turned to Anio, her voice calm but carefully measured.

"Why do you need both necklaces?"

Anio's gaze snapped toward her, suspicion flickering in his dark eyes.

"Should I be worried about your loyalty?" A cold thread of fear curled through Sonya's gut.

Did he sense my doubt?

She forced a light laugh, shaking her head casually.

"Of course not. I'm just asking, that's all."

He studied her in silence.

The pause stretched, heavy and suffocating.

Then, finally, he spoke.

"It's as I said. The pair of necklaces will bring the greatest power. Not just here, but to the other world as well."

His lips curled into a smirk.

"We'll have it all at our fingertips."

Sonya nodded, holding his gaze, her smile tight and forced.

Pretend you believe him.

But inside, her thoughts spiraled.

He's lying.

This wasn't just about helping Andrea.

It wasn't even about the power they'd gain in this world.

It was bigger.

Much bigger.

If the necklaces were as powerful as he claimed, then he wasn't just planning domination. He was planning conquest. Across worlds.

A creeping chill ran through her.

And if he succeeded, if he truly possessed both necklaces...

There would be no stopping him.

She swallowed hard, forcing her expression to remain neutral.

Anio's energy had shifted. His anticipation was near manic now.

He's waited too long for this.

And now that it was within reach...

He was dangerous.

Andrea re-entered the room, her expression focused.

She was ready.

With a wave of his hand, Anio erased the facial bruises from her earlier accident.

Her leg still ached. A dull buzz from the lingering alcohol still hummed in her head.

She had a mission.

A purpose.

And for the first time in years, a path forward.

A quiet relief settled over her. She was leaving all the chaos behind.

She would succeed.

No matter what.

Squaring her shoulders, she stepped into the center of the room.

Sonya studied her briefly, then frowned.

"No, that's not right."

She gestured toward Andrea's hair.

"I'll grab a comb."

She turned to leave.

But just as she reached the doorway...

She heard it.

Anio's voice.

Low. Commanding. Absolute.

"When you show the store owner the necklace. As soon as the blue and red light radiates from it... You must kill her. Bring a weapon. She must not live."

Sonya froze.

Her breath caught in her throat.

What?

Behind her, Andrea gasped.

Her face drained of color.

"You... you want me to kill someone?"

Anio turned to her, gaze cold and unwavering.

His voice cut through the air like a blade.

"You must. After you complete the act, you'll have nothing to worry about. No one will come after you. You'll be free to live as you wish."

Andrea stared at him, stunned.

Her heart pounded in her chest.

She wasn't a killer.

She had never killed anyone.

Then again...

Molly.

Rachel.

She drew in a shaky breath, her hands curling at her sides.

The thought pressed its way to the surface, the one thing she could cling to. The one justification she could believe in:

That wasn't her fault.

Rachel had tried to control her.

David had followed her.

They should have known better.

Slowly, Andrea's expression hardened.

She nodded.

"Alright. I'll do it."

Just outside the room, Sonya stood frozen.

She knew Anio had waited for her to leave before giving Andrea that order.

Lying, manipulating, stealing, those were one thing.

But killing?

Sonya's pulse pounded in her ears as a chilling realization settled over her like ice.

What if the store owner is Tanya?

A sharp breath caught in her chest.

Just then, Sonya returned, comb in hand.

Without a word, she began brushing Andrea's hair, shaping it to resemble the other version.

Her hands moved automatically, but inside, her mind screamed.

She didn't want to do this.

She didn't want any part of this.

But it was too late.

Andrea was ready.

Anio gave a single nod, then waved a hand over her, his fingers moving with unnatural precision.

Sonya stepped back as a swirling blue haze engulfed Andrea.

Her heart pounded.

For a split second, a wild urge clawed at her...

Step into the haze. Follow her. Go home.

But before she could act on it, Andrea was gone.

The space where she'd stood was now empty.

Just air.

Just silence.

Sonya stared, unblinking.

The room felt quieter.

Colder.

Anio's narrowed eyes flicked toward her.

"What are you waiting for?"

Sonya turned, pulse still racing.

"Where's Andri? Why didn't she appear here?"

Anio laughed, a low, amused sound.

"Ah... is that what you were expecting?"

He shook his head, smirking.

"I have no use for her, other than getting her out of the way so Andrea can complete her mission."

Sonya's stomach twisted.

"Did you kill her?" she asked, carefully.

Anio scoffed. "Hardly."

He waved a hand, dismissive.

"I left her on a park bench."

His tone was casual, like he'd misplaced a book.

"You should go now. Make sure she appears as expected. I'll send you a few seconds ahead of her."

Sonya hesitated.

"Why me? What do you want me to do... once I'm there?"

Anio's expression was unreadable.

"Nothing."

A beat of silence.

Then, his voice dropped, quiet, cold.

"Just confirm that she's there. I don't want any... unforeseen problems."

His eyes darkened.

"If she appears as expected, you can leave."

The silence between them was heavy, fraught.

Sonya nodded once.

Quickly, she slipped into her disguise...

The worn-out teeth. The tangled wig.

The tattered, dirt-streaked jacket.

Each piece dulled her light, returning her to the version of herself he expected to see.

Anio flicked his wrist.

And just like that...

She was gone.

⚬

At Sunrise Park, Sonya blinked and found herself standing near a bench.

Above her, the red-hued sky stretched endlessly.

The air was thick, heavy.

Like a storm waiting to break.

Then...

Just as Anio had said...

Andri appeared.

One second, the bench was empty.

The next...

She was there.

Sonya remained still—watching.

Andri lifted her head slowly, eyes wide.

Her lips parted. Her expression froze.

She was seeing the red sky for the first time.

A sky that wasn't hers.

Sonya watched, and a twinge stirred in her chest.

Almost...

Pity.

This version of Andrea, Andri.

Had no idea what had just happened to her.

No idea that she had been plucked out of her world with blue skies... only to land in a place that wasn't her own.

No idea she was about to be accused of a crime she didn't commit.

And worst of all...

No idea she might never make it home.

Sonya turned, her breath caught in her throat.

She tore her gaze away... and walked off.

Forcing herself not to look back.

Chapter 19

Blue Earth 2017–December, Ridgefield, Nebraska

Drew and I had been together for over a year, though, for most of that time, he'd been away.

His mother had fallen ill, and he stayed with her in Florida to care for her. He managed to come back twice for short visits, but the majority of our relationship had been built on late-night phone calls, text messages filled with longing, and video chats that never felt like enough.

Two months ago, he finally returned to Ridgefield. His mother had passed away, and after handling her affairs, he was free to come home for good. Since then, we'd hardly spent a moment apart.

As I was putting away the lunch dishes, Drew walked in, just like he did every day.

Without a word, he came up behind me, wrapping his arms around me and pulling me close. A familiar warmth settled over me as I smiled, resting my hands on his.

He brushed my hair aside, his touch gentle, and because he was so much taller than me, he had to bend down to nuzzle his face into my neck. The sensation sent a shiver down my spine, the kind that reminded me just how much I'd missed him.

I turned in his embrace, ready to kiss him, when...

"Mommy, Molly's here!"

Lanix's excited voice rang out as he burst through the door. His steps faltered, and his bright expression dimmed as his gaze landed on Drew. His eyes narrowed.

"You were trying to kiss her? That's my mom! And you were trying to kiss her. I saw you."

Neither of us said anything at first, caught off guard by the unexpected shift in his tone. Drew and I exchanged glances, surprised that Lanix seemed bothered by it.

He frowned, arms crossing as he stood there, waiting, expecting one of us to respond.

Before either of us could find the right words, Molly walked in. The air shifted.

Whatever protest Lanix had brewing seemed to slip from his mind as he turned toward his sister, his momentary irritation forgotten.

For now.

It was winter break, and both Molly and Lanix would be home for a couple of weeks. Relief washed over me, the same way it always did when Molly arrived safely from college. I guess it's just a mom thing.

"How was the trip?" I asked.

"Good. Long, as always," Molly replied with a tired smile.

Once she settled in, Drew headed downstairs to repair a shelf in Lanix's room, always finding ways to be helpful around the house.

The rest of us gathered in the living room, hot chocolate for Molly and Lanix, and tea for Mom and me.

As we sipped, we made plans to put up the Christmas tree the next day.

Molly was excited to bake cookies, a tradition she loved.

Outside, the mid-December air was crisp, but the forecast promised cold, clear skies, perfect for a cozy weekend at home.

"You should go for a drive tomorrow, Mom," Molly suggested. "You love those long, quiet trips in the countryside."

"I'm not sure," I replied hesitantly.

It's true that I love traveling alone, but now I'd rather have Drew with me, I thought.

"Come on. I'll stay with Grandma," she insisted. "The weather's good, no rain or snow, and let's be honest, you don't get this offer often!" Molly teased, laughing.

She wasn't wrong. Midwest weather could turn in an instant. Molly, always fascinated by weather patterns, loved tracking storms and watching clouds form.

"Alright," I said with a smile. "I'll head out after breakfast and be back before dinner."

"So, you won't help with the Christmas tree?" Lanix asked, frowning.

"No, but Grandma can help you.

You know she loves that," I replied.

Lanix rolled his eyes. I shot him a look. "Hey, don't start," I warned, voice sharper than intended. "She can't help it if she doesn't remember how to do things. She's my mom, and I don't like it when you're rude!"

A brief silence hung in the air before Molly interjected, "I'll make sure Grandma helps me, Mom."

I turned to her with a grateful smile, placing a hand on her shoulder. "Thank you, Molly."

Lanix looked up at me, his big blue eyes shimmering with guilt, his baby-soft face framed by tousled, sandy-blonde hair. His expression softened.

"I'm sorry, Mommy."

"Thank you for apologizing," I said, leaning down to press a kiss to his forehead.

I get defensive when someone speaks negatively about Mom. She's been an incredibly loving mother, always there for me and my siblings.

Molly and Lanix know this, but Lanix has a habit of pushing buttons just to get a reaction. It can be frustrating, but I know he doesn't mean any harm.

Mom was there for us in every way when we needed her most. Now it's my turn to be there for her. I feel blessed to have retired early and moved to this quiet rural home, where I can raise Lanix and care for Mom as her illness progresses.

⸻◆⸻

As Molly, Lanix, and Mom spent time in the living room, I made my way downstairs.

Drew looked up as I descended, and the moment his eyes met mine, he flashed me the biggest grin.

Every time he did that, my heart leaped.

I closed the space between us, and he wrapped his arms around me, holding me close.

Pressing his forehead against mine, he murmured, "The other day, when we were asking our favorite colors, favorite foods... I asked you about your hopes and dreams. You mentioned a dream that left you reeling, filled with emotions you couldn't quite describe. So, tell me, was it a good dream? One you'd count among your hopes?"

I hesitated, thinking.

"I wouldn't say it was part of my hopes. It's just that when you mentioned dreams, it reminded me of one I had last year."

"Do you want to tell me about it?" he asked gently.

I smiled. "I will, but not right now. I don't want to waste these stolen moments talking about a dream."

He was just about to kiss me when, at the same time, we both glanced up toward the stairs, making sure nobody was there, making sure Lanix wasn't there.

We burst into quiet laughter.

Our smiles faded as he leaned in, brushing his lips against mine.

His warmth melted into me, and within moments, the kiss deepened.

We lost ourselves in it, stealing minutes like reckless teenagers sneaking behind the gym.

When we finally pulled away, he gazed down at me, his dark eyes full of something both playful and tender.

His voice was low, almost a whisper.

"Come over for dinner later? I'll cook for you."

My eyes widened. "Really? You'll cook?"

He smirked.

"Yeah. We can go to Jay's Market and grab what we need to make tacos."

I raised an eyebrow. "*We*? I thought you said *you* were going to cook?"

He leaned in, his breath warm against my ear.

"*We'll* go to the store, and *I'll* do the cooking," he whispered.

I tilted my head, grinning. "Well, Mr. Andrew Romero, since Molly's here with Mom and Lanix, I do believe I'll accept your offer," I said, slipping into a playful Southern drawl.

Drew chuckled, matching my tone.

"Oh, we're using full names now? Well then, Ms. Andrea Perez, dinner at my house it is. And, by the way, I kinda like that our names are similar."

I laughed, giving him a light nudge.

"Well, don't get used to it. I might just call you Romero from now on."

He raised an eyebrow, a playful glint in his eyes. "Um... I think not."

I smirked and pulled him closer, letting my hands rest on his chest.

"Well then, I'll see you later."

He smiled, his arms slipping around my waist. "It's a date."

Our eyes met, and for a moment, the world seemed to fade away, leaving just the two of us in that small, perfect bubble.

I couldn't help but grin, feeling that familiar flutter in my chest.

Ding, ding! The sound of the doorbell chimed as the front door opened.

In walked my sister, Leanne, Christmas gifts in hand, with her son, Josh, following close behind.

As sisters, we shared the same dark brown hair and light complexion. Her straight hair cascaded to her mid-back, while mine fell just past my shoulders in soft layers, accented with subtle blonde highlights. Now in our fifties, the inevitable grays had started creeping in, though we did our best to keep them at bay with a bit of hair dye.

Leanne had been widowed for many years. Her husband, Randy Coleman, was the love of her life. Tragically, he was killed in 1995 during a parachuting accident when his chute failed to open. At the time, their son, Josh, was just twelve years old.

Two months ago, Leanne retired from her job in California and moved to a town near ours in Nebraska, where Josh had already been living. We've loved having them close by.

Josh is a joy to be around: fun, adventurous, and fearless to a fault. He's the type who charges into situations headfirst and figures things out later. He can fix just about anything, whether it's a busted electronic device or a complex construction project; he always knows what to do. But his talents don't stop there; he's also an exceptional musician, effortlessly switching between guitar and keyboard.

Standing at 6'1," with piercing blue eyes and dark hair, Josh has a presence that's hard to ignore. There's something about him that turns heads wherever he goes, and without fail, women go crazy over him.

He was currently living with his girlfriend, Patricia, a beautiful local nurse.

"Surprise!" Leanne said cheerfully as she stepped inside to greet Mom and the kids.

Startled, I looked at her.

"I didn't expect you until tomorrow to help with the tree."

"Josh and I decided at the last minute to come and spend the night tonight. Hope you don't mind?"

I waved a hand dismissively.

"Of course not. Besides, I'm glad you're here. I have a dinner date with Drew tonight."

Leanne tilted her head.

"So, does that mean I get to sleep in your bed tonight?" she teased.

Although I didn't expect it, I felt my cheeks warm. I quickly glanced around to make sure Lanix wasn't nearby, then leaned in and whispered,

"I think it's safe to say you can sleep in my bed tonight."

Leanne grinned. "You're in love."

I smiled, blushing again, and whispered, "Maybe."

I turned to Josh.

"Where's Patricia?" I asked.

"She's at the annual nurses' conference in Colorado for the week," he replied.

"In that weather?" I said, surprised.

Josh raised an eyebrow, a smirk tugging at his lips.

"That was my question too. Colorado is getting pounded with snow. I tried to talk her out of it, but she was stubborn."

I glanced at Josh, and at the same moment, he looked at me with a knowing expression, as if we were conspiring about something.

"So, you're free for the week?" I asked.

"Pretty much. Why? What's on your mind?"

"Let's take a ride to Lincoln. There's a new-age store called Mystic Crossroads that I've been wanting to check out," I said.

"Sounds good," Josh agreed with a nod.

"Molly gave me a free day to drive tomorrow, so we can head out then," I added with a smile.

"Mom, since Aunt Leanne is here, do you mind if I tag along?" Molly asked.

Leanne smiled. "Go. I'll stay here with Mom and Lanix. We'll decorate the Christmas tree."

I turned to Josh and Molly. "We're on for Lincoln tomorrow."

Josh leaned back and asked, "Is Drew coming with us?"

"I'll ask him tonight. We're having dinner together," I answered.

Josh narrowed his eyes, teasing glint in them.

"So... are you staying the night with Drew?"

I stiffened, blushing.

Josh laughed. "I got my answer."

I shot him a look. "I can't discuss my love life with my nephew."

Josh chuckled. "Yeah, whatever."

We both laughed.

Drew and I had just finished dinner at his house. After we put the dishes away, he grabbed two cold beers from the fridge, turned on what he calls "chill" music, and we sat down on the living room couch.

"So, your sister decided to come by early?" he asked.

"Yeah," I answered. "She wants to spend time with my mother. Leanne is hoping Mom doesn't forget her."

He sat back on the couch, placed his arm around me, and pulled me close, my head resting against his chest.

"So... what was the dream about?" Drew asked, trying to change the mood.

I hesitated. He noticed.

"You don't have to tell me," he said gently. "Was it about a past love?"

I could tell he was probably regretting asking, probably not wanting to hear the answer.

I smiled. "No. No past loves. It was about a past son."

He turned to look at me, confused.

"What does that mean?"

I told him about the experience I'd had when I was pregnant in 1985, how I had been expecting a baby, and then suddenly, I wasn't. I explained how mysterious it had been, how there had never been an explanation.

"I actually had a dream that I met that same child as an adult," I said. "He was a man. He lived in Texas."

Drew's brow furrowed.

"How did you know he was your long-lost baby?"

I exhaled slowly.

"I just knew. I knew he was my son, but I didn't know how I knew." My voice softened. "David. His name is David."

I explained to Drew that the man in my dream had been born right around the time I was due. I told him how, somehow, I just knew he had three daughters, even though they hadn't appeared in the dream.

"The weird thing is, I knew we were in Texas, but I've never been to Texas. It didn't feel like a dream... it felt real."

He raised an eyebrow. "That dream really made a big impression on you, huh?"

I took a sip of my beer, gathering my thoughts before answering.

"Yeah, it did. But honestly... it wasn't just the dream itself. It's what my mother said after I told her about it. That's what really got me thinking."

He leaned in, curious now.

"What did she say?"

I hesitated, the memory tugging at me, and set my beer down.

"She said sometimes dreams are more than just dreams. That they can be glimpses of something real, something we're meant to remember, that maybe God gave me a chance to meet the son that wasn't born in this life."

He looked at me thoughtfully, his expression softening.

"Sounds like your mom might be onto something."

I gave a small, uneasy smile. "Yeah... that's what scares me."

We sat in silence for a while, each lost in thought. Then I looked at him and asked,

"Oh, tomorrow, Josh, Molly, and I are driving to Lincoln. Would you like to come along?"

"Ah, I can't. I've got some repairs to do at Jay's Market tomorrow,"

I chuckled. "I thought you weren't taking handyman jobs anymore?"

"Yeah, I know. Bobby asked me for help on a project, and I told him I would. Besides paying us, they offered us discounts. How can I turn that down?" he said with a smirk.

Just then, Drew rose from the couch, extended his hand to me, and asked, "Would you like to dance?"

At first, I was startled, but then I heard the song playing.

Josh Turner's "*Your Man*" floated through the speakers.

I looked up at him, and through the flickering candlelight, shadows danced across his face. His grin was unmistakable—seductive and full of intention.

I rose from the couch and stepped into his arms.

We slow danced for a while, both lost in the quiet intimacy of simply being close.

Then, with his index finger, he gently lifted my chin.

I looked up at him, and he said, low and softly,

"I love you, Andri. I think you know that, right?"

Love? He said *love.*

I did know.

I planted a gentle kiss on his lips and whispered,

"And I love *you*. But I think you know that, too."

He grinned.

Oh, that grin.

Another song began to play: The O'Jays, *"Let Me Make Love to You."*

We looked at each other, matching grins spreading across our faces.

He blew out the candle, then danced me into his bedroom, kicking the door shut behind us.

Chapter 20

The next morning, Josh, Molly, and I set off for Lincoln. I felt good about Leanne staying with Mom, so the timing worked out perfectly.

About an hour into the drive, we stopped for breakfast and coffee, enjoying music and conversation along the way.

"So, what's going on with Patricia?" I asked.

Josh, hands on the wheel, glanced at me briefly. "I doubt she's really spending the week at some conference in Colorado. I have my suspicions, but I don't want to be that guy: paranoid, full of questions and accusations without any real proof."

"Sometimes you have to trust your instincts," I said. "And it sounds like you've got a pretty strong hunch."

Josh sighed, then shifted the conversation. "So, what are you hoping to find at Mystic Crossroads?"

"I'm not really sure," I admitted. "The idea just came to me yesterday when you arrived. I guess I'll figure it out when I get there."

⁕

After a long drive, we finally arrived. The store was larger than I expected. Its exterior unassuming, but its interior packed with fascinating trinkets and oddities.

Sitting on the counter was a sleek black cat with hypnotic blue eyes. Its gaze locked onto mine, holding me spellbound for a moment before I shook it off and began browsing.

The store was full of beautiful crystals, books, and artifacts, but nothing truly caught my eye. I admired plenty of items, but I didn't feel compelled to buy anything.

I didn't know what I was there for. As I wandered the aisles, a nagging question formed in my mind: *Why did I come here? What am I looking for?*

Eventually, I spotted Josh at the cashier counter and walked over.

"What are you buying?"

He held up a delicate figurine, the crystal catching the light. "I found this angel for Patricia," he said.

I examined it, smiling. "That's nice. She's going to love it."

Josh glanced at my empty hands. "You're not buying anything?" he asked, sounding surprised.

I opened my mouth to reply when the cashier interrupted. "I'll wrap that for you," she said, taking the figurine from Josh.

As she placed the small, wrapped package in a bag, her eyes shifted to me and froze. Her expression changed in an instant. Her face went pale, as if she'd just seen a ghost.

Startled, I stiffened, instinctively mirroring her reaction. She quickly looked away, avoiding my gaze as she handed the bag to Josh.

After the transaction, we walked toward the door, but I could feel her eyes boring into the back of my head.

The sensation unsettled me. I stopped abruptly and turned around.

"Excuse me," I said, my voice firmer than I intended. "Why did you look at me like that? Do I know you?"

Her face tightened, and for a moment, she seemed at a loss for words. The air between us grew tense, and I couldn't shake the feeling that whatever her answer might be, it would change everything.

I kept my gaze fixed on her, trying to figure out if I knew her. She looked to be in her late sixties or early seventies, with long white hair cascading down her back. She was short and a little plump, but her soft, kind gray eyes eased my uneasiness, if only slightly.

The woman asked us to follow her. She led us to a small alcove in the store.

"Shannon," she called out.

As soon as the name left her mouth, a young woman appeared, petite and pretty, with curly light blond hair piled into a messy bun on top of her head.

Josh took notice. He definitely did. But then he remembered Patricia and quickly snapped out of his devilish thoughts.

"Mind the store for a while," the older woman said.

Shannon nodded without a word, giving Josh a quick glance and then us a polite smile before heading toward the counter.

The older woman motioned for us to continue following her deeper into the alcove, where shelves crowded with peculiar trinkets and aged books seemed to swallow the light.

"My name is Tanya Mercer. I own this store," she began, her voice steady but tinged with hesitation. "I apologize if I startled you earlier, but what I need to talk to you about... you probably won't believe."

She glanced at Josh and Molly, uncertain.

"What you have to say, you can say in front of them. They're family," I assured her.

Tanya nodded, taking a deep breath. "Alright. I'll put it all out there, and if you have questions, please wait until the end."

"Okay," I replied.

Tanya began speaking, her words weaving an unbelievable tale. She spoke of another world: a parallel world with a sky tinted red, a stark contrast to our blue. She described it as a place of unease, where most people lived under an oppressive heaviness, something inexplicably tied to the crimson sky.

She hesitated for a moment before continuing. "There's someone who lives there, a woman named Andrea."

Tanya's voice lowered slightly. "Andrea is a version of you, but... she's not like you. She's... well, she's not a good person."

I shot a glance at Josh. He raised his eyebrows, intrigued but clearly skeptical. I could tell he found the story entertaining, but he didn't believe it was real.

Then a thought hit me like a thunderclap.

How does she know my real name?

Tanya spoke of the bad woman living in this Red Earth: Andrea.

The idea left me reeling. The surreal nature of her words clashing with the stark certainty in her voice.

"Wait!" I blurted. "Why are you telling me this? Why me?"

Tanya hesitated, then exhaled. "Because a dark force is working to switch you with the other you, your counterpart from the Red Earth." Her voice was grave, her eyes holding a flicker of regret. "And unfortunately, one of those working with the dark force is my twin sister."

I stared at her, stunned. "Your sister?"

Tanya gave a tight nod. "Yes. And I wish it weren't true."

Josh and I exchanged uncertain glances, doubt creeping in.

"How do you even know all this?" I asked. "Did your sister tell you?"

"No, she can't." Tanya shook her head. "She's trapped in the Red Earth. It's a long story, but I was told by my contact. He's not from this world. He knows what they're planning." She lowered her voice. "We're all in danger."

Josh arched an eyebrow, clearly skeptical. He shot me a look, then turned to Tanya with a smirk.

"Alright," he said, humoring her. "So, when exactly is this switch supposed to happen?"

Tanya's expression remained unwavering. "The moment she stepped into this store."

Molly let out a small gasp. Josh instinctively pulled her closer, wrapping an arm around her as if to shield her. He gave her a reassuring glance, silently telling her: *Don't worry. None of this is real.*

Still, he turned back to Tanya, his tone firm. "Listen, I don't care what kind of 'forces' you're talking about. I'm not going to let anybody mess with my aunt."

I forced a breath and gestured around. "Well, as you all can see, I'm still here."

Josh huffed. "Okay, this is getting way too weird for me. Let's go."

We turned toward the door, eager to step out of the strange atmosphere inside the shop.

Just as we reached the entrance, a voice called out behind us.

"Wait, your package!"

Josh sighed and turned back toward the counter. Molly followed, using the moment as an excuse to give the black cat lounging there one last affectionate scratch behind the ears.

Since I was already by the door, I decided to head to the car and start the heater for us.

As soon as I stepped outside, a strange sensation washed over me, an odd feeling, a red haze.

The haze thickened rapidly, swallowing the street, the buildings, the cars. It grew so dense that I could no longer see anything beyond it. Everything vanished into a suffocating mist. Dizziness hit me like a wave. Disoriented, I panicked. I didn't know what was happening to me. My vision blurred; my breath quickened.

Then, through the swirling haze, I caught a glimpse of a bench.

And the next thing I knew, I was sitting on it.

Red Earth 2017—December, Gilson, Texas

The spinning sensation faded, the haze lifting like a slow curtain.

I was in a park.

But the first thing I noticed wasn't the trees, the grass, or the people.

It was the sky.

It was red.

The sun shone bright, but an eerie orange hue clung to it, staining the daylight in an unnatural way.

It wasn't dark, not exactly, but unsettling, like looking at the world through a tinted lens.

It was hard to explain.

At first, I thought maybe there was a fire nearby, that smoke had tainted the sky.

But I didn't smell smoke.

I turned my head.

To my left, a woman walked a dog on a leash, moving as if nothing were wrong.

To my right, an old woman stood by a nearby bench.

She was filthy. Her gray hair matted in clumps.

She shuffled away, but not before glancing back at me.

She smiled.

A chilling, devious smile, revealing a missing tooth.

A shiver ran through me.

I clutched my shoulder bag close.

I was scared.

The world sounded normal: birds chirping, dogs barking, distant voices carried on the breeze.

A car rumbled by, tires humming against the pavement.

Yet everything felt off.

I turned slowly, my pulse thrumming in my ears.

Across the street, the buildings stood in eerie stillness.

They looked wrong.

As if someone had sketched them hastily, then abandoned the drawing midway.

The edges lacked sharpness, the details smudged, as if the world had been constructed in a rush and left unfinished.

Even the colors seemed muted, duller than they should be.

The air pressed against my skin: thick, heavy, oppressive.

The weight of it made my breath feel shallow, my movements sluggish, as though I had waded into something denser than oxygen.

Then it hit me.

Tanya had warned me. I will be switched.

The words replayed in my mind like a distant echo, a prophecy I had dismissed.

But now, as I stood in this incomplete, unsettling version of reality, the truth settled into my bones like ice.

If it was true, and I was beginning to believe it was, then the other version of me was there.

Somewhere in this distorted place, she was walking in my life, living in my world.

Panic clawed at the edges of my mind, but I shoved it down.

I had to pretend.

No fear; no hesitation.

If I broke, if I showed any sign that I didn't belong, I had no doubt that this world, whatever it was, would swallow me whole.

I needed a plan.

Should I find shelter?

A safe place to think?

Or was I already being watched?

I reached into my bag, fumbling through its contents.

My fingers brushed against familiar objects until they landed on my cell phone.

I pulled it out and checked the screen.

No service.

Just great. I sighed, frustration curling through me.

Digging deeper into my bag, I found my battery power bank charger.

My phone was at 63 percent.

Somehow, that small detail brought a flicker of comfort, a tether to something familiar in an unfamiliar world.

Then, a dull ache began pressing against my temples, a headache creeping in, slow and relentless.

I felt uneasy. Stressed.

No wonder. I was standing in a place, a world, where I knew not a single soul.

I was beginning to feel hungry and thirsty.

Would they accept bank cards here?

Or would cash work?

⎯⎯◦⎯⎯

Across the street, I spotted a diner and made my way toward the corner, waiting for the light to change.

A few people stood beside me, their faces blank and distant.

I offered a polite smile, but they only scowled in return, no friendliness, not a hint of warmth.

Everyone looked defeated, like life had drained the spirit right out of them.

Somewhere nearby, I heard a radio. No, wait. A boom box?

Someone was actually carrying one on their shoulder.

The news crackled through the speakers, reporting a fatal accident just outside of town.

Oh, how sad, I thought. *I wonder what happened.*

Then, a different thought struck me: *What year is this?*

The question gnawed at me as I stepped into a nearby convenience store.

The air smelled faintly of stale coffee and something fried.

Glancing around, my eyes landed on a magazine rack.

My stomach dropped.

Elvis Presley.

There he was, older, singing a duet with Dolly Parton on the cover. Both looked aged, weathered by time.

I blinked, taking it in. Just like the boom box, like a puzzle piece that didn't fit, but nobody else seemed to notice.

I scanned the store.

No one was on a cell phone.

Actually, I hadn't seen a single one. Not in a hand, not on a counter, not even peeking out of a pocket.

The question crept back into my mind: What year is it in this strange place?

It looked like the *1980s*, except for the hairstyles… and the SUVs.

I glanced at the magazine rack.

December 2017 edition.

People moved sluggishly, their faces hardened, sour.

A dull ache pressed against my temples again, an oppressive weight, a sensation I couldn't shake.

I walked to the cashier counter, pretending to browse, but really, I was watching.

I needed to see what kind of currency they were using.

Cash and coins.

But they weren't U.S. dollars, or at least, not any I'd ever seen before.

A tight knot formed in my stomach.

Maybe the diner will give me something to eat if I clean or wash dishes for them.

At this point, I had no other choice.

I walked out of the convenience store and two doors down into the diner.

"There's a wait for tables, but you can seat yourself at the counter if you want," the waitress said.

She wasn't very welcoming.

I nodded and headed for the counter, where two men sat eating in silence.

Their eyes were fixed on the TV mounted in the corner.

The news was on.

A fatal accident.

The same one I'd heard about on the boom box.

The reporter's voice was steady, detached:

"The female driver, suspected of being intoxicated, fled the scene. Police are still searching for her."

A *chill* ran down my spine.

"Her son, who arrived at the scene earlier, stated that his mother was driving at a high rate of speed when she missed a turn. The vehicle rolled, killing the suspect's twenty-three-year-old daughter. Another woman remains in critical condition."

I swallowed hard.

Wow. Her daughter was the same age as Molly.

What kind of mother does that?

I shook my head in disgust. Some people don't deserve to be parents.

The waitress approached, wiping her hands on her apron. "Would you like anything to drink?"

I hesitated. This was my chance. I needed to know if my money was valid here.

"I'm not from around here," I said carefully. "Will you accept my cash?"

Reaching into my bag, I pulled out a few dollar bills and held them out.

She took them, studying the paper with a frown.

"Why does this say 'The United States of America' on it?" she asked, suspicion creeping into her voice. "I thought you said you weren't from around here."

Her gaze narrowed. "Your money looks different."

Then, her eyes snapped back to mine.

"Is this counterfeit?"

I stiffened. "No! Of course not," I shot back, too quickly, my voice cracking.

From the corner of my eye, I noticed the two men at the counter had stopped eating.

They were staring.

Something felt wrong.

A flicker of movement on the TV above the counter caught my attention. I glanced up.

My own face stared back at me.

The news anchor's voice was calm, detached:

"The suspect's name is Andrea Perez. If you encounter her, contact the authorities immediately. Do not approach. She may be dangerous."

The room went silent.

I could feel it. Every single pair of eyes in the diner was now on me.

My pulse slammed against my ribs.

Run.

I bolted for the door.

"Hey!" someone shouted behind me. A chair scraped against the floor.

I didn't stop.

How could I explain?

How could I tell them it wasn't me?

I kept my head down, pushing through the crowded sidewalk. I could feel people watching. Judging. Whispering.

Glancing up, I spotted police patrol cars creeping through the streets.

They were looking for me.

I turned down a side street, forcing myself to keep a steady pace. After a few blocks, I ducked around a corner and stopped.

Peering back, my stomach twisted.

Two police cars had just pulled up in front of the diner.

Damn it!

I wasn't much of a runner, but thank God I had my sneakers on.

I took off, cutting across a vacant lot, my breath burning in my chest.

Trees loomed ahead.

I ran straight into them, weaving between thick trunks until I found a spot deep enough to hide.

Pressing my back against a tree, I clutched my bag and tried to catch my breath.

I don't know where to go. I don't know what to do.

I'm so screwed.

The sky was dimming, shadows stretching across the wooded terrain.

Panic clawed at my chest as my mind conjured images of wild animals slinking through the trees, venomous snakes coiling beneath the brush, unseen spiders creeping nearby.

I had to get out before darkness swallowed everything.

Carefully, I maneuvered through the trees, dried leaves crackling beneath my hesitant steps.

The sound of running water echoed nearby, maybe a stream cutting through the land.

Relief flickered in my chest when I spotted an open clearing ahead.

I quickened my pace, desperate to escape the tangled woods.

But as I stepped into the clearing, dread knotted in my stomach.

I was back where I started.

The park.

I froze.

If the police were searching for me, stepping out into the open would be a mistake.

My pulse pounded as I stood motionless, debating my next move.

Then... Impact.

Chapter 21

A force slammed into me from behind, sending me face-first into the dirt.

The world tilted as pain jolted through my body.

Dazed, I turned my head, my breath hitching at the sight of a man's sneakers inches from my face.

I followed the shoes upward, locking onto a man looming over me, his eyes burning with fury.

"Get up!" he barked.

Terror spiked through me. My limbs fumbled beneath me as I scrambled to stand, my breath shaky.

A warm trickle slid from my nose: blood.

"You have nothing to say to me?" His voice was tight with restrained anger.

We stood beneath the veil of the trees, just shy of the open park where anyone could see us. The moonlight cast silver streaks through the branches, illuminating his face.

There was something familiar about him, but I couldn't place it.

No, *that didn't make sense.*

How could I recognize someone from this world?

When I didn't answer, his rage ignited. He shoved me hard against a tree, his hand closing around my throat.

Panic surged through me as my airway constricted. I could barely breathe. My fingers clawed weakly at his grip, but he was too strong. Tears welled in my eyes, blurring the moonlight filtering through the branches.

His voice was low, seething. "How would you like it if I killed you? The way you killed your own daughter?"

My breath hitched as his grip loosened just slightly, enough for me to suck in a ragged gasp.

"Oh. Oh... now you're crying?" he mocked, his voice dripping with disgust. "Yeah, save it. I don't believe your crocodile tears for a second."

With a final shove, he let me go.

I stumbled forward, coughing violently, my lungs burning as I fought for air. Pain radiated through my throat, raw and pulsing.

I raised a trembling hand to my face, and when I pulled it away, my fingers were smeared with blood.

My nose.

I blinked up at him, my vision swimming.

His fury was carved into every line of his face, but beneath the fire, there was something else.

Something broken.

That's when it hit me.

He thought I was her.

The woman they're searching for.

The car accident.

The other version of me.

His version.

Andrea.

Oh no. He thinks I killed Molly. His Molly.

Panic surged through me as I lifted a trembling hand, motioning for him to stop. His fiery gaze bore into me, unyielding.

He didn't care that I was hurt.

He didn't care about anything except his own fury.

"I'm not who you think I am," I rasped, my voice hoarse and raw.

The moment the words left my mouth, I regretted them.

His expression darkened instantly.

In a flash, he shoved me back against the tree.

Pain shot through my shoulder, but I clenched my jaw, refusing to show weakness.

"Don't bullshit me, Andrea," he snarled, his voice low and laced with rage. "I'm immune to your games."

I swallowed hard. I had to make him listen.

"Can I prove it?" I blurted, desperation creeping into my tone.

His eyes narrowed. "Prove what?"

"Will you allow me to prove who I am?"

A tense silence stretched between us. His disgust didn't waver, but for a second, he just stared at me, as if weighing the possibility.

Then his expression hardened.

"No," his voice was ice. "Let's go. I'm turning you in, and I hope they put you under the jail and throw away the key forever."

He grabbed my arm and started pushing me toward the open park.

Every time I slowed, hesitated, or tried to resist, he shoved me forward again, harder each time.

I had to think fast.

I had never in my life been manhandled like this. The sheer force, the lack of hesitation, it left me in disbelief.

Who was this man?

Why was he so furious over what happened to this Molly?

Was he her husband? Her boyfriend? Just a good friend?

Then suddenly, it hit me: my phone.

My pictures.

If I could show him, maybe I could convince him I wasn't her.

I stopped abruptly.

He gave me a shove, lighter than before, but still firm.

"Let me show you my proof," I said quickly. "If you're not satisfied with it, then I'll go with you."

He rolled his eyes, exasperated.

"Please," I pleaded, locking eyes with him.

His expression flickered, just for a second. His head tilted slightly, as if something wasn't adding up.

I wasn't sure if that was a good sign.

"Humor me," he muttered, his tone mocking. "Show me what you've got."

His face was hard, impatient. He wasn't expecting anything convincing.

I reached into my shoulder bag.

He flinched.

"What are you reaching for?" he asked sharply, his body tensing.

I froze, realizing he thought I might be pulling out a weapon.

Slowly, carefully, I pulled out my phone, raising it where he could see. "It's just my phone, see?" I turned the screen toward him.

He didn't react. Not at first.

I pressed the photo icon, and his eyes tracked the movement warily. "What are you doing?" he asked, suspicion thick in his voice. "What is that?"

His reaction made me pause.

Did he... not know what a cell phone was?

I'd already noticed the pay phones. The boom box. The absence of modern technology.

Maybe in this world, people only had landlines.

I hesitated before pressing forward, opening my photo gallery.

Scrolling through the images, I showed him picture after picture: Molly and me. Mom and me. My home. My car.

A shot of Lanix hopping onto his school bus.

Leanne and Josh.

Our pets: Chulo and Catfish.

His eyes followed the screen, his face unreadable. But something shifted. A slight flicker in his expression.

He blinked, just once, his gaze briefly lingering on one of the pictures.

A photo of us outside on a bright afternoon.

The sky behind us was a brilliant blue.

He didn't say anything about it, didn't even let his expression change too much, but I saw it.

He noticed.

Then his expression darkened.

Suspicion clouded his gaze.

"What is this, Andrea?" his voice was low, edged with something dangerous. "What kind of trick are you pulling?"

"It's not a trick," I said firmly.

I took a breath, knowing what I was about to say would sound insane.

"My name is Andrea Perez, but I go by Andri. I'm not from here. Not from this world."

I held his gaze, willing him to listen.

"I'm from Earth, but not this one. My Earth has blue skies, not red. Somehow, I was switched with your Andrea. I don't know how, but it happened. And now I'm stuck here, and I don't know how to get back."

He shook his head, as if snapping himself out of a daze. He took a step back, his expression unreadable.

But I sensed something.

Hesitation. Maybe even fear.

Then, suddenly, he grabbed my arm and yanked me back into the trees.

"I'm not saying I believe you," he whispered, his voice lower now, more cautious. "But I don't know what that thing was you just showed me, with all those pictures."

He hesitated. "Pictures of Molly. Hugging that little boy you said is your son. Your mother... you look just like her."

His grip on my arm loosened, but he didn't let go.

His voice dropped even lower, as if he didn't want anyone else to hear.

"And that picture of your sister..." His brows furrowed. "I never knew you to have a sister. But..."

He looked away, muttering almost to himself. "She looks like she could be your sister."

His silence stretched. He stared at me, searching, analyzing.

I took my chance.

"Can I ask you something?" I said, my voice trembling but determined.

He nodded warily.

"Who are you?" I asked, the words hanging in the cool night air as I tried to pierce through the mystery of his anger.

The shock on his face was beyond anything I could have imagined.

"Who... *am I*?" he repeated, disbelief tightening his voice. "You don't know who I am?"

I held his gaze.

"No."

His expression tightened as he studied me, searching for a crack, for any sign that I was lying.

Silence stretched between us, heavy and tense.

Then, finally, he spoke, his voice low, almost pained.

"I'm David."

There was a shift in his posture, subtle but noticeable, a flicker of something vulnerable beneath the hardened exterior.

But he was still guarded.

I took a slow breath, choosing my next words carefully.

"Okay, David... who were you to Molly? A husband? Boyfriend?"

My tone was measured, cautious. I didn't want to set him off again.

But I needed to know.

He took a step back, exhaling sharply as he looked away.

His entire face changed, grief settling into his features like a shadow.

He ran a hand through his hair, as if trying to steady himself.

"I'm... *was*... Molly's brother," he finally said, his voice tight.

His gaze flickered upward, like he was trying to stop himself from breaking.

My breath caught in my throat.

My eyes widened, my mouth parting in stunned realization.

The dream.

The dream I had last year.

It was him.

David.

Oh my God.

He caught my reaction instantly, his brows drawing together. "What is it?" he asked, suspicion creeping into his voice.

I stared at him, still processing, still trying to make sense of it. "You," I whispered. "I saw you in a dream. It was... a strange dream."

His expression hardened. "You saw me in a dream?" He shook his head, clearly insulted. "But besides that, you don't know me?"

I had no answer.

His frustration flared. "You claim you're from another Earth," he said, voice sharp, "but I saw pictures of Molly there. If she's there... wouldn't I be there too?"

I met his eyes, my own confusion deepening.

"Why would you be there?"

His face went blank.

Then, something flickered across his features: shock, disbelief.

"Because..." His voice dropped. "Wouldn't I be your son?"

A chill ran through me.

The son in my dream.

The dream that had haunted me, because I knew him, but I didn't.

My pulse pounded. I swallowed hard, struggling to ground myself. My mind raced, trying to connect the dots, trying to make sense of something that shouldn't even be possible.

"David," I said suddenly, my voice almost unsteady. "What state are we in?"

His frown deepened. "State? Why?"

I didn't answer.

For a moment, he just looked at me.

Then, simply, he said,

"Texas."

"Texas..." I whispered to myself.

David heard me. He took a step closer, his eyes narrowing. "What is this all about?" he demanded.

I looked up at him, my mind still reeling.

Then, to his surprise, I smiled.

I told him about my dream, the strange, vivid encounter where I had met him in a place I knew was Texas, though I had never been there.

I described how I had dropped Molly off with him, how I had felt confused because I didn't know him, and yet, I did.

I hesitated before continuing. "I asked you for your birthday in the dream. You told me. And that's when I felt it, this shock, this deep knowing. Like it meant something more."

David listened intently, his face unreadable.

I told him how, in the dream, he had asked me why I hadn't raised him.

"I had no answer," I admitted. "Because I know I raised my children. And any children I would've had, I would definitely love them and raise them. It felt like I was living in two worlds at once."

David exhaled, closing his eyes momentarily.

When he spoke, his voice was laced with exhaustion. "Andrea... um, I mean, Andri, I've been through a lot in my life. More than I'd wish on anyone."

He pressed his palms to his temples, as if trying to stave off a headache. His voice was strained when he continued.

"Today has been the worst day of my life. Everything I just witnessed. Losing my sister. Chasing after you, only to find out you might not even be her. Then you show me some kind of device with pictures, people you claim are your family, Molly, but not my Molly.

And then to hear that... that I don't exist in your world?"

His breath wavered slightly. "I don't know why that's such a big deal, but it is. Somehow, I feel it. Like I'm reaching for something that keeps slipping away."

My chest tightened at his words.

"I'm sorry, David," I said softly. "I'm so sorry this happened to you."

He just looked at me, shaking his head slightly before asking, "So... all you know of me is from a dream?"

I hesitated.

"Well... there was more to the dream than what I told you."

His head tilted slightly. "What else?"

I swallowed hard, then continued.

"At the end of my dream, I kept wondering why I didn't raise you. And then I saw my ex-mother-in-law holding you... stealing you away from me."

A shudder ran through me at the memory.

"She had this look, this eerie grin, mocking me. It was chilling. I didn't know what to make of it then. But now, meeting you in person, it's..." I shook my head. "It's a miracle. But then again, me just being here, I wouldn't exactly call it a miracle. More like something unnatural.

And how Andrea managed to trade places with me..." My voice hardened. "I don't know how, but it pisses me off."

David's eyes widened. "Traded places? How do you know that?"

I told him everything.

About Tanya and Mystic Crossroads in Lincoln. About the things she had said, the warnings I had ignored.

I told him about suddenly appearing on the park bench, the diner, the news story about the accident, and how the police were looking for me.

David ran a hand down his face, shaking his head.

"Andri... I..." He exhaled. "This is too much. I have to go. I just... I need to go."

Concern tugged at me as I studied his face under the pale moonlight.

He looked wrecked. Ragged. Exhausted.

His entire world had been turned upside down, and now, I had shoved my impossible truth into the mix.

He took a step back.

Then another.

And then, without another word, he turned and disappeared into the trees.

I was alone again.

***

Dried blood crusted on my face, my body aching from being shoved, tackled, dragged. I was exhausted. Hungry, thirsty. But I didn't dare sit down, didn't dare rest. If the police were looking for me, the last thing I needed was to be spotted on that same park bench.

I stood there for a long time, just trying to think, trying to figure out what to do next.

Then I heard it.

A rustling in the trees.

I froze, my heart slamming against my ribs. For a moment, I thought it was David returning, and I felt my body begin to relax.

But when I turned around...

It wasn't David.

The burst of static cut through the air, followed by a garbled voice on a handheld radio, something about a "10-20" and "requesting backup."

There were two of them.

Police officers.

Shit.

Chapter 22

Blue Earth 2017–Lincoln, Nebraska

Inside Mystic Crossroads, Josh clutched his package and motioned for Molly to follow as they headed for the exit.

Just as they reached the front door, Tanya suddenly yelped,

"Wait!"

Josh turned, narrowing his eyes as she hurried toward them.

"If you need help with her, you can get it from her mother," Tanya said cryptically.

Josh frowned. "What are you talking about?"

Tanya held his gaze for a moment before repeating, "Her mother. She will know."

Then, without another word, Tanya turned and walked away.

Josh and Molly exchanged puzzled looks before stepping outside.

The moment they did, Andrea was there.

What they didn't know: this wasn't their Andri.

This was Andrea from Red Earth.

She stood near the entrance, her back against the wall, her posture unnaturally stiff.

Her expression was unreadable, like she had been caught off guard.

Josh's eyes narrowed the second he saw her. Something was off.

"What's the matter? Are you okay?" His voice was gentle, but beneath it, there was an edge of concern.

Andrea blinked.

She studied him, her gaze lingering too long, as if searching for recognition that didn't come.

Who is this man?

His concern unsettled her.

He was good-looking, but why did he care? She had no memory of him. No connection.

And yet, he stood there, looking at her like she was someone who mattered to him.

"Yes, I'm fine," she said, forcing a smile.

Josh glanced down at his hands, then back at her, suspicion mixed with a hint of worry in his eyes.

"I guess you had to wait out here since I had your car keys in my pocket," he said, his tone cautious.

Andrea nodded.

Molly tilted her head, her brow furrowing.

"Mom, I thought you were wearing your blue jacket. Why do you have a sweater on? It's cold."

Andrea's breath hitched.

Mom.

The word hit her like a physical blow. She turned toward Molly, her stomach twisting.

The image of the sheet, *that* sheet, flashed in her mind. The one that had once covered her daughter's still body.

But it was her. Alive. Here. She wasn't dead.

Molly, not her Molly, not really, stood right in front of her.

Flesh and blood. Breathing. Moving.

She wasn't just a memory. Not just a photograph burned into her mind.

She was here. Real. Alive.

And she belonged to the other Andrea. The one they call Andri.

Andrea's throat tightened. She wanted to say something, anything, but she couldn't.

She had imagined this moment so many times.

But now that it was real, the weight of it crushed her.

Josh frowned, his gaze sharpening as he took her in more closely.

"You look buzzed. Are you sure you're okay?"

Andrea snapped back into the moment. "I'm good," she said quickly, *too quickly.*

Her voice was too bright, too eager to smooth over any suspicion.

Josh didn't look convinced, but he exhaled, rubbing his hands together against the cold.

"Well, let's go."

Andrea hesitated but followed as they began walking.

She had no idea where they were going, how they were getting there, or who the hell this man even was.

Husband? Boyfriend? Someone else?

Then Molly's voice broke through her thoughts.

"Mom, why are you limping?"

Andrea stiffened. *Limping? Damn.*

She scrambled for an excuse. "Oh, ah... I think I pulled a muscle."

Her mind raced, emotions spiraling out of control.

She knew where she was. And she knew why.

Anio had given her a mission.

The drive was long, but she learned his name by listening carefully to his conversations with Molly.

Josh.

That was his name.

She had to fake it.

Had to pretend to be this version of her, the Andri from this Earth.

This Earth with a beautiful blue sky. The clouds were milky white. The buildings sharp and symmetrical.

And the air...

The air was lighter. It felt different. Cleaner.

A strange calmness settled over her, making her want to sleep.

She let her eyelids drift closed for a moment.

Then the car slowed.

"Aunt Andri, wake up. We're here," Josh said, nudging her lightly.

Aunt Andri?

Her thoughts reeled.

So, I'm his aunt... or rather, she is.

Before she could react, Molly's voice cut in.

"Josh, your package!" she said, handing it to him with a grin.

Josh chuckled. "Why do I keep forgetting the package?"

Andrea barely registered their exchange.

Josh. My nephew, her nephew.

She let the information settle as they stepped out of the car.

They walked toward the house, and Andrea forced herself to move naturally, as if she belonged here.

But as she took in her surroundings, doubt crept up her spine.

The house was small, isolated, surrounded by rolling hills.

Is this really her house?

The question echoed in her mind.

The front door swung open, and a young boy stood there, peering up at her. A small dog barked excitedly at his feet.

Molly and Josh stepped inside like it was nothing, chatting easily as they walked past the boy.

Andrea hesitated.

The boy stood there, holding the door open, waiting.

His eyes searched her face.

"Mommy, aren't you gonna come in?"

Andrea's breath caught in her throat.

Mommy?

Her heartbeat pounded in her ears.

I... uh... she has another son?

Stepping inside, she took in the scene around her. The house was larger than it looked from the outside.

Josh sat at the dining table, deep in conversation with a woman.

Near the rocking chair, an elderly lady sat watching TV, an orange tabby cat curled up in her lap.

Everything was too normal. Too familiar, but only to them.

Meanwhile, Andrea felt like an intruder in her own life.

She lowered herself onto the couch, her body still weak from the alcohol and the car crash.

She felt like a guest in someone else's home.

And now she had to figure out how to blend in.

Because she didn't know who these women were.

And worst of all, she didn't know this boy.

Just then, the young boy tugged at Andrea's sleeve.

"Mommy, can you make me some hot chocolate?"

Andrea opened her mouth, but before she could respond, the woman who had been talking with Josh stood up.

"Oh, I already started making it for him, I'll get it," she said with a gentle smile.

Andrea's breath hitched.

That voice. That face.

She shook as she stared at the woman.

Leanne?

No, it can't be.

Andrea sat frozen, her body tense, afraid to speak.

If she said the wrong thing, she'd give herself away.

Seeing Molly had been shocking enough, but this?

Leanne.

Her sister.

The only person she had ever truly cared about. The sister she had lost all those years ago.

But in this world, this Andrea—*Andri*, had both Molly and Leanne.

She had this home.

She had family.

Molly walked back into the living room and stopped beside the elderly woman in the rocking chair.

"Grandma, do you want me to feed Chulo?"

Andrea's head snapped up. *Grandma?*

The old woman looked at Molly, her eyes warm, familiar.

Andrea's heart nearly stopped.

It's... my mother?

Nora?

Oh my God.

Her chest tightened.

A dizzy, light-headed feeling crept over her as she struggled to breathe.

Josh must have noticed.

"Aunt Andri," he said, watching her closely. "You haven't said a word since we got here. And you've been acting weird since we left Lincoln. Are you sure you're okay?"

Before Andrea could think of an excuse, Leanne stepped into the room.

She had heard Josh's concern and was now looking at Andrea with quiet worry of her own.

"You should lay down," Leanne said softly.

Andrea nodded and rose from the couch, but as she did, her eyes flicked toward Nora.

The old woman was watching her. Something in her gaze made Andrea feel uneasy.

Does she know?

The thought made her nervous.

She forced herself to turn away and walk toward the hallway, but a new problem hit her.

She had no idea where to go.

Where is her room?

Before she could hesitate too long, Molly brushed past her.

"Oh, I was using your computer. Let me grab my notebook," she said casually, hurrying into a bedroom.

Computer? She had no idea what that even meant.

Andrea followed her, taking in the space as discreetly as she could.

Molly snatched her notebook off the desk and smiled.

"Sweet dreams, Mom."

Then, just like that, she was gone.

The door shut behind her, leaving Andrea alone.

She sank onto the bed, exhaling shakily.

Molly. Leanne. Nora.

Her mind struggled to process it. Just hours ago, Molly was dead. And Leanne, her sister, had been gone for years.

She had to fight every urge not to break down and hug her.

It was surreal seeing older versions of Leanne and Nora.

They had been dead for so long.

Where is this version of David?

The thought flickered through her mind before she pushed it away.

Focus.

If she was going to gain all the power Anio promised her, Andrea had to succeed.

She would stay here under this beautiful blue sky, live like a queen.

And she would make damn sure *Andri* stayed in the Red Earth, and never returned.

This was her world now, *her* Earth.

And she had a mission.

Everything else, Molly, Leanne, Nora, none of it mattered.

What mattered was getting that necklace.

For Anio.

Chapter 23

Andrea opened her eyes to the soft glow of sunlight streaming through the large bedroom window.

Morning.

For a moment, she was disoriented.

Where am I?

Then, it came back to her.

She had lain down for a nap the day before, but had ended up sleeping through the night, still dressed in the same clothes.

Just then, the soft creak of the bedroom door broke the silence.

It slowly opened.

The boy stepped inside, moving toward her with careful, deliberate steps.

He smiled.

"Good morning, Mom."

Andrea stared at him, her expression blank.

He climbed onto the bed beside her, wrapping his arms around her in a gentle hug.

Then, pressing a kiss to her cheek, he said softly, "I love you."

Andrea stiffened.

The warmth, the affection, it was foreign to her.

She wasn't used to this.

She sat up abruptly, putting space between them. "I have to get up. I slept too long," she muttered.

The boy didn't argue.

He simply nodded, got up, and walked out of the room.

As Andrea swung her legs over the side of the bed, she made a decision.

She would go through the drawers, find something to wear.

And while she was at it, maybe she'd find the necklace.

Andrea spent the day familiarizing herself with her surroundings, careful not to raise suspicion.

By quietly listening to their conversations, she picked up details about the household.

The boy, her son, was named *Lanix.*

The dog and cat were *Chulo* and *Catfish.*

She studied this version of Molly, noting how eerily similar she was to her own Molly: same personality, same demeanor.

The only difference was the life they had lived.

Leanne and Josh seemed to live elsewhere. They hadn't been around.

Lost in thought, Andrea barely noticed Molly appear beside her until she spoke.

"Mom, Grandma's hungry."

Andrea turned to her with a blank stare, her expression unreadable.

So? What do you want me to do about it?

As if reading her mind, Molly added, "You know she can't cook for herself."

She stared at Andrea, tilting her head slightly, suspicion creeping into her expression.

"I can cook dinner if you don't feel like it," she added slowly, "but normally, you insist on cooking."

Andrea clenched her jaw.

Is Andri a damn saint? she thought bitterly.

I need to find that necklace fast and get the hell out of here.

Still, since this Molly was eerily like her own, she might be easy to manipulate.

"Would you please?" Andrea said, feigning weariness. "I just have a headache today."

But she caught concern flicker in Molly's eyes.

Quickly, she added, "Those darn allergies."

Relief settled over Molly's face. "Okay, I'll make my favorite."

"Your favorite?" Andrea echoed, trying to mask her unfamiliarity.

Molly frowned. "Mom... you know my favorite is chicken Alfredo."

After dinner, Andrea gathered the dishes and washed them, keeping an ear on Lanix and Molly as they watched TV with Nora.

From their conversation, she learned that Nora had dementia.

That's just as well, Andrea thought. *I don't need her getting in my way while I search the house.*

"Mom," Molly called from the living room. "Aunt Leanne just texted me. She says she's been trying to call you, but you're not picking up."

Andrea turned, frowning.

"Texted me? What does that mean?"

Molly narrowed her eyes.

"Seriously? Where's your phone?"

Andrea glanced around the kitchen and living room.

Good question. Where is the phone?

She had no idea.

But before she could come up with an excuse, she saw Molly pull out a small, box-like device.

A tiny TV?

Andrea watched as Molly tapped the screen and then, to her shock, spoke into it.

Andrea forced herself not to look confused.

Molly handed the device to her.

Following her lead, Andrea brought it to her ear, mimicking what she had seen.

"Andri? Why aren't you answering your phone?"

It was Leanne.

Her voice came through the device, no cord, no wall connection, just... floating sound.

Andrea stared at the glowing screen, which displayed *Aunt Leanne* and a string of numbers.

Thinking fast, she replied, "I must have lost it."

Leanne laughed.

"Lost what? Your phone or your mind?"

Andrea said nothing.

"Where was the last place you remember seeing it?" Leanne asked.

"I don't remember," Andrea replied with a shrug. "Besides, what's the big deal?"

"Oh my God!" Leanne gasped, her voice laced with innocent sarcasm. "You don't just lose something that expensive and shrug it off like it's nothing."

Andrea wasn't sure if Leanne was teasing or just being a bitch.

She wasn't even sure of the nature of their relationship.

Before she could respond, Leanne added,

"Only dumb fucks lose their cell phones."

Andrea heard a slight chuckle from her.

Banter. Sibling banter.

Something she had never experienced before.

A small smile tugged at her lips.

"I guess I'm a dumb fuck then."

Leanne carried on nonchalantly.

"We're picking up Molly tomorrow. We're stopping at Geyer's to grab a few things. Do you need anything?"

Andrea had no idea what the hell *Geyer's* was.

She shook her head. "No. But... are you taking the boy too?"

Leanne hesitated. "The boy? You mean Lanix?"

"Oh yeah, Lanix," Andrea said quickly.

Leanne scoffed. "Andri, you're weird. Anyway, no. Lanix hates shopping. You know that. He thinks it's girly stuff."

Andrea had been hoping they'd take Lanix.

It would have been the perfect chance to search the house.

"What about Mom?" she asked. "Will you take her?"

"No, we're planning to walk around a bit, and Mom gets tired easily," Leanne replied. "Besides, I took her to the antique store a few days ago. Remember?"

"Oh, right. The antique store," Andrea said, pretending to recall.

"Well, have a good time," she said, eager to end the conversation.

"Okay. Tell Molly we'll be there at 8:30, and she better be ready."

"I will," Andrea replied.

She watched as Molly slid the little phone into her pocket. Then she turned to Andrea.

"She said you need to be ready at 8:30."

Molly gave a quick nod and disappeared into the basement.

Good. At least she'll be out of the way tomorrow, Andrea thought.

She had already torn apart Andri's bedroom searching for the necklace.

Anio had shown it to her once, but only briefly.

Would she even recognize it if she saw it again?

The next morning, after Molly left with Leanne and Josh, Andrea seized the opportunity.

Just as she was about to head to Molly's room to rummage through her belongings, Lanix walked into the living room.

"Mom, are you gonna make breakfast?" he asked carefully, his voice tinged with uncertainty.

He had noticed the shift.

How cold she had become.

How distant.

As if she didn't even like him.

Andrea spun on her heels, irritated.

"Make breakfast for yourself. Who do you think I am, your maid?"

Lanix stared at her, stunned.

The sting of her words hit him hard, tears threatening to rise, though he tried to blink them away.

"What about Grandma?" he asked hesitantly.

Andrea narrowed her eyes.

"What about her?"

"She's... she's hungry," he murmured, unsure of her reaction.

Andrea scoffed.

"Then make her breakfast too. I'm not her maid either."

Her voice was sharp. Final.

She resented the charade, the act of playing a caring daughter. A loving mother.

Oh, hell no.

She never liked Nora.

And the boy?

Lanix isn't my son.

Lanix swallowed hard and turned away, blinking back tears as he turned to walk toward the kitchen.

"Lanix," she called softly.

He stopped and looked back. She wasn't looking at him. Her eyes were fixed on a photo hanging in the hallway.

"Who are the men in this picture?" she asked, pointing.

"That's Uncle Joe and Uncle Michael."

"Who is Uncle Michael?" she asked, narrowing her eyes as if she didn't believe him.

Lanix shifted uncomfortably. "Your brother," he said, trying not to sound annoyed.

Andrea turned fully toward him now. "Where's *your* brother, David?"

Her gaze sharpened, waiting, *pressing.*

Lanix stared at her, stunned. Then he slowly shook his head. "I don't know any David."

Without another word, she turned and headed for the basement.

Lanix just stood there for a moment to process. "*That was weird,*" he thought. And then he made his way into the kitchen.

He made a simple breakfast for himself and Nora: cereal, toast, and a small glass of orange juice, then carried it to his grandmother's room.

Nora sat in her armchair watching TV.

Lanix joined her, quietly eating beside her.

Then, suddenly, a noise echoed from the basement.

A commotion.

He froze, his grip tightening around the spoon.

He knew exactly who it was.

"*Mom,*" he thought.

But the last thing he wanted to do was go down there and find out what she was up to.

⸻

Andrea came up empty-handed.

No necklace in Molly's room. At least, not the one she was looking for.

Though she did find some cash, which she casually slipped into her pocket.

Heading for the stairs, she hesitated, then turned toward Lanix's room.

She rifled through his belongings, not expecting to find the necklace, but checking anyway.

Nothing.

Then it hit her.

Nora.

Andrea stormed up the stairs from the basement, like a woman on a mission.

In the kitchen, Lanix had just finished clearing the breakfast dishes when he noticed her march past him without a word.

She walked straight to Nora's room, her footsteps heavy with determination.

Andrea entered.

And froze.

Nora sat in her rocking chair. The television was off.

Silent. Watching. Her eyes followed Andrea with an unsettling intensity.

Andrea shivered.

That look.

It was confident. Knowing. *Does she know who I really am?*

Andrea took a step forward.

Nora tilted her head slightly, her gaze never wavering.

Andrea scowled.

"What are you looking at, Nora?" she snapped.

Nora didn't answer.

Andrea clenched her jaw.

"You're going to tell me where that necklace is."

Silence.

Andrea stormed to Nora's purse, dumping its contents onto the bed, rifling through everything.

Nothing.

Frustration burned through her.

She moved to the dresser, yanking out drawers, tossing their contents aside.

"I think you understand why I'm here," she said coolly.

"If you just tell me where the necklace is, I'll be on my way.

You won't ever see me again."

Still, Nora said nothing. Andrea's patience snapped.

"Get up."

Nora rose slowly from her chair.

Andrea yanked off the seat cushion, feeling around for anything hidden.

Nothing.

Cursing under her breath, she turned to the nightstands.

Nora's eyes never left her.

Andrea stiffened.

"Stop looking at me like that! You're creeping me out!" she shouted.

From the hallway, Lanix heard the yelling. His stomach tightened.

He stepped cautiously toward the open door, listening to the rummaging, swearing.

Then, Andrea's voice, sharp and angry.

Lanix stepped inside just in time to see Andrea shove Nora onto the bed.

His heart lurched.

"Mom! Don't push Grandma!" he cried, his voice cracking with emotion.

His small body trembled with anger, tears welling in his eyes.

He had never seen his mother act like this before.

Andrea ignored him.

She ripped open the nightstand drawer Nora had been standing in front of.

And there it was.

The necklace.

Her breath caught.

This was it.

The same necklace Anio had shown her. Andrea grabbed it, gripping it tightly in her fist.

Lanix, still shaken, helped Nora sit up.

But he was in Andrea's way.

Without thinking, she shoved him aside.

He stumbled but didn't fall. His young face twisted in hurt and disbelief.

Then, something inside him snapped. He pushed back hard.

Andrea stumbled, stunned. Her face burned with rage.

Without hesitation, she struck him.

The slap echoed through the room.

Lanix cried out, stumbling back onto the bed, clutching his cheek.

Nora gasped and lunged at Andrea, striking her arms with frail but determined hands.

Andrea barely flinched.

Eyes blazing, she turned to Nora and raised her hand again, this time with full intent.

Lanix looked up just as she stepped toward Nora.

Panic surged through him.

He scrambled to his feet, desperate to protect his grandmother.

But before Andrea could swing, a sudden force slammed into her, sending her flying across the room.

She crashed against the wall and crumpled to the floor.

Dazed, she looked up, fury burning in her eyes, ready to retaliate.

But it wasn't Nora standing there.

And it wasn't Lanix.

It was Molly.

Molly stood there, breathing hard, her fists clenched, her face red with rage.

Just two minutes earlier, Molly had been dropped off by Leanne and Josh.

She stepped into the house and immediately heard it.

Shouting.

Screaming.

Crying.

Leanne and Josh were still outside.

The sounds were coming from Grandma's room.

Molly rushed to the doorway, just in time to see Andrea slap Lanix. She froze, momentarily paralyzed by shock.

Then she saw Andrea raise her hand toward Nora.

And she ran.

Shoving Andrea with all her strength, she sent her crashing into the wall.

And now, standing over her, Molly was shaking with fury. Molly had never seen herself this livid.

Leanne stepped into the room, her voice sharp.

"What the hell is going on?"

Andrea's head snapped toward her.

For a split second, she hesitated.

Then she bolted.

Shoving past Leanne, she sprinted down the hall, the necklace clutched tightly in her fist.

She made it to the mudroom, nearly stumbling in her rush.

Keys. She needed the car keys.

Her eyes locked onto them, dangling by the door.

Andrea snatched the keys.

She knew which car belonged to Andri.

The Ford.

✦

Josh was outside as Andrea burst through the side door.

He said something, but she didn't hear him.

She didn't care.

Leanne was right behind her.

"Andri!" she shouted.

Andrea ignored her, yanking open the car door and throwing herself inside.

The engine roared to life. Leanne dashed forward, but it was too late.

Andrea was already speeding away.

"Hmm... what just happened?"

Josh's voice rang out, loud and confused.

His words cut through the air, loud enough to make sure Leanne could hear him.

Leanne walked back toward him, still shaken.

Molly approached, guiding Nora by the hand, her arm wrapped protectively around Lanix.

His face was red from the slap, his expression a mix of hurt and disbelief.

Leanne exhaled.

"I'm not exactly sure."

Josh turned his gaze to Molly.

With teary eyes, she said,

"It was so weird... I think something is wrong with Mom. She... she slapped Lanix.

And she was about to slap Grandma... when I pushed her down."

Molly stared straight ahead, as if trying to make sense of it all.

Lanix looked up at Josh, his voice small but firm.

"Mom has been mean lately.

She was looking through everyone's room... for a necklace."

Josh's brow furrowed.

"A necklace?"

He took a few steps away, staring out at the rolling country hills, lost in thought.

Leanne glanced at him, then turned to Molly.

"He's thinking."

"I'm sure he's trying to figure out how to handle this."

Suddenly, Nora's expression shifted.

The vacant haze of dementia lifted, replaced with something sharp and knowing.

She straightened slightly.

"Leanne, Josh, Molly, come here."

Everyone froze.

Molly's breath hitched.

Lanix stiffened.

Leanne and Josh exchanged bewildered glances.

Slowly, they stepped forward.

Nora turned to Leanne, her voice steady. "Mija, your sister needs help."

Leanne blinked.

"Yeah, obviously."

Josh hesitated.

"Grandma... what kind of help? How can we help her?"

Nora looked straight at him, her eyes piercing.

"That woman... she is not really Andri.

She's someone else."

Silence.

Leanne frowned.

"Mom... you mean, like, she just hasn't been herself lately?"

Nora shook her head. "No, that's not what I mean. I mean the woman that was here, the one who looks like Andri? It's not her."

A shiver ran down Molly's spine.

Nora's voice dropped lower. "But I've been expecting her."

Leanne's confusion deepened. She tilted her head.

"Expecting... her?" she asked, dragging out the word in disbelief.

Molly and Josh locked eyes at the same time. The answer hit them in unison.

Josh whispered, "The switch."

Molly's eyes went wide. "Oh my God. It has to be! What are we gonna do?"

Leanne and Lanix exchanged glances, utterly bewildered.

Is everyone losing their minds? Leanne thought.

She pulled Lanix closer, kissing the top of his head, hoping he wouldn't be too upset by the conversation.

Molly turned to Josh.

"Tanya said her mother would help."

Josh nodded. "And she just did by telling us that it wasn't Andri. That means it has to be the switch. From Red Earth."

Molly's face filled with grief.

She glanced at Lanix, then gestured for Josh to step away with her.

Her voice was shaky when she spoke.

"Josh, what should we do? Grandma says she needs help... but how can we even do that?"

"*We* aren't doing anything. *I* will take care of it." Josh placed a reassuring hand on her shoulder.

"She does need help. I just... I need to think."

He exhaled and walked a few more yards away, staring at nothing.

Thinking about everything.

Leanne noticed him standing alone, his gaze fixed straight ahead.

That's how he figures things out, she thought.

Turning to Molly and Lanix, she kept her voice steady. "Don't worry. Josh will figure it out.

You know he always does. We'll find your mom and get her the help she needs."

Leanne turned and guided Nora back into the house, settling her into her chair and turning on the TV.

Chulo and Catfish lay curled up in their beds beside Nora, undisturbed by the tension in the air.

Lanix climbed onto the couch, intending to watch TV, but quickly drifted off to sleep.

Leanne led Molly into the kitchen and turned to her, arms crossed.

"Okay, have you and Josh lost your minds too? What was all that cryptic code talk about?"

Molly shook her head.

"It wasn't code."

She took a deep breath and told Leanne everything.

Mystic Crossroads in Lincoln.

Tanya.

The Red Earth.

The switch.

Leanne's eyebrows shot up.

"You didn't actually believe it, did you?"

Molly hesitated. "No. None of us did... at first. But what else could it be?"

Leanne ran a hand over her head, exhaling sharply.

Her voice cracked. "God, Molly... if this is true... then where the hell is my sister?" Her voice trailed off, the weight of it all settling in.

Chapter 24

Josh walked into the kitchen through the side door.

Leanne and Molly looked up, waiting, wondering what he had come up with.

"We need to call Tanya," Josh said.

"We have to at least see if she can help us."

Molly nodded in agreement.

Leanne turned to Josh.

"Molly told me everything. Why didn't you tell me before?"

Josh folded his arms.

"Honestly? I didn't think much of it. I thought she was batshit crazy."

Molly sighed.

"I did too."

Josh pulled out his phone and looked up the number for the shop.

Then he hit dial.

After a few rings, a voice answered.

"This is Tanya."

Josh wasted no time.

"Tanya, my name is Josh. I was there the other day with my aunt and cousin. You told my aunt about Red Earth. Do you remember?"

A brief pause.

"I do," Tanya said, her tone cautious.

Josh quickly explained everything: the fight, Andri's strange behavior, and, most importantly, what Nora had revealed.

A beat of silence.

Then Tanya murmured, more to herself than to him,

"So... it's happened then."

Josh frowned.

"Where is she now?" Tanya asked, her voice suddenly tense.

"We don't know," Josh admitted.

"She took off in my aunt's car."

Tanya's voice sharpened.

"How long ago?"

Sensing her urgency, Josh glanced at his phone.

"About thirty minutes ago. Why?"

He could hear Tanya mumbling under her breath, but he couldn't make out the words.

Then she spoke, her voice unsteady.

"Josh, you need to get here as fast as you can. It's a matter of life and death. No time to explain."

Josh's grip tightened around the phone.

"Should I bring anything?"

"Yes. Bring weapons. Hide them on your body somewhere. Anything else you might need, I have here. Just hurry."

Josh hesitated.

"Life and death for who?"

Tanya's voice was grim.

"For your aunt Andri and for myself. She's probably on her way here to kill me as we speak."

A chill ran through Josh.

Tanya exhaled sharply.

"And Josh... I know I asked you to hurry,

but please drive safely."

Josh wanted to ask more questions, but now wasn't the time.

He ended the call.

He turned to Molly and Leanne.

"I have to go. Tanya needs my help if we're going to find Aunt Andri."

Josh already knew he had his knives stashed in the car.

He hurried outside, opened the door, and pulled them out.

He adjusted the Cold Steel SRK on his right hip, the familiar weight grounding him.

Just behind him, secured horizontally along the small of his back, rested his Buck 119 in its leather sheath, hidden but ready.

He grabbed his flashlight, just in case.

His left hip holster was still strapped to his belt, but the gun? Still at home.

No time to go back for it now.

It would only slow him down.

He reached into the back seat for his jacket.

Then, moving quickly to the trunk, he lifted the hidden box beneath a pile of tools,

his just-in-case items.

Josh adjusted his jacket, feeling the familiar weight press against the fabric.

✔ Right pocket: flashbang. Small but effective. A quick escape if things got messy.

✔ Left pocket: smoke grenade. Discreet, but powerful enough to cover his tracks.

He wasn't planning on using them.

But he never went anywhere without a backup plan.

Josh was ready.

He climbed into the driver's seat, but as soon as he started the engine, Molly, Leanne, and Nora walked over.

Molly opened the passenger door and slid inside.

"I'm coming with you."

Josh turned to argue, but before he could speak, Nora stepped up to the car.

"I am too."

Josh shook his head.

"No way."

"Yes way," she said.

He sighed, exasperated.

"Grandma, this could be dangerous."

Nora grinned.

"I know. That's why I'm coming along."

Josh looked at Leanne for backup.

She just shrugged.

"They both insisted. Sorry."

Josh groaned, rubbing a hand over his face.

"Fine. Whatever. No more time to waste."

He threw the car into gear and took off.

Andrea drove the Ford, speeding down the street.

But when she noticed she wasn't being followed, she slowed and turned into the Ridgefield Hardware & Supply.

The bell above the door chimed as she stepped inside Ridgefield Hardware &
Supply.

The smell of sawdust, metal, and something faintly oily filled the air.

A few customers milled about: a man in overalls inspecting a rack of flashlights,
an older woman chatting with the cashier about her fence repair.

She didn't belong here.

But she smiled anyway.

Calm. Collected.

Just another local woman stopping by for supplies.

She walked with purpose, her boots clicking against the scuffed linoleum as she
made her way to the hunting and outdoors section.

The knives were in a locked case, but she wasn't looking at those.

A display rack stood beside it: hunting knives in plastic packaging, the kind meant
for easy grab-and-go purchases.

One in particular caught her eye.

A fixed-blade hunting knife.

Black handle. Sleek stainless-steel blade. And most importantly, a sheath.

Her fingers ghosted over the package, as if debating a purchase.

No one was watching.

Or so she thought.

From across the store, Drew saw her.

He had been standing by the plumbing aisle, searching for a replacement part,
when he glanced up and froze. *Andri.*

Relief hit him first. *There she is.*

Then confusion. *Why is she here?*

Then, alarm.

He saw her hand move.

Saw the way she picked up the package with the hunting knife, turned it over as
if inspecting it...

And then, in a single, fluid motion, slipped it beneath her coat.

Drew's stomach twisted.

What the hell?

He froze, watching as she grabbed a roll of duct tape from the shelf and walked
toward the counter.

The cashier, a graying man in his sixties, probably the owner, glanced up and
offered a nod.

"Afternoon, Andri. Just the tape?"

Andrea tilted her head, smiling.

"Just the tape."

Drew didn't move.

He should say something. He should call her out.

But he didn't.

He just watched.

The old man rang her up, gave her some change, and handed her the bag.

"You have a good day now."

Andrea nodded, turned toward the door, and walked out, the plastic package pressed against her ribs.

Drew exhaled slowly.

Then he followed her.

She opened the car door.

The door slammed shut.

Andrea stiffened. Her grip tightened around her keys.

Drew stood there, his hand flat against the metal, his face carved in stone.

She had no idea who he was.

But *he* knew *her*.

And worse, he was looking at her like she mattered.

Like she was someone he loved.

She turned her wrist, trying to subtly unlock the door.

His hand pressed against it again.

His voice was low. Measured.

"Why'd you steal the knife, Andri?"

Andrea froze.

Her mind raced. *Lie. Play it off. Run.*

But before she could speak, Drew stepped closer.

He searched her face, frowning.

Something was wrong.

"You've been avoiding me," he said softly, almost hesitant. "You won't answer my calls. You won't text back."

His voice wavered, like he was trying to find his footing in a conversation he didn't understand.

Andrea forced a casual chuckle.

"Oh. Right. Sorry. Been busy."

"Andri, what's going on?"

Andrea just stared, saying nothing.

Drew swallowed hard.

"I don't get it. Just two nights ago, we talked about our future. You stayed over. We—"

He exhaled sharply, shaking his head.

"You told me you loved me."

Andrea's lips parted slightly.

Oh. Shit.

This guy wasn't just some past fling.

Andri was in deep with him.

Drew's face tightened.

"And I was going to—" He cut himself off, raking a hand through his hair. His voice dropped to barely a whisper.

"I was going to ask you to marry me."

Silence.

Andrea blinked.

Then she laughed.

Not a soft chuckle. Not a nervous, awkward giggle.

A cold, mocking laugh.

Drew went still.

"What?" he murmured, barely audible.

Andrea smirked.

"Are you serious?"

Something inside Drew fractured.

His hands clenched into fists.

"What's wrong with you?" he demanded. "Why are you acting like this?"

For a fleeting moment, Andrea considered dragging this good-looking, tall man with dark hair, graying sides, and that deep sexy voice into the back seat for a bit of fun.

But there was no time for that. She was on a mission.

Maybe later, she thought with a sly grin.

Andrea rolled her eyes.

"Acting like what? Not some lovesick fool?"

She leaned in slightly, her voice low, every word sharpened to wound.

"You actually thought I'd marry you? God, how pathetic can you be?"

A sharp inhale.

Drew took a step back.

Andrea could see it: the moment his world tilted.

The hurt. The disbelief. The pain he couldn't hide.

Then a voice from behind him.

"Drew? Everything okay?"

Andrea's gaze flicked past him.

Another man approached: tall, mid-30s, wearing a work vest. His build suggested he could hold his own.

A coworker, likely working with Drew on a project at Jay's Market.

Drew turned slightly, but his eyes never left Andrea.

"Yeah, Bobby," he muttered, though his voice was anything but steady. "It's fine."

Andrea smirked, seizing the moment.

"Oh, I get it." She crossed her arms. "You're embarrassed."

Drew's jaw tightened.

Andrea stepped forward, closing the space between them. Her voice dropped to a cruel whisper.

"You really thought I was in love with you, didn't you?"

Drew's breath hitched.

She let out a soft, mocking sigh, shaking her head.

"You were just easy."

Drew flinched like she'd slapped him.

Bobby frowned, stepping closer.

"Hey. What's going on?"

Andrea's smirk widened.

Perfect. She wanted an audience.

"Nothing," she said with a shrug, letting her eyes skim over Drew like he was beneath her.

"He just got a little too attached. Thought we had some big romance."

She let out a fake, disappointed sigh.

"I was just using you, sweetheart. That's all it ever was."

Silence.

Drew just... stood there.

For a split second, Andrea almost thought she saw something snap inside him.

Bobby stepped forward.

"Damn, Andri, are you serious? This is messed up."

Andrea smirked. She had won.

She unlocked the car, slid inside, gave Bobby a flirty wink...

And before either of them could stop her, she was gone.

In the rearview mirror, she caught one last glimpse of Drew.

Standing there. Completely shattered.

And it made her smile.

Blue Earth 2017—December, Lincoln, Nebraska

When Josh, Molly, and Nora arrived at Mystic Crossroads, Josh parked the car and jumped out, rushing around to open the doors for Molly and Nora.

Molly helped Nora out, and Josh took off toward the store, moving fast.

Tanya hurried to meet him as he stepped inside.

"She's not here yet," she said quickly, eyes darting toward the door. "But I know she'll be here soon."

Josh wanted to ask how she knew, but there was no time.

Molly entered with Nora just as Tanya and Nora locked eyes.

Nora gave Tanya a small, knowing nod.

Molly caught it.

Her brows furrowed. *That's odd.*

Right after that nod, Molly noticed something shift in Tanya's face.

Her expression remained neutral...

But her eyes, *they were smiling.*

What the hell was that about? Molly wondered, suspicion creeping in.

Josh, oblivious to the exchange, turned to Tanya.

"Now what? Do I hide behind something and take her down when she comes in? Or wait until she tries to attack you?"

Tanya shook her head.

"No. We need to lock the doors, keep her from coming in at all. Now's not the time for the confrontation."

Josh furrowed his brows.

"Confrontation?"

Tanya nodded, her eyes fixed on the door.

"It has to be planned just right... if we're going to trap Anio."

Josh and Molly exchanged confused glances.

Neither of them knew who Anio was.

Tanya took a step toward the front, then froze.

Through the glass, she spotted Andrea.

Walking straight toward the shop.

Tanya's breath hitched.

"Too late, she's here! Quick, get to the back!"

They rushed toward the rear room as Tanya's assistant, Shannon, calmly stepped up to the counter.

The bell above the door jingled.

Andrea entered.

Shannon greeted her with an easy smile.

"Hey there."

Andrea didn't return it.

Her tone was sharp.

"Is the owner in?"

"No, she's out today," Shannon replied smoothly. "Can I help you with something?"

Andrea frowned.

"When do you expect her back?"

Shannon kept her voice casual.

"Tomorrow afternoon."

Andrea's eyes narrowed.

"Tomorrow?"

"Yes."

A faint thud from the back. Molly nearly knocked over a package. Josh caught it just in time.

Andrea's gaze snapped back to Shannon, suspicion creeping into her expression.

"Is somebody back there?"

Shannon didn't flinch.

"Just a cat."

Andrea's lip curled slightly.

"A cat?"

Shannon nodded, firm and unbothered.

Andrea took a slow step forward. "So, if I went back there right now," she said coolly, "I'd just find a cat?"

Shannon held her gaze. "There's only a cat back there. And anyway, the back is for employees only."

In the Back Room, Tanya moved quickly, eyes scanning.

They needed a distraction. Her gaze landed on the black cat.

She gently nudged it toward the curtain separating the back from the front.

The cat padded forward, tail high, and slipped through the fabric.

In the Store, Andrea barely had time to react before the cat leapt onto the counter, landing with the grace of something that clearly believed it owned the place.

"Hello, Shade," Shannon said with a fond smile.

"Shade?" Andrea asked, her eyes still fixed on the feline.

"Yes, her name is Shade," Shannon replied.

The cat stared at Andrea. Unblinking.

Its eyes, *bright, icy blue*, locked onto hers.

Andrea froze. A strange pull gripped her mind.

Dizzy. Lightheaded. The room wavered. The walls warped around her. The shelves distorted.

Her breath hitched.

What the hell was that?

She blinked hard, shaking her head.

The haze lifted.

She exhaled sharply, fingers twitching.

What just happened?

"Fine," she muttered. "I'll be back tomorrow."

She turned toward the door, then hesitated.

One last glance.

First at Shannon.

Then at the cat. Its blue eyes still locked on her.

A chill skittered down her spine.

Damn cat.

Then she walked out.

Shannon let out the breath she hadn't realized she was holding.

"Jesus," she whispered.

Tanya walked over and placed a firm hand on her shoulder.

"Shannon, you were amazing. Thank you."

Shannon managed a faint smile, relieved. It was over for now.

Josh exhaled, running a hand through his hair.

"Now what? We come back tomorrow?"

Tanya shook her head. "No."

Josh frowned. "No? Then what?"

Tanya's expression darkened. "You have to find your aunt before it's too late."

Josh's stomach clenched. "Too late for what?"

Tanya met his eyes, steady and serious.

"If you don't find her and get her back here on time, she could end up in prison. And if that happens... she may never come back."

Josh's brows shot up. "Prison? You're serious? How? When?"

Tanya's voice was calm, but firm.

"Josh, there's no time for questions. I'm sending you to Red Earth, to the exact coordinates where she'll be the moment you land."

"Red Earth?" He blinked. "Are you shittin' me right now?"

She stepped closer.

"If you have your weapons, good. But don't kill unless you have no choice."

Before Josh could respond, Molly stepped forward.

"I'm going with him."

Josh turned, ready to argue, but she repeated herself, firmer this time.

"I'm going with you."

He shook his head.

"No way, Molly. It could be dangerous."

Molly squared her shoulders.

"I don't care. We're talking about my mom. If she's trapped over there, I'm not sitting here doing nothing."

Josh exhaled sharply, rubbing a hand over his face.

"Molly..."

Tanya lifted a hand, stopping the argument before it escalated.

"Molly," she said evenly, "this isn't just a simple trip. You'd be stepping into a world that isn't yours. A world where things feel... off, where even the air is different. The people aren't like the ones here."

Teary-eyed, Molly's jaw tightened.

"I don't care. I'm going."

Josh muttered a curse under his breath and shot Tanya a look, silently begging for backup.

But Tanya let out a sigh and nodded.

"She's right."

Josh's head snapped up.

"What?"

Tanya met his glare without flinching.

"She has a reason to be there. And frankly... it might be better if you both go."

Josh groaned, rubbing the back of his neck. He looked at Tanya again, then turned slowly to Molly.

"I don't need someone falling apart on me out there," he said. "This isn't a rescue mission for a crying girl. We're walking into danger, and I need backup I can trust."

Molly stood her ground; eyes locked on his.

He sighed, defeated.

"Alright. But you wipe those tears, Molly. You soldier up, you hear me? I need to know you've got my back. And if things go sideways, you listen to me. No questions. No arguments."

Molly nodded without hesitation. Tanya stepped forward.

"Then it's settled. We don't have much time. Follow me."

She turned and walked toward the back of the shop.

Josh and Molly exchanged a glance before following.

Tanya handed Molly a compact laser stun gun.

"Hold on to this," she instructed. "Just aim and press the button. Make sure the laser is locked on the target. Aim for the legs if they're standing. It can take down two people at once if they're close together."

Molly nodded, slipping it into her pocket.

Next, Tanya grabbed a cloth shoulder bag and handed it to her.

"Wear this under your jacket. It has food and water rations, just in case."

Josh looked over.

"What about Grandma? She's definitely not coming with us."

Tanya smiled.

"No. She'll stay here with me. I'll keep her comfortable. She'll be fine."

Molly hesitated.

"But... she has dementia and..."

Tanya cut her off gently.

"She'll be fine. Trust me."

Molly exhaled slowly.

"Okay. But how do we get back?"

Tanya pulled out a small handheld mirror, its glass protected by a cover.

"When it's time to return, make sure you're all together. Press your finger to the glass and slide it down. You should see a blue haze. You might feel a little disoriented, but that's normal. Just stay close. Everyone has to be inside the haze."

She looked at both of them, serious now.

"The haze isn't instant. It takes time to swirl, for the portal to fully open and close. Make sure you give yourself enough time, especially if you're trying to escape."

She handed Molly a waistband pouch.

"Keep the mirror in here."

Molly tucked it inside and secured the strap around her waist, covering it with her shirt.

Tanya took a breath, eyes on them both. "It's time."

Josh and Molly stood side by side. A red haze rose around them. The world swirled.

Their vision blurred.

A rush of nausea.

A hard landing.

Chapter 25

Red Earth 2017—December, Gilson, Texas

Andri

I stood there as two police officers emerged from behind the trees.

Unsure of my next move, I debated: should I try to reason with them, or just run?

No.

Running wasn't an option.

At 53, I couldn't outrun them.

So I stayed where I was, waiting for their next move.

"Are you Andrea Perez?" Officer One asked, his tone sharp and no-nonsense, making it clear that lying wasn't on the table.

"I... I'm Andri," I said carefully.

Officer Two chuckled darkly. "Well, well. We found you. You know what happens to pieces of shit like you in prison? You'll find out soon enough."

Before I could respond, Officer One stepped forward and snapped cold steel handcuffs around my wrists.

Then, out of nowhere, Officer Two drove his boot into my stomach.

Not hard enough to cause real damage, but enough to knock the breath out of me.

"What the hell are you doing?" Officer One snapped, glancing over.

"She's pathetic," Officer Two sneered. "Her son said she was drunk, stole a car, and ran from the scene. Like a selfish coward. You're lucky he didn't find you first. I've never seen anyone as pissed off as he was. Can't say I blame him."

Then, he grabbed a fistful of my hair and yanked me forward.

Pain exploded across my scalp, blinding for a moment. Tears sprang to my eyes.

"Hey, take it easy," Officer One muttered. "She's cuffed. She can walk."

I turned and glared at Officer Two.

"Yeah, I can walk! I don't need you pulling my—"

Before I could finish, his hand cracked across my face.

The sting burned deep. I turned to Officer One, desperate. "You saw that, didn't you?"

He smirked.

"Nope. Didn't see a thing."

The bastard.

Officer One knew exactly what was happening, but he didn't care.

I sighed. There was no point in pleading.

Then chaos.

Both officers hit the ground with muffled grunts.

They groaned, reaching for their weapons.

My pulse spiked.

Two figures emerged from the trees, their silhouettes shifting in the moonlight that danced through wind-swept leaves.

Josh. And Molly.

Josh and Molly

The first thing Josh registered was the crisp night air.

The second: the rough ground beneath him.

They were in a wooded area, their backs pressed against the base of a tree.

Josh groaned, pushed himself upright, and then reached down to help Molly to her feet.

"You okay?" he whispered.

Molly nodded. "Yeah. I'm good."

They both instinctively lowered their voices.

Josh turned to her, serious. "Remember what I taught you and Lanix, no matter what happens, keep a clear head. Do not show fear. Never panic. Panic gets people killed."

Molly met his eyes and nodded.

Josh narrowed his gaze. "Say it back."

Molly took a breath.

"Keep a clear head. Show no fear. Never panic."

Josh exhaled, satisfied.

Moonlight filtered through the trees, casting long shadows. It was just enough to see, but out of habit, he reached for his flashlight.

"She has to be around here somewhere," he whispered. "Tanya said she'd send us right to Andri."

He was just about to click it on.

Voices.

Josh froze.

Shhh. He pressed a finger to his lips and tucked the flashlight away.

They peeked through the brush.

Three figures.

Two in uniform.

One being pushed forward.

Hands cuffed behind her back.

Aunt Andri.

Josh's jaw tightened. *"Damn."*

He turned to Molly, voice low but clear. "Get the taser ready. Wait until they're close together. Fire when I say."

Molly nodded, pulling out the taser, hands steady. She took aim.

The officers moved closer.

"Now."

Molly fired.

Both officers dropped at the same time.

Josh grinned.

"Good job."

He moved toward Andri.

"Let's get your mom out of here."

Andri

With my hands still cuffed behind me, I dropped to my knees in shock.

The officers were down.

Josh moved fast, precise, snatching both weapons before they could reach them.

Molly stood nearby, holding a strange device, its red laser flickering across the fallen men.

They looked just as stunned as I felt.

Josh tossed one baton deep into the woods and kept the other.

He tucked one pistol into his waistband and flung the other out of reach.

"What did you do to them?" I asked, breathless.

Josh flashed a grin. "They're fine, just stunned."

My eyes widened. "But how?"

"Tanya," he said simply, as if that explained everything.

Of course.

The woman who warned me about this place, about the switch.

And I hadn't believed her.

"We don't have time for this," Josh said, already moving. "Let's get out of here before more show up."

He helped me to my feet and turned to the officers. "Which one cuffed you?"

I nodded toward Officer One.

Josh dug through the duty belt, found the key, and unlocked my cuffs.

Then he turned, ready to restrain Officer Two.

That's when it happened.

Officer Two lashed out, grabbing Molly's ankle and yanking her down.

She cried out, landing hard on the ground.

Josh spun. "Let her go!" he barked, stepping forward.

But the officer held tight.

His free hand snapped out and snatched the taser from the dirt.

He turned it on Josh, face twisted with satisfaction.

Molly struggled beneath him, trying to wrench free.

He shoved her aside.

She flew backward and hit the ground hard.

Josh froze.

The device was aimed right at him.

In that split second, I could see him calculating how to move, how to protect both Molly and me.

Officer Two sneered. "Now you're gonna know what it's like to get shot with this."

Across the clearing, Officer One, still cuffed, struggled to sit up.

"Just shoot him," he barked. "What are you waiting for?"

Officer Two adjusted his grip.

Then, suddenly, the taser gun flew from his hand.

It hit the ground near Josh's feet with a dull thud.

All heads turned.

A man stood at the edge of the trees.
Someone Josh didn't recognize.
But I did.
My heart lurched.
I couldn't believe my eyes.
A smiled spread across my face.
He came back.
"It's David!" I cried out.

David

He was exhausted.
Overwhelmed.
Filled with regret.
He had left her.
Andri.
But after walking away, something gnawed at him.
She had shown him those pictures, those strange, impossibly real images.
Deep down, he had known she wasn't his mother.
She wasn't *Andrea.*
She was *Andri.*
And she was kind.
He saw it in her face when he told her how broken he was.
When he said it was the worst day of his life.
She had genuinely cared.
And she had told him she was from an Earth with a blue sky, something he'd scoffed at, thought was ridiculous. But then he saw it. In photo after photo, there it was, vast, open, and achingly blue. And in that moment, everything shifted. Because that sky didn't exist in his world, but it did in hers.
And he had left her.
Now, David was back, retracing his steps, desperate to fix the damage he'd caused.
He heard voices before he saw them.
Two officers.
Restrained.
But one of them was pointing a weapon.
And standing there... was Andri.
Cuffed.

Surrounded.

His stomach dropped.

This is my fault.

Then the moonlight shifted, revealing a face: *Josh.*

David froze.

It was the man from the photographs.

The one Andri had called her nephew.

His gaze darted. He spotted another figure in the shadows.

A girl. Young. Watching. Silent.

David crept forward, putting a finger to his lips, signaling her to stay quiet.

She nodded, eyes wide.

Then, in one smooth motion, he lunged from the brush.

And kicked the taser clean from the officer's grip.

------⋅◆⋅------

"David? Who's David? And how does Aunt Andri know him?" Josh wondered.

He didn't have time to ask, not while the officers were still twitching on the ground.

"I'll cuff this one," Josh said briskly.

David nodded and knelt, pulling the handcuffs from the officer's belt and handing them to Josh.

The officer's legs jerked again, his muscles fighting the stun.

Josh didn't flinch. He pinned the man's arms and secured the cuffs behind his back, double-checking the fit, tight but not cruel.

David stood, brushing dirt from his hands, and turned to me.

"Are you okay?"

I nodded, though my hands trembled. Not from cold, but from the overwhelming shock of everything that had just happened.

I still couldn't believe they were here. Josh. Molly. And David.

Josh's voice cut through the fog. "We have to go."

"Where?" I asked, looking to him for direction.

He shook his head. "I don't know."

We moved farther from the officers. Once we were out of earshot, David said, "Follow me. I know just the place."

Josh's jaw tightened. He didn't know David and clearly didn't trust him. But we had no better option.

We followed.

David led us through the trees, not down a path, but weaving through brush and low branches like someone who knew the terrain.

"Cops are everywhere," he muttered.

I wasn't sure where he was taking us, but something in me trusted him instinctively.

Josh, on the other hand, was clearly on edge. His eyes bounced between me, Molly, and David, calculating every risk.

"I think we're far enough away. We're all together now, so we can go back. Molly, get the mirror," Josh said.

Molly reached under her jacket and began to pull it out, but then—rustling.

Leaves shifting. Movement behind us.

Josh stiffened. "No time. Keep walking," he whispered.

We picked up the pace, hearts pounding, barely speaking.

The only sounds were our breaths and the crunch of dried leaves beneath our feet.

Then we heard it.

The faint rush of water.

A clearing opened before us. A narrow wooden bridge stretched across a small creek.

It looked old, like something from a forgotten century. Worn planks. Sagging rail.

Josh hesitated, but there was no time to weigh options.

We crossed.

The bridge groaned beneath our weight, but it held.

On the other side, Josh slowed and turned toward David.

"Where are you taking us?" Josh asked, narrowing his eyes.

David's tone was calm but firm. "There's a small cabin not far from here. My grandfather used to bring me here when I was a kid. It's part of our family trust now. Nobody will find us there. It's completely off-grid. We'll be safe there."

The trees thickened again, swallowing the light. The moon cast silver stripes on the forest floor.

Josh didn't say anything. His instincts screamed caution, but the logic was sound. We had nowhere else to go.

Finally, a shadowy shape emerged from the brush. A structure. So well hidden, it would've vanished entirely in the dark if we hadn't been looking.

David stepped up to the door and tried the knob.

Locked.

He knelt, lifted a loose board near the base of the porch, and retrieved a key.

Click.

The door creaked open.

Josh switched on his flashlight as we stepped inside.

The cabin was... surprising.

No cobwebs. No thick dust. No rodent nests.

Just clean wood floors, finished walls, a small wood-burning stove in one corner, and a sink near the back wall.

No toilet.

There were four chairs around a solid oak table.

We each took one. Josh adjusted the flashlight, aiming it across the table.

And landed the beam squarely on Molly's face.

David looked up.

And froze.

The blood drained from his face.

He stared at her like he'd just seen a ghost.

For a moment, I thought he was going to fall right off the chair.

Oh my God. He's seeing Molly. He just lost her today, watched her die, and now here she is, sitting right in front of him.

I'd been so focused on escaping that I hadn't even considered how he would react.

Josh and Molly exchanged confused glances.

"What's wrong?" Josh asked, frowning.

I hesitated, unsure if David wanted me to answer.

David exhaled sharply, running a shaky hand through his hair. His expression shifted, the initial shock melting into something unreadable.

"Of course she's not the same..." he murmured.

"Of course what?" Josh pressed, irritation creeping into his tone.

David rubbed his face, as if trying to wake himself from a dream.

Josh, growing impatient, leaned forward. "Look, dude, if you're about to lose it on us..."

"Josh, please," I cut in. "Give him a chance to explain."

Josh huffed, but leaned back, arms crossed. "Fine. Explain."

David hadn't taken his eyes off Molly. She was clearly unsettled, glancing at me, then Josh, searching for some kind of answer.

I turned to David. "Would you like me to tell them?"

He gave a small nod, but I could see the exhaustion in his face, the weight of everything pressing down on him.

So, I explained.

I told them about the accident. About Andrea's reckless, drunken driving. The crash. The car flipping. The horror of it. And how David had witnessed it all.

How, in his world, Molly had died.

His sister was gone.

But now, here she was. Alive.

For him, that was impossible.

Molly's eyes widened as I recounted what had happened. I explained how furious David had been, how he'd searched for Andrea, his mother, driven by rage and grief. But instead of finding her, he'd found me.

"He thought I was her," I said. "And he unleashed all that anger on me... until I showed him your picture on my phone."

David exhaled, his voice quieter now. "I didn't get a good look at... Molly until now. So, sorry if I made you uncomfortable."

Josh glanced over at me, his gaze hardening. "What do you mean, unleashed all that anger on you?"

Before I could answer, he turned to David, studying him. Then his voice sharpened. "So... did this happen before or after the cops showed up?"

David met his stare. "Before."

Josh's expression darkened. "Then why the hell was my aunt alone with those officers? Where were you?" His voice rose, anger bubbling to the surface.

I opened my mouth to step in, but David lifted a hand, stopping me. His eyes locked onto Josh's, steady and unflinching.

"Because," David said, his voice measured but firm, "what she told me, on top of what I'd just witnessed, losing my sister, it was too much. I had to get out of there. So I left."

Josh's entire body tensed, fury overtaking him. He shot up from his chair, fists clenched.

David stood too, just as fast.

Now they were face-to-face.

The air in the cabin thickened, charged with unspoken rage, grief, and something else, something dangerously close to a breaking point.

"You didn't help her!" Josh shouted, dragging out the words, his voice shaking with fury.

David's eyes darkened. "I came back to apologize for hurting her," he shot back. "And if it weren't for me, you wouldn't have been able to help her at all."

Josh's jaw tightened. "Hurt her? What do you mean by that?" His gaze snapped to me.

I rolled my eyes, suppressing a groan. Great. Just what I needed. I'd hoped Josh would assume the officers were responsible for my bruises and bloody nose. But now? David had just handed him the truth on a silver platter.

David, unbothered, answered evenly. "I came back to apologize for roughing her up... and was going to offer her a place to stay until she could find her way home."

Josh's expression shifted, surprise flickering across his face, as if he couldn't decide whether David was reckless, shameless, or just plain stupid for admitting it.

The air between them crackled.

Josh shoved David.

Caught off guard, David's hip slammed into the table.

Josh's eyes burned, his expression nearly unrecognizable, like something had taken hold of him. He stepped forward, ready to shove him again.

David didn't back down. Instead, he closed the distance between them, nose to nose.

"Nobody puts their hands on my aunt like that," Josh growled, his voice low, controlled, but dripping with menace.

Before David could react, Josh swung, his fist connecting with David's jaw.

David staggered but didn't fall. Josh was already winding up for another hit when David struck back, driving a powerful kick into Josh's leg.

Josh collapsed with a grunt.

He looked up, seething, catching the brief flicker of David's gaze shifting toward me. That split second was all he needed.

With a swift motion, Josh swiped his leg out, knocking David's feet from under him.

David hit the floor.

I shot to my feet, my irritation flaring. "Are you two done acting like little boys?"

Silence.

Both men breathed heavily, locked in a tense standoff.

I exhaled sharply, leveling my gaze at Josh.

"I know you're looking out for me, and I appreciate it. But David lost his sister today. His mother, Andrea, wasn't just drunk driving, Josh. She ran from the scene. She left Molly to die. She saved herself like a coward."

I glanced at David, then back at Josh.

"So, no, it wasn't me he was after. It was her. And in his eyes, I was her. He had no way of knowing otherwise."

David pushed himself up, brushing off the fall. After a pause, he turned to Josh and offered his hand.

A silent truce.

Josh hesitated. Then, grudgingly, he took it as he limped toward the chair.

They both sat back down. The tension was still thick, but no longer explosive.

David exhaled, rubbing his jaw before meeting Josh's eyes.

"I've never in my life hit a woman. But in that moment, she wasn't a woman to me. She was a killer. A demon."

Then he turned to me, his eyes raw, filled with regret, sorrow... maybe even longing.

"I'm deeply sorry. I wish... I wish you were my mother instead of her."

A heavy silence settled over us.

Josh let out a breath and gave a slow nod.

"I guess... I would've done the same. But I gotta say, your Earth sucks."

He extended his hand.

David hesitated, just for a second, then took it.

Their hands clasped in a firm shake, an unspoken agreement between two men bound by grief, rage, and something neither of them could fully explain.

"Well," Josh said, leaning back. "Let's go home."

Molly glanced around. "I'm starving. Can we eat first?"

"Yeah, I'm hungry too," Josh agreed.

David shifted. "Sorry, but there's no food..."

His voice trailed off as Molly pulled out the rations Tanya had packed. Water bottles, protein bars, and a few other essentials.

She had thought of everything.

Even this.

Chapter 26

After the meal, Molly wiped her hands and looked at David.

"Is there a bathroom?"

David shook his head. "Nope. No toilet here."

Molly and I exchanged a look.

I raised a brow. "So, there's a *sink,* but no *toilet?*"

David chuckled. "This place was mostly used by guys. We just... went outside."

Molly and I stared at him, unimpressed.

Noticing our expressions, David quickly added, "I can fill a couple of buckets with water. You can use the closet for privacy and, uh... toss it outside."

Josh smirked.

I shot him a glare.

After the dreadful, but necessary, experience, Josh stood up and stretched.

"Well, now that we've eaten and..." he glanced at Molly and me with a smirk. "...taken care of business, it's time for us to leave."

Molly practically jumped from her chair. "I agree!" she said, a little too excited.

We all stood, and I turned to Josh.

"So, we have a way home, then?"

Josh nodded. "Yeah. Tanya gave us a mirror. It'll take us back. But we'll need to go outside for this. The cabin's gonna fill with that weird haze."

David's eyes widened. *"You're leaving? Now?"*

His voice held a note of hesitation, like he wasn't quite ready to let us go.

Josh turned to him. "Yeah. We all have to be together for it to work, and now we are."

David's gaze flicked to Molly. He hesitated, then softly asked, "Can I give you a hug?"

Molly's expression warmed, and she reached out her arms.

David stepped forward, closing the distance. He wrapped her in a tight embrace and pressed a gentle kiss to her forehead.

"Thank you, Molly," he murmured. "I'm so glad you came here. Just seeing you… it's lessened my grief. I'll always miss my Molly, but at least I know *you're* alive… that helps."

He pulled back and smiled down at her before releasing her.

Molly's eyes glistened with unshed tears. She turned to me, searching my face.

"Mom… it's him, isn't it?"

I tilted my head, thrown by the question. "Who, Molly? What are you talking about?"

She met my gaze, her voice barely above a whisper.

"The dream. It's him."

Her eyes flickered toward David. "The baby that was stolen from you."

I hesitated, my heart pounding. This wasn't the time for this conversation. Not now. Not here.

But I knew she was right.

Before I could respond, David spoke.

"Yes. I'm him," he said, his voice steady but filled with something deeper, something certain. "I'm the son she dreamed about. Your brother."

He turned to me, his eyes searching mine.

"The dream you told me about… I know about it because I was there."

My breath hitched. My brows drew together.

"Well, yes, you were there when I told you about the dream. What are you trying to say?"

David took a step closer.

"No. I was there, in the dream. I remember the day you were dropping off Molly. Only… it wasn't supposed to be you. It was supposed to be my mother."

He swallowed hard, eyes locked onto mine.

"But I noticed your confusion. I asked you questions you couldn't answer. I asked why you didn't raise me."

The room seemed to shrink around us, the weight of his words pressing in.

David exhaled, his voice softer now.

"But now I understand. It was you who dropped Molly off that day. I don't know how, but it was you. It's like, for that moment, the two of you, Andrea and you, merged."

My eyes burned with tears as I stared at him.

He understood.

He got it.

And in that moment, the impossible felt real.

———◆———

Knock. Knock. Knock.

Then, pounding.

Someone was at the door.

We all froze. My heart slammed against my ribs. *Police?*

Josh, knife in hand, moved swiftly to the small window. He peered out, his body tight with tension.

"I thought you said nobody would find us here," Josh said, irritation lacing his voice.

David ignored the jab. "What do you see?"

"It's a woman. An older lady," Josh murmured.

David stepped closer. "Is she alone?"

Josh squinted. "I think so."

David nodded. "Okay. Stand by in case I need you."

Josh frowned. "What are you gonna do?"

David didn't answer.

In one swift motion, he swung the door open, grabbed the woman by the shoulder, and yanked her inside. The door slammed shut behind her.

She gasped, her wide eyes darting between us, startled by the sudden action.

Josh scowled. "What the hell was that about?"

David exhaled sharply. "In case it was a trap. Better to pull her in and shut the door than *risk an ambush.*"

He turned to the woman, his tone softening.

"I'm sorry. I hope I didn't hurt you."

The old woman waved off the apology, barely reacting as her sharp gaze swept the room.

"We don't have much time," she said urgently. "We have to work quickly."

David narrowed his eyes. "Work at what?"

She spun to face him, locking eyes.

Her gaze unnerving. For a moment, he tensed.

"I did a terrible disservice to you, young man," she said. Then she turned to me, her expression steeped in regret.

"And what I did to you was atrocious. I regret it terribly."

Before I could speak, she pressed on, her voice firm.

"But there's no time for that now. You need to know: the police are searching for the four of you. They'll be here soon."

Josh's eyes darkened. "How do you know? Did they follow you?"

"No," she shook her head. "They don't know I'm here."

A prickle ran down my spine. Something about her felt *familiar*.

"Josh," I said, my voice barely above a whisper, "raise the flashlight a little higher."

He did.

And then I saw her.

I stiffened. My stomach dropped.

It's her.

"You..." I breathed, shock tightening my throat. "You're Tanya's twin sister."

Molly and Josh's eyes widened in disbelief.

The woman nodded. "Yes. My name is Sonya."

A wave of suspicion crashed over me. My lips pressed into a thin line.

"You helped with the switch," I said coldly. "Why should we trust you?"

Sonya exhaled. "I can't convince you to trust me," she said. "But my sister's life is in danger. I don't want her killed. Part of Andrea's mission is to eliminate Tanya."

A chill ran through me.

"I need to stop that," she continued. "And I also have to make sure Anio doesn't get his hands on the necklace."

She opened her fist, revealing the object she'd been gripping tightly.

A necklace.

My breath caught. I knew that necklace.

"Wait... that looks just like my mother's!" I blurted.

Sonya's gaze sharpened. "Because Andrea is after both. She plans to kill Tanya and steal your mother's necklace. I have to stop her."

Josh scoffed. "Too late. She already stole it. Tanya sent us here right after to bring my aunt back."

Sonya's jaw tightened. "Then we don't have much time."

She took a breath and clutched the necklace again. "Anio ordered me to hold this for him until he came back for it."

We didn't move. We didn't speak. We still didn't know who Anio was, but something in Sonya's voice kept us listening.

"None of this will make sense right now," she admitted. "But I have to go back with you. I need to stop Andrea from killing my sister. And I need to keep Anio from getting this necklace."

David folded his arms and let out a bitter chuckle. "You mean *my* mother? She's up to no good *again?* And now she's stealing necklaces too? What's next?"

His laugh was hollow, empty.

Sonya turned to him, her voice grave. "Andrea... is not your real mother."

David shook his head, his face tightening in disbelief. "What are you talking about? If she's not, then who is?"

Sonya shifted her gaze to me.

"Andri," she said quietly, nodding toward me, "this woman, she is your biological mother."

The air shifted.

A stunned silence fell over the room.

David's brows furrowed. His mouth opened slightly, as if he wanted to speak but couldn't find the words.

Sonya pressed on. "She never gave birth to you because you were stolen from her womb. You were..." she hesitated. "...transported into the womb of Andrea from this Earth."

The words hit me like a punch to the chest.

The memory crashed back: the joy of pregnancy, the aching emptiness that followed. No miscarriage. No explanation. Just... gone.

David's face went pale. "That's... that's not possible."

"I know it's hard to believe," Sonya said gently. "I would explain everything, but there isn't time. I am sorry for my part in it."

She took a breath and continued. "Here's the short version: Andrea wanted to manipulate Victor into taking her back. She wished to be pregnant with his child. Anio granted that wish, but the only way to do it... was to steal a child from her counterpart. Because he knew Andrea was selfish enough to be used as his tool later. That child was stolen from... Andri."

Sonya turned to David, her voice softening. "That child... was you."

My breath hitched.

My heart pounded as I whispered, "How? How was it done?"

Sonya met my eyes.

"Magic," she said simply. "Just like everything else that's happening now."

I searched her face for a lie, but all I saw was guilt and weariness.

"I'm from your Earth too," she added quietly. "I wasn't a good sister to Tanya. I was jealous. I stole her necklace... and it transported me here."

"I've been stuck here ever since," she said, her voice low. "Doing Anio's bidding."

She turned once more to David. "You must come with us. This isn't your true home. You belong with them. With your real family."

David shook his head, his jaw tight. "No. Out of the question. I have my daughters; I'm all they have since their mother abandoned them."

Sonya's expression softened, though her tone remained firm. "Your headaches... they're caused by being here. This isn't your natural home. Bring your daughters with you. They're a part of you. They'll adapt. But we have to go now. The police will be here soon."

Josh frowned. "How do you know the police are coming?"

Sonya turned and smirked. "How does Tanya know things?"

Josh studied her for a moment, then nodded. "Fair point."

I shook my head, still skeptical. "But how can David come with us if his daughters aren't here?"

Sonya's gaze held mine. "He'll find his way home."

Before I could ask more, she added, "My power is limited, but I can transport David out of this cabin to his house. We don't want the police finding him here."

In an instant, David vanished.

Josh and Molly stood there, mouths open, eyes wide.

Sonya turned to us, urgency in her tone. "We have to move now."

Panic surged through me. "Wait! Where is he? What did you do?"

Sonya barely glanced at me. "I told you, he's safe. At home. But we don't have time for questions. We have to go."

I hesitated, unease twisting in my gut. "I have serious reservations about bringing you with us," I said, my voice sharp. "You've done some terrible things."

Josh nodded. "Yeah. We're not taking you."

Molly folded her arms. "Agreed."

Sonya turned to Molly. "Do you have the mirror Tanya gave you?"

Molly's posture stiffened. She glanced between Josh and me, her eyes narrowing. "Why do you want to know?"

"I need the mirror," Sonya said, extending her hand.

Molly looked at her palm, then gave a nervous laugh. "Yeah... I'm *not* handing it to you."

Josh scoffed. "You're out of your mind if you think we're just going to give it up."

Sonya only smiled. "Never mind. I just wanted to know if she had it."

Then her expression changed; her eyes narrowed; her voice urgent. "We have to go. NOW!"

Josh hesitated, but something in her tone propelled him forward. "Fine. We're going, but you're not coming with us."

Sonya ignored him.

We rushed outside.

Molly reached into her waistband. Empty.

She checked her pocket, fingers fumbling. Nothing.

Her breath caught. She tried the other one.

Still nothing.

Frantic now, she tore through the food bag, shoving aside ration packs and water pouches.

No mirror. A chill ran down my spine.

Then, sirens in the distance. The police were closing in.

We could see shadows shifting between the trees, weapons drawn.

A voice boomed from a bullhorn:

"This is the police! Put your hands up and get on the ground. NOW!"

The moment weighed heavy. Officers didn't move, didn't flinch. Fingers hovered near triggers.

"Do it now! Hands where we can see them!" I froze, then slowly raised my hands.

Molly stood beside me, her breathing shallow, wide eyes locked on the officers. Sonya was tense but composed a few feet away.

Josh, still near the cabin door, was too far, too exposed.

We all lowered ourselves to the ground in sync.

But as Josh crouched, I saw it, the flicker of movement as his hand slipped into his coat pocket.

In one smooth motion, he pulled out the flashbang.

Before I could say a word, he tossed it toward the trees.

A heartbeat later.

BOOM!

A blinding white light erupted, swallowing the night. A deafening blast tore through the air, disorienting the officers and sending shouts of confusion echoing through the trees.

It was our chance.

Josh sprinted toward us, his movements sharp and desperate.

Molly and I panicked as she frantically searched for the mirror. "I can't find it!" she gasped.

Before fear could take hold, Sonya bolted toward us, clutching the necklace. She activated the globe, and instantly, the blue haze swirled to life, wrapping around us like a veil.

Josh was only steps away when—

Pop!

A gunshot cracked through the night.

Josh went down, hitting the ground just inches from the haze, groaning in pain.

Molly, in tears, lunged for him, her hand outstretched, her fingertips just barely brushed his.

Desperate, she made a split-second decision. She stepped out of the haze.

I screamed, "Molly, no!"

But she wasn't listening. She wouldn't leave him behind.

I rushed to the edge of the haze, trying to grab her, to help pull Josh in, but he was too far. Molly edged closer to him.

"Molly, what are you doing? Go!" Josh rasped, eyes squeezed shut against the pain.

He continued, "Molly, you're not a crying girl. You're a soldier, remember?" he snapped. "No questions. No arguments."

She hesitated, still trying to drag him in.

Sonya reacted instantly, rushing after Molly, just as another shot rang out.

Pop!

Missed.

Sonya moved fast. She bolted toward them.

Pop!

Another shot rang out.

Sonya jerked back, a sharp gasp escaping her lips. Blood bloomed across her chest.

Josh roared in pain and fury. "Let me go! Get in the haze, NOW!" His voice cracked with authority.

Tears streamed down Molly's face, but this time she obeyed. She stumbled back into the haze, just as another bullet sliced through the air, missing her by inches.

Sonya, gasping for breath, dragged herself forward inch by inch and made it inside.

The haze thickened, twisting around us, pulling us deeper into its grasp.

Through the swirling light, Sonya's trembling fingers secured the necklace around her neck.

And then... Everything spun.

Disoriented and weightless, we were pulled into the unknown.

Chapter 27

Blue Earth 2017–December, Lincoln, Nebraska

Tanya

Today was the day. The confrontation.

Andrea was coming, and Tanya knew exactly why.

She had seen it. Andrea's intent, the malice laced through her arrival.

Nora had spent the night at Tanya's place, a quiet apartment tucked behind the shop.

Molly had been worried, but Tanya had reassured her: *"I'll keep her safe."*

But it wasn't just about safety. Tanya knew the real reason Nora had to be there.

Now, she settled Nora into the back room with Shannon. Shade, the shop's black cat, leapt onto Nora's lap, curling up as if sensing the stillness in the air.

Tanya gave Shannon a steady look. "Be sure to have Nora ready."

Shannon nodded. "I will."

Tanya stepped away, her mind focused. She needed a plan.

Andrea would come armed, likely with a knife.

In a quiet alcove at the back of the shop, Tanya inhaled deeply. With careful precision, she pulled out a small, handheld mirror.

She closed her eyes and began to chant, her voice low and rhythmic, threading through the air like a current of unseen power:

"Light of worlds, hear my call,

Anio, guide me, one and all.

To restore balance, to shield against darkness..."

As the words faded into stillness, she traced her finger along the mirror's surface. Slowly, the glass shimmered, Anio's ethereal image appearing within. His eyes, warm and enigmatic, met hers.

"Anio," Tanya whispered, "how can I protect myself from Andrea? She's coming to end my life."

A gentle smile curved his lips. "Fear not, Tanya. You will not be harmed. Her designs will crumble."

His calm confidence reassured her. Tanya allowed herself a brief smile. "Thank you... for your love and guidance through all these years."

Anio's expression grew solemn. "You and Nora are cherished fragments of *Anio*, among many who watch over this world. When you chose to live as humans, we remained beside you."

"You were entrusted with the sacred necklaces, each globe holding the power of worlds. But when the second globe was given to you, a dark fragment escaped, driven by greed and power. Banished to the red world, his strength was limited, but now he schemes to claim the second globe. We must not let him succeed."

"Is everything in order?" Anio asked, though Tanya sensed he already knew the answer.

"Yes," she said. "Nora is standing by. As soon as Andrea steps inside, Shannon will close the store. I just hope Molly, Josh, and Andri return soon."

Anio's gaze shifted, as if seeing beyond time. "They are treading the path as we speak. Trials remain, but I do not doubt their strength. The river carves stone not by force, but by persistence."

Tanya's reflection flickered, her worry showing in the mirror's light. "Is there anything we can do to help them?"

Anio offered a knowing smile. "Our place is here. This moment must unfold as it was meant to. The balance is delicate, and the cost of failure, too great."

His expression changed, sensing something. "Do not despair. A hand unseen moves in their favor. Help will come, just when it's most needed."

❖

A few minutes later, Shannon spotted Andrea approaching the storefront; she remained near the entrance, pretending to tidy the shelves. When their eyes met, Shannon gave Tanya a subtle nod, then slipped behind the curtain into the back room.

Andrea stepped inside.

Shannon greeted her with a polite smile. "Hello again."

Andrea didn't return it. "Is the owner in?"

"Yes. I'll get her." Shannon moved behind the counter and disappeared, joining Nora in the back.

Moments later, Tanya emerged, her expression calm and composed as she stepped behind the counter. "Hello, I'm Tanya, the owner. Can I help you?"

She noted Andrea's eyes darting around the shop. *She's sizing up the space,* Tanya thought. *The counter isn't ideal for whatever she's planning.*

Andrea's lips were tight. "I have something that might interest you."

Tanya raised an eyebrow, stepping around the counter as if intrigued. In reality, she was positioning Andrea with her back to the curtain.

Here we go, Tanya thought, steadying herself.

Andrea reached into her coat pocket and pulled out a necklace. Tanya's breath caught. It looked nearly identical to the real one. A brilliant move on Nora's part to have a decoy. *Where did she even find that?*

Andrea held it up, the orb catching the dim light.

Behind her, hidden by the curtain, Nora raised the real necklace.

Tanya's eyes flicked past Andrea to the glowing orb in Nora's hands. The necklace pulsed in blue and red haze, beginning to swirl around them.

Andrea believed she had triggered the phenomenon.

But Tanya knew better.

The moment the true necklace was revealed, the air thickened, charged with energy. A mist of blue and red surged forth like living fire.

Tanya's pulse quickened.

Then, movement.

Andrea's hand. Rising.

The glint of steel.

The knife.

Tanya inhaled sharply but did not flinch. *Her designs will crumble,* Anio had told her. And so she stood firm.

Then, suddenly, Andrea hesitated. Her arm wavered, then lowered. Confusion clouded her face as she scanned the room, her eyes darting toward the haze. A flicker of unease crossed her features. Without a word, she tucked the knife back under her coat.

She didn't understand what had just happened.

But Tanya did.

A few seconds later, the air trembled as Anio materialized through the portal. His grin was unsettling; his presence a weight that pressed against the room. This was Anio, but not *her* Anio. Darkness exuded from him like a thick, suffocating aura.

His feet hovered above the floor, just like her Anio had done when she met him on the Arizona mountain all those years ago.

But this one?

No. He was different. Wrong. This was the fractured shadow, the dark fragment of the Anio who had broken away, consumed by greed. Just as her Anio had warned her.

Andrea hesitated, then forced a smile. Her voice was small, eager to please.

"I showed her the necklace... just like you told me to."

Anio's gaze swept over Tanya before settling on Andrea. His expression darkened.

"You have not completed the mission."

Andrea swallowed hard, hands gripping the fabric of her coat.

"I... I tried! But she, she disappeared! I didn't see her. But I can do it now!"

Anio's stare bore into her for a moment before he gave a slow, measured nod. "Then proceed."

Tanya tensed as Andrea reached beneath her coat, fingers seeking the blade.

Her breath caught.

Nothing.

The knife was gone.

Andrea's eyes darted up, terror creeping into her expression. *"I don't have it,"* she whispered, panic flaring in her voice. *"I don't know where..."*

Before she could finish, the air shifted again.

Another presence.

A second haze swirled into existence right beside Anio, blue light curling like smoke.

The portal had opened again.

Andri

We crashed onto the floor of Mystic Crossroads.

The world around us spun, disorienting. I barely had time to process the shift before I realized where we were.

Blood pooled beside us, Sonya's wound still fresh.

Molly sat on the floor, sobbing, her body trembling from the shock.

And then I noticed him.

An imposing being floated beside us. His presence overwhelming. Otherworldly.

I sucked in a breath, heart pounding. *What the hell is that?*

Slowly, I lifted my gaze and locked eyes with Tanya.

Her expression was frozen in shock.

Then, my gaze shifted to her.

Andrea.

The other me.

The sight was jarring, unnatural. Standing face-to-face with another version of myself felt like staring into a warped reflection.

I could tell she felt the same. The way she stiffened. The flicker of disbelief in her eyes as she hesitated, momentarily stunned by my arrival.

She was wearing my clothes. My favorite boots. One of my shoulder bags slung casually over her arm.

For a fleeting moment, we simply stared at each other.

Both of us realizing only one of us belonged here.

She, Andrea, lifted the necklace in her hand, holding it up for Anio to see.

His grin widened.

He reached out, fingers curling expectantly.

Andrea hesitated. Not wanting to get too close, she tossed the necklace toward him. It hit the floor, landing just beneath his floating form.

But he didn't pick it up. Not yet.

His gaze shifted.

Sonya.

She lay wounded on the ground, her breath shallow, *another* necklace glinting at her chest.

Anio's expression changed, darkening with greed. His eyes gleamed with ravenous hunger.

"Give it to me," he commanded.

Tanya's eyes widened. She spotted her twin sister bleeding on the floor. She rushed forward, but Anio blocked her path, his presence like an invisible wall.

Desperate, Tanya shouted, "Shannon! Call an ambulance!"

But Sonya, summoning what little strength she had left, cut through the chaos.

"No. *Absolutely* no ambulance."

Tanya's voice cracked with emotion. "Please, let me help you!"

Sonya shook her head, defiant despite the agony. "No!"

Barely conscious, she reached for the necklace at her throat. With trembling fingers, she pulled it over her head.

Anio drifted closer, his presence weighing down the air.

He extended his hand, waiting.

"Sonya, no! Don't give it to him!" Tanya cried, lunging forward.

Anio turned his head, barely acknowledging her.

With a flick of his hand, an unseen force slammed into Tanya, hurling her backward.

Chapter 28

Tanya hit the floor with a painful thud, gasping as the air was knocked from her lungs.

Sonya stood frozen, the necklace clenched tightly in her trembling hand. Her eyes locked on Anio.

The room felt suspended in time, the moment hanging in a fragile, breathless silence.

Anio loomed over her, his outstretched palm radiating greed.

She moved slowly, deliberately, as if about to hand it to him.

He leaned in, hungry, desperate.

But in a sudden burst of defiance, Sonya hurled the necklace across the floor.

It skidded away.

Tanya reacted instantly. She lunged, snatching it up before Anio could process what had happened.

For a moment, the room stood still, stunned silence.

Then Anio's expression twisted. Betrayal.

His glare snapped back to Sonya, fury contorting his face.

After everything he had done for her.

With a snarl, he grabbed the necklace Andrea had given him earlier.

His fingers curled around it...

But something was off.

A flicker of confusion crossed his face.

He examined it more closely.

Fake.

A low, guttural growl rumbled from his throat.

"No... it can't be."

His head whipped toward Andrea, eyes ablaze.

"You betrayed me, too?" His voice dripped with venom.

Andrea's face drained of color, fear creeping into her features.

"No! I—I took that necklace from Nora! It can't be fake!" Her voice shook, teetering between panic and disbelief.

But Anio barely heard her.

His rage burned through whatever restraint remained.

He turned sharply, eyes locking onto Tanya.

The real necklace gleaming in her hands.

"Give it to me."

His voice was low. Dangerous.

Tanya shook her head. Once.

Anio's eyes darkened.

She took a cautious step back.

We all watched in silent horror as Anio began to rise, floating toward her, his presence suffocating, his intent unmistakable.

Then he froze.

His brow furrowed. Confusion flickered.

From behind the curtain, Nora stepped forward.

She moved with quiet purpose, the necklace dangling from her hand.

My breath caught.

"Mom, no..."

Panic surged through me. I grabbed Molly's hand, ready to rush forward, but Tanya's firm grip stopped me.

She leaned in and whispered, "It's okay."

But was it?

Anio's confusion shifted into excitement.

The real necklace. Finally.

Two women stood between him and ultimate power.

Two mere mortals.

Taking it from them should be easy.

He drifted toward them, slow and deliberate, predatory.

Then he stopped.

His breath hitched. His eyes widened.

No.

It couldn't be.

His body stiffened as realization crashed over him like a tidal wave.

They were here.

The ones he had escaped.

The ones he had severed himself from.

He was no longer one of them.
No longer just a fragment.
And now...
They had come for him.

Before Tanya and Nora, a soft, luminous glow filled the space.

We watched in silent awe as multiple beings emerged from the light, their forms fluid but distinct.

Their presence radiated peace, an overwhelming sense of balance.

Slowly, they began to merge into one.

It was breathtaking.

I glanced at Nora. She was smiling.

And in that moment, I knew.

This was him.

The being she'd always spoken of...

The one from the mountain in Superior, Arizona.

Back then, my siblings and I had never truly believed her.

We thought she'd embellished the story, that maybe she'd met a wise old man who lived near her childhood home.

But she'd been telling the truth all along.

A warmth spread through me.

I smiled back at her, my heart full.

Without hesitation, Nora turned to Anio, her Anio, and placed the necklace in his hands.

Then Tanya stepped forward, gently placing the second necklace, the one Sonya had tossed, into his grasp.

Across the room, Dark Anio's face contorted in utter defeat.

He knew.

He finally knew.

The truth.

The necklaces, his key to ultimate power, were out of reach. Forever.

The realization settled over him like a crushing weight.

His shoulders sagged.

The darkness that once made him formidable now faded, dull and flickering.

Too bad Andrea failed to kill her, he thought bitterly.

And then it happened.
He was no longer floating.
His feet touched the ground.
For the first time, he was grounded.
Mortal.

A rustling movement caught my attention.
Andrea.
She was inching toward the front door, slow and cautious, hoping to slip away unnoticed.
Before she could reach it, Shannon's voice rang out.
"That door is locked," she called, her tone smug. "And without the key..."
She folded her arms and tilted her head.
"I'm afraid you're stuck with us."
Andrea froze.
Shannon smirked, her expression mocking.
Then, suddenly, silence fell over the shop.
The air thickened, charged with something unseen, as if the very walls were holding their breath.
Anio of Light spoke.
His voice, serene yet bearing the weight of eternity, echoed through the room like the whisper of distant stars.
He turned to his fallen fragment; each word laced with ancient power.
"You have sown discord, drenched the world in the suffering of the innocent, all for your own twisted desires. Your path has come to its end. You are banished, returned to the Earth beneath the crimson sky, where only the dim light will reach."
Dark Anio stiffened.
The weight of his fate pressed down like a crushing stone.
No escape.
No power.
Only the red world, his prison.
He staggered, trembling.
"No..."
The word slipped from his lips, barely a whisper.
His breath came in short, uneven gasps.
Panic spread across his face.

"Please..." he choked. "I swear, I'll never use magic for ill again! Just... just give me one more chance!"

But his plea fell on deaf ears.

The judgment was final.

As Dark Anio trembled, power draining from him, Tanya was already moving, rushing to Sonya's side.

Shannon knelt beside her, pressing a blood-soaked towel against the wound.

Tanya's breath caught. "Sonya! I didn't realize you were shot! Who did this?"

"It doesn't matter," Sonya murmured, her voice weak but steady.

Tanya turned sharply. "Shannon, call for an ambulance."

Then, softer, pleading, "Sonya, you can't expect us not to get help for you. Please... let us do something."

Shannon shook her head, her voice tight with frustration. "I already told her I would. But the moment I turned to call, she begged me not to."

Tanya's eyes burned. She gripped Sonya's hand, her voice trembling. "You stubborn fool... we're getting you help."

Sonya managed a weak smile.

She shook her head, barely lifting it.

"No ambulance," she whispered.

Her breath came in shallow, strained gasps.

"I'm not living through this... and you know it."

Tanya did know it.

Sonya managed a faint smile. "Besides... how are you going to explain these Anios to the paramedics?"

Sonya's eyes met hers, filled with pain, but not just from the wound.

"When I heard about the plan to kill you, I had to come," she said, voice quivering, body trembling with the effort. "I couldn't let him, couldn't let Anio get his hands on both necklaces."

But she wasn't finished.

She forced herself to go on.

"I wasn't a good sister to you," she admitted, barely audible. "If it weren't for me, none of this would be happening. My jealousy... my selfishness... I set all of this in motion. I'm so sorry. Please... forgive me."

Her voice faded.

Her strength slipped away.

Tanya's grip on her hand tightened.

"There's nothing to forgive."

Soft, yet firm. A truth.

Tanya smiled through her tears, offering her sister something she had never given before: peace.

She held Sonya's hand a little longer, unwilling to let go. For the first time in years, she didn't feel angry, just... sad.

I stepped closer, glancing between them.

"It's over," I said softly. "Anio and Andrea have been banished back to the Earth beneath the red sky. He's powerless now. And Andrea... she'll probably end up in prison."

Just then, Anio of Light floated toward us, his presence both calming and commanding.

Tanya turned to him, hope flickering in her tear-filled eyes.

"*Anio*... is there anything you can do for her?"

Her voice trembled, pleading, desperate.

We all waited.

Holding our breath.

Hoping.

Before he could respond, Sonya's voice cut through the silence.

"No."

It was weak, but firm, laced with finality.

She slowly turned her head toward Tanya, eyes filled with something deeper than pain...

Acceptance.

"I think we've had enough magic, don't you?" she whispered.

"We've allowed it to alter our lives for far too long... let's not let it alter our deaths."

With that, she closed her eyes.

A final breath escaped her lips, soft, fleeting.

And then... she was gone.

A heavy silence settled over the room.

Tanya's grip on her sister's hand tightened, as if holding on could bring her back.

But there was no magic, no force in the universe, that could change this.

I knelt beside her, my voice gentle.

"Tanya... she wasn't truly helping that monster. She was trapped."

Tanya didn't look up, but I saw the slight tremble in her fingers as she brushed a strand of Sonya's hair from her face.

"She tried to save Molly back there," I whispered. "She got shot doing it."

I swallowed hard.

"She came back to save you... and *both* of our worlds."

Tanya let out a shaky breath.

Sonya's final act hadn't been one of betrayal.

It had been one of redemption.

———⋯———

As Tanya grieved for her twin sister, Anio reached out and gently lifted her chin.

His touch was as light as a whisper, his eyes filled with ageless wisdom, otherworldly and calm.

"Do not weep for her," he said, his voice resonant and comforting. "She lives, just not here. She walks another path now, in another place, another time.

There, she does good works to redeem her soul. And in time, her purpose will become clear.

That is why she would not allow you to seek help; she knew her journey did not end here. It was her choice, freely made. And I honored it."

Tanya's tears slowed. Though sorrow still clung to her heart, a flicker of hope stirred within her.

Somewhere out there, Sonya was finding her way...

Perhaps even preparing to help others in ways Tanya could not yet imagine.

Molly and I stood holding each other, bound by our own grief.

Tanya turned to me and asked softly, "Josh?"

A cry escaped from Molly, and I simply shook my head.

Tanya, eyes brimming with tears, mouthed the words, "I'm sorry."

The weight of Josh's absence pressed down on us, squeezing the air from our lungs and knotting our throats with sorrow.

And as the reality sank in, I felt it...

The universe had torn my heart apart all over again.

David, the baby I'd lost all those years ago...

He was alive.

Right there.

Within reach.

Yet just as quickly as I'd found him, fate had stolen him from me once more.

The pain of that truth settled deep in my bones.

A grief within grief, something I couldn't begin to unravel.

In that moment, I realized something:

Grief wasn't just pain.

It was love with nowhere to go.

And as we stood there, sharing the ache of missing them,

I knew...

No matter how much time passed, a part of us would always be standing right there.

In the place where love and loss collided.

Chapter 29

Red Earth 2018–January, Gilson, Texas

Josh had just been released from the hospital.

Handcuffed to a wheelchair, he was carefully transferred onto the bed in his new jail cell by a detention officer.

Outside the cell, two officers stood near the bars, deliberately discussing him within earshot.

"So, that's the guy, huh?" one muttered.

"Yeah," the other replied. "You heard about him, right? Threw a flashbang at the officers as a distraction; three of them got away."

The first officer let out a low whistle, shaking his head with a trace of admiration.

"After he was shot and hit the ground, Officers Andrews and White were closing in on him. And he lobbed a smoke grenade. Then he ran."

The second officer chuckled, mirroring the sentiment.

"Nobody in the department had ever seen anything like it. Officer White said he felt like he was in a movie!"

He shook his head, still in disbelief.

"You should've seen the knives he had concealed. This guy's obviously not from around here."

The first officer scoffed.

"Must've been on a mission, for sure."

Laughter followed, echoing down the corridor.

It died down as one of the officers turned back to Josh, his tone shifting.

"How far did you think you were gonna get with a bullet in your shoulder? You're lucky it only hit muscle."

Josh didn't respond.

Exhausted, he lay back and closed his eyes.

His thoughts drifted to the days after he ran from the police.

The days he spent on the run were the worst of his life; wounded, exhausted, always looking over his shoulder.

He had hidden in abandoned homes and shacks, his body wracked with pain from the gunshot wound.

Desperation had driven him to steal clothes from a yard, some to wear, others to press against the injury.

But it wasn't enough.

Blood seeped through the fabric.

Soon, the wound festered.

The infection burned beneath his skin.

He was miserable.

Hunger gnawed at him, forcing him to blend in with the homeless, accepting meals and water from charity workers.

Even the city itself felt wrong.

The buildings leaned precariously, as if they might collapse at any moment.

There were no cell phones, only old radios with long antennas... crackling in the background like distant ghosts.

He missed his family.

His mother, Leanne, must be frantic.

And Patricia... *did she even miss him?*

Josh swallowed hard.

"Please, God, don't let me be stuck here," he murmured.

David

David sat on his porch chair as dusk settled. The air cool but not cold.

Across from him, his daughter Daphne sat cross-legged, absorbed in her coloring book, lost in her own little world.

He smiled quietly, watching her.

The girls were growing up so fast.

Paula was twelve now, and both Daphne and Delilah were ten. They were his only family left.

Sure, Aunt Bridgette was still out there somewhere.

But after what Sonya had told him, she no longer felt like family at all.

Sonya had insisted his real family belonged to another Earth. She had urged him to join them.

And he wanted that.

A loving family.

A mother who truly cared.

The chance to have Molly again.

And Josh...

It would've been nice to have a cousin like him.

Fearless.

Protective.

Always looking out for his own.

But that life wasn't his.

"They're gone now," he murmured. "I hope they're happy to be home."

A bittersweet smile played on his lips as the thought settled, both comforting and aching all at once.

"Dad?"

Paula's voice pulled David from his thoughts.

He blinked, shaking his head. "What?"

She walked over and wrapped her arms around his neck in a quick hug.

"Dad, I'm bored."

David furrowed his brow. "Bored? Books, coloring, and baking don't interest you anymore?" He smirked.

Paula pulled back slightly, rolling her eyes, then suddenly perked up.

"Baking does!" she yelped, excited.

David chuckled.

"Alright then. Let's get started."

He rose from his chair, following her inside.

But she stopped him.

"Dad, I want to bake with Connie," Paula said softly, as if worried she might hurt his feelings.

David, noting her careful tone, kept his smile.

"Connie? You mean Mrs. Fernandez?"

Paula hesitated. "Dad, um... I hope you don't get mad, but Delilah and I already called her.

I told her it was okay with you."

She frowned, bracing for his reaction.

Before he could respond, Daphne chimed in, "I want to go to Connie's house!"

David raised a brow. "Why do you call her Connie? Don't you think that's disrespectful?"

All three girls answered at once, nearly in unison: "She asked us to call her Connie."

David exhaled, shaking his head with a chuckle. "Well then, Connie it is."

"Dad, me and Paula already packed our overnight bag," Delilah announced.

David raised a brow. *"It's Paula and I*, not me and Paula.

And did you say overnight?

You never mentioned staying over. Is Connie okay with that?"

Paula chimed in, "Daddy, it's already getting dark outside, so it makes sense."

David nodded. "True enough."

Then, turning to Daphne, he added, "You'd better run inside and pack a bag. You don't want to be left out."

Daphne didn't need to be told twice. She dashed inside.

⚬

When Connie pulled up, she stepped out of the car with an ease that belied her years. In her early seventies, she was as active and sharp as ever; her small frame moving with quiet confidence. Short gray hair framed her face, neatly combed and paired with a no-nonsense air that had earned both respect and affection from those who knew her.

She made her way toward the porch, where the girls were already waiting with their bags. David walked to the front door to greet her. She gave him a nod before turning to the girls.

"Girls, the doors are unlocked. Go ahead and get settled in the car. I'd like to speak with your dad for a few minutes."

The girls raced to the car, each scrambling for the coveted front seat.

Connie turned to David, her expression serious.

Before she could speak, he held up a hand. "Look, I'm sorry if the girls put you on the spot..."

"No, no," Connie shook her head. "I was happy when they called. I love having them."

She hesitated, then added, "I want to talk with you about something else."

David tensed, uncertain of what was coming next.

Connie met his gaze, her voice gentle but firm.

"Mijo, I've known your family for a long time. I always tried to be there for Victor and Bridgette. But now, I'm here for you and the girls."

"Connie, I'll never understand how someone like *Julia* could've ever been your friend," David said, shaking his head.

Connie looked away for a moment before meeting his eyes again.

"Mijo, Julia was never a friend to anyone. It didn't take me long to figure that out. But once I did, I stuck around for Victor and Bridgette."

She paused, studying David's reaction before continuing.

"I know you've been through a lot, but I noticed something... during winter break, you never left the house. The girls told me you were home the whole time."

Her voice softened.

"Are you okay?"

David rubbed his temples, trying to stave off another headache.

He forced a smile, but it didn't quite reach his eyes.

"I'm okay. Just a lot to sort through, trying to get things in perspective." He exhaled. "I'm ready to start looking for a job. I don't like living off the family trust fund... it just doesn't feel right."

Connie's lips curved into a small smile.

"There's something else," she said. "Have you been listening to the news lately?"

David shrugged. "No, I don't anymore. It's always so negative."

"Well," Connie continued, "I thought you should know; they caught the man they were searching for."

David's brow furrowed. "A man? Who?"

Connie tilted her head slightly. "Hmm... I guess you didn't know. The police caught the man who was trying to help your mother, ah, Andrea, escape."

David's eyes widened in disbelief.

Josh.

His chest tightened.

"What? What happened?" he asked quickly.

Connie exhaled. "They think there were three other people involved, possibly four. Two were reported as female. They allegedly tried to help Andrea escape and reportedly assaulted two police officers."

David's stomach knotted as she continued.

"When the police caught up to them, the man deployed some kind of smoke bomb. He was shot, and they believe another person, a female, was also hit."

She paused, noticing the color drain from David's face. His breathing quickened.

"Should I continue?" she asked gently.

David swallowed hard. "Yes. But... what happened to the female who was shot?" His voice was tight with anticipation.

Connie hesitated before answering. "They don't know."

David's heart pounded.

"After the smoke bomb went off, the women escaped.

They haven't been found yet, but the police are still searching. Apparently, the man managed to surprise the officers with another smoke bomb and escaped despite his injury. They caught him a few days later. He was just released from the hospital."

David's mind raced. "He's in jail? Here in Gilson?"

Connie tilted her head. "Of course, he's in Gilson."

David forced himself to stay calm. He offered a measured nod.

"Connie, thank you for the information. I guess I'll start watching the news."

He forced a strained smile.

"Don't worry, Connie. I've disowned Andrea *completely*.

This won't have any adverse effect on me."

But his mind was already elsewhere.

He needed a moment to think.

Sensing his need for space, Connie offered a gentle smile.

"I'll bring the girls back around three-ish."

"Perfect," David said. "I have some errands to run, so three-ish works."

Connie nodded and made her way down the steps toward the car.

Just as she reached the driveway, David called after her. "Connie!"

She paused, turning back.

He met her gaze. "Thank you for being there for me and the girls."

Connie's lips curved into a soft smile. She gave him a small nod of acknowledgment before slipping into the car and driving off.

Shaken by the news, David retreated to his room.

Josh had been caught.

A lump formed in his throat as his thoughts swirled.

If Josh was caught... then where were Andri and Molly?

And the mysterious fourth person, was it me? Or Sonya?

He paced the room, running a hand through his hair, struggling to focus.

Ah, Josh. I've got to get him out somehow, he thought.

That was his top priority. But before he could make a plan, another thought gnawed at him...

Could the police identify him?

What if they came here to search?

His jacket. His breath hitched. *I need to get rid of it... just in case.*

He rushed to his closet, pushing past shirts, sweaters, and jackets until he found it.

His mind flashed back to that night...

Meeting Andri, Molly, and Josh.

And then Sonya.

Strange, mysterious Sonya.

The last thing he remembered was her voice:

"I have only limited power, but I can transport David out of this cabin to his house. We don't need the police finding him here."

After those words...

Nothing.

The next thing he knew, he had woken up in his bed.

Fully clothed.

David pulled the jacket off the hanger and laid it on his bed.

He stared at it, trying to figure out how to get rid of it.

He slipped his hand into the right pocket.

Then the left pocket.

Something caught his fingers.

He frowned. *"What is this?"* he muttered.

It was a small pouch.

Frowning deeper, David opened it and pulled out its contents...

A little round mirror.

He turned it over in his hands, wondering how it had found its way into his pocket.

Strange.

Lifting the mirror to his face, he barely had a moment to process what he saw before his reflection distorted.

Startled, he quickly set it down on the bed and turned to the wall-mounted mirror across the room.

His reflection there was perfectly normal.

For a long moment, he simply stared at the small mirror on his bed, suspicion gnawing at him.

Is this even a mirror?

Curiosity won out. He picked it up again and peered into it.

Once more, his reflection warped, unnerving and unnatural.

His pulse quickened. He hesitantly tapped the glass with his index finger.

To his shock, a light blue haze began to rise from within the mirror. It lingered in the air for only a moment before fading away.

David jolted back, dropping the mirror onto the bed.

"Whoa! What was that?"

He cautiously picked it up again and hurriedly slipped it back into the pouch, shoving it into his nightstand drawer.

He sat on the edge of the bed, staring at the drawer. His heart was still pounding.

What the hell had he just seen?

He rubbed his temples, trying to make sense of it, but no answers came.

The Next Morning, David woke just before dawn.

After a warm shower, he made coffee and poured himself a cup, deciding to drink it outside while watching the sunrise.

He set the cup down on the side table and grabbed a sweater from the front closet.

Coffee in hand, he opened the front door...

And froze.

His eyes locked onto a pair of legs stretched out on the futon.

Jeans. Ankle boots.

Someone was there.

Alarmed, he stepped back inside, setting down his coffee.

His breath hitched as he peeked through the window, needing to double-check what he had just seen.

There was definitely someone there.

A female.

His stomach dropped.

Andrea.

David hesitated.

Was it Andri or Andrea?

It couldn't be his real mother, Andri.

She wouldn't know where he lived.

Only that demon Andrea knew his address.

It had to be her.

Without hesitation, he rushed to the kitchen drawer and pulled out two large zip ties.

Moving quietly, he slipped onto the porch, the first light of dawn creeping over the horizon.

His movements were slow, methodical.

Carefully, he fastened a zip tie around Andrea's ankles.

She didn't stir.

Holding his breath, he reached for her hands…

Her eyes flew open.

A flash of shock widened them as she stared up at him.

In the dim morning light, David took in her tired gaze and the strands of gray in her hair.

Definitely the demon.

She jerked forward, trying to sit up, but her bound legs held her in place.

"What the fuck?" she gasped, twisting to look up at him, confusion flickering across her face.

That voice. That reaction.

Confirmed.

This was Andrea.

David's expression hardened.

"Andrea, what the hell are you doing here?"

She swallowed, desperation creeping into her voice.

"David, please. I don't have anywhere to go. I have no one. Please help me! I'm your mother."

Her plea hung in the air.

But David wasn't buying it.

Anger. Rage. And something else.

It surged through him, tightening his chest.

His piercing gaze bore into Andrea, making her flinch.

Struggling to keep his emotions in check, he spat:

"You have no one because of you! And my mother? No, you're not my mother. You stole me from Andri."

His voice was low but seething with fury.

Andrea's shock deepened.

"How could you know about that? I wasn't the one who did it; it was Sonya and Anio!"

"Sonya told me," David snapped.

Andrea blinked, confusion clouding her expression.

"Sonya's dead."

David's breath caught. His anger faltered.

"What do you mean, dead? How would you know?"

Andrea hesitated. Then her voice wavered.

"I was... away for a while. Sonya showed up there. She was shot in the chest. I don't know who did it. She was dying when I left. She probably died shortly after."

She stared up at David, fear creeping into her expression.

David narrowed his eyes.

"Away for a while, huh? Where?"

Andrea's voice dropped to a whisper.

"You wouldn't believe me if I told you."

David let out a humorless chuckle, thick with disgust.

"Let me guess, you transported to another world to steal a necklace and... kill a woman, all the while not giving a shit about what you did to Molly and Rachel, and the hell you put Andri through. How am I doing so far?"

Andrea, wide-eyed, remained silent.

"Where did you see Sonya?" David demanded.

After a pause, she replied hesitantly,

"I saw her in a city called Lincoln. She was there with... Molly, and the other me... Andri."

Her voice trailed off.

David struggled to conceal his relief. *They made it back.*

"So, what happened? Why are you back here?" he pressed, eyes locked on hers.

She murmured,

"I... I was sent back."

David chuckled, the disgust returning to his tone.

"I can't say I blame them. However, I'm glad you're back. It goes along with my plan perfectly."

Andrea slumped down, defeated.

David grabbed her wrist and tied her hands in front of her.

In a low whisper, she asked,

"Why are you doing this?"

David locked eyes with her.

"I just told you. It's part of my plan. So, now we're going for a ride."

Andrea didn't dare ask anything further.

Fear had silenced her completely.

Chapter 30

David had two priorities; turn Andrea in and see Josh.

He pulled into the parking lot of the Gilson Police Department. Chose a spot closest to the entrance.

In the back seat, Andrea lay bound, her wrists and ankles secured with zip ties.

He opened the door and glanced at her.

"We're here. The police department, your new home for now."

Andrea rolled her eyes.

David smirked.

Without another word, he shut the door and strode toward the front desk window.

A woman behind the glass looked up as he approached.

"Can I help you?" she asked.

David met her gaze.

"I'm here to make a citizen's arrest."

Her eyes widened slightly.

"Is the person here?"

"Yes," David confirmed. "But I'd like an officer's help in bringing her inside."

"*Her?*" she asked.

David nodded.

The woman studied him for a moment, as if trying to gauge whether he was serious.

David didn't waver.

Finally, she asked, "Sir, what's your name?"

He hesitated.

Before he could respond, an officer stepped up to the window.

"Is there a problem here?" the officer asked, his gaze sharp.

David kept his voice steady.

"Not at all."

The officer stared him down, suspicion flickering in his eyes.

"So, what's your name?" he asked again, his tone firmer this time.

David felt the weight of the moment settle over him.

He hesitated. But answered quickly.

"I'm David. Now, am I going to get help here or not?"

The officer folded his arms, eyeing him.

"David, *huh?*"

Before David could respond, another officer approached from behind.

"You wanna come with me?" the second officer asked, his tone unreadable.

David sized him up.

"Where to, Officer?"

The officer smirked slightly.

"We just want to have a little chat, is all."

David noticed the first officer, now standing beside him, clearly trying to intimidate him.

Stay calm.

Keeping his voice steady, David said,

"I'm here on a citizen's arrest. I have a prisoner in my car outside."

One officer scoffed.

"Oh yeah? And who's your prisoner?" His tone dripped with sarcasm.

David's jaw tightened.

"*Look,* I told you my name. What's yours?"

The first officer squared his shoulders.

"I'm Officer Andrews."

The second officer, still watching David closely, added,

"I'm Detective Marquez. So again, who's your prisoner?"

David met his gaze.

"Andrea Perez. I found her sleeping on my porch."

Detective Marquez shot a glance at Officer Andrews, then asked,

"Is your car locked?"

"Yes," David replied.

"Which car is it?" Marquez pressed.

David took a slow breath.

"I'll unlock the door."

He turned toward the exit, but Officer Andrews stepped in front of him.

His eyes narrowed.

"What's going on?" David asked, tension rising in his gut.

Just then, another officer approached.

Detective Marquez didn't take his eyes off David.

"David, we believe you may be involved in a crime."

His tone was measured but firm.

"The officers will escort you to an interview room. You're not under arrest, just detained."

David's jaw tightened.

"What crime?"

Marquez offered a vague smile.

"We'll discuss that with you. But right now, we need your car keys. We'll bring them back to you shortly."

David hesitated.

"It's the dark blue sedan, *just outside the door."*

He didn't like this.

But refusing would only make things worse.

Reluctantly, he handed the keys to Officer Andrews.

A woman in plain clothes approached them.

She introduced herself as Detective Janowski, then leaned in to whisper with Detective Marquez. David couldn't make out what they were saying.

He turned his head just in time to see Officer Andrews escorting Andrea down the opposite hall, toward the booking room.

She glanced back and *glared* at him.

It was a glare unlike anything David had ever seen before.

Something cold, almost inhuman, radiated from her stare.

That glare alone made David *damn* grateful she was no longer free. He wasn't sure what kind of danger he might be in if she were.

Detective Marquez placed a hand on David's upper arm. "Let's go."

Without another word, the detectives escorted him down the hall.

———— ◈ ————

Two Hours Later, David sat in a stark, windowless room; the fluorescent lights above him buzzing faintly.

Across the table, Detective Marquez and Detective Janowski leaned forward, their gazes fixed on him. And for two long hours, they had fired off the same questions. Over and over. Poking, prodding, waiting for him to slip.

Now, Marquez folded his hands, his voice cool.

"Are you ready to tell us what really happened, the truth?"

David exhaled slowly, then leaned back in his chair.

"I don't know what happened." His tone was even. Unshaken.

"I wasn't there."

Yet, in his mind, he knew he had been.

Detective Janowski leaned forward, eyes locked onto his.

"Two officers have identified you as the one who kicked a weapon from an officer's hand to help Andrea Perez escape."

Her voice was steady, almost disappointed.

"Frankly, we're surprised. You were present at the accident and fully cooperated with the police, so why would you help her escape, and even assist in subduing the officers?"

David scoffed.

"It *wasn't* me. So, if you're going to arrest me, then do it."

His gaze sharpened.

"I don't understand how your officers claim to have identified me. I hadn't seen Andrea until she showed up on my doorstep this morning. Why would I bring her in if I was trying to help her? It just doesn't add up, does it?"

Inside, he seethed.

God, I'm lying through my teeth!

Detective Marquez studied him for a long moment before speaking.

"Both officers claim that when you appeared, they heard Andrea say, 'It's David.'"

He paused, letting the weight of the statement settle.

"Why would she say that?"

Because it was me, David thought.

But his expression didn't waver.

Instead, he leaned back slightly and said coolly,

"Detective, you'll have to ask her. But good luck with that. We all know there's something off about her."

Then, with deliberate calm, he asked,

"If you're not arresting me, am I still being detained?"

Detective Janowski exhaled.

"Just a few more questions."

David's mind raced. It was time to pull *the chief card.*

Todd Edmonds.

Chief of Police, Gilson PD.

Before Janowski could continue, David cut in.

"I'd like to speak with Chief Edmonds, please."

The two detectives exchanged a look.

A silent conversation passed between them.

Then Marquez smirked slightly.

"That's not how it works here."

David locked eyes with him, unwavering.

"He'll want to talk to me. Ask him."

Chief Edmonds agreed to see David, who insisted they speak privately in his office, away from the recorded interview rooms.

As soon as the door shut, David offered a confident smile.

"Chief Edmonds, I appreciate you taking the time to see me. You understand why your detectives are grilling me, don't you?"

The chief studied him for a moment.

"I do."

David leaned forward slightly.

"Well, you also know that I turned Andrea in this morning under a citizen's arrest, right?"

Chief Edmonds leaned back in his chair, folding his arms.

"Yes, I'm aware."

David exhaled, keeping his voice smooth.

"They claim two of your officers can identify me as helping Andrea escape, which, of course, is absurd. Don't you think?"

He paused, watching for a reaction.

"They say Andrea called him 'David.' Well, I'm not the only David in this town. And from what I understand, it was dark."

He let that sink in before continuing.

"So tell me, do you really believe they can positively identify me? Is there any other evidence?"

Leaning back, he allowed a smug smile to play on his lips.

Chief Edmonds narrowed his eyes, clearly unimpressed with David's calculated reasoning.

After a long pause, he said,

"The only reason I agreed to talk to you is because your grandfather was a friend of mine."

"Yes, I know," David said, completely unfazed.

He leaned forward again, keeping his gaze locked on the chief.

"I figured you to be a man of reason. Call your detectives off; there's no evidence I was there."

His stare remained unwavering.

An awkward silence stretched between them before Chief Edmonds finally exhaled.

"Okay." His voice was clipped. "But if they find evidence, I won't stop them. And let's be clear, I'm only doing this because of your grandfather. Nothing else."

His patience was wearing thin.

"Now, leave my office. And don't think for a second you can come to me for favors."

David remained seated.

Edmonds' jaw tightened.

"I said *leave*," he barked.

Still, David didn't move. Instead, he calmly replied.

"I will. But first, I need a favor."

Chief Edmonds scoffed, shaking his head in disbelief.

"Another favor? Are you kidding me? Get out."

David smirked.

"You said you were only doing this because of my grandfather. But let's be honest, calling off your detectives isn't a favor."

He held the chief's gaze.

"You're doing it because you know there's no evidence."

His voice was calm. Deliberate.

"The favor I'm asking for... is as a friend of my grandfather."

Chief Edmonds' expression hardened.

"No. Don't pull this shit on me, boy," he snapped, anger flashing in his eyes.

David didn't flinch. His gaze darkened as he leaned in slightly.

"My grandfather wasn't just a friend," he said, voice low and measured.

"You did business together, and you know it. You did big favors for him."

Edmonds shifted in his seat, visibly uneasy.

His jaw clenched.

How much does this kid actually know?

Finally, he exhaled sharply.

"What kind of favor?"

David didn't hesitate.

"I want to visit the man in jail who's accused of helping Andrea escape."

Chief Edmonds' eyebrows furrowed.

"Now, why would you want to see him? Do you know him?" His tone was accusatory, eyes narrowing.

David smirked, unfazed.

"Nothing nefarious, Chief. I just want to have a simple conversation with the man who tried to help my demon mother escape."

He shrugged casually.

"I want to ask him how he knows her and why he would risk helping her."

Then, in one fluid motion, David stood from his chair, leaning forward with both hands planted firmly on the desk, his voice dropped: controlled, deliberate.

"Don't forget, Chief. I just buried my little sister the other day. All because of Andrea. Don't you think I deserve *this*?"

A muscle in Edmonds' jaw twitched. His face flushed red.

A tense silence hung between them before he finally exhaled sharply.

"Just this once. But I'll have them post a detention officer—"

David cut him off smoothly.

"No detention officers. They can watch from afar, but I don't want them standing around."

A flicker of irritation crossed the Chief's face. But David had already won.

With a gruff sigh, Edmonds picked up the phone.

"Get me the jail," he muttered, waving David away dismissively.

David nodded in acknowledgment and left the office.

As he walked down the hall toward the jail, he passed the detectives, flashing them a smug smile.

But the moment he turned the corner, his expression faded. Disgust churned in his gut.

He hated playing this game.

Twisting words.

Pushing buttons.

"I'm not *that kind* of person," he muttered under his breath.

But deep down, he knew the truth.

He had to be that person, at least for now.

Because whatever it took, he was going to see Josh.

———◦———

At the jail, a detention officer unlocked Josh's cell.

Josh lay stretched out on the bottom bunk, a book in his hands.

"Five minutes," the officer said before stepping a few yards away, keeping an eye on them but staying out of earshot.

Josh glanced up, pleasantly surprised.

David winked, a silent cue.

Josh caught it and gave a subtle nod in return.

David folded his arms, adopting a casual stance.

"So, you're the one who helped her escape?" His voice was deliberate, just loud enough for prying ears.

Then, in a quick, hushed tone, he added,

"I found a weird mirror in my jacket pocket. Would you know anything about that?"

Josh didn't miss a beat.

Just as loudly he replied,

"Yeah, I helped her."

Then, lowering his voice, he muttered,

"It's probably the mirror Tanya gave us to return. Molly lost it that night, so Sonya used her crystal necklace to activate the portal."

David's mind raced, but before he could process it, a detention officer passed by.

Keeping up appearances, David said at a casual volume,

"So, how did you meet her?"

Then, in a whisper,

"I'll be back tomorrow. I'll try to sneak the mirror in. You need to get home."

Josh's eyes widened slightly.

David didn't give him time to dwell.

"I hope you know how to work it."

Josh met his gaze, steady now.

"I do."

"Time's up," the detention officer announced, unlocking the cell door.

David gave a brief nod.

"Thanks for the information."

Then, without another word, he turned and walked out.

Josh watched him go before climbing back onto the bunk. He picked up his book, but his mind was racing.

He hoped David would bring the mirror.

This Earth was hell.

That awful red sky.

But how was David planning to bring a mirror in here?

And more importantly, how did the mirror end up in David's pocket in the first place?

He didn't have to wonder for long.

A slow grin spread across his face.

Sonya.

Who else?

The next morning, David made two phone calls.

The first was to Rachel. She was home from the hospital, recuperating.

Hearing she was doing well brought him a sense of relief.

The second was to Connie.

Once the calls were made, he gathered the girls.

They headed out the door, climbed into the car, buckled their seatbelts, and settled in.

David started the engine and pulled away, his mind already focused on *what lay ahead.*

"Where are we going, Dad?" Paula asked.

"Yeah, Daddy, where are we going?" Daphne chimed in.

David smiled but kept his eyes on the road.

"Girls, I promised. I'll explain when we get there."

The girls exchanged curious glances but didn't press further.

A few minutes later, David pulled into the parking lot and switched off the engine.

The girls looked around, confused.

"Dad, why are we at the police department?" Paula asked, frowning.

David turned in his seat, meeting the eyes of all three girls.

Clearing his throat, he said carefully,

"I just found out that I have a cousin."

Daphne's brow furrowed. "A cousin?"

David nodded.

"He's part of our family, and I'd like to take you girls to meet him."

Paula's eyes widened.

"And he's here? At the police department?"

David chuckled lightly.

"Yes, he's in jail."

Three sets of eyes stared at him in shock.

Before they could react, he added,

"But he's only there because he tried to help someone the police were after. He didn't know how serious the situation was, and when he tried to leave, they caught him. It was all a misunderstanding. He shouldn't be in jail. I want to help him get home."

The girls remained quiet, absorbing his words.

Paula tilted her head.

"What's his name?"

David smiled slightly.

"His name is Josh. You girls can call him Uncle Josh."

Delilah's face lit up.

"Okay, let's go meet Uncle Josh!" she exclaimed, eyes sparkling with excitement.

David's expression turned serious.

"Not just yet. I have more to tell you."

The girls immediately sat up straighter, their full attention on him.

"When we go in, I have to speak with a man. You girls will wait in the lobby, and I expect you to be on your best behavior."

He hesitated before continuing.

"There might be some... disagreements, but I need you to do as I say. No questions."

A brief pause.

He wasn't sure how to explain the next part.

Finally, he outlined the plan. The girls nodded, agreeing to follow along.

Inside the Police Station, the lobby was stale and uninviting, the overhead lights buzzing faintly.

David led the girls to a row of chairs.

"Stay here," he instructed.

With that, he strode toward the reception window.

The same woman sat behind the glass, her expression shifting the moment she saw him.

She knew who he was.

"Can I help you?" she asked.

David nodded.

"I'd like to speak with Chief Edmonds, *please.*"

The woman's eyebrows lifted slightly.

"Do you have an appointment?"

A pang of reluctance hit him.

He didn't like lying.

Didn't like manipulating.

But he knew it had to be done.

"Yes, I do," he said smoothly.

She didn't look convinced.

"Just a minute."

Picking up the phone, she turned slightly, speaking in low tones.

David couldn't make out the conversation.

After a moment, she covered the receiver and asked,

"What is your name?"

David held her gaze.

"Tell him I'm Felipe Costa's grandson."

A beat.

"David."

His voice was calm, controlled.

But he knew full well he didn't actually have an appointment.

"Sir, I'm sorry, but the Chief doesn't have an appointment scheduled with you today," she said, her tone firm but polite.

David grinned.

"Could you tell him I'll only take a few minutes? And that it's *important* business."

She hesitated, then resumed her conversation on the phone.

David couldn't hear the details, but he didn't need to.

He knew the chief would reconsider.

Chapter 31

The chief stormed into the lobby, his face contorted with fury. He fixed his gaze on David, who sat calmly with three young girls.

Rising from his chair, David smiled.

"These are my daughters. Girls, say hello to the Chief."

In unison, the girls greeted him with sweet smiles.

The chief, uncertain of what to think, attempted a smile but only managed a slight curve of his lips.

"Hello," he said, his tone cautious, then turning to David with a questioning look.

"What do you want to talk to me about?" the chief asked aloud, crossing his arms over his chest.

"Not here. In your office?" David replied, a smirk tugging at his lips.

The chief shot him a fiery glare, anger flaring in his eyes, trying to intimidate. But instead, he exhaled sharply and gestured toward the door.

"Let's step outside."

They moved away from the entrance, the red sky hidden beneath a thick layer of clouds. Both men glanced around, ensuring no one was within earshot before speaking.

"Whatever you have to say, get to the point. I don't have time for this," the chief barked.

David didn't hesitate.

"I want to visit Mr. Coleman."

The chief narrowed his eyes, tilting his head.

"Mr. Coleman?" His voice dripped with suspicion.

David remained silent.

The chief's gaze sharpened.

"Is that his name? Coleman?"

"Yes," David replied coolly.

The chief studied him, searching for any sign of deception.

"How do you know? Did he tell you his name?"

He was fishing, trying to manipulate David into revealing what he knew about the man they were holding in jail.

David met his gaze without flinching.

"I found out he's related to me, a cousin." A pause. "I brought my daughters to meet him."

Chief Edmonds' expression darkened with fury, his face twisting in rage.

"Are you shitting me? Why the hell would you bring children to meet that loser? And what makes you think you have the right to visit him, much less bring your daughters?"

David kept his composure.

"No, I'm *not* shitting you. I told you. I brought my daughters because he's family. That's something we don't have much of around here anymore. And I think you'll want to do me this favor."

The chief bristled, his anger boiling over.

"No! Absolutely not. I told you not to come to me for any more favors."

He waved a dismissive hand and turned to walk away.

David couldn't let him go. He *needed* to see Josh.

As Chief Edmonds strode off, David raised his voice just enough to be heard.

"Todd Edmonds... ahem, I mean Chief Edmonds. I heard you acquired a few cows to graze on all that land. And a new horse."

The chief halted mid-step. His shoulders stiffened before he slowly turned back to face David. His eyes burned with suspicion.

"And what's it to you?" he asked, his tone edged with warning.

"Well, let's just say I know about a certain business deal between you and my grandfather," David said, a slow grin spreading across his face.

Chief Edmonds' expression darkened, shifting between anger and appre-hension.

"And what exactly do you *think* you know about it?"

"I don't think. I *know*," David countered smoothly.

"I know the terms of the deal. I know it was carried out. My grandfather waived the lease fee for one year on the eight acres you'd been leasing from him. But then he died four months later... and you haven't paid a dime since."

He tilted his head slightly, feigning curiosity.

"Hmm... what's it been now? Seven... eight years? That's quite a sum owed to the Costa Family Trust."

David had no way of knowing for sure whether Chief Edmonds had been making payments, but the flicker of panic in the chief's eyes told him everything he needed to know; he was onto something.

Edmonds narrowed his eyes, then scoffed, masking his unease with arrogance.

"That's none of your business. That's between me and Bridgette Costa."

David arched a brow, letting the silence stretch.

"Why my Aunt Bridgette? I'm the trustee of the Costa Family Trust. But you wouldn't know that, would you? Since you never bothered to contact me to make payments."

Chief Edmonds' eyes widened slightly.

"You're the trustee?"

"The one and only. Besides," David said confidently, "I'm sure you know my aunt's been missing for some years now?"

Edmonds clenched his jaw, his irritation evident.

"What do you want from me?" he asked, his voice tight with anger, hating that David now had the upper hand.

"Now we're talking," David replied smugly. He was just about to manipulate this man again.

His conscience pricked at him with a pang of guilt.

But it had to be done.

He had learned these tactics from his grandmother, Julia; he'd watched her outmaneuver people without a shred of remorse. And then there was Andrea. She hadn't raised him, but in the few times he was around her, she always seemed ready to use people for her own benefit.

It's disgusting, he thought. *And yet, here I am, about to do the same.*

Chief Edmonds stood silently, waiting for David to continue.

"You let me and my daughters visit Mr. Coleman," David said, his voice steady, "and I'll consider forgetting about the back payments you owe."

Suspicious, Chief Edmonds narrowed his eyes.

"Hmm... why do you need to see him so badly that you're willing to forget thousands of dollars?"

David chuckled.

"It'd cost me about that much to pay my attorney. And trust me, I will if I have to."

He let that sink in before adding.

"And don't forget, I know what the deal was between you and my grandfather, Felipe."

He paused, then met the chief's gaze.

"I'll admit, I'm not proud of my grandfather for being part of the..." His voice trailed off. "Dirty deed."

David studied him closely, watching for any reaction.

In truth, he didn't know exactly what the deal was, but knowing his grandfather and knowing he had waived lease fees for a year, David was certain it was something underhanded.

After his grandfather died, he had come across Felipe's notes about the lease while helping Aunt Bridgette pack up his things. It was enough to piece together that something wasn't right.

David refocused on the chief.

"So, do we have a deal?"

"Are you trying to blackmail me?" the chief asked, eyes narrowing as he attempted to intimidate him.

David chuckled.

"I wouldn't call it blackmail. It's more like something for something, you know, quid pro quo."

Chief Edmonds exhaled sharply.

"I don't see how I can let you visit him and bring your daughters without raising questions from my staff."

"Simple," David said smoothly.

"Have one of your officers bring Mr. Coleman out of his cell and into the visiting area. Use two of your most trusted men, the ones who won't question you."

The chief folded his arms, unconvinced.

"I don't buy it. I don't believe your only motive is for your girls to meet some long-lost cousin. What are you really up to?"

His voice was laced with suspicion.

David held his ground.

"Calm down. You're the one who benefits the most from this deal. When I told my daughters they had a family member here, they were excited to meet him. I'm not about to let them down."

He shrugged.

"So yeah, to me, the deal is worth it."

The chief fell silent, lost in thought.

David recognized the hesitation and wisely chose not to interrupt.

Chief Edmonds knew David was up to something, and he didn't like it. But then greed settled in. If he agreed, he wouldn't have to repay the back fees. His shady deal with Felipe would remain buried.

And really, what choice did he have?

He hated being in this position.

"Fine," he said at last. "I'll allow it. But I need two things from you."

His voice carried an authoritative edge, an attempt to maintain control, to make it seem like he was the one dictating terms.

But they both knew better.

David tilted his head slightly.

"What?"

"One, you keep your mouth shut about my dealings with Felipe. Two, since your Mr. Coleman has refused to identify himself, I want his full name and where he's from."

David nodded.

"I won't say a word about your dealings. And as for Coleman, the only thing I've learned is that his name is Josh Coleman. He's from Nebraska."

He saw no harm in revealing this much.

Soon, none of it would matter.

Once he handed Josh the mirror, the portal would open, and Josh would be gone. These people would never see him again.

Chief Edmonds studied him for a moment, then gave a firm nod.

"You and your daughters will be searched before you go in."

David's expression darkened.

"They can search me, but no one is laying a hand on my daughters," he warned.

His voice was calm but edged with steel.

"I would never put them in danger. They aren't armed."

"Five minutes. That's all you're getting. This is very risky for me," Chief Edmonds said.

He continued.

"Coleman will be brought into the visiting area, but he stays behind bars. I'll have two detention officers present, and—"

David cut him off.

"No. I don't want them too close. They can watch from the corner of the room."

The chief scoffed.

"You expect me to let you into the visiting room without proper supervision?"

He narrowed his eyes.

"Do you realize how suspicious your demands sound?"

David held his ground.

"Fine. You can have your guards inside, but they don't hover around my girls," he said firmly.

Chief Edmonds gave a sharp nod.

"And Coleman stays behind bars."

David exhaled.

"Agreed."

They walked back inside.

In the lobby, the girls sat quietly in their chairs.

Delilah had a small purse strapped over her shoulder, decorated with images of a popular cartoon cat. She and Daphne busied themselves with tiny, palm-sized dolls, their fingers moving absently over the plastic figures. Nearby, Paula held up a compact mirror, pretending to apply lipstick, though the lipstick itself was just a molded piece of plastic.

In truth, they felt ridiculous.

Embarrassed, even.

These were toys meant for much younger children.

But this was part of the plan they had worked out with their father in the parking lot.

They weren't about to let him down.

So they played their roles perfectly.

The chief walked toward the secured doors while David remained in the lobby with the girls.

"You're doing great," he said, keeping his voice low. "Keep playing."

Then, lowering his tone even further, he added,

"When we go in to see Josh, there's going to be some strange smoke. I think it'll be blue. Don't be alarmed. It's normal. Part of the plan. Okay?"

Paula's brows furrowed.

"Smoke? Will there be a fire?"

"No, just smoke… well, more like a blue haze. At least, that's what I was told," David reassured her.

Daphne glanced up at him, curiosity flickering in her eyes.

"Why will it be there? What does it do?"

David placed a steady hand on her small shoulder.

"I was told it might make people feel a little dizzy and groggy at first, but then it passes."

Before they could ask any more questions, Chief Edmonds strode back into the lobby with an officer at his side.

He gestured for them to follow.

David watched as the girls quickly stashed their dolls, compact mirror, and fake lipstick into Delilah's small purse before rising to their feet.

They followed the officer down a dim hallway and into an interview room. Chief Edmonds turned to them.

"Officer Tejeda will lead you to the visiting area," he said, then fixed his gaze on David.

"But first, he'll search you."

David gave a small nod. He had expected this.

The officer patted him down as the girls exchanged confused glances.

"Daddy, why..." Delilah started, but David quickly raised a finger to his lips, silencing her with a subtle gesture.

"It's called a search," he said calmly. "Nothing to worry about."

"She won't be bringing that purse in. She'll have to set it right here," Officer Tejeda said, his tone firm but not unkind.

David turned to Chief Edmonds, a hint of frustration in his voice.

"Come on, they're just kids. The toys are harmless. You've seen them. It keeps them preoccupied."

Chief Edmonds glanced at Officer Tejeda, then gave him a slight nod.

Once the search was complete, Officer Tejeda led them to another door, not the one they had entered from.

They followed him through a series of hallways and locked doors, the sterile atmosphere of the facility pressing in around them.

Chapter 32

F inally, they arrived at the visiting area.

Three chairs were arranged in front of a set of bars. On the other side sat a single chair, meant for the inmate.

The officer gestured for them to sit. It was clear these seats had been set just for them.

David discreetly scanned the room, noting Officer Tejeda's position. Across from him, another officer stood watch, stationed on the opposite side.

Subtly, David gave the girls their cue.

Slowly, they pulled out their dolls, the fake plastic lipstick, and the small mirror, but this time, the mirror wasn't the same one from the lobby.

Paula knew to be careful. She had been instructed not to touch the glass. She handled it exactly as David had told her.

David's plan was simple: the girls would appear to be playing so that the officers, and the Chief, wouldn't question the mirror in Paula's hand.

One of the officers stepped forward, ready to confiscate the purse and its contents. But before he could, Officer Tejeda gave a slight shake of his head.

Leave it alone.

Just then, Josh was led into the room.

His posture was stiff, expression unreadable, as he walked to the chair behind the bars. The escorting officer followed, securing one of Josh's wrists to the armrest before stepping back. Dressed in pale gray jail garb, Josh sat still, his eyes scanning the group seated across from him until they landed on the three little girls beside David.

"Yours?" Josh asked, his voice quiet, almost disbelieving.

"Yes," David answered.

Then, Josh's gaze shifted, landing on the mirror.

David knew exactly what he was looking at.

"We only have five minutes," he murmured.

Josh met his gaze, tense, as if silently asking, *how are you going to get it to me?*

David scooted his chair slightly closer to the bars that separated them. The girls did the same, their eyes fixed on him with quiet anticipation.

———◆———

Meanwhile, back at the Chief's office, Chief Edmonds had assigned someone to dig into the Costa Family Trust, and someone else to investigate a Josh or Joshua Coleman in Nebraska.

The results came back quickly.

There were four males by that name in Nebraska.

Two were in their seventies. One was in his twenties. And the last was a five-year-old child.

The one in his twenties was of African descent.

Just then, the Chief's phone rang. He snatched it up.

"Yes? What did you find out?"

A moment later, he shot up from his chair, his face contorted in fury.

"Are you sure?" he barked into the receiver.

Slamming the phone down, he immediately picked it back up and punched in another number.

"Send Wade and Angie to my office, *now!*" he snapped, his voice sharp and unwavering.

Officers Wade Huynh and Angie Weldon rushed into the office.

Chief Edmonds rose from his chair. His expression darkened.

"Follow me. We're taking someone in," he ordered.

Without hesitation, they hurried out the door, making their way toward the visiting area.

Edmonds' fury simmered just beneath the surface; his suspicions had just been confirmed.

This so-called Josh Coleman from Nebraska didn't exist.

And David Costa?

He wasn't the trustee of the Costa Family Trust. He never had been. That role still belonged to Bridgette Costa.

David had pulled one over on him.

But not for long.

He wasn't getting away with this.

"What are we charging him with?" Wade asked, brows furrowed.

Chief Edmonds shot him a sharp look.

"We'll think of something," he said, dismissively.

The Chief knew David knew too much.

So, he had other plans for David, permanent ones.

Then, turning to Angie, he added,

"His three young kids are with him. I need you to get them out of there as soon as we arrive."

Angie's eyes widened in surprise.

"Children? In the visiting area?"

Chief Edmonds raised an eyebrow, a silent warning not to question it.

In the visiting area, his pulse pounded in his ears.

They had one shot at this.

David introduced the twins to Josh, doing his best to keep his voice steady.

"This is Paula," he said, nodding toward his eldest.

Paula glanced at David, seeking reassurance.

David gave her a small, encouraging nod.

She stepped forward, her expression calm, but her fingers trembled slightly as she slid her hand through the bars to shake Josh's.

"No shaking hands," Officer Tejeda barked.

All eyes flicked to him.

"Oh, we didn't know that," David said quickly, his tone light and casual.

The girls echoed him with innocent expressions.

It was all part of the distraction, just as he'd instructed.

Paula moved fast.

With a flick of her wrist, she slid the mirror from her sleeve. Pressed it into Josh's palm.

She followed the plan *to the letter*, just as David had drilled into them.

Josh clenched his fingers around the small object, barely breathing.

Heart hammering, he let the mirror slip from his grip, dropping it onto his lap.

With a controlled motion, he pressed his thighs together, trapping it between them.

David swallowed hard, forcing himself to stay calm.

He could feel sweat trickling down his back.

Across from him, Josh looked composed, but David knew better.

He was sweating too.

Then, the worst happened.

The detention officer behind Josh shifted.

His eyes narrowed.

Had he seen?

The officer took a step forward, boots heavy against the floor.

"Open your hands," he ordered.

Josh obeyed, lifting his cuffed wrist and holding the other palm open and still.

The officer's gaze lingered.

Then, with a grunt, he stepped back, seemingly satisfied.

David let out a slow breath.

Too close.

Then, BANG!

The door to the visiting area slammed open, striking the wall with a jarring crack.

The officers in the room snapped into defense mode, hands shifting toward their weapons, until they saw who it was.

⸺◆⸺

Chief Edmonds stormed in, his glare locking onto David with the heat of a firestorm.

David's stomach dropped.

Angie stepped forward, her voice firm and commanding.

"Girls, come with me."

David shot to his feet, and the girls instinctively clung to him, their small fingers digging into his shirt.

The air in the room shifted.

The officers braced.

David could see it, the tightening of shoulders, the subtle movements, the weight shifting onto the balls of their feet.

They were about to take him down.

He flicked a quick glance at Josh, then rolled his eyes downward.

A silent command.

Now.

Josh swallowed hard, pulse hammering as he understood the signal.

"Girls, we just want to talk to your dad," Wade said, his voice smooth but firm. "Let go of him, and this nice officer will take you to get some hot chocolate."

The girls didn't move.

They clung to David even tighter.

Josh barely registered the exchange; his focus was locked on Chief Edmonds, just as the Chief gave a subtle nod to the detention officer behind him.

Shit.

They were about to drag him back to his cell.

The officer stepped forward, keys jingling as he reached for Josh's cuff.

Josh didn't resist. He let the officer unlock it. Waited. Timed it just right.

The moment the metal restraint loosened, before the officer could tighten his grip to guide him back...

Now!

Josh's hand shot down, grabbing the mirror from between his thighs.

With a sharp inhale, he sprang from the chair, ignoring the startled shouts behind him.

He lifted the mirror, tapped the glass with his finger, then dragged it downward in one smooth motion.

For a heartbeat, nothing happened.

Then...

A shimmering blue haze crackled across the surface.

The air *shifted.* The atmosphere *thickened.*

The officers hesitated, eyes widening as the unnatural glow spread outward.

No turning back now.

Angie pried at the girls' hands, trying to loosen their desperate grip on David.

Meanwhile, Wade clamped a firm hold on David's upper arm, ready to haul him away.

David's pulse pounded in his ears. His head throbbed as he flicked a glance over his shoulder.

The blue haze was expanding—thick, electric, alive.

He stepped back, pressing closer to the bars.

They needed to be near Josh if they were going to get out of this.

It was the only way.

Across the room, chaos erupted.

The detention officer wrestled with Josh, yanking at his arm to drag him back to his cell.

Josh, still recovering from the gunshot wound in his shoulder, gritted his teeth and resisted, muscles coiled with urgency. Then, with a sudden surge of strength, he drove his fist into the officer's jaw. The man dropped instantly.

Another officer rushed in. Skidded to a stop. Eyes wide with terror at the swirling haze.

He hesitated, fear overriding duty.

Josh pressed against the bars, trying to get as close to David and the girls as possible.

The portal churned like a living storm.

The girls panicked, their screams cutting through the air.

"It won't hurt you!" David reassured them, though his own heart raced.

Angie yanked Daphne away from the haze, ripping her small arm free just in time.

Daphne let out a *bloodcurdling scream.* David's instincts roared to life.

Frantic, he shoved Paula and Delilah against the bars, shielding them as he stepped out of the haze.

Instinctively, Josh grabbed the girls by the shoulders through the bars to keep them close.

The officers stood frozen, eyes darting between each other, their expressions screaming the same question: *What the hell is happening?*

The swirling blue mist thickened. Twisted like a vortex.

"David! Get back in!" Josh shouted.

Angie, convinced she was saving Daphne from some kind of unknown horror, dragged her farther away.

The little girl's terrified wails tore through David's chest. *Enough.*

David lunged, grabbing Angie's wrist in a vice grip. His fingers dug in, forcing her to release Daphne.

The portal was closing. Wade moved fast, lunging to grab David just as he yanked Daphne into his arms.

Too late.

David ripped free of Wade's grasp and threw himself into the haze with Daphne, just as the shimmering portal snapped shut behind them.

Silence crashed into the room like a thunderclap. Chief Edmonds and his officers stood there, unmoving, staring at the empty space where, just seconds ago, David, Josh, and the girls had been.

They were gone.

Chapter 33

Blue Earth 2018–January, Ridgefield, Nebraska

Andri

It had been two weeks since everything happened, but the weight of it still pressed down on us.

Coming home without Josh was a devastation none of us were prepared for.

Molly and I carried the unbearable truth: he had been shot before we crossed the portal.

We didn't know if he had survived, and we made a silent agreement not to tell Leanne.

It's bad enough to know he's trapped on Red Earth, but for her to think he might be dead would break her completely.

Grief had become our shadow, stretching long over the days and settling into every quiet moment.

We had spent two weeks mourning, drowning in sorrow. Yet somehow, life kept moving.

We knew we had to find a way to do the same.

But today was no different than the days before: tears, exhaustion, and the hollow ache of loss.

All of us felt it.

Except for Mom.

She drifted in and out of her own world, untouched by the weight we carried.

Maybe that was a mercy.

My brother Joe is flying in from California today.

Normally, his visits were something to look forward to, something that pulled us together.

But today, it was just another day soaked in grief, the kind that doesn't fade, but instead settles deeper into your bones.

The night we came home, without Josh, I called Joe.

We explained everything. Of course, he didn't believe me at first.

Who would?

But Leanne and Molly confirmed it, and Joe, knowing what he knows about our family, understood.

He didn't ask many questions after that.

He just booked a flight and told us he was coming.

My brother Michael was out of the country, working on a project in Scotland.

We decided not to tell him about Josh until he returned to the States.

Besides, I doubt he would believe it anyway.

Molly sat curled in the corner of the couch, her arms wrapped tightly around her knees, rocking slightly, as if the motion might somehow undo what had happened.

Her eyes were red and swollen, dark circles beneath them, a testament to sleepless nights and restless thoughts.

I could see it in the way she clenched her jaw, in how her fingers dug into her arms.

She blamed herself.

She hadn't said it out loud.

But I knew.

I could hear it in the heavy silence that filled the room every time Molly exhaled.

The what-ifs were crushing her.

Maybe she could've convinced Josh not to go.

Maybe she could've stopped him.

Maybe if she'd been just a little braver, a little stronger... he'd still be here.

She was drowning in guilt, and I had no idea how to pull her out of it.

Leanne sat at the dining table, staring into a cup of tea as if it held all the answers she'd never find.

Her fingers traced the rim, slow and absentminded. Her face was blank, but her body was stiff.

She hadn't spoken in hours.

Her only child.

Her son.

The one she had raised, protected, and cherished, gone.

The worst part was the not knowing.

The thought that he might be stuck in that wretched world, never to see home again.

It hollowed her out, leaving behind nothing but the fragile shell of the woman she once was.

She'd asked me if Tanya, or her angel, Anio, could help bring him home.

But Tanya told me she couldn't. She had no way to reach him.

Still, Tanya remained hopeful.

She believed Josh would find his way back.

I knew Leanne was trying to stay strong, but the cracks were showing.

I wanted to tell her Josh was smart. That if anyone could find a way back, it was him.

But she wasn't ready to hear it.

Not yet.

Not while she was still lost in the worst kind of grief, the kind without closure.

Nora sat across from Leanne, her thin hands resting lightly on the table.

She hadn't said much, just watched us, her clouded eyes taking everything in.

And then, in a rare moment of clarity, she spoke.

"He will make his way home."

Leanne's head snapped up, her lips parting slightly. But she said nothing.

Molly wiped her eyes and sniffled. "Grandma..."

But Nora only smiled faintly, as if she knew something we didn't.

Then, just as quickly as the light had come, it faded, and she drifted back into her usual confusion.

I swallowed hard, unsure whether to believe the words she'd just spoken, or dismiss them as another one of her moments.

Lanix shifted near the doorway, his expression conflicted.

He had loved Josh, respected him. But more than anything, he hated seeing us like this broken, lost.

Clearing his throat hesitantly, he offered, "Can I get anyone something? Maybe some breakfast? Or coffee? Tea? Anything?"

His voice was soft, uncertain, like he didn't know whether comfort in such a small form even mattered.

No one answered.

The grief in the room was too thick to respond.

But I saw Leanne's tired nod.

I saw the way Molly briefly met his eyes before looking away.

Even in loss, Lanix was trying.

And that was more than most could do.

And then... there was me.

I had no words for the grief curling inside my chest.

No way to make sense of it.

Josh had gone there for me.

If it weren't for me, he wouldn't be trapped.

He'd be home. Safe. Living his life.

And David...

Sonya's words echoed in my mind:

You must come with us. This is not your real home. You belong with them. With your real family.

I wanted him to come with us. So badly.

But it was impossible.

He'd never leave his daughters. And I would never ask him to.

I had lost him.

Again.

The son I never got to hold.

The son I only found when it was too late.

And now... he was gone.

I squeezed my eyes shut, swallowing the sob clawing its way up my throat.

There was no fixing this.

No undoing what had been done.

The loss sat heavy in my bones, settling into places that would never feel whole again.

And then... there was Drew.

He hadn't answered my calls.

My texts went unread.

He wasn't even opening his door.

I didn't know what had happened, but whatever it was, it only compounded the weight of my already broken heart.

It had been two weeks, and I missed him more than I wanted to admit.

I stood at the kitchen window, staring out at nothing, lost in thought, not really seeing anything at all.

A sudden, bitter laugh snapped me back. I turned to see Leanne shaking her head, eyes fixed on her phone.

"What is it?" I asked, my voice hoarse.

She let out a short, humorless sound before tossing the phone onto the table.

"Patricia wasted no time moving on. She's already with someone new."

I frowned, picking up the phone. The picture was clear, Patricia, smiling and nestled close to another man, his arm draped possessively around her.

I blinked. "It's only been a couple of weeks."

Leanne snorted. "I suspect it's been a lot longer than that. Josh thought so too." Josh had loved her.

I didn't have the energy to be angry, but something twisted inside me.

He'd risked everything, for me, for his family.

And she... she had already moved on.

I set the phone down, exhaling slowly. "He deserved better."

Leanne nodded, her eyes darkened with shadow. "Yeah. He did."

And then I heard her cry, a hard, soul-piercing cry. "I want him back! I just want him to come home, Andri!" Her voice was loud. I got up from my chair and placed my hand on her shoulder and said, "I know...I know, me too." I felt so helpless. It was crushing. Molly walked over to Leanne and gave her a hug. Now both were crying on each other's shoulders.

Lanix ran to grab tissues for us.

And then Nora came up to us. With one hand, she clutched the silver cross at her neck, and with the other, she tapped each of us lightly on the crown of our heads and whispered:

"Que Nuestra Señora del Consuelo los abrace con su amor y les dé paz."

May Our Lady of Consolation embrace you with her love and give you peace. Her voice was soft, almost like a lullaby. The warmth in her tone said everything.

We heard a car pull up the driveway.

Joe was here.

Leanne and I walked to the door as he climbed the steps.

He didn't hesitate. Before he even reached us, he opened his arms wide.

Without a word, we both stepped into the hug, each taking a side, holding onto him like an anchor.

There was nothing to say.

No words could fix what had been broken.

I pulled away first, stepping aside to let him focus on Leanne.

She had lost her son. This moment belonged to her.

Joe wrapped his arms around her, holding her tightly, as if somehow, he could take away even a fraction of her pain.

When he finally stepped inside, he greeted Molly with a warm embrace, then moved to Mom, wrapping her fragile frame in his arms.

She blinked up at him, momentarily confused. Then she smiled, as if recalling something distant and beautiful.

The house was still heavy with grief, but for the first time in weeks, it felt like we weren't carrying it alone.

I offered Joe the guest bedroom in the basement.

"I'll get my bags out of the rental car and go down for a nap," he said, his voice thick with exhaustion.

I nodded. There wasn't much else to say.

As I walked into the kitchen, I paused, watching Lanix at the counter.

He was heating water, carefully placing a tea bag into a cup.

His small hands moved with quiet determination.

He turned and looked at me.

"Mom, does Grandma use sugar in her tea?"

I smiled at him, but inside, my heart sank.

He was trying so hard to be strong, for me, for all of us.

But he was just a child.

He shouldn't have to carry this.

Shouldn't be the one offering comfort while the rest of us were unraveling.

I swallowed the lump in my throat.

I had to get it together.

For him.

He didn't need another grieving soul.

He needed his mother.

I could be that.

I *would* be that.

The next morning, I woke to a bright, beautiful sunrise.

How can there be beauty shining on this house of sorrow? I wondered.

I got up, showered, got dressed, and walked into the living room.

Lanix was on the couch, watching TV.

"Have you had breakfast?" I asked.

"Molly made Grandma and me eggs and toast," he replied.

"Good. I'm going to the market for orange juice. Want to come along?"

Lanix barely looked up, his attention locked on the screen. "No, Mom. I'm watching my show, and..."

He lifted a tall glass. "I have my chocolate milk."

I smiled at his chocolate milk mustache.

And then I turned and walked out the door and headed straight to my car.

As I let the engine warm up, my mind drifted to Drew.

Instead of heading straight to the market, I found myself driving past his house.

I froze.

A *For Rent* sign stood on the lawn. What?

My heart lurched.

His truck was in the driveway. He was home.

Frowning, I pulled over to the curb and walked up to his front door.

I knocked.

No answer.

Chapter 34

I knocked again, harder this time. Louder.

Again and again until finally the door flew open.

Drew stood there, jaw clenched, his expression shadowed with anger.

"What do you want?"

I didn't hesitate. "You're renting your house? Are you moving?"

"That's the plan," he snapped, his voice sharp, laced with sarcasm.

I blinked, taken aback. "Are you... angry with me for some reason?"

His glare hardened, fury flashing in his eyes. "Are you kidding me right now? After everything you said and did that day, you're really standing here asking if I'm angry?"

Confusion tightened in my chest. "Drew, what exactly did I say or do?" I demanded.

"The last time I talked to you was the night I stayed over with you. You weren't angry. You weren't upset. You even texted me the next morning to make sure I got home okay."

I hesitated, pulse quickening. "I texted you on my way to Lincoln, and..."

My voice trailed off as his expression shifted.

The fury in his eyes flickered, turning wary. Confused.

He just stared at me, guarded now.

"Oh no," I murmured, more to myself than to him.

But he heard it.

"Oh no, *what?*" he snapped, his irritation sharpening.

I swallowed. "Drew..."

My throat tightened.

"I know I told you the last time I saw you was the night I stayed over. But when was the last time *you* saw me?" I asked, hesitant but firm.

Drew's eyes darkened. "Andri, don't play games with me. Do you even hear how fucking stupid this sounds right now?"

He let out a bitter laugh, shaking his head.

"Oh, and by the way, I went back to the hardware store. The one where you stole the knife."

My stomach dropped.

"I covered for you," he said through clenched teeth.

"I told old Craig you meant to buy it. That you had it in your hand and forgot. I said you asked me to come back and pay for it. I even apologized for the... so-called mistake."

That's when it hit me.

He had encountered *Andrea*.

God knows what she'd said. What she'd done.

She'd poisoned everything.

That bitch. I hoped, truly hoped, she was rotting in prison.

I looked up at him, my chest aching with regret. "Drew... I need to talk to you about something."

He tilted his head, narrowing his eyes. "Talk? About what?"

I saw it in his face. He was about to send me away. Shut the door. Cut me off.

Panic surged in my chest, and before I could stop myself, the truth tumbled out.

"I didn't steal the knife. And I wasn't the one you encountered."

His mouth parted slightly. The anger in his eyes morphed into disbelief.

Then came the laugh, sharp and humorless.

"Oh really? Then who was it? Your long-lost twin sister?"

The jab was deliberate. He didn't expect an answer. He was mocking me.

As Drew started to close the door, I shot my foot forward, wedging it in before he could shut me out.

He exhaled sharply, opening his mouth to say something, but I beat him to it.

"Yes."

I met his gaze, unwavering.

"A twin sister. Well... something like that."

Confusion deepened in his features, irritation giving way to uncertainty.

He straightened, posture rigid. His neck remained still, head locked forward, his eyes looked down at me, fixed on mine.

"Something like that?" he echoed, voice low, edged with suspicion. "Explain."

Good. At least he was listening, giving me a moment.

But how the hell was I supposed to explain something this insane?

I hesitated, scrambling for the right words. I could try to soften it, spin it, make it sound somewhat reasonable... but there was no reasonable way to say this.

And no matter how impossible it sounded, I couldn't lie.

I took a slow breath, bracing myself. "Drew, when I went to Lincoln... something happened to me."

No easing into it. Just say it.

"Let me start by saying what I'm about to tell you will sound unbelievable. Impossible."

His expression shifted, just slightly. A flicker of concern behind the guarded suspicion.

"Something happened to you?" he asked, his voice quieter now. "What kind of something?"

So I told him.

Everything.

Tanya. Mystic Crossroads.

Red Earth. Sonya. Anio.

Andrea. David.

All of it.

Drew didn't interrupt. But I could tell he wanted to, jaw tight, arms folded, knee bouncing in that barely perceptible way that only happens when someone's about to snap.

By the time I finished, we were sitting side by side on his porch chairs. The cold had crept in unnoticed. The kind of chill that settles deep, like grief.

I hadn't felt it until then.

Judging by his silence, he hadn't either.

I studied his face, searching for anything, disbelief, fear, mockery, something.

Would he ask questions? Call me insane? Tell me to get off his porch?

Instead, he just stared at me. Expression unreadable.

Like I'd just told him a bedtime story. And he was waiting for the part where it all made sense.

But this wasn't a story.

And there was no neat ending.

I waited.

At last, he spoke.

"Andri..."

His voice was careful. Deliberate.

"For as long as I've known you, I've never seen you act like this. And I've sure as hell never heard anything this outrageous."

He let out a sharp breath, shaking his head.

"You're right. What you just told me is impossible. Unbelievable."

He narrowed his eyes slightly.

"My question is... how the hell do you expect me to believe any of this?"

Something in me stirred: frustration, desperation, maybe both. I held his gaze.

"Look, I know how it sounds. But I'm telling you the truth."

My voice was steady, but raw.

"When have you ever known me to steal anything? A knife, of all things?"

I moved a bit closer.

"And whatever she, Andrea, said to you that day... did it sound like me?"

His expression flickered.

Just for a second.

Doubt.

I pressed on.

"That night, I told you I loved you... and I meant it. I still do."

I swallowed hard, willing him to see the truth in my eyes, feel it in every word.

"Drew, I don't know how to make you believe the impossible.

But if you come to my house, you'll see..."

My voice broke slightly.

"You'll see all of us. Grieving Josh. You'll see me grieving David. Losing him... again."

Nothing. Just silence.

I stood, hands clenched at my sides, and met his gaze one last time before turning away.

I walked to my car and didn't look back.

I had told him the truth. That was all I could do.

And yet... deep down, I wanted him to stop me. To pull me close. To hold me. But he didn't.

Because he didn't believe me.

⁕

The late afternoon sun hung low in the sky, casting golden light across the backyard. The scent of sizzling burgers filled the air as Joe stood over the grill, flipping patties with practiced ease. He hadn't said much about why he decided to cook, but we all knew. No one had been cooking much lately. Meals had become an afterthought, something to pick at, not prepare.

Joe, being Joe, had stepped in without a word.

"Burgers are almost done!" he called over his shoulder, forcing a bit of cheer into his voice. It was his way of lightening the mood, trying to pull us out of the fog of grief we'd been drowning in.

Next to him, Lanix watched closely, his small hands gripping the spatula as Joe guided him. "See, you want to press just a little, but not too much," Joe said, nodding toward the patty. "Otherwise, you lose all the good juices."

Lanix nodded seriously, mimicking Joe's movements as he flipped a burger. Joe grinned and gave him a pat on the back. "You're a natural, kiddo."

Molly set out the paper plates and plastic silverware on the folding table while I arranged the cans of soda and bottles of water. Leanne walked out of the house carrying a large container of potato salad, Joe's last-minute addition to the meal.

She set it down with a small nod. "Figured we needed something to go with the burgers."

Joe grinned. "See? Now it's a proper barbecue."

The conversation was light, casual, but I could feel the heaviness lingering beneath it all.

We were outside together, but still carrying the weight of loss.

The sounds of spatulas scraping, soda cans popping open, and the low murmur of voices filled the space between us.

It was almost normal. Almost.

Then we heard the sound of a vehicle pulling into the driveway.

A black pickup truck.

We all turned to look.

It was Drew.

I wasn't sure why he was here. Was he coming to say goodbye?

I braced for the blow.

As he stepped out of the truck, I walked toward him, meeting him halfway.

We both glanced around, instinctively making sure we were out of earshot.

He exhaled, rubbing the back of his neck before finally speaking.

"Andri, I don't know what to think about the... the explanation." His voice was hesitant, but not dismissive. "But what I do know is this..." He met my eyes. "The woman at the hardware store... the one who looked exactly like you, sounded like you, driving your car..." He shook his head. "That couldn't have been you."

He looked past me, his gaze settling on my family gathered around the patio. His expression softened.

"And seeing them now," he continued, "I can feel it. The grief. The sorrow. Whatever happened... I can see it was real."

I swallowed the lump in my throat and slowly reached out my hand. He hesitated only a moment before placing his hand in mine.

We didn't need words. We just stood there, holding hands, sharing a quiet understanding.

I smiled. "Come on, join us."

Hand in hand, we walked toward my family.

After we finished eating burgers, we sat around, talking and letting the evening settle around us.

Leanne began clearing the table, gathering plates and cups. She was just about to head inside to bring out dessert when...

The distant sound of tires crunching on gravel cut through the quiet.

A minivan rounded the circular path, rolling to a slow stop behind Drew's truck.

The driver's side door opened. Tanya stepped out.

Molly and I exchanged glances, confusion flickering across her face. What was she doing here?

Before I could fully process it, the passenger door swung open, and Josh stepped out, grinning.

For a split second, the world held still. Then everything else blurred into nothing but him.

The paper plate I'd been holding slipped from my hands, drifting to the ground in slow motion. The scent of burgers still lingered in the air, mixing with the crispness of the evening, but all I could see was him.

"Josh?" Leanne's voice cracked, barely above a whisper.

Then the moment shattered.

Leanne rushed forward, wrapping her arms around him before he could take another step. The sound she made was part sob, part laughter, as if she couldn't quite believe he was real.

Molly was next, gripping his arm, her face buried in his shoulder.

Joe clapped him on the back, murmuring something low and gruff, but the emotion in his voice was unmistakable.

Lanix hesitated at first, standing near the table, his hands fidgeting at his sides. Then, all at once, he darted forward and hugged Josh around the waist, holding on tightly.

"I knew you'd come back," he whispered.

Josh ruffled his hair and chuckled. "Of course, buddy. You didn't think I'd stay gone forever, did you?"

Nearby, Nora sat in her chair, watching with a soft, knowing smile. She didn't seem surprised. Didn't question what was happening. She simply opened her arms when Josh turned to her.

"Grandma," he murmured, kneeling beside her chair as she cradled his face in her hands.

"You came home," she said, her voice clear, as if for this moment all of her mind was present.

He leaned in, pressing a kiss to her temple before pulling her into a hug.

I stood there, breath caught somewhere between a sob and a prayer. My chest was tight, my heart pounding, trying to catch up with the impossible sight in front of me.

Our Josh.

Alive. Whole.

But just beyond him, something shifted in the corner of my vision.

Someone else.

A tall figure lingered near the minivan, standing slightly apart from the others. Watching. Waiting.

My heart stuttered.

David.

Time slowed again. The sounds faded to nothing but the rushing in my ears.

My son.

My boy.

But he wasn't alone.

Three girls stood beside him, hesitant but close, their eyes flicking between the chaos of Josh's reunion and me.

I didn't need anyone to tell me who they were.

My granddaughters.

My throat closed, my legs rooted to the ground. For so long, I had lost him, and now, here he was. With the daughters I only dreamed of seeing.

Around me, the family watched in silence, their joy quieting as they sensed the shift.

Josh turned back to us then, his smile faltering when he saw my expression. He glanced toward David, then back at me.

He gave a small nod. Not one of introduction, but of understanding.

With tears in my eyes and joy in my heart, I stepped forward.

Epilogue

It's been three months since Josh, David, and the girls came home. Those dark weeks of grief and despair have quickly been replaced with something else: happiness, love, and family.

Molly has adjusted well, all things considered. Josh's homecoming was her cure.

Josh and Patricia are no longer together, though he took it better than we expected.

He'd seen it coming, had already made peace with it before his journey.

Let's just say his nights haven't exactly been lonely.

Drew found a renter for his house, David, who now works as an assistant manager for a growing real estate brokerage.

And thanks to Anio, all the legal documentation for David and the girls has been taken care of.

As for Drew, he moved in with me. We plan to get married soon. No date set yet, but it will be a quiet event. Just family.

And Nora? Well, Nora is still Nora.

She hasn't had another lucid moment since that day, but she was present when we needed her most.

Now, it's her time to be cared for, to receive the love she's always given.

Every Saturday, Leanne, Josh, David, and the girls come over for family fun.

Mom and I enjoy our teatime on the porch, watching our growing family laugh and play together.

In the kitchen, Molly and the girls bake, giggles mingling with the warm, comforting aroma of cookies and her favorite chicken Alfredo. She's so proud of how quickly they've mastered the recipe.

Inside, Lanix and David are locked in a friendly competition, battling it out on the game console, Lanix determined to keep his winning streak alive.

Out by the dartboard, no matter how hard they try, neither Josh nor Drew can ever manage to beat Leanne.

On one of those Saturdays, I found David sitting on the porch steps, his gaze lifted to the sky, a blue sky. His sky.

His shoulders were relaxed, and there was a calmness about him that I hadn't seen before. He looked at peace. I couldn't help but smile.

Stepping outside, I walked over and sat beside him. He scooted to make room without breaking his gaze from the sky. Before settling in, I wrapped my arms around him and kissed his forehead, just as I do with all my children, no matter how old they are.

I sat down and said softly, "David, even though I didn't raise you, I feel the same way about you as I do Molly and Lanix. And now, I'm a grandmother to three beautiful girls. They are my heart."

David turned to me, eyes watery. "Andri, I'm so very grateful that you're my mother. I can't begin to tell you how happy we are here, with you, with my real family, under this beautiful blue sky. I know it's only been three months, but it feels like that life was all just a dream. A nightmare. And since we've arrived... I haven't had one headache."

His words pierced straight through me, filling my heart with a bittersweet ache, joy and sorrow all tangled together.

I brushed a strand of his dark hair from his face and cupped his cheek, my thumb tracing the faint lines of worry that still lingered.

"You deserve this peace, David. You and the girls. You've been through so much. But you're home now. You're safe."

He gave a half-smile, wiping at his eyes, and I pulled him close, resting my head on his shoulder. A gentle breeze ruffled his hair as we sat together, soaking in the moment, the sky stretching wide and limitless above us.

I couldn't help but tease, smiling against his shoulder. "But David, are you ever gonna call me 'Mom'?"

He hesitated, his smile softening, almost wistful. "Hmm, Mom... That's gonna take some getting used to. I've never called anybody 'Mom' before."

His words hung in the air, bittersweet and full of all the years he'd missed. My heart squeezed, aching for the boy who never got to feel the comfort of a mother's love.

I reached out and touched his arm, feeling the warmth of his presence and the fragile hope in his eyes.

"It's okay," I whispered, giving his arm a gentle squeeze. "Take all the time you need. I'll be here whenever you're ready."

He gave me a small, grateful smile, and I leaned in to kiss his forehead once more. The wind stirred around us, rustling the leaves like a soft lullaby. In that moment, I knew, no matter how long it took, I'd wait for him to feel it. To know, deep down, that he finally had a mom who loved him.

But I could see it: the emotion building in his eyes again. It was too much, too fast. He was feeling everything, and I picked up on it.

So, I changed the subject.

I chuckled softly, trying to lighten the mood. "Well, I didn't just come out here to tell you how much I love you."

David looked at me, curious. "No?"

I grinned. "There's something else."

His expression shifted, open, eager. "What?"

Just then, Molly walked over. David scooted to make room, and she nestled beside him, resting her head on his shoulder.

I took a steady breath, bracing for his reaction. "Your grandparents, Julia and Felipe, they're alive. And they're healthy."

David's eyes widened. "Wait, what?"

I nodded. "And your dad, Victor, too."

For a moment, he just stared, trying to grasp the impossible truth.

"The Julia you knew was bitter and calculating," I said. "But this Julia? I think you'll be pleasantly surprised."

David let out a shaky breath, then grinned. "I want to meet them."

I exhaled, smirking. "Sure, but..." I paused.

His grin faded. "But what?"

I raised an eyebrow. "I'd like to see how we're supposed to explain all this to them, explain *you.*"

David blinked. And then he laughed, a real, deep, genuine laugh.

For the first time in a long time, everything felt right.

———— ◦◦◦ ————

"Andri!" Leanne called from the patio, her voice urgent.

I turned. "What is it?"

She barely caught her breath before blurting out, "I saw your phone light up on the table, so I picked it up and answered it. It was Tanya. She's pulling up any minute. In fact, that's her."

All eyes turned toward the driveway as the familiar minivan rolled to a stop. Josh, Molly, and Leanne stepped forward as Tanya climbed out from the driver's side. The air shifted, charged with something unseen, a quiet energy thrumming beneath the ordinary evening.

We gathered around, instinctively sensing that something significant was about to happen.

Tanya's gaze was calm, but behind it was something knowing, something deeper.

"I brought someone with me," she said.

She reached into a small pouch and withdrew a mirror. At first glance, it looked simple, plain. But as soon as it caught the light, its surface shimmered like water under moonlight.

Josh, Molly, and David froze. Their eyes widened in recognition. They knew this object.

Tanya pressed a single finger to the glass and slid it downward.

A ripple spread across the mirror's surface, like a veil parting.

And then... there was someone there.

A hazy, shifting figure. Twisting at first, blurred and unreal...

Until it wasn't.

A white glow illuminated the space around us, soft yet powerful.

Floating above the earth, his feet untouched by the ground, stood an old man with long, salt-and-pepper hair tied back. His robe was woven from light itself, shifting with hues beyond human comprehension. His gaze, warm yet infinite, swept over us.

"Anio."

Nora's voice trembled with joy. She beamed, her face alight with recognition.

The rest of us stood frozen, watching as Anio's radiant presence seemed to slow time itself.

Drew was suddenly beside me, his arm around my shoulder, glancing at me with wide, stunned eyes.

Leanne's breath hitched. She took an unsteady step forward, her wide eyes locked on the glowing figure.

"It's... it's you," she whispered, her voice barely above a breath.

A knowing smile played on Anio's lips. "Do you remember me, Leanne?"

Silence blanketed us. Even the children, who had been laughing moments before, fell still.

Leanne's eyes scanned his face, her expression tight with the effort of retrieving a memory long buried in time.

Tanya turned to Anio, and with quiet reverence, handed him the mirror.

The moment the glass touched his hands, it erupted in color, vivid, brilliant hues unlike anything we'd ever seen on this earth. It wasn't just light. It was alive. Moving. Shifting between dimensions beyond our understanding.

Anio floated closer to Leanne, his presence neither imposing nor distant, but familiar, like he had never truly been gone.

"You remember when I came to teach you."

His voice was both a whisper and a force, filling the space around us.

Leanne's hands trembled at her sides.

She remembered.

But she remembered him differently, wearing a top hat, a waistcoat, and a bow tie around his neck, as if he belonged to another time.

He extended his glowing hand, offering her the mirror.

"It now belongs to you. Use it wisely."

Leanne hesitated, staring at it, the swirling light reflecting in her wide eyes. Slowly, deliberately, she reached out and took it. A warmth seeped through her fingers, like a heartbeat in the glass.

And then... Anio was gone.

Silence settled. Heavy. Profound.

As if the very air held its breath.

Leanne stood rooted in place, the mirror clutched to her chest, while the rest of the family watched in stunned stillness. No one spoke, but their eyes were wide with awe and disbelief, as if they had just witnessed something beyond the realm of human understanding.

And in that moment, Leanne knew she wasn't alone.

Surrounded by family, bound by love and trust, she felt something awaken inside her.

A sense of purpose.

One that had been waiting for this very moment.

Next in the Series: *Mystic Crossroads*

Acknowledgements

This book would not have been possible without the unwavering support of my mother, Elodia, whose love and guidance taught me to embrace my experience and beyond the ordinary.

To my children: you are my world, my greatest blessings. Your constant support gave me the strength to keep going.

And to Chulo and Catfish, our faithful companions, thank you for leaving paw prints on my heart.

To my siblings, thank you for reminding me to embrace the unknown and for sharing your incredible experiences.

To my beta readers, Lena, Deb, and Syl: your insights helped mold this story into what it is today.

To Kurt and Bill. Thank you for being my sound board and for listening to my ideas, no matter how far-fetched they seemed. Your encouragement means more than you know.

To the book cover artist, Sienna Rose, thank you for bringing this story to life visually.

To audiobook narrator Amelia Hugh, thank you for bringing this story to life through your wonderful narration.

Lastly, to the readers, thank you.
I hope this story stays with you long after the final page.
With all my heart, thank you.

After this book was completed, I learned to the devastating flood in Kerrville, Texas, the town that inspired fictional Gilson. My heart goes out to the people there, especially those who lost loved ones.